PRAISE FOR

CHOSEN BY BLOOD

"Virna DePaul creates the perfect blend of danger, intrigue, and romance. You won't be able to put this book down."
                    —Brenda Novak, *New York Times* bestselling author

"Virna DePaul is amazing! *Chosen by Blood* is a unique, hot, spellbinding treat for all paranormal romance fans. I can't wait for the next book in the series!"
                    —Lori Foster, *New York Times* bestselling author

"Sexy, suspenseful, and very, very smart. I couldn't put it down."   —Eileen Rendahl, national bestselling author

"DePaul's debut novel, *Chosen by Blood*, snaps, crackles, and pops with action, adventure, and a heart-pounding romance. She builds an intriguing world populated by fascinating characters. You won't want to miss this one!"
                    —Karin Tabke, award-winning author

CHOSEN BY FATE

Virna DePaul

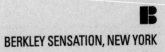

BERKLEY SENSATION, NEW YORK

THE BERKLEY PUBLISHING GROUP
Published by the Penguin Group
Penguin Group (USA) Inc.
375 Hudson Street, New York, New York 10014, USA

Penguin Group (Canada), 90 Eglinton Avenue East, Suite 700, Toronto, Ontario M4P 2Y3, Canada
(a division of Pearson Penguin Canada Inc.)
Penguin Books Ltd., 80 Strand, London WC2R 0RL, England
Penguin Group Ireland, 25 St. Stephen's Green, Dublin 2, Ireland (a division of Penguin Books Ltd.)
Penguin Group (Australia), 250 Camberwell Road, Camberwell, Victoria 3124, Australia
(a division of Pearson Australia Group Pty. Ltd.)
Penguin Books India Pvt. Ltd., 11 Community Centre, Panchsheel Park, New Delhi—110 017, India
Penguin Group (NZ), 67 Apollo Drive, Rosedale, Auckland 0632, New Zealand
(a division of Pearson New Zealand Ltd.)
Penguin Books (South Africa) (Pty.) Ltd., 24 Sturdee Avenue, Rosebank, Johannesburg 2196,
South Africa

Penguin Books Ltd., Registered Offices: 80 Strand, London WC2R 0RL, England

This is a work of fiction. Names, characters, places, and incidents either are the product of the author's imagination or are used fictitiously, and any resemblance to actual persons, living or dead, business establishments, events, or locales is entirely coincidental. The publisher does not have any control over and does not assume any responsibility for author or third-party websites or their content.

CHOSEN BY FATE

A Berkley Sensation Book / published by arrangement with the author

PRINTING HISTORY
Berkley Sensation mass-market edition / October 2011

Copyright © 2011 by Virna DePaul.
Excerpt from *All That Bleeds* by Kimberly Frost copyright © by Kimberly Chambers.
Cover art by Tony Mauro.
Cover design by Rita Frangie.
Interior text design by Tiffany Estreicher.

ISBN: 978-0-425-24399-2

BERKLEY SENSATION®
Berkley Sensation Books are published by The Berkley Publishing Group,
a division of Penguin Group (USA) Inc.,
375 Hudson Street, New York, New York 10014.
BERKLEY SENSATION® is a registered trademark of Penguin Group (USA) Inc.
The "B" design is a trademark of Penguin Group (USA) Inc.

PRINTED IN THE UNITED STATES OF AMERICA

10 9 8 7 6 5 4 3 2 1

*To my boys, Joshua, Ethan, and Zachary.
Dream big, love hard, be happy, and know
I'm forever grateful for the privilege of being
your mother. You make me so proud!*

ACKNOWLEDGMENTS

As always, I want to thank my friends and family for their support. I'm blessed to work with my agent, Holly Root, and my editor, Leis Pederson, as well as have the support of my critique partners and countless professionals at Berkley Publishing. Most of all, thanks to Craig for being my rock, my safe harbor, my anchor, and my wings. I love you!

PROLOGUE

Caleb O'Flare recognized the man as a Fed the second he stepped into the Kiva Bar.

Amid the roughly hewn furniture and scattering of primitive blankets on the wall, the guy's pin-striped suit, conservative tie, and dark aviator glasses were dead giveaways. He was as out of place on the dusty reservation as a drag queen hanging with a pack of Navy SEALs.

Still, when the man removed his glasses, Caleb saw a weary experience edging his expression. He'd seen action on the field, not just behind a desk. He might even have fought in the War when Caleb had. If so, he deserved Caleb's respect.

It didn't matter.

Respect wasn't the issue. Trust was. And Caleb didn't trust anyone anymore, especially not a Fed.

As Secret Agent Man scanned the bar, Caleb purposely slouched lower in his seat—attitude, not evasion—spread his thighs wider, and nearly drained the rest of the whiskey he'd been nursing. He signaled the bartender, Nick, for another drink, then picked up his glass again.

The last drops of whiskey warmed his stomach, and unbelievably managed to make him feel almost mellow. The Fed spoke and that mellowness quickly faded.

"Caleb O'Flare."

The man stated his name with an arrogant certainty rather than pose it as a question. Caleb swiped the back of his hand across his heavily whiskered jaw. Deliberately, he let loose an insolent burp. He grinned at the expression of distaste that washed over the man's features even as he heard a snort and chuckle behind him.

"Whassa matter?" he said, purposely slurring his words. "Didn't you do your intel? I'm half-Indian and half-Irish. You had to know the chances of finding me shit-faced were esp . . . est . . . extremely high."

Another burp escaped him, this one so prolonged that the man narrowed his eyes.

"I'm Kyle Mahone, director of the FBI's Special Ops Tactical Division. I'm here to offer you a job."

Abdomen muscles tightening, Caleb tilted his head to one side in an exaggerated manner and stared silently at Mahone. Neither of them blinked.

"Here you go." Nick handed him a stiff one.

"Thanks, Nick," Caleb said softly, taking the drink from his friend. He drained it in one swallow before silently placing the glass down. He twirled the glass in small circles against the scarred, wooden tabletop. Minutes ticked by.

He had to give Mahone credit.

The man didn't shuffle his feet or try to break the awkward silence. He stayed put. Still. Until Caleb finally met his gaze once more.

"Somehow I don't think you're here because of my medical skills, and as I told you people years ago, I'm out of the torturing business." He spoke clearly, loudly, knowing his statement would raise questions in the minds of the three other people in the bar, but also knowing none of them would dare question him about it.

Although he wasn't expecting Mahone to look shocked by his verbal volley, neither was he expecting the man to keep his expression so bland. The word "torture" tended to make most people uncomfortable, even when they'd been the ones committing it.

Unofficially, of course.

"We're asking you to join a team. One made up of Otherborn and humans."

Now it was Caleb who struggled to keep his expression

composed. This had to be a joke. Or a trap. Since humans first discovered the Otherborn almost a decade ago, there'd been attempts to befriend and integrate them, with the ultimate result being the Second Civil War and countless deaths among all the races. Yes, peace had eventually been declared, segregation had been outlawed, and progress had been made, but mistrust and bitterness still divided humans and Otherborn by miles.

A combined team of Otherborn and humans? Who'd authorized that debacle? Not Mahone. As a Bureau director, he was powerful, but not that powerful. The green light would have had to come from a higher-up. Hell, probably from the President of the United States himself.

But why? He couldn't see the Feds voluntarily working with Others unless it was to manipulate them.

"Peace is tenuous. A Para-Ops team is our best way of protecting it. The team's tasks will be varied. Force will be used only when necessary."

His pulse accelerating with his irritation, Caleb caught Nick's eye. "I've heard that line before."

"I'm sure you have, but you haven't heard it from me."

He snorted. "Meaning you'd never ask me to lie, cheat, or steal to get the U.S. government what it wants?"

Mahone's face tightened fractionally. "I didn't say that. But this time, the judgment calls will be made by you. You and your team," he amended.

Caleb's "team" had once been the U.S. Army. He'd been a medic, mostly. Other times . . .

Maybe he should have guessed what they'd use him for, but he hadn't. Not until . . .

Nick delivered Caleb another drink, this time with a glare of disapproval. Caleb ignored him. He stared at the drink, then cleared his throat. He told himself he was asking out of curiosity, not because he was considering the job offer. Even so, he couldn't deny the way his heart was pounding with excitement or the way his blood was rushing through his veins with a vigor he hadn't felt in years.

Five years to be exact.

"So what kind of Others are we talking about? Weres?"

Mahone's nod wasn't a surprise. Weres were the most aggressive Others, natural-born warriors. "Vamps?"

"A dharmire."

Caleb straightened in his chair. "Knox Devereaux?" he guessed, thinking of the one dharmire the FBI would be most interested in. While the rest of his vamp clan was wasting away thanks to an engineered vaccine, which prevented human blood from nourishing vamps, Devereaux ironically thrived because he *had* human blood running through his veins. What good was being immortal when it meant an eternity of starvation or, in Devereaux's case, an eternity of watching those you love starve? If the FBI had convinced Devereaux to join its ranks, it was because it had something invaluable to offer in return. Sure enough, Mahone gave a terse nod, and Caleb whistled. "Wow. You're recruiting big, Mahone." Sprawling back in his chair with his legs stretched in front of him, Caleb folded his hands behind his head, blinking when his surroundings faded in and out. It was a sign that he was drinking too much, but he pushed through the haze. "So what do you want with little old me?"

"Don't play coy," Mahone snapped. "You're a healer whose talent is as unique as it is inexplicable. You were a vocal supporter of Otherborn rights, even during the War. Plus you're skilled in chemical weaponry. That's a talent we can use—*if* it's needed," he emphasized.

"Any felines on this team?" Caleb taunted, already knowing the answer.

"No."

He reached for his drink and took a swallow, draining more than half of it. "Smart, considering so many of them want to kill me."

"Given how out of shape you've become, O'Flare, killing you might not be as hard as one would've thought."

Mahone's caustic statement almost made Caleb laugh. Almost. "Reconsidering your offer?"

"Considering accepting?"

Staring down a man who was far more sober than him turned out to be fairly difficult. "So who else?"

After a brief pause, Mahone said, "Two females. I'm targeting a mage and a wraith."

"A wraith?" He frowned. He'd never seen one, not in all his travels or years of service. But he'd heard about them. No pulse. No blood. No body heat or need to eat. What they did have was a common gender—female—and a whole lot of angry going on. Oh, and immortality. "Some dead chick? I thought the few in that species were isolated up in Maine, in that compound they'd built."

"This one's an independent thinker."

Right.

Or, put another way, she was an especially heinous bitch who couldn't be killed and who wouldn't die.

Nice.

Caleb studied Mahone. "By the look on your face, the ghost troubles you. Why?"

"Let's just say she has an agenda, one I'm not sure I can help her with."

"So your role is to fulfill agendas?" He smirked. "What's mine?"

"What do you want?"

Caleb raised a brow at the man's bravado. "Nothing you can give me."

"Not even a name?"

What the hell was Mahone getting at? "What name?"

"The name of the person who masterminded Elijah's death."

Shock rattled through Caleb like Mahone's words were a ball and Caleb the pinball machine.

Elijah—the feline prince. The bastards. Set him up and then use the situation to bribe him? He stood, palms pressed on the table, and sent Mahone a silent though unmistakable message: Do. Not. Fuck. With. Me. "Haven't you heard? Elijah's death was accidental. A foreseeable one, given he was being tortured at the time. But then, that was my doing, right? After all, I'm the one who could've stopped the questioning by confirming whether he was answering truthfully or not." Caleb pounded the table so hard it shook. "No one masterminded his death, and the person universally blamed is *me*. Some made-up name isn't worth anything at this point."

Mahone shrugged with an obvious lack of concern. "Maybe. Or maybe the use of torture as a last resort was really an intentional execution, and your role began and ended as a convenient scapegoat."

Caleb laughed, the sound mockingly bitter. Shaking his head, he sat down again. "How convenient. Too bad no one's ever posited that theory before."

"And that means it's not true? Pity, but maybe you're not as smart as I thought you were, O'Flare."

"I'm plenty smart enough to smell crap when I hear it," he muttered. "Go sell it to someone else." He reached for his glass, then was shocked when Mahone reached out and tossed the contents on the floor.

Deliberately, Mahone set the glass back on the table. "You've had enough, son."

Son? Mahone couldn't be more than ten years his senior. Staring first at the man, then at the glass, Caleb gripped the edges of the table and struggled for restraint. The intensity of his emotions made his voice shake. "Get me another drink. Now." But even as he uttered the command, shame washed over him. Shame because he needed the liquor with a biting intensity. Shame because he knew he was pissing away what could be his last chance to do something worthwhile with the rest of his life. But then he remembered . . .

"You saved lives, O'Flare. Fought for what was right."

Caleb shook his head, rejecting his mind's recollection of all the gruesome images it had collected over the years. "I don't know what's right anymore. And I took lives, too."

"A few in combat. When you had no choice."

"I had a choice toward the end."

Mahone sighed. "One. One life. And it wasn't deliberate."

"One. One hundred. One thousand. Deliberate or not." He swallowed hard. "Doesn't matter. Culpability isn't based on quantity. At least, not in my world."

"All the more reason for you to get involved in what I'm offering. And you're right about one thing. I don't have proof that Prince Elijah was murdered, but I'm following a lead. If it pans out, you can be privy to the information I collect or not. Serve on the team, and I give you an IOU. If you decide you want something other than my intel, and it's within my power to give it to you, it's yours."

Caleb ripped his gaze from the empty glass to stare at Mahone. An IOU could come in handy someday, but that was assuming Mahone was a man of his word.

"So what's it to be, O'Flare?" Mahone pressed. "You can take another drink, or you can listen to what I have to say. What I have to offer. If you want to tell me to piss off, at least do it with all the information. That's something you didn't have before, isn't it?"

The low blow took Caleb unawares. No, he hadn't known

Elijah was the prisoner being tortured for information or that his own refusal to act as a human lie detector would result in Elijah's death. In his mind, doing the latter had been tantamount to condoning the methods used to extract Elijah's confession. A lot of good Caleb's principles had done Elijah in the end.

He hadn't known Elijah very long before the War had started, but in the months he'd dated Elijah's sister, Natia, they'd formed a swift bond. Caleb had liked Elijah's humor and charm, and he'd respected Elijah's loyalty to his family, especially to his sisters, whom he'd doted on. Despite Caleb's place of honor within the reservation, his position as shaman had distanced him from his people. In many ways, being around the royal feline family had fed Caleb's need for normalcy and affection and acceptance, things he'd missed after his mother and father had died. In truth, if forced to choose between his friendship with Elijah and his relationship with Natia, Caleb would have chosen the friendship. In the end, he'd lost both. He'd lost everything.

Caleb's gaze returned once more to the glass on the table, then to the bottles of liquor Nick kept stored behind the bar. The amber liquid called to him, promising not forgetfulness but a type of lessening.

Forgetfulness was what he craved.

If he couldn't have that . . .

Destiny.

The vision came upon him without warning, causing Caleb to close his eyes. He heard the whispers of his ancestors. He saw six auras, their forms ebbing and flowing, first together and then apart, pulsing so their energies sparked a riotous kaleidoscope of colors. His was there, burning a bright green, gravitating toward another shadow comprised of darkest black and purest white, the colors not cleanly divided but rather bleeding into one another.

Destiny.

Cursing softly, he opened his eyes, willing the whispers and vision away.

He had no idea what it meant. Whether the shadow's duality represented another being or another manifestation of himself—light and dark, good and evil, healer and murderer.

As Mahone studied him with a cocked brow, Caleb sighed. He didn't know what the vision meant, but he knew it had something to do with Mahone and the team he was forming. Caleb had a role in it, and for the first time in a long time, his body sizzled with anticipation.

Of course, he couldn't let Mahone know that.

Kicking out the chair in front of him, he jerked his head toward Mahone, then the chair. "Talk fast before I change my mind."

ONE

SEVERAL WEEKS LATER
AN ABANDONED WAREHOUSE
WASHINGTON, D.C.

Caleb's hands moved swiftly and efficiently as he set up the mobile radar equipment he'd spread out on the roof. The building below his feet had been swept and a perimeter established. Now all Caleb had to do was determine who was in the room with Mahone and whether Mahone was still alive.

Briefly, he glanced at Ethan Riley, leader of Hope Restored Team Blue, and the four men, skilled in entry and perimeter surveillance, who'd accompanied them here. Only hours had passed since Caleb had left his teammates in the Vamp Council's chambers in Oregon and, despite the grueling activity of the last few days—which had included parachuting into North Korea, hiking miles in the snow, rescuing several Otherborn, and tracking down what just might be an antidote to the vamp vaccine— Caleb felt the same focused energy he always did when on a mission. "Did you get in touch with the Para-Ops team?"

Riley looked up from checking his rifle. "They've detained the vampire Dante Prime. Devereaux tried to teleport here, but he'd depleted his powers in Korea . . ."

Caleb snorted. "No shit." Although vamps could teleport to and from anywhere in the world, provided they'd been there before, that kind of travel drained them. Before Knox Devereaux and the rest of the team had interrupted the Vamp Council to question Dante Prime for treason and conspiracy to commit murder, the dharmire had spent several hours teleporting between North Korea and the U.S. Each time, he'd carried a wounded Otherborn or one of his team members back with him. Beat him how the vamp was even capable of talking at this point. Add everything else that had happened to him—

"Is it true you found his father? And that he'd been turned into a vampire?"

Caleb didn't even look up. The Para-Ops team had trained with Team Blue's aerial experts before dropping into North Korea. At the time, Knox's father hadn't even been on their radar—and for good reason—since everyone believed he was dead. How the hell news of Jacques Devereaux's return had spread so fast, Caleb didn't know. Still, Riley had to know how fruitless his question was. "No comment."

He sensed Riley wince. "Sorry."

Caleb shrugged. Just because a person expected a particular result didn't mean he shouldn't try to get around it. Caleb was always trying to get a different reaction from his teammate Wraith, regardless of how unlikely that was. For one horrific moment, Caleb felt the same fear that had constricted his chest when he'd realized Wraith planned to blow herself up to get them inside the North Korean compound. It wasn't easy, but he pushed the feeling away.

Wraith was okay. He'd seen that for himself. He'd felt it when he'd pushed her down and covered her body with his. He'd savored it when she'd kissed him back, right before she'd kneed him in the balls.

Clearing his throat, he returned his attention to Riley and the other man's apology. "No worries. I'm as human as you, remember?"

Now it was Riley who snorted, prompting Caleb to smile tightly.

Okay, so maybe he wasn't quite as human as Riley. They shared the same DNA, but being able to communicate with his ancestors, hear the Great Song, and occasionally walk the Otherworld made him a little different.

Different didn't always mean better.

His fingers moved faster. Almost there. Glancing at his watch,

Caleb clenched his teeth. A bead of sweat trickled down his temple. He knew they couldn't go in blind, but—

"What about your wraith? Was she what you expected her to be?"

Caleb paused for only a fraction of a second before continuing his task. "She's not my wraith. She's a wraith who decided to keep the name 'Wraith' just to be ornery. And she's exactly what I expected her to be." What he didn't say was that she was also far more than he'd expected. A heinous bitch, yes, but one whose attitude and mouth were designed to hide something textured and complex and—

Disgusted with himself, Caleb pressed his lips together and once again pushed thoughts of Wraith out of his head.

Get Mahone out. That's all he could think about right now.

"Finally!" Snapping the last wire in place, Caleb flipped on the power and adjusted the radar settings, then scanned the building's interior until the radar picked up body heat. "Bingo."

Caleb immediately zoomed the camera in and got a good look at Mahone.

Dear Essenia, he thought, automatically invoking the name of the Earth Goddess to give him strength. Although humans believed Essenia was an Otherborn deity, few knew Earth People—like Caleb's own Native American tribe—had prayed to the same deity for centuries. Besides, from what Caleb saw, Mahone needed all the prayers he could get.

With his wrists shackled to chains hanging from the ceiling, Mahone looked like he'd gotten into a fight with a chipper machine and lost. His face and body were covered in blood, and what was left of his clothes hung in shreds from his battered body. From his position on the rooftop above, Caleb once again adjusted the settings on the mobile radar equipment. His adjustments made the image on the screen zoom out, losing detail and focus until it captured the entire room, providing grainy outlines of Mahone, a desk, a table, and one other individual whose silver hair, height, and slim build proclaimed him to be a vampire.

When Caleb and the five members of Hope Restored Team Blue had arrived at the isolated warehouse twenty minutes earlier, Caleb had figured Knox, leader of the Para-Ops team, had made a mistake by not sending any Others with him. That, or Knox simply had faith in Caleb's ability to take down anything that got in their way, human or not. Either way, Caleb was getting Mahone out, and he planned for both of them to be breathing when he did it.

Caleb thought of the first time he'd met Mahone and the vision he'd had. He'd had the same vision several times since, and the moment he'd met Wraith, he'd become convinced that the black-and-white aura that hovered near his own had to be hers. Upon their meeting, he'd felt a sizzling arc of connection that had only intensified with time. Apparently she hadn't. In fact, she seemed to have no use for him and spent most of her time pushing him away. Maybe the aura belonged to Mahone, instead, and the vision had been a premonition of this very moment—Mahone straddling the line between life and death, waiting to see whether Caleb could save him.

Luckily for both of them, Caleb had come prepared.

He looked at Riley. The man might be a little chattier than Caleb liked, but he'd had no problem taking Caleb's lead on the current mission. He was smart and he was a clean shot. That's all that mattered right now. "Mahone's in bad shape. We need to get in there fast. I'm hoping the vamp will teleport as soon as he knows he has company, but I need you and your team to cover me in case he decides to stick around. Are your shooters set up around the perimeter of the room?"

"They've all checked in and are in the crawl space with their weapons ready."

"Obviously your bullets won't kill him, but along with the Hyperion gas, they may buy me enough time to get to Mahone and extract him."

"How long does it take for the Hyperion to immobilize a vampire?"

The Hyperion was something Caleb had developed toward the end of the War. The government hadn't known about it, and he'd only used it a few times before peace had been declared. The testing he'd conducted had been limited, but he felt fairly confident it would work.

At this point, he figured his odds of getting out with Mahone were only slightly below average. "Usually about sixty seconds, but that's with a vamp who's been weakened by the effects of the vampire vaccine. From the looks of this one, he's had pure blood recently. Still, he might not be at full strength."

"If the vamp's immobilized by the Hyperion, how do we keep him contained while we take him in?"

"We don't. That's not what we're here for. Our sole objective is to rescue Mahone."

Riley nodded, but looked troubled. "You said he's doing bad . . ."

Caleb tried to keep his expression blank. "Doing bad" was an understatement. Mahone probably had less than five minutes of life left in his broken body. "Just get me to him. I'll take care of it from there. You ready?"

Riley communicated with his men, then nodded. "It's a go."

Slipping the small gas pellet from his pocket, Caleb held it up. "Remember, you have to stay back. Help me hold back the vamp, then get your men out. You're maintaining the perimeter, not going in. This gas immobilizes vamps and weres, but it does far worse to humans once enough of it is absorbed in the bloodstream."

"What about you?"

"I've built up a resistance. It's not extensive, but it'll give me the five minutes I need. If we don't make it out, it'll take two hours for the gas to dissipate. Don't come into the room until that much time has passed. Understood?"

Riley nodded and held out his hand. O'Flare shook it, then strode to the door that would lead him from the roof to the room below. He moved quietly, his breathing low and shallow, his gun held at the ready with the gas pellet in his other hand. He'd activate it as soon as he got close enough that it could work its magic on the vampire.

When he entered the room, he immediately saw Mahone. Even the radar's enhanced imaging hadn't prepared him. The vampire wasn't touching him, but Mahone's facial features were contorted in agony, his body writhing and jerking even as he remained silent. Fuck, Caleb thought when he saw the blood seeping out of Mahone's eyes and ears.

"Hey, vamp." He shouted at the same time he threw the pellet, which would emit a toxic but invisible gas. The vampire whirled around, his eyes flashing red the instant he saw Caleb. The vampire bared his fangs and came at him, his feet gliding above the ground. Caleb fired a round directly at his chest, causing him to fall back. At the same time, Riley and his men fired, as well. As the vamp jerked with the impact of the bullets, O'Flare ran for Mahone. He reached up and felt his pulse.

It was barely there. Caleb felt the man's life literally bleeding out of him.

Laying his hands on Mahone's bloody chest, Caleb closed his eyes. Bullets still fired around him, some coming too damn close. Damn it, Riley's men had to get out before the gas reached them in the crawl space. "Get out!" he yelled.

"The vampire teleported," Riley shouted. "We're clear."

With a sigh of relief, Caleb willed his consciousness into a trance and called to his ancestors for their healing help. He saw them in the colors that swirled behind his eyelids and felt their presence in the heat that immediately suffused his body. Their voices chanted, low and soothing, directing him to keep one hand directly over Mahone's heart and the other over his eyes. Caleb willed the healing heat building within his body to transfer to Mahone. As it did, he took some of Mahone's pain into himself.

He felt his own heartbeat slow.

His limbs weakened.

His body began to shake with the effort of remaining upright, and he forced even breaths, sensing he needed to maintain contact far longer than he ever had.

Come on, come on, he urged himself. Hang in there.

The dizziness came next. Then the nausea. He could feel his lungs filling with the gas that swirled around them and knew his time was running out.

His body jerked as he coughed, and the movement threatened to pull his hands away from Mahone.

They had to get out of there, but if he disconnected too soon, it would all be for nothing. Mahone would die. Hell, Caleb would probably die, as well, too weak from the healing to get out on his own.

But then he felt Mahone's chest rising strongly and his pulse beating regularly, and he knew the healing had worked. The heat slowly left his body, and the voices of his ancestors faded. Caleb whispered his thanks, then opened his eyes. Swiftly, he reached up and unhooked Mahone's chains from the manacles around his wrists. Mahone groaned and slumped over just as Caleb caught him and threw him fireman-style over his shoulder.

Caleb staggered a few steps before he turned, intending to carry Mahone to the doorway. Halfway there, his knees buckled.

He lost his grip on Mahone, and the man slipped and rolled a couple of feet away. Grunting, Caleb fell on all fours, his head hanging, his lungs seizing up.

He'd waited too long. They were both going to die in this warehouse, just like the FBI scientists who'd discovered the vamp antidote only to be killed because of it. He looked up, eyes watering, searching the room, thankful that Team Blue had obeyed his orders even as he regretted the fact no one was going to be able to help him.

But then he saw her. Wraith. Running toward him. He tried to open his mouth. To yell at her to stop.

His heart squeezed. Damn her for putting herself at such risk. He didn't know how the gas would affect a wraith. Since it worked so well on vamps, immortality had nothing to do with the effects. But he couldn't make a sound, and Wraith kept coming. She knelt beside him and pulled him up. She was yelling something, and he tried to make it out.

". . . have to walk! I need to get Mahone. Can you walk, O'Flare?"

She was glancing frantically between him and Mahone, the indecision on her face readily apparent. She couldn't carry them both out of there before the gas ended them.

"Leave me . . ." he tried to say, but again no sound came out. It didn't matter. Wraith understood.

She grabbed him by his shirt and shook him, hanging on when he began to slide, practically keeping him on his feet. "No fucking way, O'Flare. I didn't survive Korea just to come back and lose you in the States. Stay on your feet and move. You're walking out of here. Got it?"

The vehemence in her voice roused him enough to nod. She released him, and although he swayed on his feet, he didn't fall. Quickly, she grabbed Mahone, carrying him in the same lift O'Flare had used. Then, amazingly, she positioned herself next to him and ordered, "Lean against me if you need to. Start walking. Now."

Caleb walked. He didn't know how he did it, but he managed to put one foot in front of the other. At one point, he did have to lean on her, and he sensed how it slowed her down, but she didn't move away. She stayed with him.

Until they made it out into the open air. He heard shouts and the sound of stomping feet just as he collapsed.

When he came to, he was being loaded into an ambulance. Riley's face hovered above him. "Mahone?" Caleb rasped out.

"Still alive," Riley said. "But I don't know if he's going to stay that way."

From the worried expression on the man's face, Caleb knew his own chance of survival was also in question.

"Wraith?" he asked, grabbing on to the man's shirt when he didn't answer. "What about the wraith?"

Riley shook his head. "I don't know. She passed out, same as you. No pulse, remember? No breath. No way to tell if she's alive or dead. They took her in another cab. Your guess is as good as mine."

TWO

First it had been vamps and weres. Then felines and mages. Then finally wraiths and shape-shifters. One by one, the Otherborn had been discovered by humans. Over the next five years, they'd run the gamut of emotions together: fear and exhilaration, hope and despair, suspicion and hostility.

And then, just when the fighting had ended and Mahone had taken a breath, amazed that he'd managed to survive it all, he'd been visited by a Goddess with plans to annihilate every living creature on earth. Even more surprising, she'd apparently believed that *he*, Kyle Mahone, generic human, FBI grunt, and all-around fuck-up at heart, held the key to stopping her.

By the look on her face right now, she no longer did.

Even as Mahone stared at the Goddess Essenia, sensation and thoughts numbed by drugs immediately flared to life. White-hot pain made him jerk and gasp, while at the same time his mind, his soul, his being—whatever the hell one chose to label his life force—greedily latched on to the feelings that had never been so crystal clear with purpose. He felt the zing of blood pumping through his veins, the crackle of neurons firing in his brain, and the powerful beat of his heart thudding in his chest cavity. Every cell inside him shouted. He lived. He breathed. He existed. At the same time, he was consumed by a heady, life-altering knowledge, one granted to him by the being who'd appeared in his room.

He lived, but only because she permitted it.

He lived, but only because she had the power to sustain life or end it.

He knew she wanted to end it.

Despite everything he and the Para-Ops team had done in the past two months to fulfill the bargain he'd struck with her, he sensed her resolve. Her disappointment. In him. In all of her children.

Growling at the knowledge, he forced his eyes to remain open. He stared despite the light that surrounded her, so intense that most were blind to it unless she chose to reveal herself. Yet again, he was stunned by the power of her visage, one so beautiful and so frightening it made him think of Medusa, the creature with snakes for hair and the ability to turn any man who looked directly at her into stone.

Her soft, melodious laugh drifted toward him. The sound was ethereal. Soothing. Mahone actually felt his wounds healing. Pain ebbed, replaced by a pleasure so intense it made his body shudder in near orgasmic pulses. He threw back his head and groaned, his body arching off the bed so that only his skull and heels made contact with the mattress.

"Medusa was but a myth, Human. Yet another boogeyman created by your kind to fulfill its need for darkness and violence." Essenia drifted closer to him and waved her hand over his body. The riotous sensations quivering through his muscles ceased until he once more lay in the bed, the sweat on his brow and the dull, medicated pain of his wounds a blessing. "Your wounds are just another manifestation of the inability of my offspring to exist in peace. No matter how I try, no matter the chances I've granted, it is always the same."

Gut clenching with the effort it cost him, Mahone forced himself to sit up. "The team . . ." he gasped. "We accomplished our first mission. We proved humans and Otherborn can work together."

The being shook her head. "Even your statement highlights the chasm between my children. And your mission? One small victory drowned by a sea of greed and violence. Look what happened to you in the process. Your success cannot make up for centuries of deception and violence."

"It doesn't have to," Mahone reasoned desperately. "The prophecy doesn't speak of the whole world, nor the whole nation. Only of six. The ability of six, each from different races, to unite with one purpose. To act as one for the greater good of all."

"Something they have not yet been able to achieve," she reminded him. "With respect to the dharmire and his mate? I never doubted they would unite. The others?" She laughed again, but this time the sound was rife with rancor. "Give it up, Mahone. They are too caught up in their own agendas. Their own pain."

Mahone automatically thought of the two Para-Ops team members who posed the greatest challenge, but plowed ahead anyway. "They can come together. They will."

"Wraith? Dex? You don't know the darkness inside them, Mahone. Even with the information your men have collected, you have only the barest hint of a clue. No, you made a mistake when you chose them."

"Wraith has proven herself. She's put herself in danger time and again. To help others. O'Flare. Me."

She shook off his arguments with a wave of her hand. "I think it's best we stop playing this game and start over. Humanity has proven itself unworthy of the gifts I have bestowed upon it. I have come to a decision, but I will make your end painless. You, who have endeavored to serve me, will—"

Enraged, Mahone pulled at the tubes and needles piercing his skin, immediately causing several machines next to the bed to beep in alarm. He stood, swayed on his feet, then steadied himself with one arm braced against the bed. Breathing hard and fighting the nausea that twisted in his gut, he nonetheless forced himself to walk closer to the glowing, celestial being. "It's not your decision to make," he rasped. "You are bound by the agreement we made. I have done what you asked of me, and so must you. You—"

He felt her fury in the blast of heat she threw at him, knocking him off his feet and back onto the bed. Then she was upon him, hovering over him, doing what, for lack of a better description, could only be seen as straddling his body. "I created you," she hissed. "I am required to do nothing. Do you think O'Flare could have rescued you, with Wraith's help or not, if I hadn't wanted him to? I am the law and I make the law."

At her statement, a flash of skepticism ran through him. Just as he had before, when she'd shown herself to him before Caleb's rescue, he wondered who she answered to. Somehow he knew, even if she made the law, someone or something had the power to veto her decisions. Even now, a tinge of desperation edged her words, telling him that her threats were a way to maintain control, to keep her cover as the most powerful deity so he wouldn't guess that something else, something darker and more ominous, threatened them. Where his idea of God fit into all this, he couldn't know. But Essenia *wanted* Mahone to contradict her, to persuade her to give her children another chance, so that's what he tried to do.

"You made the law," Mahone gasped, failing to look away even as blisters began to mark his face. "You laid down your decree. Even you must follow it; otherwise, your word has no worth. Your existence no meaning. Your prophecy is recorded in the mage's texts, and you sought me out, not the other way around. Now you want to change the rules?"

The heat emanating from her grew more intense. His hospital gown and the sheets twisted around him began to smolder. His already-chapped lips split, and he could suddenly taste his own blood. Maybe he'd been wrong after all. Maybe the Goddess really wasn't feigning her bad intentions. He forced back an agonized, terror-filled scream, refusing to give her the satisfaction of hearing it.

But then the heat waned as she backed away.

He could see his words had swayed her, so he kept talking, his voice harsh in his parched throat. "You gave me one year to prove that my team can make an impact. We can help your children once again live in peace, despite the darkness that will always be among them and within them. Perfection wasn't our deal, nor is it demanded by the prophecy. We need only show a tipping of the scales in favor of the goodness of humanity."

Essenia's renewed anger flashed through the room once again, and he involuntarily closed his eyes against the horror of it.

He heard her voice reverberate around him. Inside him. "Why do you continue to rally for them? I've taken everything away from you, Mahone. Any chance of the life you hoped to spend with Bianca. Yet you fight for your survival. For that of your kindred."

At the thought of Bianca, another kind of pain shot through him. Why did he fight for the survival of humanity when there were times he himself believed they were lost? Maybe for the very reason Bianca, the vampire Queen and Knox Devereaux's mother, had been reunited with her husband and why he could accept it.

Hope.

"You question my persistence? Even though you chose me and won't tell me why? I don't know what answer you want. All I know is you created us." Or had some hand in that creation, he thought. "You imbued us with both strengths and weaknesses, but with one strength above all. The ability to learn. To change. To grow. We might not be doing it with the speed you wish, we might have fucked up again and again, but we deserve another chance. Please."

For several long minutes, she said nothing. Then she waved her hand, silencing the beeping machines abruptly. She nodded, causing him to shudder in relief.

"Very well. Continue with this game, but the outcome won't change. Humanity is lost, Mahone. You cling to visions of what could have been, just as I once did."

"Just hold to our bargain. Let my team show you what they're capable of."

"The bargain stands. For now. You have until the end of one year. Then humanity will fall in order to be reborn."

THREE

It was finally happening.

Wraith's appearance was changing. In less than a year's time, she'd be dead.

Almost a month had passed since the Para-Ops team had recovered the vamp antidote, rescued a dozen Otherborn, and returned from Korea to rescue Mahone. Then, of course, she'd survived Caleb's toxic gas—Essenia wouldn't want her to miss what came next.

As Wraith stared in the bathroom mirror, she could hear the sounds of the others moving down the hall, packing up their things, getting ready for some well-earned R & R at Knox's big estate in the Vamp Dome. Felicia and Knox had left the week before to oversee the wedding preparations. Although the rest of the Para-Ops team had stayed behind, they'd barely seen each other. For the past few mornings, she'd heard the roar of Dex's Harley as he tore out of the compound before dawn, not returning until dark. When the were did return, he glowered at his team members as he grabbed a beer and whatever else he could find in the kitchen, then slammed into his room. Lucy and Caleb had spent the week visiting Mahone in the hospital or seeing family. Wraith had noticed, however, that although they didn't bother her, one of her team members had always stayed behind when the other was gone.

As if they didn't trust her to be alone.

Wraith shook her head, an ugly jeer twisting her expression. Apparently, blowing herself up *and* rushing into a room filled with toxic gas had been too much to take, even when she'd had no other choice. In doing the first, she'd gotten the team inside the North Korean compound that housed the vamp antidote. And in doing the second, she'd saved both Caleb and Mahone. But instead of high-fiving her for her bravery and quick thinking, Lucy and Caleb obviously thought she was suicidal.

The thought instantly sobered her.

If they only knew.

". . . felines are a menace to you and your children. Their very nature has ensured they're more animal than not."

Words drifted toward Wraith from the other room. She left the bathroom and walked up to the TV. The local news was playing, broadcasting the most recent rant by Harry Jenkins, pulpit leader and Otherborn basher. None of the Others, however—not even the vampires—got as much heat from Jenkins as the felines did. Given the fact that a feline betrayed and delivered Wraith into the hands of a sadist, Jenkins's vendetta against the race shouldn't have bothered her, but it did. The man was a small-minded bigot who lived to spread misinformation and fear. No matter what her past was, she judged individuals by their actions, not their DNA. At least, she tried.

". . . are controlled by their urge to fornicate, and they don't care who it's with—man, woman, child."

At Jenkins's words, Wraith snorted and angrily punched the power button on the TV so the screen went blank. Another second of listening to that stuff, and she'd be tempted to track the man down and make sure he never made such ridiculous statements again. Because racial hatred against one Otherborn race ultimately spread to the others; even if Wraith, as a dead human, wasn't technically an Otherborn, she'd probably faced more judgment and discrimination than any of them.

She returned to the bathroom, stared into the mirror once more, and considered the havoc Jenkins could wreak if he knew that wraiths, the creatures who'd been granted a second chance at life, and an immortal one at that, came with an expiration date.

In Korea, she hadn't yet seen any changes, but the possibility had been there. Now she knew it was more than a possibility.

Raising a steady hand to her face, she smoothed a finger over her hairline, where her bluish-hued skin normally met stark white hair. Today, her hair was longer—no longer spiky so much as shaggy—and was showing a hint of color: faint, dark root that no one else would ever notice.

But she saw it. And she knew exactly what it meant.

She was changing, and as much as she wanted to, she couldn't ignore the timing. Thirty-eight days ago had been the tenth anniversary of her "die day," or, as most wraiths called it, the day of her transitioning. She was the oldest known wraith in America, and like the few that had come before her, she was about to meet her fate.

It wasn't until after the War, when they'd begun cohabitating in their compound in Maine, that the wraiths had realized their numbers were dwindling. An odd thing for immortals. One wraith had noted something interesting—that the "ability" for wraiths to die seemed to have only one thing in common: Dying only happened between a wraith's tenth and eleventh transition year, after a wraith started to regain more and more physical human traits. Of course, when that theory had been developed, Wraith had already abandoned Maine for the familiarity of Los Angeles. She'd still heard the rumors, though. Then she'd seen it for herself—a wraith she'd met only once before, one who was several years older than herself, and thus would have been almost eleven years old in wraith life, dead, lying in the back alley of a Texas bar, blood seeping out of her wounds. She'd accepted the rumors for what they were then—truth.

That had changed in the last few months. The longer she'd spent on the Para-Ops team and with her team members, something had changed inside her.

She'd weakened. Begun to hope. Begun to think maybe the rumors had been wrong . . .

They weren't, she told herself brutally.

Over the next year, she would gradually lose her immortality. Before the year was up, she would die.

She laughed harshly at her image in the mirror.

It was perfect. Just perfect.

The latest cosmic joke added to the crappy luck that amounted to her doomed existence.

Ten years ago, she awoke with no memory. Then she'd discovered she was a freak. And not just a freak by human standards, but by the whole damn world's, Otherborn included. Vamps, weres, and mages looked more normal than she did. Unlike her, they ate. Slept. They had heartbeats and observable brain waves *and* blood.

They were alive. She, on the other hand . . .

She was the walking dead, her outer shell visibly announcing it even as she felt the same emotions everyone else did. The difference was, she couldn't do anything about them. Not the softer ones anyway. Not when everyone around her either feared her or wanted to use her to increase their bank account, feed their sick, sexual fetishes, or learn the secret to immortality. Who knew being dead could be so handy—for the living, anyway?

When she'd figured that out, she'd *wanted* to die. She'd tried to kill herself several times only to learn that, while she couldn't die, she could feel pain. Even worse, when her body had regenerated after a particularly vicious suicide attempt, it had upped the stakes. From then on, a simple touch from someone else was painful. The infliction of a deliberate wound was excruciating agony.

Her body's way of saying, "Go ahead, try to kill me, I'll make you pay."

Apparently, suicidal tendencies were another thing wraiths had in common, because every wraith she'd ever met suffered the same curse. Either that, or pain from touch was a generic punishment for a variety of one's crimes against the Gods and nature.

She'd sought comfort in the beginning. Companionship. She'd gotten both to some degree, only to be betrayed. It had taken two years of captivity and the threat of Otherborn eradication before she'd learned to put her immortality to good use during the War. After peace had been declared and she'd confirmed that living among other wraiths wasn't for her, she'd learned to exist alone. To survive. With no place to call home. No one to call family or friend.

And now, just when she'd become part of a team and had begun to think that maybe, just maybe, she had some purpose for being here, the Goddess Essenia was fucking her over again.

She could actually envision the bitch, an impossibly beautiful creature, dangling Wraith's immortality in front of her while taunting, "I'm going to take it away, only you won't know when. Could be today. Could be next month. But before this year is up, it'll all be over.

"*You'll* be over."

A harsh thump tore Wraith from her thoughts. With a gasp, she pulled her fist back from the mirror, which now sported a long, jagged crack down its center. Pain radiated from her fist, down her arm, and up into her temple. As she watched, several cuts on her hand began fusing together, then disappeared completely.

She'd been pounding on the mirror, she realized, and hadn't even known it.

Just like the crazy creature she was.

A low moan slipped out of her before she could stifle the sound. Her knees grew rubbery, causing her to grip the sides of the sink to keep upright. She flinched when someone knocked on the door of the adjacent bedroom. Automatically, she turned toward the sound.

"Wraith? Are you okay?"

Caleb. She pressed her lips together, tamping down her foolish urge to run to the door and throw herself into his arms. Ever since she'd helped him get Mahone out of that warehouse, he'd kept his distance from her. But he'd watched her, too. Constantly. Desire continued to heat his gaze whenever he looked at her, and she'd had to work doubly hard to make sure the same desire wasn't evident in her own eyes. "I . . . I'm fine," she croaked out.

"Let me in."

His gruff command was enough to shock her back to her senses. Straightening, she moved into the bedroom and glared at the door. How dare he command her to do anything? Despite riding to his rescue, she hadn't forgotten how less than a month ago he'd played them all, feeding her information and pretending to find answers that he and Mahone had known all along. "I said I'm fine."

There was a pause, and then he said, "Open the door, or I'll break it down."

His quiet assertion stunned her even more, and to her horror, she felt an immediate surge of lust. Her perpetually cold body suddenly prickled with heat. Her nipples hardened, and the flesh between her thighs ached, adding to all the aches she normally lived with.

It was so unfair, to only feel warmth when she was turned on. Because she couldn't do anything to satisfy her desire, being aroused inevitably meant more pain, a hollow ache in her gut that grew steadily worse until she wanted to curl into a ball and scream.

Instantly, she remembered the first and only time Caleb had kissed her, and how, even though they'd been wrestling in the snow at the time, the press of his body against hers had heated her skin, making her feel sensations that she'd only grieved more once they were gone. She'd told herself then that her response, the thing that had made her stop fighting and willingly open her mouth for the invasion of his tongue, was a result of having just been blown apart and fused back together. That would be enough to make anyone act out of character.

Yet, she knew, if he kissed her now, she wouldn't be able to stop herself from responding again. She'd felt need like that before. First it had been the need for pain. Then the need for drugs to numb the pain. In both cases, she'd become dependent on both. Until she'd been nothing but a mindless shell.

The idea of craving something like that again scared her more than dying. As long as she was strong, with only herself to worry about, she could deal with whatever BS fate threw her way. If she allowed herself to care about someone else, to depend on them for her survival or to have them depend on her . . . ?

She couldn't. She wouldn't.

If she died today, so be it. The only regret she'd have was not knowing who she'd been. That would, however, be a *huge* regret. She wanted, no, *needed*, to know why. Why the last ten years had happened. But more importantly, who was she? Who had she left behind? She'd tried to find out, but at every turn, she came up empty. No one knew her. Even her fingerprints were gone. It was as if she'd never existed.

But she knew she *had*. And she *had* to know who she was.

Now, more than ever, she needed to act fast. She needed to get answers while she had the chance. She couldn't control much in her world, but regretting or not regretting her own actions was something she could.

So she wasn't going to let Caleb O'Flare in her room, despite her instinctive need to meet aggression with aggression and desire with desire. Besides, she reasoned, Caleb's attraction to her was as temporary as it was predictable. He was a healer, and that was the only reason he felt anything for her. He wanted to help her, just as he would want to help any wounded creature. But what he didn't know about her was that she was incapable of being helped.

Even as she stepped toward the door and wearily leaned her forehead against it, she threatened, "Do that, and I'll make sure you can't dance at Knox's wedding, let alone nail any of the desperate females I'm sure will be there. I'm busy and I don't have time for your immature games, Caleb. Go find Lucy and bother her." She raised her head, knowing it would take more to get him to leave. Suddenly inspired, she taunted, "Better yet, why don't you go run to Mahone and report what I've been doing. Isn't he due some information by now?"

She held her proverbial breath when he didn't immediately respond. Told herself it was impossible to feel someone's hurt through the thick, wooden door that separated them.

She felt it anyway. Lightly resting her palm flat on the door, she imagined him standing on the other side, a man almost too beautiful for his own good. In a moment of weakness, she'd asked Lucy to describe what Caleb looked like in colors—something wraiths couldn't see. It hadn't been just the words Lucy had used but the tone of her voice that confirmed she wasn't the only female to find Caleb attractive. Slumberous green eyes. Silky caramel-and-toffee-colored hair with just enough wave to make Lucy itch to touch it. Bronzed skin. Wraith knew for herself he had a broad, rangy body and was good at hiding who he really was. He liked to play the laid-back, charming ladies' man, yet she sensed the inner darkness he tried to hide. Not dark intent, but the darkness of pain.

She knew from the files she'd hacked months ago what he'd been accused of—torturing Otherborn soldiers during the War. She'd known the instant she'd met him it wasn't true. She hadn't needed to be psychic, either. Caleb's goodness was as visible on him as death was on her.

"I don't know why I even bother," she heard him mutter.

The fall of his footsteps as he walked away were quick, as if he couldn't get away from her fast enough. Opening her eyes, she turned and scanned her small dorm room. It was as barren and as impersonal as it had been the day she moved into it, even though she hadn't packed up a single thing. She could leave this instant if she needed to, with no regrets.

That was how it had to be. How it *would* be.

The sooner Caleb accepted that, the better off they'd both be.

The wall of monitors was as high-tech as one could get. Twelve flat-screen panels broadcasted the images of the most powerful humans living in the United States. And each and every one of them was relying on Isaac Smith to restore order to a world gone mad.

"Tell us, Isaac. Did you deliver our message to Mr. Jenkins?"

Isaac resisted the urge to smooth a hand over his bald head or fiddle with his glasses. Instead, he leaned against his cane and took several steps closer to the bank of monitors on the wall—in particular, the screen transmitting the face of the Quorum's sole female member. "To the letter, Ms. Athena."

Although the raven-haired woman was beautiful enough to deserve the name of a Greek Goddess, Isaac couldn't help thinking "Hera" would have been a more appropriate pseudonym. After all, Hera had ruled Mt. Olympus by Zeus's side, and it was becoming clear that, while the Quorum was supposed to be ruled equally by all its members, the human female was slowly taking a leadership role. When she advised, few argued with her.

"But did he *hear* you, Isaac?"

Isaac sighed and turned to Mr. Apollo's image. How to respond? Apollo was one of the few Quorum members who enjoyed butting heads with Athena. Although Isaac had no reason to believe they'd ever met face-to-face, the hostility between the two seemed to indicate it was so. Of course, that would mean a major Quorum rule had been broken. If such a thing was ever proven, both would be eliminated. None of the twelve members of the Quorum's Board of Directors were ever supposed to meet, and none were supposed to know the others' true identities. Each human had been awarded a spot on the board by virtue of one thing—the amount of money in his or her bank account. Money, after all, was power, and when it came to stripping Otherborn of the rights granted to U.S. citizens, huge amounts of both were absolute necessities.

"Mr. Jenkins indicated a certain amount of . . . displeasure at the Quorum's attempt to control his right to free speech. He said if we were truly interested in eradicating an Otherborn presence in North America, we certainly wouldn't want to quash his attempts—heavy-handed though they may be—at shedding light on the feline race's inherent sinfulness."

"In other words," Apollo murmured, "no."

"I'm afraid not, sir. Mr. Jenkins strongly feels he needs to warn humans about the feline heat and the fact it turns feline females into, and I quote, 'immoral whores and sexual predators.'"

"His methods may not be the best, but he certainly is an outstanding judge of character," Athena interjected. Several of the Quorum members laughed while Apollo scowled like a recalcitrant little boy.

"He needs to be reined in, Athena. He's stirring up the public, and by bringing so much attention to the felines, he's undermining our plans. Plans, I might remind you, that require a more subtle hand than Jenkins is capable of." When Athena remained silent, Apollo snapped, "Help me out here, Hades. Do you agree with me or not?"

Mr. Hades sucked in his weak chin and said, "What's there to agree with? Jenkins is a vulgar bigot with no agenda other than hate-mongering. I don't believe, however, he's influential enough to interfere with our ultimate objective. I say the more hate he can stir up for the felines, the easier it will make things for us in the end."

Only Isaac saw the way Apollo's face flushed with anger. "Damn it! That's not what you said yesterday, Hades, before you—"

"Gentlemen," Athena interrupted, her voice betraying both amusement and resolve. "I believe we should leave Mr. Jenkins to his own devices for a while longer until we're given proof that his role as a feline oppressor is somehow damaging the Quorum's objectives. Does everyone other than Apollo agree?"

As Isaac recorded the votes and Apollo seethed quietly, the other ten members of the Quorum cast their agreement.

"So it's settled," Athena said. "Thank you, gentlemen." Ten of the twelve monitors flickered to dark, and Isaac powered them down and made sure they were indeed unable to transmit either video or audio. Only when he nodded did Athena recommence speaking. "What of our other problem, Isaac?"

Earlier, out of earshot of the other Quorum members, Athena

had referred to a "whoring human female who was a traitor to her race by publicly worshipping at the feet of Otherborn savages and doing their bidding for them." Isaac assumed this female was the "other problem" Athena had spoken of.

"It's being taken care of, ma'am."

"Good."

Hesitantly, Isaac's gaze moved to the only other lit monitor. The man staring back at him never failed to make his skin crawl. It wasn't so much the thick, bumpy scars on his face that caused Isaac's involuntary response, but his flat, icy stare. It was devoid of all emotion, even the arrogance or hate that often lit the eyes of many of the Quorum's members.

This man didn't hate. The word was too weak for what he felt. What he wanted.

His goal wasn't just to strip the Otherborn of their civil rights. If he had his way, he'd make every one of them suffer the pain of a thousand deaths. And that went double for any female human who'd dare take an Otherborn for her mate.

Even if that human female was his own daughter.

FOUR

It was a hell of a celebration.

Not every day did a vamp, especially one of royal lineage, marry a human. As witnesses to the momentous union of Knox Devereaux and Felicia Locke, new friends and old had been allowed inside the Vamp Dome, the stronghold and sanctuary of the Devereaux clan, which included most of the vamps in the United States.

To someone who'd never been inside, like Caleb, it was a mind-boggling experience. The Dome was a massive enclosed territory that operated as a structured, peaceful society with top-notch security; it was part of the United States, but clearly separate from it. Much like Caleb's own reservation, he figured. Unlike his reservation, however, the Dome didn't suffer from poverty or a fractured community. Rather, it had hundreds of posh residences within its borders; its own government buildings, including a courthouse and jail; and at its hub, the resplendent home of the royal Devereaux family, the clan's leaders.

The royal ballroom was big and opulent but not garish. Marble floors with some kind of black accent screamed money, while the curtains, oversized artwork, and multitude of flowers, both inside and out, radiated class. No expense had been spared on the food, decor, or the diverse guest list, which had meant flying in countless numbers of individuals from abroad. Even the President of the United States, Cameron Morrison, and his wife, Vanessa Morrison, had extended their congratulations to Devereaux and his bride.

There was no denying that vamps knew how to throw one hell of a party.

The grand affair, however, wasn't just a wedding celebration, but a celebration of a family united despite centuries of lies. It was also a celebration of success and salvation. Or at least the beginnings of it.

Even now, Caleb could hardly believe it.

They'd done it. The Para-Ops team had successfully completed its first mission. It had brought back the vamp antidote from North Korea, and the Goddess Essenia willing, hundreds of vampires would soon be recovering from a decade of starvation. Better yet, they'd completed their mission without losing anyone on the team, Mahone included. It was a heady victory, even if it did mean the Para-Ops team's job had just gotten a helluva lot harder.

Already, despite their attempts to contain the information, rumors about the antidote had been leaked to the public. Those who opposed the administration of the antidote were protesting, stirring fears of what would happen once vampires again attained their full strength.

Unfortunately, those fears weren't completely unfounded.

Since most of the guests in the Dome were vampires, one didn't have to look far to see the ravages the antidote was intended to fight. Despite their fancy clothes, it was clear most of the vampires were sick. Starving. Some looked better than others, indicating some still had access to immaculates, humans with pure blood. Whether the number of humans with full blood had increased recently due to the discovery of the antidote was an unspoken question, but Caleb believed the answer was a resounding yes. Although the antidote was being withheld due to the possibility of dangerous side effects—to the humans taking it, most likely—he knew there were humans who'd be willing to take their chances if it meant saving someone they loved.

Felicia Locke would certainly take her chances over and over again, and nothing Knox Devereaux could say or do would be able to sway her from that course. Unfortunately, most humans couldn't accept the willingness of their kind to sacrifice themselves for *vampires*. One had only to look at Knox Devereaux or his mother and father, vamps who were close to their full strength, to see the threat they inherently posed to humans.

Taking the antidote that would once again allow human blood to nourish a vamp was going to be strictly voluntary, but there was always the risk that if the antidote got into the wrong hands, it could be wielded to create victims rather than donors. That risk, however, wasn't worth the destruction of an entire race of innocents, Caleb thought, but some would never accept that.

Plus, although Knox had caught one of the vampires responsible for the disappearance of the antidote as well as Mahone's capture, they hadn't been able to find the individuals who'd been pulling the strings. They knew whoever it was had to be well-organized and heavily funded, but at this point that was all they knew.

Still, Caleb tried to push aside his thoughts and focus solely on the beauty of his surroundings and on the pleasure of dancing with the female in his arms.

If it weren't for their complicated past, Princess Natia would be exactly the kind of female Caleb needed after the hellish last few weeks. Generous. Feminine. And she was sexy as hell, all curves and fragrant, soft skin, with long hair ribboned with shades of gold, toffee, and espresso.

Right now, those curves and soft skin were pressed against him, making his blood heat and his mind race with memories of what their bodies had once done to each other. But he'd already been having doubts about his and Natia's compatibility before Elijah had died, and Caleb's role in Elijah's death had severed whatever bond they'd had left. Even despite her recent words of faith in him—specifically, her belief that he hadn't had anything to do with her brother's death—and despite the affection he still held for her, he knew getting involved again wasn't what he wanted.

Caleb was a different man now. Yes, he'd managed to heal a great deal since joining the Para-Ops team. In playing the easygoing charmer, he didn't have to pretend quite as often. That part of Caleb's personality was returning more and more on its own, but his past was still there. The betrayal. The blood. With Mahone's promise to uncover the truth about Elijah's death, Caleb found his pain lessening with every day that passed. Instinctively, he knew Natia wasn't supposed to be part of his healing. It was better to leave her in the past, where she belonged. But he didn't want to hurt her, either, and her own clan had been experiencing difficulties . . .

He frowned when the slow music changed to something with a rocking beat and he heard a female whoop.

Wraith.

His gaze instantly found her on the other side of the dance floor, surrounded by a veritable smorgasbord of Otherborn representatives: vamps, mages, felines, and weres. Given the strong smell of roses Caleb had detected earlier, Knox had even invited a shape-shifter or two. Even so, despite the variances each race brought to the table, Wraith stuck out like a neon light in a vast wasteland of darkness.

His teammate was dressed as she always was—skin-tight black leather, four-inch blue stilettos, shockingly white, spiky pixie hair that was in extreme contrast to her bluish skin—yet she looked nothing like the female he was used to seeing. He'd only seen a genuine smile on her face one other time, and that had been in response to music, as well.

This time, her smile seemed to be equally prompted by the stranger—a tall, broader-than-average vamp—she was dancing with. Although he couldn't see them, Caleb imagined that her eerily hazed-over eyes, covered as usual by her big Ray-Ban sunglasses, were focused on the vamp's handsome face.

Mixed feelings swept through Caleb. Anger. Confusion. Resignation. At one time, he'd wanted to be someone who could make her smile, but she'd never let him close enough to try.

If his own pain was a raging river slowly growing calmer, Wraith's was a lit fuse ready to blow, taking everyone around her with it.

She didn't trust or rely on anyone easily. The fact that he'd betrayed her for Mahone had only been the nail in the coffin as far as she was concerned. But that hadn't stopped her from endangering her own life to save the two of them. That was something he'd never forget, even though she clearly wanted him to.

"Caleb, I was wondering . . ."

He returned his attention to Natia, surprised by his annoyance. He'd wanted to watch Wraith dance a little longer. Make sure she and the male didn't get any closer, or else—

Or else what? He mentally snorted. Would he walk over like a jealous lover and challenge the vamp to a duel? It was a ridiculous thought. Nonetheless, he looked over at Wraith again, only vaguely listening to what Natia was saying.

". . . you can come to dinner and meet with Mother. Try one more time to explain. What do you think?"

His jaw tightened when Wraith's dance partner placed a hand on her waist, caressing her over her leather jacket. Swallowing the growl of displeasure rising in his throat, Caleb shook his head and turned back to Natia. "I'm sorry, sweet. What were you asking?"

She frowned. "I was saying, why don't you come up to my room for a drink? We can spend the night together. Then tomorrow we can fly to Los Angeles and you can have dinner with Mother."

His brows rose, but not because of her suggestion that they spend the night together. He'd known that's where Natia was headed. But as for dinner with "Mother" . . . He'd rather be back in that warehouse taking his chances with the Hyperion gas. "Your mother hates me, Natia. As do most of your clan. Given what's happened recently to your cousins, they'll be even more suspicious of outsiders, let alone someone accused of killing Elijah."

Natia looked away at the mention of her brother's name, but then met Caleb's gaze once more. "The drug rapes occurred while you were in Korea, Caleb. Even Mother wouldn't accuse you of having something to do with that. And as for Elijah . . ." She bit her lip and trailed a hand down his arm. "I should have stood by you. Announced my faith in you. But I was so upset. I didn't know who to trust or . . ." Tears filled her eyes. Seeing her genuine regret, Caleb sighed.

He hugged her close, and she wrapped her arms around him. Her sweet, familiar scent filled his lungs, making him reconsider. Perhaps he should take her up on her invitation. Lose himself in her sweet body and then try, one more time, to talk to her mother . . .

But it suddenly occurred to him that sweetness didn't hold the appeal for him that it once might have. He wanted more. He wanted complexity. Shadows. A bitterness to make the pleasure of being in a woman's arms and inside her body all the more intense. And he didn't want to convince someone to have faith in him. He wanted more than that.

As he slowly pulled away from Natia's embrace, his gaze once again swept to Wraith.

Dumb shit, he berated himself. She's dead. She's beyond bitter. And most of all, she's not interested.

"Caleb? Are you even listening to me? What's gotten into you?"

He forced himself to turn back to Natia. She was pissed, her gaze moving from Caleb to Wraith with clear jealousy. Not good. A feline who thought her territory was being poached on was volatile and unpredictable. And even though he was no longer her territory, that wouldn't stop Natia from confronting Wraith. Caleb actually shuddered as he imagined what the two females could do to one another. The scene wouldn't be something Knox or Felicia would appreciate, that was for sure. Taking Natia's hand, he raised it to his lips and kissed it. "You're a guest of the Devereaux clan, aren't you? Because a drink is sounding really nice."

It was both truth and lie. A drink did sound nice, but he hadn't fallen off the wagon since joining the team. Granted, he was on vacation now, but he knew how easily one drink could turn into two, and that into a desperate need for more. Still, the longer he watched Wraith and that vamp, the more convinced he became that a drink would do far more good than not. That some *needs* were far more dangerous than others.

Natia beamed, all thoughts of Wraith apparently forgotten. "Yes. I'll . . . I'll be waiting for you. Give me ten minutes to get ready."

"Sure."

As she walked away, her security team moved like stealthy specters, shadowing her even as they blended in with the crowd. Caleb told himself to go with her. At the very least, to wait out the ten minutes on the patio, where he could get some fresh air. She might be expecting more than he was willing to give her, but at least she would be out of Wraith's vicinity. They could talk, and he'd figure out what to do then. Cursing beneath his breath, he strode toward the doors leading to the gardens outside.

He paused. He looked back. He gritted his teeth.

The vamp had his hands all over Wraith. On her bare skin now—caressing the vulnerable flesh at her throat.

Like the rest of her kind, Wraith was thought to have been human at one time until she appeared on earth, the living dead with no pulse, and no memory of who or what she was. There were many mysteries surrounding her kind, but one thing was universally known—touching their bare skin caused them pain.

He knew the vampire's prolonged touch had to be hurting Wraith like hell, but she took it, peering up at the vamp flirtatiously, a raw, sexual smile on her lips. The vamp's hand moved, and Caleb saw her cringe—an imperceptible flinch that highlighted the lines of distress near her eyes. Instantly, he thought of the scars on her throat and how they'd gotten there.

He took a swift look around the room, instinctively searching for his team to help out Wraith. The were, Dex Hunt, hadn't bothered showing up, and he didn't know where Lucy was. Mahone had left. Knox and Felicia hadn't arrived after the ceremony, but he knew Knox didn't give a damn how rude that might seem. The dharmire had finally won the body, heart, and soul of his human female and would likely have to be dragged away before he left her bed. Although Knox's parents, Bianca and Jacques Devereaux, were here, they were dancing under the watchful eyes of their guards, with no reason to suspect a wedding guest was being hurt by one of their clan.

Without hesitating, Caleb moved across the room.

"You know I can make it worth your time, Wraith. I've done it before."

Wraith shot Colt a practiced smile. "By 'it,' you mean making me come?"

Eyes narrowing, the vamp she hadn't seen for two years returned her smile with one of his own. "Making a wraith, and particularly you, come isn't an easy feat, so I wouldn't speak so dismissively if I were you." Once more, he rubbed the side of her neck with his thumb, but she barely noticed the sting of pain, let alone felt any pleasure.

It was as if she were completely dead now, not even able to recall the memory of physical pleasure Colt had once given her. She leaned away from his touch.

"We did it a few times. It means nothing. Leave it in the

past, Colt, where it belongs. Things are different now." She was clean, for one. Plus, she'd long grown accustomed to doing without a male's touch.

Instinctively, her gaze fluttered to Caleb, who was grinning and flirting with an exotic and buxom feline on the dance floor. A feline *princess*, she'd been told, named Natia. Due to the film over her eyes, she couldn't tell what color the female's hair was—it looked like several shades of gray, just like everything else in her life.

"Yes, I can see they are," Colt murmured, then tilted his head to Caleb and the feline. "She's gorgeous, but no match for you, doll."

At Colt's knowing tone, Wraith snapped her gaze back to his. She knew that if it were possible for her to flush, she'd be doing it right now. As it was, she struggled to keep her expression free of guilt. "Look, I don't know why you're here or how you knew where to find me, but if Knox finds out, he'll—"

Colt chuckled. "He'll what? He's heir apparent to the royal vamp throne. It's his wedding, and he invited the whole clan, Wraith. I'm part of the clan. You being here is raising more questions than my presence. Most of these folks probably have never even seen a wraith."

She ground her teeth at his condescending tone. "Does he know what you do?"

"Just what do I do?"

She looked at him chidingly. "You might be part of Knox's clan, but that's where your similarity ends. Knox is loyal to his family. To his people. To his wife. Your only loyalty is to the highest bidder for whatever you're peddling nowadays."

He hummed and smoothed his hand down her hair, his eyes challenging her to retaliate. She wanted to, but she was wise enough to know the power he held over her. The power to expose her for the weak coward she truly was. "What you say is the absolute truth, Wraith. And I've always been very loyal to you, haven't I?" Dropping his hand to the small of her back and pulling her close enough that she could feel his arousal against her stomach, he said, "I got you away from Ramsey, didn't I? Showed you how pleasure was so much better than pain. But I understand . . . You've been without for a long time. Now that I'm back, there's no need for that to continue." He bent over her so that his lips hovered over her earlobe. He raked his fangs against her. "Come on, baby. I've got what you need. As soon as you taste it again, you'll remember why it's so good. Why we were so good together and can be again."

Closing her eyes, Wraith swallowed hard. His voice was cajoling, his tone a dark, sinful urge. She felt herself lean against him as memories washed over her. Their shared past was one filled with darkness and pain, just as every part of her life was, but it was also the only time in the past ten years that she'd ever experienced pure physical pleasure. The drugs Colt had access to were the only things that had allowed her to feel pure pleasure at being touched. But they had also left her stoned. Disoriented. In an altered state for days.

That was what a wraith's options were for avoiding pain. Complete isolation or complete addiction.

Colt was right. He had saved her to some degree. He'd helped her see that what she'd had with Ramsey Monroe wasn't real and wasn't all there was to life. But what he'd introduced her to had been just as limiting. Just as destructive. Still, despite her addiction to Colt and the drugs, she'd finally managed to extract herself from their grip. It had taken time, and then Mahone had found her. Given her the opportunity to once again do something different. This time, something good.

She wanted to keep doing good with the little time she had left. She also wanted to get the information she needed to leave this life with some semblance of peace.

She wanted those things more than she needed to ease her pain. More than she needed sex. More than she needed to be touched.

She eased away from Colt and shot another glance toward Caleb. Only he wasn't there. Scanning the room, she saw him beside the patio doors. Watching her.

Or at least that's what she thought at first.

Behind her sunglasses, her eyes rounded in surprise. Caleb was alone now. The feline had disappeared. But he wasn't looking at her. He was looking at Colt and at the hand that, even now, was once again stroking her neck.

Amazing, she thought. She'd been wrong about her inability to feel pleasure without the aid of drugs.

She felt pleasure now.

A pleasure that was sweeping through her because she recognized the look on Caleb's face.

Pure, murderous rage mixed with possessive jealousy.

All three—his rage, his jealousy, and her pleasure—flared and became more intense the second he began to walk toward her.

"Wraith." Her name fell harshly from Caleb's lips as he approached her.

Typically, Wraith ignored him, but as she continued to dance with the big vamp beside her, her smile turned from seductive to cool. Yeah, she'd heard him all right.

As always, he was assaulted by the dual need to kiss her and shake her. Then kiss her some more. She'd been alternately ignoring him and hissing at him from the start. Learning he'd betrayed her had only made her double her efforts. After Korea, he'd thought he'd have the chance to fix things between them, but the moment had never seemed right. She'd seemed to withdraw into herself even more, locking herself in her room for such prolonged periods of time that he and Lucy had wondered what she was doing that she couldn't do in front of them. They'd taken turns hanging back, but except for the one time he'd heard a crash in her room, she'd been eerily quiet.

The day he'd threatened to break her door down had been a crossroads for him. When he'd said it, he'd meant it. He'd been damn sick of her running away from him when he knew she was as attracted to him as he was to her. But when she'd spit back, absolutely no softening in her voice, he'd wondered what the hell he was doing. What the hell he hoped to gain from breaking down her defenses.

No, he couldn't deny that he lusted after this female. He'd wanted her from the second she'd straddled his lap and shoved a gun in his face, hissing and cussing a blue streak in order to hide the fear and pain inside her.

But he'd finally forced himself to accept it—his attraction to her was as fruitless as it was inexplicable. She couldn't be touched without experiencing pain. That was actually the least of her problems. Even so, Caleb had sworn never to be the cause of an innocent's pain again.

Ever.

That said, he'd be damned if he'd let someone hurt her when he could stop it.

He turned to the vamp. "Get lost. I need to talk to Wraith."

The vamp, who was taller than him by a good three inches, wasn't easily intimidated. "Wraith's just fine. Real fine. I'm not going anywhere." Once more, his hand moved to caress Wraith's neck.

Quick as a snake, Caleb grabbed the vamp's wrist and shoved him back. The vamp growled and his eyes flashed red.

Conversation in the ballroom stilled. Dancers paused. The air in the room grew tense. The vamp tsked. "You're going to regret that . . ."

Casually, Wraith glanced at him. "You heard him, Colt. Leave us. Please."

Shock made Caleb's head jerk back. He'd never heard Wraith say "please" before. He'd also never heard her speak to someone in such a familiar, intimate tone. Rage spiraled through him. When he saw Colt clench his fists and unsheathe his fangs, Caleb stepped in front of Wraith, more than willing to give the vamp what he was asking for.

The vamp's eyes followed Caleb's movement. He lifted a brow and smirked. Instantly, his eyes faded to their normal color, pitch black with silver pupils. "We'll talk later, Wraith," the vamp crooned. He swept his hand toward her. "Good luck, my friend." With a mocking smile, he left.

Wraith didn't even bother watching his exit. Hands on hips, she scowled at Caleb. "What the hell are you doing, O'Flare?"

He got in her face, the tips of his shoes nearly touching hers. "You always let vamps caress your throat despite the fact you don't have any blood to give?"

She stood her ground and arched a brow. "It wasn't blood he was after."

Taking a deep breath, he stepped back. Slowly, the conversation and music started again.

Caleb ran a hand through his hair. "He had his hands on you," he bit out. "He was hurting you."

She looked stunned, then snorted and rolled her eyes. "I hurt all the time. Some types of 'hurt' are better than others," she drawled, "and there are plenty of males willing to make me hurt good."

Her words gave him pause. He'd heard the stories about wraiths and their attraction to BDSM. He supposed it was a testament to the strength of a creature's sex drive—how they wanted sex, even if pain came with it. But in the case of wraiths, there was no kink involved—they simply had no other choice.

He remembered touching her throat just before they'd left for North Korea, examining the old scars from the paralyzing collar she'd been forced to wear so some freak could experiment on her. He'd been careful. Gentle. But even that fluttering touch had caused her pain. No matter how she tried to dismiss it now, he'd seen her tremble and flinch away from the vamp's touch, too.

She obviously took his silence for disbelief. "What, you don't think men have touched me before? Fucked me? Because plenty have. What do you care anyway? I saw your little princess leave, and she looked ready for some action. You better get to her."

He'd been dismissed. And what more could he say? He turned to leave.

"Unless . . ."

He sucked in a breath and froze. Unless what?

"Unless you want to see for yourself that I don't mind a little pain."

FIVE

Wraith saw Caleb's back muscles tense and closed her eyes.

What. Had. She. Just. Said?

One minute she'd been watching the golden boy walk away, imagining him doing the nasty with that vixen of a cat instead of just dancing with her; then, in quick unison, she'd experienced denial. Lust.

Entitlement.

Not this time, she'd thought. This time, she wasn't going to resign herself to having him walk away. Not when she might not have another chance to be with him.

Over the sounds of music and revelry, she heard him breathe a curse.

Her eyes flared open. Swallowing hard, she waited for him to laugh and walk away.

He didn't. Slowly, he turned to face her, keeping several feet between them.

"You're joking? Right?"

The way he said it, he clearly believed she was playing him. Her brain screamed for her to backtrack. To laugh it off. "Yep.

Gotcha," she'd say, then let him walk away to go fuck the feline he'd been dancing with.

But even though she opened her mouth to say just that, nothing came out.

He narrowed his eyes and took several steps closer. "Wraith?" His confusion was apparent, as was the fact he was going to reject her. "Sex hurts you. I don't see how it couldn't. I can't . . ."

She'd been waiting for his refusal, but now that it was on the tip of his tongue, she couldn't bear to hear it. One night. Was that too much to ask? A bit of forgetfulness. A hint of pleasure to go along with the pain she always carried around with her. After what she'd done, what she'd helped achieve, didn't she deserve that? She'd *blown herself up*, for God's sake.

"We don't have to have sex," she said, wanting to be with him in whatever manner she could. She needed it. Craved it. He was sexy no matter what he wore, but tonight, in his formal tux, he looked like every woman's fantasy—tightly leashed sexuality thinly disguised as charm and elegance. She'd sensed his true primal nature from the very beginning, and it had made her core ache with the need to be filled.

By him.

But even though she was willing, she knew he'd never agree. Caleb was a good man. An honorable man. A warrior, but also a healer. He could never receive pleasure from hurting her, even though there had been plenty of men who could. She could probably find one or two in this very room, in fact. But she didn't want that tonight.

There was only one man she wanted, here and now. Just once, before she died the way she should have long ago, she wanted something different—something she'd never experienced in her current form. Something she might not have experienced it in her human life. She wanted to touch and be touched by someone who cared about what *she* felt. What *she* needed.

She wanted to have sex with someone who cared about *her*. And she didn't want to be doped up on drugs in order to experience it, either.

No matter how she'd treated him, how she'd pushed him away, she knew Caleb cared for her.

So she took a chance and bargained for what she needed. "I can . . . I can touch you. I can control it. I can pleasure you," she assured him, knowing that touching him, no matter the pain it caused, would be *her* pleasure. Her nipples hardened as she imagined it. Stroking his broad shoulders and chest. Trailing trembling fingers down his abs to encircle his shaft. "I . . ."

Again, his confusion was evident. "Why would you want to do that? I thought you hated me. Were pissed at me for acting on Mahone's behalf. I mean, you saved me and Mahone, but that was the job . . ."

She scowled. Of course he'd have to bring up his betrayal. For days, she and Caleb had worked together—solving puzzles and piecing out his visions in order to track down the location of the vamp antidote—when the whole time, Mahone already had that information. He'd just been testing her, and he'd used Caleb to do so. What she'd thought had been a building trust between them had turned out to be a lie. "I do," she said. "I am. But . . ." How could she explain that while she still felt betrayed by his actions, she also understood why he'd done it. From what she knew about him, Caleb always did the hard thing, especially when it was for the good of the whole. Mahone had been right—she had been the unknown element in the group. He'd needed to test her, and Caleb had given him the means. It had pissed her off, but it hadn't made her want him any less, no matter how hard she'd tried. "Jesus, why do you have to analyze everything?"

He said nothing, not even to question her reference to a Christian God, the one she'd studied in L.A. and continued to study, drawn to the accounts of his selflessness and willingness to suffer for the redemption of others. Caleb simply studied her as if he was still trying to figure out something puzzling. His ability to remain cautious and curious when she was being burned alive by desire shamed her.

Hurt and anger made her turn away from him. "Forget it," she called over her shoulder. "I just thought you might want some R & R, too. If you don't want it with me, I'll go find someone who does. And this time, don't interfere."

She skirted around the guests on the dance floor and was almost out of the room when his voice stopped her.

"Wait."

Now it was Wraith who froze. The sound of his voice, deep and gravelly, dark in a way his cockiness and movie star good looks belied, had brought her to a halt. Slowly, she turned back to face him. Several people looked at them. Tipped their heads toward one another, most likely whispering about the handsome human male talking to the pitiful dead creature.

She didn't care.

He wanted her. She could see it in his face. In his glittering eyes where desire burned like a raging fire. In the nostrils that flared as he stared at her, his features hard. Dangerous.

Something tightened in her chest, and she felt it move to shiver along her spine as if he'd caressed it with his finger. She gasped, a sound of excitement. And fear?

The notion made her straighten her shoulders, raise her chin, and react the way she always reacted—on the offensive. "Don't think about it too long," she drawled. "I'm getting bored really fast."

But he couldn't *not* think about it. She saw it all tumbling through his mind. His doubts. His suspicions. His belief that he could just talk to her. Comfort her. And yes, maybe even experiment a little to see what caused her pain and what didn't.

Her mouth twisted at the dreaded word: "experiment."

Like she was some freak whose responses were to be judged. Analyzed. But how could she blame him? Even the idea of making out with a female without a pulse must cause him concern. She'd never been intimate with a human before. How did he know she wouldn't hurt him? Infect him, somehow? Why had she even—

He closed the distance between them and thumbed her chin up. That small contact caused a zing to shoot through her body—a jolt of pain, yes, but one tempered by the headiness of his touch.

"You should be more protective of yourself."

"What do I need to protect myself from?" she murmured, moving her jaw so his thumb caressed it. "I know you won't hurt me, not intentionally."

"And how do you know that?"

She put her hand against his chest, relishing the accelerated beat of his heart. For a moment she weakened, wanting to drop her shields and give him a little of the truth. "Give me some credit, O'Flare. I don't need to be psychic to sense the goodness inside you."

He peered at her from beneath heavy lids. "Goodness, huh?" He swiped his thumb across her lips, then slipped it into her mouth. When she gasped, he rubbed her tongue, then her lips, wetting them. "You really don't know me, do you, Wraith?" he whispered.

In response, she nipped his thumb, then laved the hurt with her tongue. His eyes went dark and smoky, making her smile. "I might come off as a total bitch, but I'm a smart one. And I don't live in denial. I know what is. And what isn't." She hesitated, then plowed on, knowing it had to be said. Caleb was too knight-in-shining-armor. He was attracted to her because he wanted to save her, she knew that. Only he couldn't.

And even if he could, she didn't want to be saved. She'd walked the earth as the living dead long enough. She was tired. So tired. Maybe tonight she could have more, but eventually . . . soon . . .

"Tonight isn't going to be more than a roll in the sack. Know that now, before things go further."

"Is that right?" he said with a mocking smile.

She narrowed her eyes at him. "Listen, O'Flare—"

"You'd best brace yourself, Wraith," he said softly, a hint of Irish and sex sneaking into his voice.

She did.

Her eyes widened.

Her muscles tensed.

Then he kissed her.

Sort of. Truth was, he hardly touched her because, as always, he didn't want to hurt her. She wanted to weep at that knowledge.

Such a good man, she thought again.

His lips barely brushed hers, but their breath mingled and their gazes locked.

For long moments, he stood close to her, grazing her mouth with whisper-soft sips and the occasional slick glide of his tongue. Raising her arms, she threaded her fingers through his hair, marveling at the soft, silky texture. He pulled his head back to stare into the dark lenses of her sunglasses, and she wished he could see past them—see past the cloudy haze that covered her eyes. She wished he could see the color of her eyes and watch her pupils dilate with the evidence of her desire, the way a normal human's pupils would.

But she knew what he'd see if he removed her glasses. Blankness. Eyes foggy and seemingly unaffected, when so much of her was churning with a restless energy she could barely contain.

He pulled away, and she barely stopped herself from grabbing for him. "I need to talk to someone," he said.

She tried to fight off a pang of jealousy. The cat. "You certain you want to do that?" she whispered, hoping she sounded seductive.

"Yes, but I won't be long. You changing your mind?"

She shook her head. No, she wasn't changing her mind. She might be a fool. She might not know what this evening was going to bring her, but she wanted to find out. She wanted him.

"Don't move and don't jerk me around, Wraith. If I find out—"

She shook her head. "I'm not. I won't. Tonight, I just want . . . I just want to forget . . . to rest . . ."

"So I'm going to be used as a sleeping pill?" he teased, his face lightening with a smile.

"I didn't say anything about sleeping, O'Flare."

His smile vanished as he sucked in a breath, eyes flashing hot with desire. Without another word, he turned around.

Holy shit. For a second there, he'd looked like he wanted to eat her alive. Suck her up and swallow her down.

She licked her lips, thinking that's exactly what she wanted to do to him.

Before she could let her doubts get the better of her, she turned around to scan the crowd. Her brows furrowed when she saw Lucy by the bar, sipping on a drink.

Had Lucy seen her and Caleb kissing? Would she be hurt when she saw them leave together? She knew the little mage had a crush on him, and for an instant, guilt made her pause. But Wraith wasn't selfless as a general rule, and that counted double when it came to her limited choices in bed partners. She liked Lucy, but not enough to give up a chance like this.

Still . . . What if sex with Caleb was addictive? What if after tonight she wanted more? She couldn't have more. She knew that. And they still had to work together.

Sensing she was close to bolting, Wraith pushed her concerns out of her head. It was too loud in here. Too . . . happy. She needed to get outside. To be alone so she could think clearly for a moment.

Desperately, she searched the room until she saw the doors leading outside. She strode toward the exit, and toward what she hoped would be clarity. Lord knows, she'd need it.

Convincing Natia that he didn't want to get back together or have sex with her had taken far longer than Caleb thought it would. Finally, he gave up trying to part on good terms.

He barely shut the door to Natia's room before the vase she'd been hefting crashed against the other side. The Were standing guard next to the door looked at him from the corner of his eye, and although the burly creature's expression didn't change, Caleb could sense the amusement radiating from him.

That had gone as badly as he'd thought it would, with Natia accusing him of fucking Wraith just to get back at her and her family. Then she'd started railing about her mother being right, that Caleb must have had something to do with Elijah's death since he clearly had no respect for the feline race as a whole . . .

Caleb sighed and pinched the bridge of his nose. He didn't mind a little spirit or outright bitchiness in a female. In fact, he preferred it. The attitude certainly made life more interesting. Even so, Natia's little temper tantrum should have had him reconsidering Wraith's offer.

It didn't. Not at all.

Natia didn't hold a candle to Wraith in the bitch category. In all their years together, despite all the fights and hysterics, Natia had never pulled a gun on him. Wraith had already done it once, and she'd probably do it a few more times before things were settled between them. He didn't care. Wraith had finally let down her guard. Admitted she needed something from him, something even more than sexual relief. She needed contact. Caring. Intimacy. And he was the man who was going to give her what she wanted. What she needed.

He started the walk from the guest quarters back to the reception area. On the way, he thought of the vamp Wraith had been dancing with. There had been a familiarity between them that indicated a past physical intimacy, whether it had been actual intercourse or not. Hell, despite Wraith's implication that she'd been fucked by a squadron of males, he didn't even know if wraiths could have intercourse. That was one of the things he was going to demand from her tonight—information. He didn't want just physical or sexual contact from her—he wanted emotional contact, as well. He wanted to know more about her, more than he'd been given in the team's personnel files. He wanted to know what she was capable of taking and what she wasn't.

He'd already figured out his healing powers were worthless with her.

Both in Korea and on the dance floor tonight, he'd tried to trance himself when he was kissing her. His healing powers had saved men whose insides had been blasted in four different directions, so why couldn't they prevent the pain Wraith felt at being touched? Only it hadn't worked.

It wasn't completely unheard of. Usually, his powers worked best when the person he was trying to heal was so far gone, their body so damaged that there was no natural mental barrier to block him. Healthy individuals, whether they knew it or not, had the power to protect themselves from the probings of the Otherworld, even when it was done for their own good. That's why possession by dead spirits was such a rare thing. It was only when people were extremely weak, their natural defenses down, that their minds would let another in.

That was also why wraiths in particular were feared by his people. They were thought to be the walking hosts of evil spirits from the Otherworld.

Caleb didn't buy it. The instant he'd met Wraith, he'd known there was nothing evil about her. She was lost and damaged, but she had goodness in her, too.

She'd proven that time and again.

The fact that he couldn't help her—heal her—rubbed him raw.

He wanted to give her more tonight than forgetfulness. Assuming he could even give her that.

SIX

Wraith stepped out into a garden. Despite the fact she saw only bare branches, she knew they were actually blooming with roses, magnolias, and camellias. She'd heard other guests commenting on their beauty, and if she concentrated, she could almost smell their distinct sweetness in the air. She stumbled slightly when she felt a warm breeze against her skin, one that actually invaded her body and stayed awhile. The warmth was gone in just a few seconds but to a being who was perpetually cold, the sensation had been a small slice of heaven. Fleeting, yes, but still something that might comfort her in the end.

Shaking her head, she stepped farther into the garden. Lucky vamps. Even though it was an early evening smack-dab in the middle of spring, the Dome would maintain this same pleasant weather—neither too hot nor too cold, whether day or night—when the rest of the state sweltered in the summer or froze in the winter. No wonder she wasn't alone. There were several individuals wandering the manicured paths, so she immediately headed around the side of the house to what looked like a delivery dock and service area. A door to what she assumed was the kitchen was closed. To her right, a dense grove of trees shaded a grass-covered knoll, the perfect spot for picnicking or playing, but also for watching the comings and goings of Knox's staff in order to gain entry into his home.

She'd have to talk to the vamp about—

Wraith's senses went on alert when she spotted movement in the trees. Although her muscles tightened, she immediately loosened them and kept walking so as to appear unconcerned. It could just be an adventurous guest who, like her, was simply looking for a little escape from the merriment inside.

That's what she'd told herself earlier, too.

Upon first arriving, she'd also felt like she was being watched. Tracked. Then, when she'd encountered Colt inside the grand house, the feeling had gone away, and she'd assumed it had been him looking for her. She no longer believed that. Wraith didn't have this kind of feeling more than once without reason.

Just to confirm it was actually her and not the house her observer was interested in, however, Wraith turned and headed back toward the gardens. She grabbed a glass of champagne from a wandering waiter. Taking her time, she strolled the gardens and pretended to indulge in the champagne. She even smiled as she passed a few of the guests, couples clearly immersed in each other rather than their surroundings. She stifled her instinctive disdain for their carelessness, then thought of Caleb. Had he returned? Was he looking for her?

She wanted to go to him, but she couldn't let this feeling of being watched go unexplored. It was more intense now. She felt someone's gaze pressing on her body. Idly, she glanced around and noticed a big, well-dressed male just behind her and to her right. He averted his gaze.

Bingo.

Putting her glass down on a stone pedestal, she made her way back toward the service area, moving behind a high retaining wall that led to an alley with a refuse area.

A few seconds later, the male stepped into view. Wraith grabbed his arm, yanked him around, and shoved him face-first into the wall. With her other hand, she shoved her pistol into his side. Hard. Although she expected him to grab at her with his other arm, he didn't. Instead, his body remained slack and he rested the palm of his free hand flat against the wall. He didn't gasp, didn't groan. He barely even seemed to breathe.

"Who are you?" she snapped.

"A friend," was his only response.

Wraith laughed. "I don't have friends. No family. No one. You wanna try again?"

"You have friends, Wraith. You've just forgotten them."

His softly spoken words and his use of her name—somehow she knew it was being used properly and not generically—gave her pause. What did he mean? Could he be referring to her past? Did this man know something about who she'd been?

For a second, she felt her guard lower, then caught herself. She shook herself mentally. Staring at his profile, she told herself to be smart. Ruthless.

Vigilant.

He had an arresting face, all sharp angles and jutting strength, and a subtle British accent that matched the simple but expensive lines of his clothes. Everything about him—from the way he moved and talked—screamed thinly disguised danger. He was trained. Deadly.

When he shifted and lightly tested the grip she had on his arm, she shoved him harder against the wall. "Try anything, *friend*, and you're dead. Are we clear?"

"Quite," he murmured.

"Spread your legs." He did. With her gun still firmly in his side, she slowly released his arm and commanded, "Both hands on the wall."

He complied readily. "Anything else?" He sounded calm. Magnanimous, even.

"Don't move. Not an inch." Swiftly, she began using her free hand to search him, starting with his legs and working up.

"No," he agreed, sounding amused. "Not an inch. But given where you're headed, one inch isn't the problem . . ."

He hissed when she shoved her hand none too gently between his legs.

"Damn it," he growled, all sound of amusement gone from his voice. "Watch what you're—"

"Shut up!" She leaned harder into him, moved her hand inside his jacket and found the holstered weapon there. Again, she waited for him to move, to try and take her down.

No way he was going to let her get his weapon, she thought. *No way.*

But he did. He just stood there while she withdrew the heavy pistol. It was a Luger, as big and sleek and expensive-looking as its owner. Shoving the gun into her front waistband, she finished her search.

"I'm not here to hurt you," he said softly.

"Uh-huh," she snorted. "What next? You're going to tell me you come in peace, right?"

"I'm not—"

Grabbing his hair, Wraith slammed his face into the wall, grinding it into the plaster and stone with enough force to make him grunt. "Don't fuck around with me. You were watching me. Why? Who sent you?"

"Again, a friend," he gritted.

Wraith cracked him on the side of his head with the butt of her gun, then spoke over his outraged growl. "Try again."

"Fine."

Before she could anticipate his movements, he knocked the back of his head into her face. Pain exploded in a profusion of black dots, momentarily blinding her. As she struggled to recover, the man kicked back, slamming her gun out of her hand before turning to tackle her. Instead of trying to break her fall, however, Wraith reached for his gun, which was still tucked into the front of her pants. When she landed, her head knocked against the unforgiving concrete. The pain almost made her black out, but she managed to stay conscious *and* keep her grip on his gun. Mercilessly, even with him on top of her, she shoved the gun into his crotch.

They stared at each other, his face directly above hers.

"You've got three seconds," she said hoarsely, "to tell me who you are before I shoot your dick off."

Unbelievably, he lifted himself onto his elbows, glanced down at the gun she held on him, and grinned. He tsked and raised his gaze to hers. "And break hundreds of women's hearts in the process?"

She narrowed her eyes, the line immediately making her think of Caleb. Like this man, Caleb wielded a playboy's charm naturally but deliberately, a front for the deadliness that infused every nerve of his body.

She punched the gun harder into the man's balls. "More like do them a huge favor. Maybe then you'll think twice before you follow a female around to—"

"Wraith?"

The soft, feminine voice behind her made her stiffen, but she didn't turn to look. Didn't take her eyes off the man on top of her. His companion might have a weapon, but she wasn't worried about that. Because if the woman had wanted Wraith dead, she'd have taken her out already. That she hadn't already done so meant she cared about the man on top of her. And his package.

"Who is she?" she snapped out.

He raised a brow. "Don't you know?"

The vague comment snapped her patience. She prepared to fire her gun.

"Wraith. Don't! Joanna. It's Joanna."

Joanna. As soon as the name was uttered, Wraith recognized the voice.

Holy hell. Joanna.

"He's with you?"

"Yes. He was watching you for *me*. For an opportunity to talk to you without being noticed."

Wraith shook her head in disbelief. For an opportunity not to get noticed? Joanna was as naïve as ever, apparently. She glared at the man, then ordered, "Get off me."

He did. Quite speedily.

Scrambling to her feet, she kept the gun trained on his chest but managed to put some distance between them.

The man rolled his shoulders, stretched his neck to one side, then the other, then raked a hand through his slightly disheveled hair. He jerked his head toward the gun. "Be careful. The safety's off."

"No shit."

Unbelievably, his mouth quirked. As if he was *amused* with her. "Oh, that's right. Joanna said you're a superspy who's very good with weapons. You just lack something when it comes to family loyalty, apparently."

"Fuck you," she muttered automatically, even though her words held little heat. Taking a steadying breath, she turned her body so she could keep him in her sights but also see the female who was standing half in shadow. "Step into the light."

She did.

Wraith swallowed hard as she took in Joanna's features. The shock of white hair. The bluish skin that was a perfect match for hers. Of course, Joanna dressed differently. Classier. Less fuck-you-and-get-the-hell-away-from-me. Joanna had always teased Wraith relentlessly about dressing like a poster child for the walking wounded. Wraith, in turn, had teased Joanna about her preference for nun's attire.

Wraith eyed the man who'd immediately moved to Joanna's side. He put a hand on her clothed shoulder and squeezed. That small connection, coupled with seeing another one of her kind, someone she'd once considered a friend, had Wraith blinking her eyes furiously.

Damn it. Apparently becoming human enough to die meant getting all the sappy human emotions, too.

Joanna smiled and opened her arms to her. "Wraith. It's so good to see you. Aren't you going to give me a hug?"

Wraith was tempted. Touching another wraith didn't cause pain. It was why many of them turned to each other for sexual release. All wraiths, however, were female. Wraith had never felt a spark of sexual feeling for another wraith, but she'd often craved a hug from one or more of her sisters. When she'd first left Maine, she'd missed that affectionate touch more than anything.

Until she'd begun to crave Caleb's touch.

Caleb. He had to be back by now. Would probably come looking for her if she didn't return soon. For some reason, the idea of him finding her gone, or even worse, finding her with Joanna, made panic shudder through her. She made sure her voice reflected none of it.

"What are you doing here, Joanna? How the hell did you get inside the Dome?"

With a frown, Joanna lowered her arms, not bothering to hide the hurt on her face.

Wraith forced herself to shrug the guilt away. "Answer me."

"I was invited."

"Bullshit."

Joanna's mouth tipped up. "Same old Wraith. Suspicious and foulmouthed. But I *was* invited. Knox Devereaux wanted to surprise you. To have one of your own kind here. A friend, he requested. I certainly fit the bill. Once."

Knox's generosity both touched and infuriated her. "He shouldn't have bothered. I don't want you here. None of you. You know that."

"Yes, you made it quite clear when you left Maine that you didn't want to be associated with your own kind anymore."

"That's not it and you know it."

"Your turning's begun."

Joanna's abrupt change of subject made Wraith frown. She shrugged. "Our intel is right. As the oldest wraith, it's my turn. So you know my leaving was better for everyone involved. I'm nothing but a liability to our kind now."

"A liability, or our only chance of survival."

"What do you mean?" Wraith asked.

"Wraith, we've never had the chance to study one of our kind so soon upon her changing, when she still retains her immortality. Maybe . . ."

Bitterness filled Wraith's mouth. So this wasn't about being missed. It was about Joanna wanting to study her. That's all she was good for, being some kind of test subject. It managed to shock her, the fact that Joanna would ask that of her when she knew exactly what Wraith had suffered in the past.

"No," Wraith said. "We're freaks. Apparently, dying is what we're meant to do. I don't want to be part of prolonging any wraith's life."

Joanna looked like she wanted to argue, but then nodded. "Fine. If you won't do it, we won't force you. I know what you're thinking, and it's not like that, Wraith. We'd never hurt you. We want you back with us where you belong. With people that care about you."

"I am with people who care about me," she said instinctively. But when Joanna scoffed, she wished she could retract the words.

"The Para-Ops team? Care for you? You're deluding yourself, Wraith."

Was that true? Did she truly believe that her team cared about her? Not because of what she could do for them, but because of who she was? She remembered how furious Caleb had been after she'd blown herself up, regenerated, and made her way back to them. He'd been so out of control that he'd forgotten the need to take care when touching her.

That meant he cared about her, didn't it? And maybe that meant the others cared for her, as well.

Widening her stance, she tightened her grip on her gun and lifted it again. "I want you both to leave and not come back. Tell the others I refuse to be a freak they can study until I'm of no use to them."

"Unlike your team, you mean? Do they even know you're turning, Wraith? What do you think is going to happen when they learn you're going to start losing your ability to regenerate? Do you think they're going to care about you then?"

If it was possible, Joanna's words were both taunting and compassionate. The man beside her, while quiet, was obviously assessing Wraith. Evaluating her. Sizing her up like this was some kind of dog and pony show. It made her feel like the freak she'd verbally rejected, something she'd never wanted to feel like again.

"Who's he?" she asked, pointing her gun at him.

"I'm hers," the man said.

Wraith nodded, trying not to feel jealous at the simple statement. "You got a name?"

He hesitated then looked at Joanna, who nodded. "Michel."

"You're human, Michel?"

"You could say that."

"So you know exactly what Joanna is asking for, right? She wants to study me because she wants to remain immortal."

"It's not mortality that comes with the turning. Not when every wraith to turn has died before her eleventh year. It's a death sentence. One I'll do anything to stop. I'll even take you down if I have to. Joanna doesn't want to use force. I'm making no promises."

"Michel . . ." Joanna said chidingly.

Wraith shook her head. "It's okay, Joanna. We understand each other. It's better that way. Now understand me. I'm going back inside. I have something extremely important to do. If you get in the way, I promise I will kill you. Both of you."

Michel's eyes flashed furiously, but Joanna just nodded. "We won't interfere. I've said what I wanted. We're heading back to Maine. I hope you'll join us there, Wraith. Soon. Come on, Michel."

Michel didn't look like he wanted to obey. Joanna tugged on his arm. "Come on!" she snapped, showing some of her natural wraith spunk.

"Yes, Michel. Listen to Joanna like a good little boy, now," Wraith taunted.

With a growl, he turned away, and they disappeared into the shadows of the trees.

Wraith stayed where she was for several minutes, her gun

pointed outward. It was only when she sensed her arm shaking that she lowered and holstered her gun, then moved swiftly back toward the gardens. She took time to gain her composure before going inside, where the party had grown even more raucous. She immediately scanned the room for Caleb.

Her mouth dried up when she saw him.

Eyes on hers, he started walking toward her. A second later, he was waylaid by someone who grabbed his arm, but Wraith barely saw that. Her gaze had focused on his chest and the dark shadow that now pulsed like a giant ink stain.

A death mark.

A death mark that hadn't been there before.

Terror made her dizzy and her knees weak. Wraiths saw death marks on people's chests all the time. It identified those with cancer. Or a brain tumor. Even the slow effects of lead poisoning. However, the mark also appeared when sudden death loomed in someone's near future, the result of events recently set in motion. In those cases, when death was situational rather than a result of illness, it was never guaranteed. Events could change. But not always.

"Wraith," she heard someone say from behind her.

She shook her head, trying to clear her fuzzy thoughts.

"Wraith."

She turned. It was Mahone, his expression one of genuine confusion. His face had almost completely healed. A few bruises were still visible, and of course, he'd scarred. But those would fade, just like hers had. "Mahone. What . . . what are you . . . ?"

"Are you okay?" The man was staring at her as if he wasn't sure what she'd do next.

She wasn't so certain, either.

Swallowing hard, she whispered, "I'm . . . I'm fine."

He didn't look convinced, but he cleared his throat. "Listen, Wraith. I'm going to brief the team on its next mission, but I need to talk with you first. There's a situation with the felines. One that just reached crisis proportions. I . . ."

Wraith heard everything he said about the recent rash of rapes against feline females. Blurrily aware, focusing on Caleb's death stain, she listened as Mahone told her that just a few hours ago, the royal feline princess Morgana had been the latest rape victim and that her mother was sure the perpetrator was human and too evasive to be working alone. She was accusing him of being law enforcement. Connected to the government. Finding the rapist was to be the Para-Ops team's highest priority, more important than their mission to find out Wraith's identity. For now, he said, trying to reassure her, but Wraith knew the truth. Her gut twisted.

Mahone's words echoed through her head as she stared at Caleb. At the death mark that hadn't been there before she'd offered to be with him. It hadn't appeared until he'd agreed to it. And until she'd run into Joanna outside.

Defeat was a dark, empty hole inside of her.

She got the message loud and clear.

The mark, coupled with Joanna's surprise appearance, told her that not only couldn't she have Caleb, she couldn't have any of it. Not a night in his arms. Not a purpose to serve. Not even a team to belong to.

She'd been a fool not to disappear when she'd reached her tenth "die day." She had no business being around others, trying to live any semblance of a life. She was dead, and she was death to anyone who got close to her.

Only she could control her fate and protect the few individuals she'd managed to connect with. By removing herself from all of them. With Joanna's words about the Para-Ops team using her and Mahone's description of a new mission, the decision was easy.

She turned back to Mahone, an angry scowl on her face, forcing her words to be hard. Unforgiving. "Forget it, Mahone. I'm not letting you use me again only to blow me off when I need something in return. I'm done."

SEVEN

Caleb saw the desire on Wraith's face a second before he saw the fear. He moved toward her, almost cursing when Knox's parents stepped in front of him. "Having a good time, Mr. O'Flare?"

He hesitated, wanting to get to Wraith fast but not wanting to be rude to the vamp Queen and King, either. "I am, ma'am. Thank you." He looked up at the tall vamp standing proudly next to Bianca Devereaux. "Sir," he said, bowing his head slightly.

"I've heard many things about you, Mr. O'Flare. Not all of them good," said Jacques Devereaux.

Caleb stiffened but didn't bother defending himself or offering any explanation. Instead, all he said was, "I'm sorry to hear that, sir."

Jacques studied him for several seconds, then smiled. "I think you should know, given my peculiar circumstances, I learned a long time ago not to believe everything I hear."

The vamp stared at Caleb for so long, he almost shuffled his feet like a little boy. Jacques Devereaux, a human when he married the vamp Queen, had been accused of betraying the vamp clan by revealing several vampire secrets during the French Revolution. Everyone close to him believed he'd been beheaded. Only centuries later did his son and wife learn that he'd survived—but only because his wife had managed to begin the process of turning him into a vamp first, risking her own life in the process.

"I believe Wraith is waiting for you," Bianca said in a knowing tone. "We won't keep you any longer."

Caleb couldn't get to Wraith fast enough, but he paused long enough to say, "Please tell Knox and Felicia, whenever they manage to show up, that we're very happy for them."

Bianca smiled. "I will. Now . . ." Bianca frowned when angry words filtered toward them. As one, they glanced over to see Wraith and Mahone in a heated discussion.

"Excuse me," Caleb said, striding toward them. He was just in time to catch Wraith's words.

"You can't argue with me, Mahone. Just fuck off. You're reneging on our deal to help some . . . some *felines* that I could care less about."

The word "felines" rolled off Wraith's tongue so disdainfully that for a moment Caleb was shocked. Not once during the time they'd been working together had he seen her reveal disdain for any particular race. Suspicion, yes, but not disdain.

In his periphery, Caleb saw Lucy rushing up to them. A quick glance confirmed she feared the worst.

"Wraith," Mahone plowed on. "The situation that's come up is critical—"

"Critical to the Para-Ops team, maybe, but not to me."

Just behind her, Caleb frowned. "What the hell does that mean?" he questioned. "You're a part of the Para-Ops team."

She didn't look at him. "Not anymore, I'm not."

Lucy gasped.

Caleb kept his gaze on Wraith. Unbelievably, she actually tried to walk away from him.

Growling, he went after her, even though he knew he shouldn't.

She was fast, so it wasn't until they were in the grand foyer that he caught up with her. He grabbed her, conscious of the feel of her distressed leather jacket in his grasp, holding on despite her automatic attempt to jerk away.

"What the hell is wrong with you? That's it? You're just going to walk? Why?"

She still refused to meet his gaze. "Mahone promised me—"

"I know," he said between clenched teeth. "He promised we'd help you find out who you are. But now, I take it, something more important than your precious identity has come up, right? Something having to do with *felines*?" He imitated the disdain with which she'd spoken the word. She scowled and he released her arm. "It can't wait? How selfish can you be?"

Something resembling hurt flashed across her face, instantly making him regret his careless words.

"Oh, I can be plenty selfish, you bastard. Years of betrayal and the need for self-preservation tends to do that to a person."

He shook his head. "So that's it? What about your offer—your need to *forget*? Are you walking away from that, too?"

She hesitated, then plastered on a mocking sneer. "You were right, O'Flare, I was playing you, and you, with your thick skull and all, fell for it. I can't say it hasn't been fun. For a little while."

She turned and walked away. She was almost to the front door when Caleb said exactly what he was thinking.

"Coward."

"Coward."

Wraith stiffened. She imagined that if she had a pulse, it would have skittered out of control, or if she wasn't freezing cold again, that she would have been suffused with an angry heat. Neither happened, but she was nonetheless pissed at his accusation.

And hurt.

Of course, she wasn't going to let *him* see that.

Pausing at the front entrance of Knox Devereaux's grand estate, her gaze met Caleb's. With the band still blasting music in the next room, she envisioned him as he'd been twenty minutes ago—lust in his eyes, his lips barely brushing hers.

He was so beautiful; he'd made her long for things she hadn't longed for in ages. She could see by his expression that he wanted to say more. She could even convince herself that he wanted her to stay, not for the good of the team or for its next mission, but because . . . because he truly cared for her. Just as she'd told Joanna.

The notion weakened her. Made her open her mouth to say . . . what? She didn't know. Something. Anything that would eradicate the lingering disdain in his gaze and make him understand that she was doing this because she cared, too. About the team, yes, but most of all, about him. "Caleb . . ." she whispered.

The sound of people running toward them made them both glance away. The feline female Caleb had been dancing with had changed out of her party dress and was wearing sleepwear, a skimpy negligee and a see-through robe that was clearly more decorative than useful. Her curves were displayed to their greatest advantage, but her face was splotchy and tear-stained, her makeup washed off, making her look vulnerable and needy. Despite the fact that she was accompanied by several large males who hovered around her, she flung herself into Caleb's arms. She was distraught. Weeping. Screaming that the bastards had gotten her sister and that Caleb would help find them, wouldn't he?

Even as a sharp pain poked at Wraith's temple and spread through her body, Caleb soothed the feline with his words and body, his voice soft and low, his arms engulfing her. It physically hurt her, Wraith thought, to see them together like that. Hurt more than anything she'd ever experienced. Because they looked right together. The feline fit in Caleb's arms in a way Wraith never could.

She mentally shook herself. It was time to stop fantasizing about what could never be. She'd joined the Para-Ops team for one reason—to find out who she was. Mahone was backing out of their deal. More importantly, she was a ticking time bomb. She couldn't make a move without knowing whether it was going to affect the well-being of everyone around her. That meant she walked away. Now.

Just as she had the thought, Caleb looked up at her. The feline's body shifted, giving Wraith a clear view of Caleb's chest. The death mark was gone.

She'd been right.

The only way to protect Caleb was to stay away from him. At least she'd figured that out, if nothing else, before it was too late.

With an imperceptible sigh of relief, Wraith lifted her hand. She blew him a taunting kiss, watching as his eyes narrowed slightly. Then, forcing herself to turn away, she walked through the door, adding an extra sway to her hips.

Playtime was over.

It was back to reality for her, and reality meant a world without Caleb O'Flare.

EIGHT

Un-fucking-believable.

An hour had passed since Wraith had walked away, but Caleb was still angry.

More than angry. He was pissed. Boiling mad.

He, who had sworn an oath to heal and had been taught by his ancestors to respect life in all its forms, was listening to the sounds of Knox and Felicia's wedding reception while wanting to rip someone apart.

Figuratively, of course.

Unfortunately, he wanted to kiss that someone even more. Deeply. Punishingly. Without restraint.

Too bad that for Wraith, kissing him like that would be about as pleasurable as an unanesthetized amputation.

But he wanted to do it anyway. He wanted to do a hell of a lot more than kiss her, and he'd been ready to do exactly that. To take her up on her offer and have sex with her, forgetting about all the reasons why he shouldn't, including his own mental health.

And that just proved what a fool he was.

She was *dead*, for God's sake. If it wasn't obvious from her blue-tinged skin, white hair, and hazy eyes, it was apparent in the coolness of her body temperature and in the persistence of her dark cynicism. Prickly and foulmouthed and about as feminine as a pair of combat boots. That was Wraith, from introduction to kiss-off.

At the time of said kiss-off, on the other hand, Natia had been practically catatonic. He'd finally convinced her to listen to her personal physician, who'd recommended a tranquilizer. She'd gone to her room to lie down, but not before extracting Caleb's promise to find her sister's rapists and make them pay. He'd watched her go with a feeling of pity, but also of dread. He'd seen the way Wraith had watched them embrace. But what was he supposed to have done? Pushed Natia away when she'd just learned her sister had been raped?

Growling, Caleb tore at the knot of his tie, then unbuttoned his formal dress shirt until he could breathe easier. When that still didn't provide him relief, he tore off his tuxedo jacket and flung it to the ground like a five-year-old having a tantrum. Staring at it, he shook his head, then started to laugh as he backed into a nearby wall. With the smooth sounds of Marvin Gaye in the background, Caleb slid slowly downward until he was crouching, head back and eyes closed. He could almost picture it now—him jumping up and down on his jacket like a rabid were just as Lucy or Knox or, God forbid, Dex walked into the small hallway just outside the Dome's grand ballroom.

He'd never be able to face them again.

As a tight smile formed on his face, he opened his eyes.

Then again, they all knew Wraith. They understood the depths of frustration to which she could bring a person. Hell, maybe they wouldn't blink an eye if he lost it after all.

She'd told him loud and clear how little he or any of the other Para-Ops team members meant to her. After everything they'd gone through together, she'd dismissed him as easily as a scrap of food, something she no longer had need for. And why? She'd turned her back on all of them because she didn't want to wait her turn in line for FBI Director Kyle Mahone's payout.

But, he reminded himself, it was a turn that was due to her.

Wraith had done what had been asked of her. Hell, he thought, shuddering at the memory of how she'd walked toward that gated compound in North Korea with explosives strapped to her torso, she'd done far more than what had been asked. All she'd asked in return was that the team find out who she was. Where she'd come from. What the hell she was doing here.

Of course she'd reacted badly when Mahone had put her off with his claim that the situation with the felines took priority. But he understood Mahone's position, as well. The felines were the most populated group of Otherborn, as well as the most united. They had pushed hardest for peace, while at the same time vowing to reinstitute the War should the government fail to protect them the way it promised. That vow had almost been tested after the death of Prince Elijah.

Unbidden, an image of his friend formed in his mind, as did the memory of their last conversation before the War had erupted.

"Our loyalty to our people is just one thing we have in common," the man had said, then laughed. "You, O'Flare, are a hound dog."

Shaking his head, Caleb pushed thoughts of his friend's grinning face away. He fought even harder to make the images of Elijah's bloodied face and body disappear. Their friendship hadn't been a deep one, nor had it been very long, but Caleb's relationship with Elijah's sister Natia had sped it along. Caleb had felt a natural affinity toward the younger man who liked to play and laugh far more than he liked to fight.

In the five years since Elijah's death, the felines had only grown more volatile. It was as if they were looking for any excuse to once again war with humans; for everyone's sake, that had to be avoided at all cost. Then there was the simple fact that a rapist was hurting females, no matter what their race. As a society, the United States couldn't let that continue.

After his part in Elijah's death, Caleb certainly owed it to the felines to help. What's more, he wanted to. Guilt filled him as he remembered the pain that had thrummed through Natia's body as he'd held her. She was close to all her sisters, but to Morgana most of all. Caleb hadn't known Morgana very well, but he remembered her being extremely shy, peeking around her mother's leg when Natia had introduced them. She couldn't be more than seventeen or eighteen years old now. The idea of her being raped by a coward who'd drugged her made him want to begin hunting him immediately. It just looked like he'd have to do it without Wraith.

Sighing, he wearily swiped his hands over his face, straightened, and snatched his jacket up. He was shrugging it on when he heard footsteps.

Mahone.

Caleb glared at the man who'd wreaked havoc on his life from the moment he'd stepped inside the reservation's bar. "Forget something?" Caleb snarled. "Or did you want just one more look at the mother of the groom so you can jack off tonight?"

The instant the words left his mouth, Caleb regretted them. Worse yet, Mahone didn't even look surprised by his vicious attack. It was a low blow, mentioning Mahone's feelings for Knox's mother, Bianca. The fact that Bianca had recently been reunited with Knox's father had to be killing the other man. "I'm sor—"

"Save it, O'Flare. I'm sure you and your teammates will get a lot of use out of that particular subject for years to come. Lucky for me, I don't give a shit. I have more important things to do than cater to your knee-jerk salvos, the first of which is to get the Para-Ops team ready for its next mission."

"Yeah, well, the Para-Ops team's numbers are fading fast," Caleb shot back. "With Knox and Felicia on sabbatical and Wraith headed for God knows where, you better hope Lucy, Dex, and I can—"

"Wraith isn't headed anywhere. Not if you or I have any say in the matter."

Caleb narrowed his eyes. "And what makes you think I want a say in anything Wraith does?"

Mahone looked at him chidingly. "Don't play games with me, O'Flare. You want Wraith around more than any of us, so you're going to do whatever you can to make sure she stays."

Trying to shrug off his displeasure that Mahone knew even a fraction of what he felt for Wraith, Caleb tried to keep his face blank. "You pitted me against her once before, remember? I'm not of a mind to put my head on that particular chopping block again."

Her offer of a booty-call aside, he knew his betrayal still weighed heavily on Wraith. Guilt ate at him, as well. He'd done what needed to be done for the benefit of the team, but he hadn't liked it.

Mahone didn't reply. He simply stared at Caleb, waiting for him to break. But Caleb didn't break easily. He turned and had actually made it to the door when Mahone said, "If you want me to beg, that's not going to happen." He paused, then said somewhat reluctantly, "But we need Wraith. This next op is sensitive, and having two females who are already familiar with each other is key to its success. So I won't beg, but I'm willing to offer an incentive."

Disbelief whipped Caleb around. "Incentive?" he snorted. "You mean you're trying your hand at bribery again? You did that to get me to join the team, and I still haven't collected."

"Yes, but I didn't have a name for you then. I do now."

Caleb sucked in his breath. "*Now* you have a name for me? Why should I believe you?"

"Who else are you going to believe, O'Flare?"

Caleb paced, cursing under his breath. Whatever name Mahone had, it was the name of someone high up. Well protected. His statements to Mahone aside, Caleb hadn't overlooked the possibility that Elijah's death might have been intentional. In following that theory, Caleb had pulled every string and used every advantage and connection he had to get a name, but it hadn't mattered. People had closed up. Gathered close. Shut the vault. No amount of money or threat of bodily harm had made a difference. For the sake of his peace of mind, he needed that name. He finally paused and stared Mahone down. "Who is it?"

Mahone shook his head. "After you bring back Wraith."

Caleb was on him in a second, pushing him against the wall. "You promised me if I joined the team—"

"I promised I'd help you find the truth. And I will. But first you need to get Wraith. After all, you're the one who chased her off in the first place."

"What the hell are you talking about?" Caleb released Mahone and stepped back. "She left when you told her you were sending us on a different mission."

"She left when *you* came back into the room. You guys have another fight or something?"

"Or something," he mumbled. His mind raced back to that moment when he'd seen her. The lust. Then the fear. Right before Bianca and Jacques had stopped him. Could Mahone be right? Had she made up an excuse to leave because she'd been afraid? Of him? But that didn't make any sense, given the way she'd propositioned him.

Mahone stared at him, waiting patiently.

"Tell me," Caleb ground out.

"Drugging and raping the feline leader's daughter and getting away with it? Untenable. We need to find the bastards, and fast, before the felines decide to take matters into their own hands. To do that, we need two Otherborn females, at least one of them disguised as a feline. They need to be comfortable with each other, able to pose as friends out for some fun on the town. Wraith and Lucy fit the bill."

Of course they did, Caleb thought. Only, he didn't see how they were going to convince Wraith she needed to come along, or for that matter, why it was so important she did. Caleb took a deep breath, keeping his gaze fixed on Mahone. "Why do you really need Wraith? And don't tell me it's so Lucy can feel comfortable. You know Lucy'll get the job done regardless, and that's all you care about."

Mahone studied him, then said, "Wraith has previous experience with the type of club we'll be targeting, as well as a prior history with one of the suspects we've identified. Her reappearance might be surprising, but it won't be overly suspicious. It can also give us an advantage."

Caleb formed his hands into fists. He knew what kind of clubs they were talking about. Sex clubs. Kinky-ass shit with private rooms, sex toys, and even an audience, if that's what someone wanted. When wraiths were involved, kink became synonymous with pain, and lots of it. Picturing Wraith involved in that made him sick.

Picturing her coming face-to-face with yet another lover, one Caleb seriously suspected had gotten off on hurting her, made him want to kill the unknown son of a bitch.

"So what's it to be?" Mahone prompted. "Because a certain name's drifting from my memory even as we speak."

"You're a fucking bastard, Mahone," Caleb snarled.

"So I've been told."

Caleb wanted to tell him to go to hell, but Mahone had planned well. Caleb wanted that name. He also wanted Wraith.

"Where is she?"

"I've got men tailing her. She got her stuff from the hotel and right now is on a bus headed for Maine."

He blinked, then slowly shook his head. "Public transportation? What the hell is she thinking?"

"She's thinking she doesn't want anything to do with us, and that goes double for any type of transportation we offered her."

"Yes, she's also pissed and wanting to fight. And what better way to pick one than on a bus? Shit."

"My thoughts exactly. Now, if you're done dancing here, go after her and bring her back."

Caleb winced, thinking of how he must have looked when he'd thrown his jacket to the ground. "Saw that, did you?"

"No worries, O'Flare. I'll keep your little secret. Believe me, I've done quite a bit of my own tantrum-throwing lately. So, do we have a deal?"

Caleb knew he should tell Mahone to go to hell and walk away, but he knew it wasn't going to happen.

Things weren't over between him and Wraith. Not this easily.

Not until he decided they were over.

"Fine." He nodded curtly. "But first I need to check on . . . a friend." He hesitated, not wanting to say Natia's name out loud for some reason.

Mahone nodded, understanding in his eyes.

Caleb continued, "I want the name the instant I get back, whether Wraith stays or not. She's too—"

"Yeah, I get it. Whether she stays or not." Mahone looked over Caleb's shoulder toward the reception room from which music was still merrily blasting. His gaze clouded. Caleb assumed it was because he'd caught sight of Bianca. Mahone's jaw firmed as he turned around. Striding toward the entrance, he spoke without turning around. "Get her, O'Flare. And get her to L.A. in the next two days."

NINE

Outside the Devereaux compound, Dex Hunt took a final drag of his cigarette before stamping it out on the rock he was sitting on. He stared at the butt, raised a brow, then stuffed the damn thing into his jacket pocket. Knox would kick his ass for littering, especially on his wedding day. The dharmire was even more fastidious than most vamps, and that was saying something.

Dex's eyes narrowed when he saw Lucy Talbot, the Para-Ops team's mage, slip onto the patio outside the ballroom. He'd seen Wraith's furious exit. O'Flare had left about twenty minutes ago, followed not long after by a grim-faced Mahone. Having gotten wind of the situation in L.A., it didn't take a genius to figure out that Wraith was royally pissed and that Mahone had just sent O'Flare to bring her back.

Snorting, he shook his head. He had to admit, O'Flare had balls. Going after Wraith after what he'd done to her? Well, he for one looked forward to seeing what kind of condition O'Flare returned in.

Glancing at the heavy steel watch on his wrist, Dex told himself he should've driven off hours ago. Hell, he should never have come. He'd known he was never going to make it to the ceremony, let alone the reception. But once he'd gotten here, he'd waited, compelled for some reason to see each of the team members.

Now that he'd seen Lucy, he knew he should leave, but he didn't. Instead, he studied her. Seeing her all dolled up in a floaty golden dress and strappy high heels, he imagined he felt the way a big brother would feel seeing his little sister dressed for the prom. Proud. Protective.

He grinned, thinking it was a good thing Lucy couldn't hear his thoughts.

She'd probably be pissed. Insulted. Spout something about being a woman, not a young girl. That's what she'd been trying to prove when she and Felicia had climbed into that extreme wrestling ring months ago. The fact that she'd stripped off her shirt and worn nothing but jeans and a bra had certainly helped prove her point.

Leaning against a column, Lucy stared out into the night, her expression almost wistful. He wondered if she was thinking of Knox and Felicia or of Caleb O'Flare. Maybe both. If she was thinking of O'Flare, she was probably thinking of Wraith, too.

But that was Lucy. Compassionate to a fault. She could consider herself in love with a man and still feel sorry that he wasn't getting together with the woman he really wanted. In this case, the woman was Wraith.

Dex cursed when Lucy straightened all of a sudden, her eyes scanning the trees where Dex sat. He knew she couldn't see him there, but for a half second, he wondered if she sensed him with some of her weird mage powers or something. He rolled his shoulders uncomfortably. He still didn't know enough about her. Didn't know enough about any of the Para-Ops team members. But he liked Lucy. Hell, he was beginning to like all of them. Even that cocky human, Caleb O'Flare.

And that's why Dex hadn't gone to Knox and Felicia's wedding. He knew from experience that the closer you got to others, the more distracted you became. The more vulnerable.

And he couldn't afford to be vulnerable.

He couldn't forget that he had his own plan, one he couldn't waver from, even if it might eventually pit him against the very people he worked with.

After one final glance in his direction, Lucy turned and strode back toward the house. When she was about five feet from the doors, she faltered and doubled over, causing Dex to curse. He threw his leg over his bike, prepared to haul ass to get to her. But when he glanced at her again, she was slowly straightening and then seemed to take several deep breaths before smoothing out her dress. She walked back inside as if nothing unusual had happened.

What the hell?

She'd been in severe pain, but it hadn't lasted long. Maybe it had been one of those female things? A cramp she wouldn't take too kindly to him asking about?

He stayed there, undecided, until he felt ridiculous. If she needed help, she had plenty of it inside. She didn't need him watching over her like an overprotective parent.

He swung his Harley onto the road that would take him out of the Dome.

Lucy was fine. He had a few days until he met up with the team in Los Angeles. Until then, he had his own intel to do.

TEN

"Saltine?"

Behind her sunglasses, Wraith squeezed her eyes shut even tighter and struggled to remain completely still. Holding her nonexistent breath, she remained curled into a ball, huddled beneath the layers of her concealing poncho and hood, her body swaying with the twists and turns of the moving bus. After several seconds, she sensed the woman standing in the aisle give up and walk away. Maybe this time, Wraith thought desperately, they'd get the hint and leave her alone.

For the past half hour, despite her best efforts to feign sleep, someone had been offering her something every five minutes. First it had been a pillow. Then a book to read.

Then a fucking lollipop.

Everything but what she wanted.

Wraith shifted slightly, her weight causing the tattered seat beneath her to squeak. What had the world come to, she thought querulously, when you couldn't even pick a fight on a Greyhound bus?

And Essenia knows she'd tried. For all of two minutes.

After leaving Knox's reception, she'd been hoping for some relief. But no, she'd boarded the only tin can on wheels that, instead of providing her with the poor, desperate, and depraved, was transporting a group of Goody Two-shoes who looked at her as if she was a bedraggled puppy in need of nurturing.

That was the last thing she wanted.

She wanted—no, needed—to let off steam. To release the pent-up frustration and resentment and fury that was threatening to eat her from the inside out. Scream out her fear before it overwhelmed her. Pummel her despair so it remained undetected by those who would capitalize on her weakness. Slam away her thoughts of what and whom she was leaving behind in order to dive headfirst into a wasteland of nothingness—the same nothingness she'd endured for over a decade.

When she hadn't gotten the fight she'd wanted, she'd spotted the poncho someone had abandoned on the bus hours earlier and figured she could at least hide herself and get some peace and quiet. Wrong again.

Swallowing hard, she involuntarily jerked at the feeling of moisture behind her lids. She hated it, but at least Caleb wasn't here to witness her making a damn fool of herself again.

Still, she was so disgusted with herself that when she sensed someone else approaching, she bolted upright and jerked her sunglasses off. "Damn it, will you—"

She stopped at the sight before her. It was a little boy, probably about nine years old, with eyes that reminded her of Caleb's. She cleared her throat and struggled to appear annoyed. "What?"

The boy didn't smile. He continued to look at her solemnly, then held his hand out. Wraith sighed and looked down, expecting to see a piece of gum or a tattered toy. Instead, what she saw made her suck in her breath and instinctively cringe away. It was a kitten. Small. Fragile. Weak-looking. "What . . . ?"

The boy took a step closer, his hand still outstretched, his near-frantic gaze pleading. Although he remained silent, his breaths heaved in and out of him in panicked bursts, making his hand shake.

A quick look around told her no one was paying attention to her for once.

"Please. Take him."

She turned back to the boy. His eyes were flooded with tears now, and the sight made her gasp. "Okay, okay. Take it easy. I'll . . . I can hold it for a minute."

With a trembling hand, she reached out, her hand hovering

over the boy's. She glanced up, confirming he indeed wanted her to take it.

The boy nodded.

Wraith gingerly picked up the small kitten that was only slightly bigger than the boy's palm. She waited for the pain, but none came.

What a cosmic joke. She hadn't felt pain when she'd petted Dex in wolf form, either, but it seemed unfair, given her history, that she'd feel no pain when a feline was involved, even one as small and innocent as this one.

Years ago, Wraith had made a mistake. A huge one. Weary and scared, she'd allowed herself to seek companionship. Friendship. She'd thought she'd found it in the form of a feline female named Maria. She'd known the feline for only a matter of days, but something about her manner had relaxed Wraith's natural defensiveness. Eventually, Maria had introduced her to a mage, an evil so dark she still felt its looming presence hovering over her at times. She'd spent the next two years imprisoned. In a constant state of pain she'd never experienced before, not even with Ramsey . . .

No! Wraith gritted her teeth, chased the ghosts away, and forced herself back to the present. To the feline that she held in the palm of her hand. The one that couldn't hurt her.

It took her several moments, but she finally managed it. Vaguely, she stared at the creature, grateful she hadn't inadvertently crushed it during her brief but troubled trip into the past.

The kitten was a newborn, probably a week old since its eyes were open, blinking owlishly up at her. Its body shivered, its fur barely providing any protection for its fragile bones. The boy studied them—her and the damn cat—for a few seconds, then smiled.

His smile was almost enough to knock her back. She instinctively looked away.

So much innocence. So much goodness and purity in that one gaze. She couldn't remember seeing it before, and seeing it now was almost painful.

She'd been innocent once. Scared. Wanting desperately to trust another. What had it gotten her? Nothing but pain and betrayal. First, the twisted relief of sexual pain with Ramsey, her first lover as a wraith. Then, betrayal by Maria. Then . . .

Tentatively, she lifted a hand to touch the scars on her neck.

Torture, she thought. An endless amount of time and pain. Of knowing she was alone. That no one cared. And that she couldn't die. No matter how much she begged and pleaded, she couldn't die. She—

Movement caught her eye as the boy moved away from her, jolting her out of her tormented memories and back to the present in which she still held the kitten. "Wait—"

The boy ignored her and returned to his seat at the front of the bus.

What was his deal? Did he really expect her to babysit while he . . . while he . . .

With a sigh of surrender, Wraith sat down, jerking when the kitten mewled and latched on to her thumb, sucking it softly before quieting. She cleared her throat and hesitantly lifted her other hand. With one finger, she rubbed the kitten's soft head. To her amazement, it began to purr, its soft rumble vibrating against her skin so that for the slightest second, she felt warm.

She stared at the kitten for over an hour, well after it closed its eyes and fell asleep. Then, even though there was no reason to do so, she closed her eyes and pretended to sleep, as well. The rhythmic sway of the bus seemed to put her into a trance until its sudden absence made her eyes fly open.

The sun was bright and intense, indicating it was likely late afternoon.

Several seats were empty. Vacated.

Jerking up, she whipped her head around. The bus was parked in a terminal and was nearly empty. The kitten's owner was gone.

She'd been so zoned out, so thrown off by the kitten in her hand that she'd left herself open to anything and anyone.

Idiot.

Cradling the kitten, she jumped to the window across the aisle and immediately spotted the boy in a crowd. "Hey, kid!" she shouted, causing the boy to look up. Wraith held out the kitten but the boy shook his head.

Within seconds, the bus started up again. Through the back window, Wraith watched the group around the boy disperse. People melted away until the boy stood out like a beacon, alone. Wraith's gaze traveled the crowd, searching for the boy's mother or aunt or family friend. No one appeared.

The bus started moving.

The boy's figure got smaller.

The cat in her palm mewled and licked her thumb. Then something even more disturbing happened. A man, beefy and angry-looking, strode up to the boy and grabbed hold of his arm.

The boy winced in obvious pain.

Wraith shook her head. "Shit."

She turned to the driver and yelled. "Stop."

The driver ignored her, even though she repeated the command several times.

Walking quickly toward the front of the bus, she shifted the kitten to her other hand and whipped her pistol out from the back of her pants.

She pointed the gun at the driver's temple. "I said to stop the fucking bus. *Now*."

ELEVEN

As she stepped off the bus, Wraith was once more hit with a blast of warmth; however, unlike the soothing sensation she'd experienced in the Devereaux garden, this warmth felt muggy. Stifling. For a moment she felt dizzy, but she shook her head, willing the feeling away as she strode toward the man who was now shaking the boy. His words were clipped and angry. ". . . ever do something so stupid again, do you hear me, Foster! I can't believe you—"

Wraith gripped the man's arm and whirled him around so suddenly that he automatically released his hold on the child. She had the barrel of her gun resting in between his eyes before his words fully faded away.

"Do. Not. Touch. Him." Wraith ground the words out, telling herself not to blow the man's brains out in front of the child. Not unless she had to.

Eyes wide, the man nearly swallowed his tongue. His gaze skittered from Wraith to the little boy.

Foster.

She said his name and the boy nodded.

"Who's meeting you here?" she asked.

"I'm—" the man began. Wraith pushed the barrel of her gun even harder into his skin.

"Shut up," she hissed. "I don't want you saying one word, do you understand?"

Pressing his lips tightly together, he nodded.

She felt a tug on her poncho and looked down.

"He's my dad," Foster said, face calm and eyes dry.

"He was hurting you," she said.

The boy just shrugged. "He's mad at me. I ran away."

She looked at the father again. "Maybe you had good reason to," she purred threateningly.

Again, the man's eyes widened as his fear increased. Wraith sniffed, but there were no sickly fumes coming from him. No hint of disease or death. He was as healthy and strong as he looked, perfectly capable of overpowering and abusing some-one as small and weak as the boy next to her.

"I did," the boy confirmed. "He was going to kill my kitten. He said it wasn't going to make it past the night, but it did. He's made it three nights. The three nights I've been gone. I showed him," the young boy said proudly.

"Good for you," Wraith said, although she eased off on the gun a little. Never taking her eyes off of the man in front of her, she said, "Foster, has your father hurt you? Do you want to leave with me?"

"No, wait—" the man began, and Wraith shook her head, cutting him off.

"Foster?" she said when he didn't answer.

She looked down and was shocked to see him smiling at her, his eyes slightly glassy now. "I knew," he whispered. "I knew when I saw you that you were the one that would take care of him. I knew I couldn't keep him. Not now. But you'll take care of him for me, won't you?"

She sighed and lowered her arm, holstering her gun. With a warning glance at the man, Wraith kneeled down in front of Foster. "Your father loves you, doesn't he, Foster?"

The boy nodded.

"And you love him? You want to stay with him?"

Again, the boy confirmed that he was, indeed, happy to be returning home.

She pretended to consider the matter for several minutes, then nodded. Standing, she held out her hand, bracing herself for the moment when the boy's touch would cause pain to zing up her arm. It was there, but faint. Barely anything given what she was used to. Animals. Kids. Apparently she could touch them without it hurting so much. Why?

But she didn't have time to dwell on that right now.

"Then I'll find a home for your kitten. Because I travel a lot, and my job, well, it's a little dangerous, so I think the kitten would be better off with someone else. Is that okay?"

Foster hesitated, twitched his mouth back and forth as he thought, then nodded.

"Good," she said. "But first you have to promise—no more running away. You talk things out with your parents when you need to. Got me?"

Foster wiped at his eyes, then ran to hug his father and nodded. "Okay."

His father watched her warily as he returned his son's hug.

Wraith pressed her lips together and jerked her chin toward the parking lot. "Go on. Get out of here. And remember, don't hurt the boy. Ever. Or you will see me again."

It took Caleb almost twenty-four hours to catch up with Wraith. When he did, it was early evening and she was sitting alone on an outdoor bench at the Rock Springs, Wyoming, Greyhound Station. She was staring at something in her cupped hands before she tucked it into the front pocket of an unfamiliar-looking poncho. It was black, of course, but looked more like wool than Wraith's standard leather. Something so insignificant, but it made her look softer. The impression of softness was magnified when, wearily, she closed her eyes and tilted her head back.

Her weariness echoed his own.

It reminded him that, despite her appearance and nonexistent vital signs, Wraith was more like him than she wanted to admit. True, she was far more stubborn than him, but today he was going to outlast her if it killed him.

"You were more difficult to find than I thought you'd be," he called, even though it was a lie. He'd known where she was every minute. Mahone had made sure of that, notifying him of her coordinates via his cell. "Must be the lack of bloody bodies I was expecting."

Wraith jerked to standing and turned to face him. Although she quickly scowled, he didn't miss the second of relief that flashed across her features. "This is becoming a refrain, but what the hell are you doing here, O'Flare?"

He snorted. "You didn't think I was going to let you go that easily, did you?"

Walking toward her, he watched her fumble for a response. Good. He liked keeping Wraith unsettled. It happened so rarely, and he needed every advantage he could get when it came to her.

"You don't 'let' me do anything, O'Flare. And I'm not coming back, so you can tell Mahone—"

"I'm not here because of Mahone."

She laughed. "Bullshit. Why else would you be here?"

Her accusation made him feel guilty for about half a second. "Mahone asked me to track you down, true. He gave me a head start on where you were. But I would have come after you anyway. You know that."

"Really? And why's that?" Cocking a brow, she propped a hand on her hip in an arrogant gesture that was quickly dispelled by the wriggling going on in her poncho pocket. Distracted, she looked down, mumbling something.

"Because I want you. And I know you want me, too. What happened, Wraith? Did you suddenly get scared it would mean more to you than you were prepared for?"

Her head snapped up. "No. Besides, you don't want me. You want to save me. So quit fucking around with me, O'Flare."

His mouth twisted in a grimace of a smile. "Poor choice of words, Wraith."

Her eyes narrowed. "You know what I mean. Don't play—"

"I know what you mean. Now why don't you tell me what the hell you've got wriggling around in your pocket so we can get to L.A. and get started on our next mission?"

Her hands came up and seemed to cup themselves protectively over the pocket lying against her stomach. It was one of those big tube pockets that a person could stick both hands in at the same time. Despite the positioning of her hands, he saw a piece of gray fur flicker in and out of the pocket, causing his brow to arch.

"Dex'll be jealous," he said wryly, even though his words made him uncomfortable. He hadn't missed the fact that she and the were had bonded in some way in North Korea, nor had he missed the fact that seeing Dex in wolf form rubbing against her leg had made him want to rip the wolf's throat out.

"Please," she snorted. "He'd have to care to be jealous. The Para-Ops team might work well together, but its members, first and foremost, care only about one thing—what we're going to get at the end of it all."

Tauntingly, he asked, "So you don't care what happens to us? Lucy? Dex?" He paused. "Me?"

She hesitated. "I . . . I didn't say that."

"Then you do care?"

She frowned and shook her head. "No . . ."

He stepped closer.

"No?"

She held up a hand, palm facing him. "Stop. I'm not playing your games. If you and the others want to do Mahone's dirty work for him and risk not getting whatever the hell it is he's promised you, then by all means, do it. I don't give second chances."

"Even though that's what you've been given?" he asked quietly.

She startled. "A second chance? Is that what you think I am?"

"You're the walking dead, Wraith. Seems like a second chance to me."

"A second chance to see the evil in the world. To hurt and be hurt. To feel"—she swallowed hard—"to feel pain." She turned away. "To be alone," she muttered.

He saw her hand move and knew she had put her hand inside her pocket to pet the furry creature she had sequestered inside there. He remembered the way she'd stroked Dex when he'd been in wolf form. How it hadn't seemed to hurt her then, either. How jealous he'd been at that realization.

"You're choosing to be alone, Wraith. Choosing to leave the team. Come back with me. Help us with this mission, and I promise I'll make sure Mahone gives you what it is you need."

"Making me promises now? And I'm supposed to believe you? After what you pulled for Mahone? You're nothing but Mahone's lackey."

"So now that bothers you? A day ago, you—"

"Don't even try. Leave. The last thing I'm going to do is help you. Any of you, let alone a bunch of felines I don't even know."

"That's it? It's all about getting what you want? Fuck the greater good?"

She looked away, but only for an instant. "That's right."

"Then you're not the person I thought you were."

"That was your first mistake, O'Flare. I'm not a person. I'm nothing. No one. You don't have to pretend you care."

"I guess not." He turned away, then stopped and turned back toward her. "Good luck, Wraith. I hope wherever you're going gives you the answers you want. And that you don't—"

She stepped toward him, frowning, her gaze on his chest. "What the . . . ? It's still there . . ." he thought she whispered, but before he could ask what she was talking about, her gaze jerked up to his. "What . . . what's happened since I've left? What's Mahone told you?" she asked.

"Excuse me?"

"Have you been briefed on the assignment?"

He stepped closer to her. "A little. Why?"

She looked away, then back toward him. "Just curious."

"Uh-huh." He tilted his head and studied her. "You were staring at my chest. Why?"

"Just admiring your muscles," she said smoothly.

He knew she was lying. "Wraith, why—"

"What is Mahone giving you to serve on the Para-Ops team, anyway?" Almost reflexively, her hands returned to her front pocket, both hands rubbing its contents.

The stroke of her fingers mesmerized him and he once again felt true jealousy for the creature she touched. He shook his head to clear it. "What?"

"You heard me."

He shrugged.

Rolling her eyes, she shook her head. "Figures. So there's nothing you want that badly?"

"You're wrong. There's something I want very badly. Sometimes you can't get what you want, no matter who's willing to give it to you." As he spoke, his gaze remained unwavering on hers. She licked her lips.

"Fine," she said, her jaw clenched.

"Fine?"

"I'll come back with you."

"Why the turnaround?"

"I just decided, you're right. Maybe a second chance is what

I've been given, and maybe it's what I should give Mahone. One more chance. Besides, something tells me sitting on a bus all the way to Maine is liable to bore me to death."

"Yeah, plus, who knows what else you're liable to pick up along the way?" His gaze once again dropped pointedly to her pocket.

"I'm not taking it with me."

He watched as her hands continued to stroke.

"Okay."

"I'm not."

"I'm not disagreeing with you. But why don't you let me hold it while you get your things?"

She hesitated, then reached in, plucked the tiny kitten out of her pocket, and gingerly handed it to him. "Careful," she whispered. "He's fragile."

Caleb nodded. "Don't worry. I'll take care of him."

And you, he thought. Whether you want me to or not.

TWELVE

"A motorcycle?" Wraith said in disbelief when she saw the slick Ducati. "You followed me on a motorcycle?"

Caleb shrugged. "What, you thought Dex was the only one who knows how to ride a bike?"

"No, but I'm not going to L.A. on a motorcycle driven by you, Dex, or anyone else."

"No kidding. That many hours with someone, and you'd surely kill your escort." He waited for her to comment on the bike's color—which he'd just realized matched the color of her electric blue shoes to a T—but she didn't. Staring at the pair of sunglasses she wore, the pair she was almost never without, regardless of the time of day or the weather, he said absently, "It'll just be to the nearest airport. We'll catch a flight from there." He'd seen her hazed-over eyes before. Knew they resembled cloudy cataracts. But he hadn't really given her vision much thought. Did she view the world differently not just because of her experiences but because of her biology?

She didn't move. Just continued to stare at the bike with something akin to horror. Her expression temporarily wrenched Caleb away from his thoughts and made him stifle a smile. "You're not afraid of the bike, are you?"

She shot him a droll look. "Of course not."

"Then it must be me you're afraid of."

"I'm more afraid of the bike than I am you, O'Flare, and I already told you, I'm not afraid of the bike."

She was afraid, all right. Maybe not of the bike, but of the contact it would force them to endure. Hell, there'd be no enduring going on for him. More like savoring. His decision to go after Wraith on the bike had been a deliberate one, which she'd probably figure out sooner than later. The question was whether she'd risk revealing her own discomfort by saying something about it. He was betting she wouldn't. "Great. Then there's no problem." He handed her a helmet. The only helmet. "Hop on."

"I don't need a helmet, O'Flare. If we crashed, you'd need it more than I would."

"Yeah, I know. I'm quite aware of how invincible you are. Please . . . just humor me."

She looked like she was going to argue with him some more, but instead she asked, "Why can't I drive?"

Instead of answering, he said, "You like the color of my bike, Wraith? It's one of my favorites."

She rolled her eyes, then nodded impatiently. "Yeah, it's gorgeous, O'Flare. Now answer my question."

"I will. But only if you answer one for me first."

"What has gotten into you? We're wasting time here." When he didn't respond, she blew out an impatient sigh and waved him on. "Ask and maybe I'll answer. Maybe I won't."

"What color is my bike?"

He saw the way she immediately closed off before she narrowed her eyes at him. "What the hell does that matter?"

He tried to remember if she'd ever commented on a color before. Referred to anything in terms of a color. She hadn't. Her response only confirmed his suspicions. "You don't know, do you? You don't see in colors, do you, Wraith?"

"You're being ridicu—"

"What do you see with those hazy eyes of yours? Do you even see the same things I do?"

She didn't make a snotty comment about his visions or dreams. "Why do you want to know?"

Because he wanted to *know* her. Know what she saw. What she felt, even if it was just pain. "You wanna drive, don't you? Let's just say I'd like to know what a person driving me around can see, that's all."

She looked dubious, then pissed, then resigned. "I see black and white. Shades of gray."

Averting her gaze, she stared into the distance, prompting him to ask, "That's the only difference?"

She glared at him and practically stamped her foot in frustration. Instead, she threw up her arms in disgust. "I see death, Caleb. Death in many forms. I see death marks on people dying. I see trees without leaves, even when others say they're there. I see the end of life, even as people try to hold on to it. I see exactly what a dead human should see. Is that honest enough for you?"

He kept his expression bland but felt the muscles in his jaw constrict. Not so much because of what she'd said, but how she said it. Sometimes, when he needled her enough, Wraith gave him a glimpse of her emotions and the pain she always bore. Even as he told himself he should stop, that it was better for her to suppress the pain on some level if she could, he couldn't help poking at her. It was when she expressed her pain and emotion that she seemed the most human, and thus the most accessible to him. Finally, he nodded. "Yes. That's honest enough." He swung onto the bike and looked expectantly at her. "Let's go."

She laughed in disbelief. "So why can't I drive?" she asked again.

"Because of Garfield, remember? The cat," he clarified when she shot him a confused look. "It seems to like you, and traveling on the motorcycle will probably freak it out at first. You'll want to comfort it, right?" He pointed to the bike. "Put it in the case right there. You'll be able to reach in and touch it if you need to."

She was frowning, probably because he'd dared to assume she'd comfort anything. But she simply slipped the cat where he'd pointed, put on the helmet, then swung onto the bike behind him. She braced herself for him to take off, but he didn't.

Without looking back at her, he said, "Oh, I should let you know some things. First, I'm particularly fond of the colors black and white. That said, I wish you could see more. The earth in full color and full bloom is an amazing sight. It's holy. Enough to make a doubter believe in something bigger at work." She jerked against him and he hesitated, then shifted around to look at her over his shoulder. "Oh, and you should get comfortable, because the nearest airport is a few hours away," he said.

That broke her out of her silence. "A few . . . ?" Her voice was tinged with something close to panic.

Smiling again, he started the motorcycle and shot away.

She'd obviously ridden a motorcycle before. She sat on the bike with ease and moved fluidly with him whenever they took a curve or turn in the road. At first, she tried to put as much distance between them as she could, but he purposely accelerated into a couple of turns until she had no choice but to lightly place her hands on either side of his waist.

An hour into the ride, he wondered if he'd made a mistake.

Despite the fresh air blasting him from all sides, and despite the fact that she barely touched him, he felt suffocated by her. By desire. By the overwhelming need to stop the bike and pull her into the grass on the side of the road and kiss her and pound into her until she screamed his name with pleasure, not in pain. Of course, that was impossible. But he still fantasized, and part of his fantasy was based on reality.

He'd kissed her before, and had felt the give of her breasts when her body had pressed against his. Her mouth had been soft and moist, which told him other places on her body would be, too.

She shifted slightly and he imagined her wriggling as she adjusted to the feel of his cock inside her. His dick grew hard. Arousal combined with the constant vibration of the motorcycle caused his balls to ache so bad he had to clench his teeth.

Another hour later, and he felt his sanity beginning to slip.

Shit. He needed to stop. Get away from her before he howled in frustration and did something really stupid. Like wrapped his arms around her and begged her to take him into her and make him forget anything or anyone else had ever existed.

Idiot, he told himself. Why couldn't he learn? She was a wraith who couldn't experience pleasure without pain. And he couldn't—wouldn't—hurt her. Besides, while he was suffering the tortures of the damned, she seemed completely at ease, her grip light and steady on him. That made him madder than anything else.

Clasping the bike's handlebars in an effort to get control of himself, Caleb took the first exit he saw. He navigated the bike toward a looming chain restaurant with the desperation of a man who'd been wandering the desert for days and had finally caught sight of shelter.

A few minutes, that's all he needed. A few minutes without her body pressed up against him, and he'd be ready to go. Ready to face whatever challenge she threw his way.

Riding with her body pressed tightly to Caleb's had given Wraith a true high. With no one to see her and every excuse to hold him and press her body against him—with their bodies fully clothed and no pain resulting from the touch—she could simply soak in the rare intimacy of being close to another. And not just anyone, but Caleb, the man she'd desired for what seemed like forever.

The bike rumbled between her thighs, exacerbating the ache caused by feeling her breasts smashed up against Caleb's broad back, and by the fact that his muscular butt was sandwiched firmly up against her pelvis. She'd never been in such close or prolonged contact with another person in her entire ten years of wraith life. There was no denying that it alternately rattled and aroused her.

For the first half hour, she'd tried to touch him as little as possible, but the bike was built for speed, something he obviously liked. She eventually gave up trying to maintain her space. Within the dark confines of the helmet that he'd insisted she wear, she closed her eyes, blocking out all sensation but the feel of him and the smooth way he maneuvered the rumbling bike across the deserted roads.

The Italian sports bike was more like a work of art than a piece of machinery. Completely different from the Harley Dex drove. Wraith wrapped her arms more tightly around Caleb and focused on the subtle movement of his muscles underneath his jacket. His hair whipped against the visor of her helmet, and she remembered how silky it had felt when he'd kissed her at Felicia and Knox's wedding. And how he'd immediately pulled away.

How would it have been if they'd finished what they'd started then? If she'd explored his body the way she'd wanted to? First, his broad shoulders and his chest. Then his flat abdomen. Then his thighs and the hard shaft between them. What would he have done if she'd pushed him back, knelt over him, and taken him inside her mouth?

The sudden swerving of the bike as Caleb took an exit for Evanston, Wyoming, interrupted Wraith's heated thoughts. Where the hell was he going? When he pulled into a restaurant parking lot, she tried to rein in her impatience. The guy was entitled to a bathroom break, for God's sake.

When he stopped the motor, she immediately swung off the bike, suddenly wanting to get as far away from him as possible. Her body buzzed with arousal, and she felt that warm whisper of air again, this time all over her body. She felt flushed and achy. For a moment, she was tempted to leave her helmet on, but she didn't want him to think she was hiding from him. So she slipped off the helmet and shook out her hair, keeping her facial expression blandly composed.

"Why'd we stop?"

He looked pissed. He got off the bike and stepped closer to her, which immediately made her want to run. She didn't like the feeling. She didn't run from confrontation, it ran from her. Still, she had to forcibly keep her feet planted where they were and remind herself that if she did run, Caleb would likely chase her down in the parking lot with all the enthusiasm of a lion hunting a gazelle.

And if he caught her . . . She could practically feel his hot breath on the nape of her neck and the sting of his teeth clamping down on the tender skin there. A shiver of delight pulsed through her at the thought. She held her breath, waiting for him to touch her. Instead, he stepped around her, keeping a careful distance between them. Without a word, he walked into the restaurant, leaving her to follow.

She chastised herself with each step she took. What was wrong with her? Attraction was one thing. But this primitive, all-encompassing neediness was uncharacteristic and unsettling. She was suddenly overcome with a desire to walk away and leave Caleb in the restaurant. She could get to the airport and L.A. on her own, couldn't she?

As soon as she asked the question, she dismissed it. There was still the damn death mark to contend with. Plus, he already thought she was afraid of him. Or, more precisely, of the attraction they shared. She wouldn't give him another reason to believe that.

THIRTEEN

The chilly blast of air-conditioning managed to clear her head. She immediately beelined for the restrooms, not because she needed to pee, because she never did, but to give herself more distance from Caleb. She splashed some water on her face, hoping the wetness would cool her thoughts, but it didn't. She cringed at her reflection in the mirror. Her hair looked greasy, and it had conformed to her scalp where the helmet had been. Her skin looked splotchy and . . .

She cursed and looked closer.

Her skin didn't just look splotchy . . . it looked . . . She blinked. It wasn't her skin that was different. It was her vision. Her skin looked shaded in places it normally wasn't. At the same time, the roots of her hair were definitely getting darker, and her eyes looked a little clearer than normal. Was some of what she was seeing, these new gradations of shadow, actually spots of color? The other changes were subtle, not likely to be something Caleb would notice. Still, the change was progressing faster than she'd thought it would.

What did that mean? That she was on an expedited course for death?

She bent and reached under her pant leg for the knife she kept strapped to her ankle. Unsheathing it, she pressed the serrated edge against her throat, just under her jaw. For a moment, she considered doing it. Slicing her throat and seeing if, this time, it would work. If it didn't, she'd what? Increase the pain she felt at another's contact? If it did, she'd bleed out and die. A blessing in some ways, yes, but she'd still die without knowing who she was.

Undecided, she closed her eyes, but they popped open when she felt the cat wriggle and change positions inside her pocket. When it mewled, she realized it must be hungry. She lowered the knife and swiftly sliced the blade against her forearm. The physical pain was minimal, and the wound instantly started to seal. For such a small wound, however, it seemed to take especially long to finish healing.

Yet more proof that her time was running out. The more human she became, the closer she moved toward mortality. To death. To her end.

Her end without Caleb.

With a sigh, she slipped her knife back into its sheath and walked back into the restaurant. There was no sign of Caleb. After looking her up and down like she was a walking insect, the hostess stammered an offer to show her to the table where Caleb sat. Annoyed that Caleb was obviously taking more than a bathroom break, Wraith thought about hissing at the hostess but dismissed the idea. Apparently, she'd lost all sense of fun.

She'd take a few seconds to get the cat some water and food, but then she wanted back on the road. She'd suffer the closeness of Caleb's body for another hour, but then she'd make sure things got back to normal. No more talk of forgetfulness or peace or possibilities. Her sole focus would be on the mission. She followed the hostess to a booth where Caleb sat, slouched and comfortable. Along the way, she felt the stares of every individual they passed. Caleb, on the other hand, seemed oblivious to the attention she was attracting.

"I'd like to get back on the road," Wraith told him.

He simply picked up his cup of coffee and stared at her as he took a sip. She rolled her eyes and gracelessly flopped onto the seat across from him. As soon as she sat down, her long legs momentarily tangled with his splayed ones, and she quickly pulled them back and to the side.

He responded to her retreat with a slight tilting of his lips.

She met Caleb's stare with her own, trying to set things on the right course. "Fill me in on the specifics of the mission."

He took another sip of coffee, then took his time answering. "There's not much to tell. Three felines have been raped, apparently with the aid of drugs, since there are huge holes in their memories. Before being raped, each feline frequented a different sex club. That's three different sex clubs in close proximity to one another, including a place called Ramsey's. There's one more club that fits the pattern. Lucy's going to act as bait, the rest of us as backup. We're going to do the club scene until we get the scum responsible. It'll be a cakewalk."

A cakewalk. That's exactly why it made no sense, even if her old lover Ramsey did own one of the four clubs Caleb was talking about. "That's it? No concerns about why Mahone is bringing in the team for this?"

"He needs Otherborn. Who else is he going to bring in?"

"Local law enforcement?"

Caleb shrugged. "Maybe he just wants the best. The felines are slow to anger, but when they do, they're vicious. If they think humans are going after their females, they won't wait very long to extract their own brand of justice."

"Which would be what?"

His expression darkened. "Let's just say the human way of torturing someone will look like child's play in comparison."

"And that's what you're trying to avoid? Because of what happened to you in the War?"

Just like that, his expression was wiped clean. He looked up when their waitress approached them. Wraith didn't miss the way she immediately perked up upon seeing Caleb. She tossed back her hair, sucked in her stomach, and stuck out her impressively perky chest. She was pretty, but Caleb barely glanced at her.

That pleased her. Why? It shouldn't matter if he slept with every woman from here to Los Angeles. But it did.

The waitress devoured Caleb with her eyes. "Can I get you . . . something, sir?"

Wraith barely restrained herself from ripping out the woman's fluttering fake eyelashes. Why didn't she just offer to get down on her knees and give him a blow job?

Wraith feigned an avid interest in the rundown diner. After a few seconds, she felt ridiculous and brought her gaze back to

Caleb, who watched her from beneath hooded eyes. He placed his order without looking away.

The waitress turned to her with lifted brows, as if she wasn't worth the effort of speaking.

"I'm dead, in case you can't tell. I don't eat."

Caleb waited until the waitress walked away before continuing their conversation. "Yeah, I want to avoid that kind of torture if I can. I'd think you would, too, given what you've been through."

Now it was her turn to look away. She didn't like the fact that he knew about the experiments. That he'd even seen the videos that Mahone had. The knowledge burrowed under her skin and poked with unerring accuracy at every vulnerable spot she had. Even a few she'd been completely unaware of. Stubbornly, she remained silent, and he seemed unwilling to push her.

It was only a matter of minutes before the waitress brought Caleb his food—eggs and bacon—and another smile. Wraith waited impatiently for her to leave.

"You have a history with the felines," she pointed out. "You used to date their princess, and it certainly looked like she was amenable to starting things up again. Why can't you go in and talk to them? Convince them to cool down?"

Caleb stopped chewing for a second and dropped his gaze to his meal. With his fork, he pierced his eggs with more force than necessary. "Believe me, the felines are the last race that would listen to anything I said, even with my prior relationship with Natia."

"Because you killed her brother?"

Caleb stopped eating, wiped his mouth, and leaned back in his chair to stare at Wraith.

Despite the shocking statement she'd just thrown down, he didn't even blink. No way was he going to give her the reaction she so clearly wanted. Instead, remembering the way she'd spoken of "felines" so disdainfully, he went digging for his own gold.

"You have your own history with the felines, don't you, Wraith? Some reason to hold a grudge. A former lover, perhaps? One who did you wrong?"

Sure enough, her expression closed up. "You're way off."

"Am I?" He studied her and she squirmed, clearly uncomfortable with the turn in the conversation.

It was her own fault, he assured himself. He hadn't been this hard this long since he was in high school. Back then, all he'd had to do was look at a woman, and he'd get a massive hard-on. Wraith always had the same effect on him. Even when she glared at him like she was doing now.

Especially when she glared at him.

Caleb had stopped at the restaurant because he'd wanted to eradicate the sexual feelings she was bringing out in him, but now he welcomed them. He'd do anything to avoid talking about Elijah. But he didn't want to be the only one on the hook. The only one who had problems. Vulnerabilities. Wraith had plenty of them, and for some reason he wanted to explore each and every one. On the night she'd offered herself to him, on the night he'd accepted, he'd wanted information just as much as he'd wanted Wraith's body. He still did.

"Tell me something . . . Are you a virgin?"

About to give the cat some food and water, she choked instead. "What?"

"I asked if you're a virgin."

"I heard you. Why the hell are you asking me that?"

"Given what you wanted from me a day ago, it seems a fair question to ask."

"Since it's not going to happen, then it's not open for discussion. It wouldn't be, anyway." She shook her head. "But to answer your childish question, I've had lovers. Were you hoping otherwise? That you've been the only guy to ever make me feel desire?"

"So you admit you desire me."

"I'm not doing anything but leaving."

Despite her threat, she didn't stand. Didn't move at all. Mildly, he said, "Give the cat some water, Wraith. I won't go there anymore, okay?"

She looked at him suspiciously, then gave the cat some water and some of Caleb's bacon. She didn't like her response to him, but he knew his ability to goad her was a direct result of the fact that she was attracted to him. And fighting it. Just like him.

"Can I ask you a question, though? All hostility aside?"

She just stared at him, which he took for her consent.

"Have any of your partners been able to touch you without causing you pain?"

She hesitated only briefly before replying, "No."

It was the answer he'd been expecting, but not the one he wanted.

She started to get up, then met his gaze directly. "It wouldn't be any different with you. No luck of the Irish, not when it comes to me. You understand that, right?"

He nodded. "Yeah. I do."

"So let's just get the mission over with, O'Flare, okay? The sooner we do, the sooner we can find out who I was, and the sooner I can leave and get back to where I belong."

"And where is that?"

"Away from you."

Amazing how those three words hurt him. Perhaps sensing that, she shook her head. "Look, let's just get going—"

Abruptly, she stopped talking. Looked over his head at something and narrowed her eyes.

Caleb tensed. "What is it?"

She looked down at him then jerked her chin in the direction of the window.

From his place in the booth, Caleb turned and saw what she was seeing. Two men messing with his bike. "Shit."

Wraith sprinted for the door with him just behind her.

"Take care of my cat," she told the wide-eyed waitress. Then she said to Caleb, "I've got the big one," as they both shot out of the restaurant.

"Of course you do," Caleb muttered.

The two men, one definitely bigger than the other, whipped around, saw them, and took off running in different directions.

Having obviously heard Caleb's comment, Wraith shot him a grin—a fucking honest-to-goodness grin—before she veered to follow her mark.

Wraith pumped her legs faster, steadily gaining ground on the man. "Stop," she yelled. "Don't make this harder on yourself."

Of course he didn't listen to her. No one ever did. Kind of hard to blame them when something that looked like her was after them.

He headed toward a steel-framed building surrounded by mounds of junked-out cars and piles of trash. When he made a sharp turn around the building, Wraith immediately stopped, drew her weapon, and put her back against the wall so she could peer around the corner and into the alley where he'd disappeared.

No sign of him. He was obviously hiding behind one of the Dumpsters that were scattered erratically down the narrow corridor.

She pulled back and shouted, "My partner and I saw you fiddling around with our bike. Just relax. You don't need this kind of trouble. Why don't you come out and talk to me?"

Silence followed for several moments before the man shouted back. "I ain't going back to jail, bitch! I'll kill you first."

"Tell you what. I have no interest in hauling you anywhere. We can figure this out. It doesn't have to get dirty." She realized as she spoke that she was applying some of Felicia's verbal judo techniques. The hostage negotiator had once taught Wraith a humiliating lesson about the benefits of using intellect as opposed to force in certain situations. At the time, Wraith had felt disdain for the human female's philosophies. Today, she'd applied Felicia's lesson without thought. Imagine that.

Holding her weapon in front of her, Wraith cautiously entered the alley, taking care to scope out any places the man could be hiding before moving forward. She heard some thuds and screams in the distance, telling her that Caleb had caught up with the man's companion.

"You hear that? Looks like your buddy is being taken down. My partner will be here soon, and then you'll have to face the both of us. You won't like that, I promise."

He didn't respond. Wraith was halfway down the alley when a door suddenly opened behind her. Wraith flinched toward the sound, just for a second, but it was long enough for the man to get a drop on her, a gun in his hand. He alternated his aim between her and the person who'd opened the door—a young, wide-eyed human kid, maybe about sixteen, dressed in stained overalls.

"Whoa. Whoa." She didn't know who she was talking to, the boy, the man, herself, or all of them. "Look. Don't do this. Like I said, I'm not here to—"

"Shut up." From the way his gun was shaking, Wraith suspected the guy was high enough on adrenaline to actually pull the trigger.

"Drop the gun or I'm gonna shoot him! Now, bitch."

On the outside, she remained calm. On the inside, because of the kid, her nerves were as jumpy as his.

"Put your gun down or I'll shoot!"

She jolted as he yelled the words. Slowly relaxing her stance, she lowered her arm, pointing her gun toward the ground but held on to the grip. The man immediately walked up to her and pushed the barrel of his gun to her head. The barrel skipped erratically against her temple as his hand continued to shake.

He was hyped up on something. Meth, probably.

She watched him as his gaze skittered nervously between her and the kid.

"Let him go. You don't need him. You don't need me."

"He said you'd be tricky," he mumbled.

"Who? Who said that?" She immediately thought of Joanna and her male companion, Michel. Had he sent someone for her after all? But she couldn't imagine Michel sending this junkie. He was too amateur. He actually thought he was going to get the best of her. If it weren't for the kid, she'd have taken him down already. Besides, Michel seemed like someone who would come after her himself.

The man glanced at her nervously. "Drop the gun first."

She nodded. Slowly bent her knees until she could place the gun on the ground.

As she straightened, she said, "Now let him go. Please."

"Go on. Get out of here," he shouted to the kid. The kid ran from the alley as if it were on fire.

Shifting her right leg slightly behind her, she held up both her hands. "So, you going to tell me who you're working for? Seeing as how you're going to kill me and all."

"I'm not supposed to kill you. We was just supposed to—"

Wraith sprung, swinging herself out of the line of fire and elbowing him in the face. Almost simultaneously, she grabbed the gun with both hands and performed a *C* move with her right leg, sweeping it 180 degrees. She violently pushed the gun toward him, and he screamed as she dislocated his trigger finger. He fired the gun, and shards of heat grazed her face. Taking advantage of his pain-induced weakness, Wraith twisted the gun so that she could control him with a reverse wristlock. With his arm locked straight, she applied enough pressure to dislocate his elbow and drive him to the ground.

She caught movement out of the corner of her eye and looked up. Caleb stood there, breathing hard, his face pale and sweaty. His mouth moved, but she couldn't hear him. The side of her face felt like someone had splashed it with gasoline and lit it on fire. Her ears were ringing from the gun being fired so close to her head. She shook her head to let him know she couldn't hear him, but almost immediately she felt her skin cooling. Her hearing corrected, but sounds were still fuzzy.

"You okay?" he asked.

She nodded. "I'm fine." Glaring down at the man, who even now was whimpering and crying as he clutched his arm, Wraith said, "Are you still more afraid of him than you are me? Because if that's the case, I'd reconsider your options really fast. Who sent you?"

He didn't say anything, but Wraith narrowed her eyes and bent closer, whispering in his ear, "Did you know wraiths live their whole lives in pain? It gives us an advantage when it comes to administering it."

If possible, he paled even more.

"Not both of you," he said. "Just you. The ghost who left the Vamp Dome."

Again, Wraith thought of Joanna and Michel. But then a thought occurred to her. She grabbed the man by his shirt. "I wasn't the only wraith at the Vamp Dome that night," she said, immediately sensing the way Caleb stiffened.

The man looked scared, then looked away. Panicked, she grabbed the man's hair and yanked his head back so he whimpered.

"Wraith . . ." Caleb said softly.

"Did you hurt her?"

"No . . . she and the man fought back. They killed one of my men."

So whoever had hired him had sent three men after her. He'd underestimated her. "How did you know *she* wasn't the right one?"

"She didn't know how to fight. Only he did."

"Bastards," Wraith spit out. "Did you hurt her? Did you?"

"No. The guy with her . . . I told you, he could fight. He protected her."

Wraith released his hair. Good. She just might like Michel after all.

"What were you looking for on the bike?" Caleb asked harshly.

"We wanted to be sure we had the right one this time. We were looking for credentials. FBI badge—"

Hissing, Wraith extracted her knife from its sheath and flipped it in her hand.

"This is the last time I'm going to ask. Who sent you?"

"I don't know!"

"I don't believe you." Wraith raised the knife, but Caleb grabbed her arm, stopping her.

"Don't, Wraith," he warned.

Her eyes widened with disbelief. "He was sent to get me. Do you think I'm going to let him live without telling me the truth about who sent him?"

"He's an idiot. Someone's using him. Besides, he's telling the truth. At least I think so. But I'll confirm it."

She wrenched her arm away from him. "And how are you going to do that?"

He didn't answer. Instead, he walked up to the man who stared fearfully up at him. "What's your name?"

When he remained silent, Caleb sighed. "Look, in case you didn't notice, I'm trying to save you some pain here. If you'd rather, I can let my friend loose and let her do whatever she wants to you."

"Doug," the man said quickly.

"Right. Doug. And your friend is Emmett."

Doug nodded frantically.

"Emmett doesn't know the name of the person giving you your orders," Caleb said. "But I need to confirm you don't know his name, either. So I'm going to lay my hands on you, and I don't want you to move a muscle, otherwise my friend here is going to gut you with her not-so-little knife and I'm going to let her. Understand, Doug?"

"Yes," he squeaked out. "I understand."

"Good." Caleb laid his hands on Doug's temples. "Ask him again," he said to Wraith. "And ask him what he knows about the feline situation and whatever else you need to know."

Unsure what was happening, Wraith hesitated, then asked, "Do you know the name of the person who ordered you to capture me?"

"No," Doug replied.

Wraith proceeded to ask him more questions: "Do you know about felines being raped? About a drug being used to rape felines? Did you hurt the wraith you followed from the Dome or her male companion? How long have you been following me? When did you get your orders? Do you know who I am? Do you know who I was before I was a wraith?"

Doug denied knowledge of the drug rapes or Wraith's identity, and he denied hurting Joanna or Michel. He said he'd gotten the call about her just after Knox's wedding. The message had been passed along anonymously, after he'd received five hundred dollars on his front stoop with the promise of five hundred more.

"Five hundred dollars?" Wraith asked in disbelief. "For a total of one grand?" She glared at Doug. "I'm insulted."

"Ask the same questions again," Caleb said.

Wraith repeated the questions. Doug repeated the answers. This continued approximately ten times. In the meantime, Wraith watched Caleb. He'd closed his eyes and his body had relaxed. His breathing evened. His color returned to normal. He looked utterly at peace. More precisely, he looked zoned out. As if he'd left his body and gone someplace else.

She didn't like it. It scared her.

"Caleb?" She prodded him for what had to be the fifth time. He didn't answer.

She grabbed his arm and shook him. "Caleb. Caleb!"

Doug's eyes were bouncing back and forth between them, and Wraith spared a glance for him when she sensed his muscles stiffen. "Don't. Remember what he said about me and my knife."

He immediately looked down at the ground and remained still.

"Caleb—" When she turned back to him, she gasped.

His eyes were open. He was breathing hard. He released Doug and stepped back. "He's telling the truth, Wraith. I promise. He's told us everything he does know. He knows nothing about the feline situation. He and his friend are hired muscle. Sent to track you down and immobilize you. Killing you wasn't on the program because whoever hired them knows you can't be killed. But you can be contained, and that's what he wanted. Now we need to go. Let the police deal with him."

It was only then that she heard the sirens wailing in the background, distant but getting closer. Caleb must have called them. She swallowed hard, trying to get over the shock of seeing Caleb go into some kind of truth detector trance. That hadn't been in his files under the heading of "special gifts," but she didn't doubt he had the gift. If he said Doug was telling the truth, Wraith believed him.

Caleb was watching her carefully, in particular the hand that held her knife. What, did he think she was still going to use it now that there was no reason to? Is that what he thought? That she killed because she liked it?

With a flurry of questions beating at her and making her feel disoriented, she sheathed her knife, noting Caleb's almost-imperceptible sigh of relief as she did so. Doug made one, too.

They both pissed her off.

She looked down at Doug and said, "Guess you're going back to jail after all, Doug. Dream of me while you're there, okay? And next time you talk to your boss, tell him I'm going to see him really soon."

FOURTEEN

For Wraith, returning to Los Angeles was a lot like returning to prison after twenty years of incarceration followed by one short month on parole—equal parts depressing and comforting.

She knew this town. Knew what to expect. How to maneuver. The best places to go to hide out. The few places she could go for help or a quiet moment of peace.

Driving along Franklin Avenue made her feel like she'd returned home—only home was an insane asylum where she not only believed the other patients were trying to kill her, but that the medical staff was, too. Everyone was a threat as far as she was concerned.

It was no wonder she jumped when Caleb gently pulled on her jacket sleeve.

"We're here," he said quietly.

She nodded and opened her door to step onto the sidewalk outside their hotel. It was a step up from the rat-infested apartments she'd rented while she'd lived here, but it wasn't exactly luxury living, either. "You'd think as a former boyfriend of the feline princess, you'd warrant enough clout to at least get us into an Embassy Suites," she said nastily.

Caleb pressed his lips together but didn't reply.

She didn't blame him, but it still pissed her off.

After their run-in with Doug and Emmett, she'd had tons of questions about Caleb's ability to discern the truth and if he had other abilities she didn't know about. But he'd shut down and hadn't wanted to talk, no matter how often she'd tried to get a rise out of him. That had included making several nasty allusions to his former relationship with Natia, the feline he'd danced with at Knox's wedding. Every time she acknowledged the existence of that previous relationship, however, she only ended up hurting herself.

Absently, she wondered if that's why she kept doing it.

"Dex and Mahone are going to meet us at the Bureau's local headquarters. I need to shower and get a meal first. How much time do you need?"

"You know I don't eat, Caleb. Are you implying I need to bathe?" she asked mildly. "Or was that an invitation to join you for either of those activities?"

He tensed, stopped, then turned to face her. The expression on his face actually made her take a step back. "Careful, Wraith. It's been a long day. Don't push me unless you want me to push back."

She glanced away and swallowed hard. "I can leave in twenty."

"I'll need closer to forty-five. Then we can share a cab—"

"You know, why don't I meet you there? I have some things to do. People to see."

"Would those things and people have anything to do with Ramsey Monroe?"

She smiled thinly. "Heard about him already, have you? So I guess it was Mahone who wanted me to come back, and not you, after all?"

"Do you really want me to answer that, Wraith?"

"No. Do you really expect me to tell you who I'm going to see? Or is there some other reason behind the third degree? You obviously thought I was willing to kill old Doug in cold blood. Are you afraid I'm an accessory to the feline rapes somehow? That I'll tip Ramsey off? Because—"

He turned away. "Go. See who you want to see. Given the fact someone's gunning for you, I'd feel better if you'd wait for me, but I have a feeling that doesn't make a difference to you, now does it? And believe it or not, I don't have the energy to argue right now."

The weariness in his voice made her frown. "Are you feeling okay? Maybe we should take more time before seeing Mahone. You can rest."

Facing her again, his brow quirked. "Worried about me?"

She was. Very worried. Couldn't he sense how worried she was? Apparently not. "Worried you're going to get Lucy or me killed. You're our backup, remember?"

"The last thing I plan on doing is leaving you hanging. In any manner whatsoever." With those enigmatic words, he strode into the hotel lobby, leaving her standing on the sidewalk to follow or not. She stood there for several undecided moments before catching the doorman's eyes.

Caleb made it seem like walking around L.A. was dangerous for her. What, did he think Doug and Emmett were the first individuals to hunt her down? Hell, she had plenty of enemies, and she'd always handled them alone. She couldn't get used to relying on Caleb now. Didn't he understand that?

"I need to leave my bag before I check in. Can you take care of it?" She handed the bag to the doorman.

"I can get you a claim ticket—"

She shook her head as she walked away, still troubled by the exhaustion that had suddenly seemed to hang on Caleb, from the lines near his eyes to the slowness of his movements. That wasn't natural for him. Usually he was so amped up with energy it made her, a creature who didn't even need to sleep, tired. Was the change related to his death mark? Or maybe she was mistaking the weariness for something different altogether. Maybe he was simply tired of her. Tired of her needling him. Tired of her prickliness and bitchiness. Tired of *her*.

Pressing her lips together, she shrugged before making a right on North Virgil.

After retrieving a pack of her favorite cinnamon gum from her pocket, she popped a piece in her mouth. Then she put on her earphones and switched on her iPod. The tunes of Bob Marley immediately calmed her, and she jacked the volume up even more, knowing from experience that the blaring sound wouldn't distract her from any potential threats. Soon, her strides lengthened, carrying her away from the human who made her long for things out of her reach and feel an emotion she tried so hard to keep away—regret.

Whatever. If he was tired of her, maybe he'd leave her alone and let her get her head on straight. Finish this damn assignment and move on.

As soon as she knew he was safe, that is.

After all, he still bore that damn death mark, and she didn't know what the hell that meant anymore. But she wasn't leaving him until she figured out why the damn thing had appeared and how she could get rid of it.

The contradictory nature of her thoughts had her cursing beneath her breath. Caleb had gotten under her skin just like the damn cat that she'd left with the waitress at the diner. The two of them had seemed happy enough when she'd checked on them, and the waitress had promised to take care of the cat. Wraith knew it wasn't a promise the waitress intended to break, given Wraith's threat to come back if she discovered otherwise. Still, it hadn't been easy driving away from the kitten. She actually missed the comfort of stroking its soft fur.

Again only wearing her leathers, she even missed the coziness of that damn poncho.

She'd miss Caleb even more when he was gone.

She walked a few more blocks until she reached her destination, an isolated area of town under a section of the 101 freeway. The littered streets were lined with auto repair shops, chain-link fences, and taxi cab companies. There were few trees. Nothing resembling a haven or sanctuary.

She pocketed her earphones and stared at the structure to her right.

The familiar brick building was still covered with grids of smoky glass windows. A large maroon awning directed visitors to a front entrance, but there were no signs identifying what they might find inside. From the outside, at least, nothing about the place had changed.

Wraith walked up to the solid black door and yanked. Locked.

She skirted around the building toward the back entrance, walking through a carpet of shrubs that clawed at her leathers. Sure enough, the back door was propped open and she could hear the rattling of dishes and the low murmur of voices from inside.

For a moment, she hesitated, wondering how smart it was to go digging into a past she'd tried so hard to forget. But she was back in L.A. for a reason. She knew perfectly well her ties with this nightclub were why Mahone had sent Caleb after her. It was where the second feline rape victim had been attacked, and there was no way Ramsey would let something like that happen in his place without following up on it. So get your ass up there and talk to him, she told herself.

Wraith strode toward the door and stopped just outside. Inside, several Hispanic men stopped washing dishes or prepping food to turn and look at her. By their wide-eyed gazes, it appeared Ramsey had decided inviting one dead chick into his establishment had been more than enough and hadn't done so again. She wondered if he still had a thing for vamps.

"Hola, señors," Wraith said, her Spanish accent flawless. "Dónde está su jefe?"

One of the men pointed to a set of interior swinging doors, and Wraith walked past them. "Gracias," she drawled, grinning darkly when she caught the gaze of one of the men attach to her ass. She might be a freak, but she was sexy enough to warrant a second glance. Some things never changed.

When she pushed open the interior doors, Wraith whistled, impressed despite herself. Apparently, the club scene was doing right by Ramsey. The last time she'd been here, the cavernous interior had been respectable but streamlined. Nothing fancy. Now, the space was highly stylized. Ultramodern. Slick. It sported at least three levels, with travertine floors and glass railings, dark wood, stainless steel, halogen lighting, and plush velvet accents.

Wraith slowly walked the floor. There were two bars, each with a black granite top that reflected the mirror of glasses overhead. Several doors peppered three long corridors, opening to spacious, soundproof rooms where private business could be conducted if that's what someone had in mind.

All in all, very upscale. Classy.

But it still smelled the same. The rank odor of cigarette smoke and lingering sweat—even blood—made Wraith's stomach turn.

"Well, well. Do my eyes deceive me, or am I being visited by a ghost? The Ghost of Christmas Past, here to show me the error of my ways? Or perhaps a ghost who's learned from her own mistakes and decided to come crawling back where she belongs?"

Stiffening, Wraith slowly turned. She smiled at the were

standing several feet away from her, but didn't move to embrace him the way she instinctively wanted to. "Crawling, Ramsey?" She pressed her lips into a pout. "I thought you knew me better than that."

"Ah, that's right." He leaned casually against one of the bars. "Crawling wasn't your thing. Usually you were immobile when you were on all fours—isn't that right, Wraith?"

His soft, taunting words immediately made her want to bash his face in. But even worse, a part of her instantly pictured her in the position he described and felt a hint—the barest hint—of longing. It was pathetic, she knew, but she chalked it up to a Pavlovian response. If Caleb O'Flare tempted her with pleasure, Ramsey Monroe would always be the male who tempted her with pain.

He wasn't very tall. A little taller than Dex. Shorter than Caleb. Unlike most of his kind, he wasn't particularly muscular. His body bordered on thin. She knew it was powerful, but a stranger wouldn't necessarily think so. Even so, Ramsey's appearance was instantly compelling. His face was equal parts angelic and devilish. He had classically honed features that made him look pretty on first glance until you really looked into his eyes and saw the shadows there. Not shadows of despair but of challenge. Hedonism. Desire. No boundaries. It was like looking into a mirror and seeing every dark, secret fantasy you'd ever had and knowing he was the person who could give it to you. But only, like he'd just said, if you were willing to crawl for him first.

She no longer was. "I'm a different person now, Ramsey. Emotionally balanced. Healthy, some might say. For a wraith, anyway. I've even joined forces with the good guys. Can you believe it?"

He straightened and shook his head. "As a matter of fact, I can't. You never liked taking orders, Wraith, even in the bedroom. I remember how long it took to get you to break. To surrender yourself to me. Do you remember how good it felt when you finally did?"

Wraith tilted her head. "Oddly enough, all I can remember is how good it felt when I finally learned the truth about you. Because it broke the hold you had on me once and for all."

"Not quite a clean break, I suppose, since here you are. Home once more."

"I'm not back for long, and I'm only here for information. When I get it, you'll never see me again."

He shook his head and tsked. "Now that's just mean." He sneered at her and jerked his head toward the raised stage in the center of the room. "I've missed you, Wraith. You still dance?"

Dance? Strip, he meant. Memories of leering faces and sweaty palms came at her like a hail of bullets. "Sure," she snorted. "I still let guys who get off on other people's pain use me for their own perverted pleasure, too."

"Hmmm." He walked toward the stage and vaulted up to palm one of the poles. "I've never found another wraith who could move like you do. Show me."

Wraith conjured up an image of herself gyrating against a pole, completely naked. But instead of remembering the way Ramsey and his customers had watched her, she imagined Caleb as the sole member of the audience. She felt a thrill of arousal, but it disappeared when Ramsey focused his gaze on her crotch. She shook her head.

"Tell you what. You strip and do a little dance for me. Then when you're done, you can tell me what you know about felines being raped. And don't even try telling me you don't know what I'm talking about. Three victims, three clubs, all within a ten-mile radius of this place. You know something, all right."

One side of Ramsey's mouth curved up as he rested his cheek against the pole. "Still as smart as ever, my dear. And of course I know something. The question is, why on earth would I tell you?"

FIFTEEN

An hour and a half after checking into his hotel room, Caleb was at the Bureau's Los Angeles headquarters, in a private conference room with Mahone and Dex. Wraith still hadn't shown up.

"It's too damn dangerous. I don't like it," Dex said for what seemed the hundredth time. His persistence wasn't half as surprising, however, as the message he was trying to jam down their throats. Caleb wondered not for the first time if he'd misjudged the were—his blatant flirting with Felicia aside, Caleb had truly believed Dex viewed the Para-Ops team's three female members in a platonic manner. Even when he'd rubbed himself all over Wraith in Korea, Caleb had suspected it had been just to get a rise out of him. Which it had.

Mahone sighed. "It's not like I'm thrilled, either, but I don't think you're giving Lucy enough credit. She can handle herself. Hell, she can psychically push someone away if he gets too close."

"You know as well as I do that her powers are limited when it comes to living matter. What more if she's drugged up on something someone slips into her drink?"

"We won't let someone get close enough to hurt her," Caleb

insisted, talking over both Mahone and the were. "Either physically or by spiking her damn drink with some drug." He turned
to Dex. "Besides, do you have any other suggestions? Are you
going to try and pass yourself off as a female feline? Because
that's about as likely as Wraith or me being able to pull it off."

Dex's answer was to flip him off.

The sound of the door opening made them all jerk around.
Wraith shot each of them a reproving glare. "You're lucky Lucy
isn't hearing this conversation, or she'd knock all your heads
together." She shut the door with an audible click. Crossing her
arms over her chest, she stared at each of them in turn.

Wraith looked as cool and confident as she always did. Under
her gaze, Mahone flushed. Dex wouldn't quite meet Wraith's
gaze. Caleb wanted to smile at Wraith's effect on them.

"What exactly is the problem here?" Wraith drawled. "Lucy
can handle parachuting into North Korea, but she'll be in mortal danger if she goes into an L.A. nightclub? If that's how little
you think of her, why the hell did you put her on the team in the
first place?"

"These aren't just any clubs, Wraith. You know that better
than any of us," Dex growled.

Wraith feigned shock. Then she narrowed her eyes and strode
brashly toward Dex. "That's right, Dex. It's a sex club." Leaning
toward him, she made a big show of talking in his ear, pseudo-
whispering, "Where people do the *nasty* in all kinds of *wicked*
ways." Straightening, she stepped back and planted her hands on
her hips. "Don't act like the thought shocks you down to your
lily-white core, you hypocrite." Her gaze shot to Mahone and
then to Caleb. He struggled to stifle a grin. "That goes double for
you two morally upstanding angels, as well."

Caleb's amusement vanished at the pure disdain in Wraith's
voice. Sure, he'd boasted at being an unrepentant lady's man,
and would often fall back on that as his cover, but he wasn't
sexually immoral. Not by a long shot.

"We're not talking about shocking me," Dex said. His fangs,
unlike a vamp's, didn't retract, and his long incisors made for
an interesting sight when coupled with his fierce glower. "We're
talking about shocking Lucy."

Openmouthed, Wraith stared at him. "You are shitting me."
She looked at Caleb. "Am I actually having this conversation?

You boneheads are afraid of shocking Lucy? Where do you think she's been living her whole life?"

"She is young," Caleb conceded before running a hand through his hair.

"She's twenty-two," Wraith retorted. "Technically, I'm only ten."

Dex snorted. "A very experienced ten. If it were you, I'd know you could take care of yourself. Hell, I'd feel more sorry for the drug pushers than for you."

"Enough," Mahone snapped. He pointed a finger at Dex. "You've voiced your concerns. Now we're going to move past them. The First Lady is meeting with the feline Queen as we speak in an effort to ease tension between the races. The President is considering forming a task force comprised of both federal and local law enforcement in the event the Para-Ops team fails to make headway on this mission. That is not going to happen. Lucy is a member of this team. The team's mission is to infiltrate the club scene and apprehend a serial rapist. With some makeup, Lucy's the best feline bait we have, and she's agreed it's our greatest chance of making quick progress in the case. However, I agree, special preparations need to be made. Lucy herself—"

"Lucy would do almost anything if she thought it would help someone," Dex said. "Even put her head on a chopping block, which is what you're essentially asking her to do."

"Where is this coming from, Dex?" Wraith asked, looking like she was confused. "Lucy has as much right to go on this mission as you do. So she's not a super-badass like the two of us—"

Affronted, Caleb opened his mouth, but she held up her hand, cutting him off. The sight of that imperious hand made his chest puff out and urged him to grab her by the wrist, drag her out of the room, and show her what a badass he could be—only with her, it would be in bed. With great effort, he shut his mouth and waved his hand in a gesture for her to proceed.

"When we're on the job, we take care of our own," she said. "And Lucy's one of ours."

"An interesting statement coming from someone who was ready to walk away from the team yesterday," Dex shot out.

That shut Wraith up for a couple seconds. She didn't look

pleased, but then Dex had simply stated what everyone already knew. Wraith glanced briefly at Caleb before responding to Dex. "I'm here now. You trust me to take care of myself in her place? Then trust me to take care of her. I'm going to be right there with her. And you guys are going to be covering our backs. All we're doing is a little low-key surveillance, trying to get the drop on a cowardly drug pusher who needs to knock out females in order to get laid. Compared to our last mission, this one should be quick and easy."

Dex said nothing. Growling, he walked out of the room instead.

"Welcome back, by the way," Mahone said. "Don't walk away from the team again, Wraith. Because it'll be the last time you do."

For a minute, she stared at the man, her expression slightly troubled. Somehow Caleb knew the look wasn't about Lucy or Dex or anything else that had just gone on, including Mahone's threat. It made Caleb's nerves jump to attention.

"So," Caleb said, testing. "Where've you been, Wraith?"

She turned, her version of a go-to-hell smile splitting her face. "I told you. Looking up old friends."

"Monroe?" he growled.

She pressed a hand to her chest, right where her heart should have been. "Is that a note of jealousy I hear, Caleb? Afraid Ramsey used our short time together to reintroduce me to the L.A. nightclub scene in all its wicked glory?" She said "wicked" in the same taunting tone she'd said "nasty" to Dex. Caleb's need for dominance rose to the surface. He was far more easygoing than Dex or their vampire leader, Knox Devereaux, but he wasn't a sissy-boy. It was time Wraith figured that out. He straightened and walked toward her, hearing Mahone's weary sigh but ignoring him.

"No," he said softly.

"Why not?"

He'd warned Wraith not to push him earlier, but obviously she hadn't gotten the message.

"Because," he said, even as he kept coming at her, forcing her to move away from him until her back was against the door. He planted his palms on either side of her head. "You still have the look of a female who hasn't been fucked in a good, long time and needs it really bad. And if you're not careful, honey, you're going to get the fucking you've clearly been asking for."

They stared at each other, neither one blinking, for what seemed like hours. Days. In the end, she blinked. She tried to cover it with another disdainful smile and a glib, "Real nice, O'Flare. Get real and get away from me," but it was a blink all the same. He knew it. And so did she.

With a satisfied smile, he pushed away from her, not missing her mumbled, "Cocky bastard." When he arched a brow, ready to call her bluff yet again, she turned to Mahone, who'd been watching them intently.

"So it'll just be the four of us? You're not bringing in subs for Felicia and Knox?"

Mahone pursed his lips, then picked up his jacket from where he'd hung it on the back of a chair. "For this assignment, four seems more than enough to get the job done. If I'm wrong, tell me now." He looked pointedly at Caleb, who remained silent.

Forcing his gaze away from Wraith, he asked, "Why was Lucy already briefed?"

"Excuse me?" Mahone asked.

Caleb smiled. He didn't buy Mahone's innocent act for one second. "Why was she briefed separately from the rest of us? Granted, being used as the primary bait entitled her to a heads-up, or at least a chance to decline, but why isn't she here now? Where is she?"

Mahone looked away and moved to the other side of the room to gather his files. "She had business to attend to, but she'll be here soon."

Dex walked back in the room, leaving the door open. It was clear he'd been listening the whole time from the hallway. The wolf had exceptional hearing. "What business does she have to attend to?" he asked.

Yet another uncharacteristic question. Caleb figured.

Mahone apparently thought so, too. "What's going on here, Dex? You and Lucy got something going on that I don't know about?"

"No," Dex said. "We don't. Not the way you're thinking."

Did Caleb imagine it, or was there a flicker of relief in Mahone's eyes just then? Maybe, but Dex kept talking, rerouting his attention.

"Regardless, what makes you think Lucy can play the femme fatale? Or am I missing something here? She's a virgin."

Wraith rounded on Dex. "How the hell would you know that?"

"How the hell could you not?"

"Let me guess, you're such a stud, you can just sense whether a woman's been fucked, right?" Although she spoke to Dex, she glanced at Caleb, apparently including him in the question.

Caleb sure hoped it wasn't for support. He shrugged sheepishly and said, "I'd put money on it."

She made a frustrated sound. "And?"

"And felines, even feline virgins, are intensely sexual creatures," he explained. "Their bodies force that upon them at an early age. Hell, once they pass the age of sixteen, they need sex on a regular basis or it causes them physical pain. Why do you think they go to these clubs in the first place?"

"If I didn't know better—that rape is about power, not sex—I'd almost wonder why someone is even bothering raping felines," Dex muttered. "When in heat, felines aren't often sexually discriminating—"

"God, you're sounding like someone I heard on TV the other day. Are you actually saying what I think you are? That these felines deserved to be raped because their race is sexually promiscuous or—"

Dex's eyes widened. "No!"

"—that a feline rape isn't a big deal?"

Caleb's eyebrows shot up. Where the hell was that coming from? Because neither he nor Dex had said that, and neither had anyone else in this room. "You're way out of line, Wraith. That wasn't what Dex was—"

Wraith turned toward him. "Of course, you know only too well the benefits of sleeping with a feline, don't you, Caleb? And not just any feline, but the feline princess."

Caleb, Dex, and Mahone fell silent. Ever since Wraith had stepped into the room, things were going from bad to worse, and Caleb wasn't even sure why. With her last statement hanging in the air, Wraith shook her head. "I . . . I don't know why I—"

"Look," Caleb interrupted, wanting to calm Wraith. "I know what Dex is getting at. It's not so much what the felines need or are looking for when they go to those clubs. It's about the guys and what *they're* looking for. What they're *expecting*. Which is uncomplicated sex with someone who wants it just as much as they do; otherwise, they wouldn't be there in the first place. Those guys aren't going to beat around the bush or make the kind of effort to get laid they might at other places. They're going be all over Lucy. Hell, they're even going to be all over you." He held up his hands at the way she narrowed her eyes in affront. "You know what I mean, Wraith. The second you or Lucy stiffen up, you're going to be made and our drug-touting rapists are going to head for the hills fast. Then the team's usefulness is toast."

"Again, what's your point?" Her gaze tore to Mahone's. "Because I know we're not wasting words for nothing. Tell me."

Mahone rubbed the back of his neck. "Well, if Lucy really is a virgin . . . And you've been—well, on your own for a while—maybe you could . . ." He cleared his throat.

"Get in some practice beforehand?" Wraith sneered. "Is that what you're saying?" Her gaze bounced to Caleb.

"I'm talking training—something akin to touch therapy or role playing—not the four of you doing the actual deed, Wraith. You'd split into pairs and—"

"And let me guess who we'd be practicing with. Lucy with Dex and me with Caleb, right?"

Even though Caleb was just as surprised by Mahone's apparent plans as Wraith was, he couldn't ignore the way his pulse began to race at her words. Not that he wasn't without conflict. Hell, he always wanted to touch Wraith, no matter where he was or who he was with or how damn fucking pissed she made him. But . . .

"Actually, I was thinking it would be the other way around."

"What?" Caleb felt the sudden rage wash over him. He probably looked all squinty-eyed, but he couldn't help himself. He didn't know when the conversation had turned to him and Dex pimping themselves out for the sake of the mission, "doing the actual deed" or not, but now that it had, he was damned if he'd listen to any talk of Wraith being with anyone but him.

"Who the hell's bright idea was this, anyway?" Dex grumbled, although he sounded slightly amused by everyone else's reactions. Again, telling. Unlike Caleb, he showed no preference for bedmates; hell, Mahone could just as easily have suggested he and Dex pair up, and Dex would probably have the same indifferent reaction.

"Actually," a soft feminine voice came from the doorway. They all turned as one to see Lucy, chin up and mouth trembling. "It was mine."

Caleb closed his eyes and felt his stomach drop.

Shit.

SIXTEEN

Knox awoke by degrees, but he knew instantly that Felicia was no longer beside him. Panic beat its familiar wings within his chest before he sat up and forced the feeling away. He hadn't imagined it, he assured himself, taking in the things she'd left strewn about the bedroom—her perfume and hairbrush set. Lotions. Jewelry. The framed picture from their wedding day.

Felicia was inside the Dome. They'd been in bed for the better part of six hours, and she was either enjoying a long soak in the spa tub she loved so much or gathering snacks in the kitchen for the both of them to eat.

Picturing her doing either eased his mind.

It was still something he was getting used to—living with her at the Dome, knowing that when he woke and went to bed, she'd be there. Feeling confident that she was safe within his care. Knowing that she touched and enjoyed all the details he'd considered in making this house a home.

Who could blame him for occasionally wondering if it was all a dream? After all, not only had he finally won the heart of the human he loved, but he had his father back. Things were as they should have always been.

His mother, Bianca, the vampire Queen, and his father,

Jacques, the human-turned-vampire who'd been unfairly branded a traitor, had been reunited.

Knox's son, Thomas, and his daughter, Joelle, were thriving. With the addition of Felicia, they were a family.

And he was happy. Happier than he ever would have dreamed possible.

Although his clan still suffered from the effects of the vamp vaccine—which had been given to humans once vampires were discovered, changing human blood so that it could no longer nourish the vamps—many of them, including his mother, had shown remarkable improvement. In part, it was because of the return of Knox's father, which, along with a regular infusion of pure blood from Felicia, had revived their Queen. It was also because they had hope now—hope that the vamp antidote the Para-Ops team had brought back from Korea would be their ultimate salvation. That they would return to strength and flourish as a race once more.

Shifting until he was flat on his back, he stretched his limbs, soaking in the feeling of the silk sheets beneath him and the realization that no matter how luxurious the fabric, it didn't come anywhere close to the softness of his wife's skin.

Smiling, he turned his face into his pillow, savoring the sound of the word "wife" even as he savored the headiness of their combined scents. Instantly, his body hardened, and he cupped his dick with his palm, stroking himself in anticipation of her return. He hadn't yet opened his eyes when he felt her body against him and her fingers brush away his. A rough moan escaped him as she began working him with her fist.

"You started without me," Felicia murmured, her chiding tone causing him to open his eyes. She was bent over him, straddling his thighs, her long hair falling across his face in a tangle of fiery silk. He cupped her face in his palms and said, "No, my love. Nothing starts until you're with me. Nothing."

The amusement on her face vanished, and her beautiful blue eyes got glassy, making his chest hurt. The bond between them was so strong, but the way she teared up at his words told him she also had trouble believing they'd made it to this moment. Married. Mated. With no guilt to burden their joy.

The only thing that had dimmed Felicia's joy on their wedding day had been regret that her parents couldn't have been there. She'd talked a little of her mother and father, who'd been dedicated to the peaceful integration of Otherborn into human society before they'd been killed in a house fire. He would have done anything to make her sadness go away. Since he couldn't, he'd sworn their future would be one to make her father proud.

Pulling her down, he kissed her, worshipping her mouth with his. Showing her with every breath and every touch how much she meant to him. The hand that still cradled his cock shifted as she guided the head to the honeyed warmth between her thighs. They both inhaled as he raised his hips, slowly pushing into her. This time he took her slowly, wanting to draw her pleasure out as long as possible so it lingered on her skin for days, wiping away even the faintest hints of doubt that she still carried with her. When she cried out her pleasure, arching her back and covering his heart with both her palms, he crooned, "That's it. I love you, baby. You'll be mine forever."

She immediately fell into a light sleep, and he held her and watched her the entire time, savoring the quivers of sensation that still trembled through them both. A long time later, a faint blinking of light caught his attention. On the night stand, he saw his phone's message light blinking. He hesitated briefly then, moving carefully so he wouldn't wake Felicia, retrieved the phone, and played the messages.

He frowned when he heard Caleb's voice. Gritted his teeth as he listened to Caleb describe the men who'd followed them to Evanston, Wyoming, with the instructions to retrieve the wraith who'd been inside the Dome. According to Caleb, Wraith had indeed met up with her friend, Joanna, the wraith Knox had cleared for entry, only to learn she'd been attacked before the men had found Wraith and Caleb in Wyoming. Although Joanna had survived, it had only been because she'd received help from a male companion.

"I'm sorry to intrude on your honeymoon," Caleb's voice continued. "You and Felicia deserve your time together. But I thought you should know that someone's watching the individuals coming and going from the Dome. I know you'll want to take precautions."

With another apology from Caleb, the message ended. Grim, Knox dialed another number and quietly gave his security team instructions. With calm, deliberate movements, he shifted back into a reclining position, still cradling Felicia.

Caleb had done the right thing by letting him know about the attack. Knox wouldn't take any chances when it came to protecting his clan and his family. His security team was now on red alert, and he'd instructed them to pull all security footage from the night of the wedding reception, even those from his guest's private quarters. It was an intrusion into their privacy, but one that was necessary at this point. If someone could get to Wraith and Caleb so easily simply because Wraith had attended a function in the Dome, then that meant they could get to others, as well, including Felicia.

He was going to make sure there was zero chance of that happening. But even as his determination fed his confidence, even as he looked down at his wife and assured himself that no living thing, whether human or Otherborn, would harm her, a different fear began to creep in.

He could protect her from others or die trying, but there was still the matter of that damn antidote . . .

When Knox had accepted Mahone's invitation to lead the Para-Ops team, it had been for two reasons: to find the missing antidote that FBI scientists had engineered to reverse the effects of the vamp vaccine, and to get closer to Felicia, the human female he'd loved for years, but whose mortality, along with his marriage and subsequent duty to marry another vamp, had kept him at a distance. During the mission, they'd learned Felicia was an immaculate—that she had pure blood—and the most likely explanation was that the FBI's lead scientist, Dr. Barker, had given her the antidote without telling her. Dr. Barker's trickery had enabled her to feed Knox, to give him the strength to get through the mission and teleport everyone back to the United States, but in the end it could also result in Felicia's death.

Because at the same time Knox had discovered Zeph's father, Dante Prime, was the traitor rather than Knox's father, Prime had claimed that the antidote had deadly side effects. Just because Prime had lied about the antidote having killed the Bureau's scientists, that didn't mean the possibility of negative side effects was eliminated. The vamp antidote hadn't been fully tested and cleared before Dr. Barker had begun administering it. Now Felicia and a handful of humans had the pure human blood that made them indispensable to vampires, but they also lived with the uncertainty of how the antidote would affect them in the long term. Even as quickly as his scientists were working to find the answer, there was no way they could fully conclude—

He jerked when he felt a hand cup his cheek. Felicia looked up at him, a frown marring her delicate brow. "You're worrying again, aren't you? Thinking about what Prime said?"

"Yes," he answered honestly, which was the only way a vamp *could* answer. Vamps couldn't lie. That didn't mean, however, that he wasn't well trained in diversion tactics. "But there was something I meant to ask you earlier . . ."

"Don't you try that with me, Knox Dev—umph."

He kissed her soundly. He'd tell her about the men who'd tracked Caleb and Wraith, but he wouldn't concern her with his own fears regarding the antidote. In the end, he was foolish for even entertaining them.

Felicia wasn't going to die because he wouldn't allow it. If it meant taking the ultimate risk and turning her into a vampire, he'd do it. No hesitation. She didn't want to talk about that option, and he wasn't pushing, but it wouldn't change his course, either.

When he'd kissed her breathless, he asked, "How much fun do you think the team is having in L.A.?" He smiled broadly. "Because I know they can't be having more fun than us."

She laughed, whooping when he scooped her up and headed toward the bathroom.

"Just what kind of fun are we in for now?"

"The kind where you lie back and let me take care of you."

She stroked his hair. "That's what you always do, my love. Take care of me."

And I always will, Knox thought. Whatever it takes.

SEVENTEEN

Aware that all eyes had shifted from Lucy to her, Wraith forced her gaze down to the floor. Even so, her body trembled with a vicious need for action. Every instinct screamed for her to move, to shove Lucy to the floor while yelling her denial, or to throw herself at Caleb and wrap herself protectively around him, announcing both her refusal to accept Lucy's so-called plan and her unspoken desire for the human male. She did neither. Instead, she just kept staring at the floor, listening to Lucy's wavering explanation.

"I'm sorry. It might seem excessive to you all, but the fact is, I'm not . . ." Lucy cleared her throat. "I'm not sexually experienced. More to the point, I'm not comfortable with anyone touching me in a sexual way. I don't want to mess things up before we even get started, so I suggested to Mahone that perhaps a little training would help. And because, well, Caleb and Wraith are always fighting, I just figured . . ."

Slowly, Wraith leveled her gaze on Lucy, causing the mage's words to falter. Oh no. She wasn't letting her get away with that feeble excuse. Not without some kind of reaction from her. Lucy knew damn well how Wraith felt about Caleb and that the last thing she'd want is to see him hooking up with another female, let alone the female teammate she'd thought at least came close to being a friend. Of course, Wraith also knew that Lucy harbored feelings for Caleb as well. She just hadn't realized how strong they were or how strong the mage's will was, either. She'd obviously fooled them all. Wraith considered her to be a youngster in many ways and had dismissed her feelings for Caleb as a schoolgirl's crush. As evidenced by his earlier protectiveness, Dex seemed to also believe that Lucy was vulnerable.

Turned out she was as manipulating and scheming as the rest of them. Score one for the mage.

As for Caleb . . .

She shifted her gaze to him, swearing that if he was looking at the mage with anything close to desire, she was going to drop him right there. Instead, he was staring back at her, his expression blank but his eyes heated. She actually gasped, because while he was indeed shooting off desire, that desire seemed to be completely directed at her.

It threw her off balance. He didn't seem to care who saw it. Who knew it. He was clearly telling her that he wanted her, not the mage. And as much as that made her want to pump her fists in the air and do a victory lap, it also quieted her instinctive feelings of possession and had her struggling to make sense of both their situation and their feelings.

What did he want from her? Because she knew what she wanted. Yes, she wanted his body. There was no doubt about that. But secretly, she wanted everything that he'd been unconsciously offering her, too. She wanted him to save her. She wanted him to ride up on his white horse and slay every dragon from her past and every one that was coming for her in her future.

She couldn't have that. She couldn't have him.

How many times would she have it shoved in her face before she accepted it?

She forced herself to walk slowly toward the mage. Everyone in the room tensed, including Lucy, but she narrowed her eyes and raised her chin. Good girl, Wraith thought. Fight for him. Show me you deserve him, and maybe, just maybe, I'll actually be able to let you have him.

She forced herself to smile and say, "That's a great idea, Lucy. Good way to think ahead." She shrugged and looked over her shoulder at Mahone. "I don't know why you thought I'd need the same training, though. Believe me, Mahone, I don't. Isn't that right, Lucy?"

Lucy flushed. "I didn't suggest you and Dex . . . train. That was Mahone's idea."

"Really? Hmmm. Well then, maybe I should take our fearless leader's advice." She turned toward Dex and threw him a come-hither glance. To her surprise, the werebeast actually looked scared of her.

"Wraith . . ." Caleb growled, causing her to stumble. Eyes forward, she told herself. Everyone's watching, Wraith.

With determination, she walked toward Dex and stared at him with challenge.

"What do you say, Dex? You up for being used? Let's show everyone just how adept I am at being touched so we can put all this bullshit aside and get on with things." She tried to keep the entreaty out of her voice, out of her eyes, but as Dex stared at her, she could almost believe he sensed it anyway. His eyes darted to Caleb, and in her peripheral vision, Caleb shook his head.

Dex's gaze came back to hers. "You're playing with fire, Wraith. You know that," he said softly—so softly she knew she was the only one who could hear him. Leaning close, she pretended to kiss his ear.

"I don't want to play, Dex," she said just as softly. "Not anymore." And she meant it. She was tired. Past tired. She wished she could lie down right now and go to sleep and never wake up.

Pulling back, she saw the understanding in his eyes. With a muffled curse, he pulled her into his arms and bent to kiss her. Wraith didn't feel pain. She didn't feel pleasure. She didn't feel anything. But for those watching, she pretended to. And one thing she'd always been good at was pretending.

As Caleb watched Wraith and Dex embrace, he actually felt something snap in his brain. He watched Dex's hands roaming Wraith's body and hers roaming over his. Distantly, he was aware of both Mahone and Lucy, still and eerily quiet beside him.

It was several minutes before Wraith pulled back and made a show of straightening her clothes. Without a word, she walked slowly past them, taking a path that left her out of Caleb's reach. Not that he made any move to reach for her. The door shut quietly behind her.

Dex was trying hard, but he didn't exactly look unaffected by Wraith's kiss. Vaguely, Caleb heard Mahone say something to Lucy, sensed him encouraging her to leave the room, and then the two of them were gone. He was shut inside the office with just Dex, the werebeast who'd just had his hands all over Wraith despite the fact he'd known Caleb was watching.

A sound, a repetitive beat, rang around him. He realized he was breathing like a horse that had just been run hard.

"She did it to push you away, you know," Dex said idly, as if they were discussing what they were going to have for lunch.

"Yeah," Caleb said. "I know." His hands clenched as he visualized strangling the life out of the were.

"And Lucy's had a crush on you from the beginning. I suppose you know that, too?"

That gave him pause. Had he? He supposed on some level he'd sensed it, but like the rest of them, he'd dismissed it easily enough, unable to take the little mage's emotions seriously. Obviously, he should have.

"I'm judging by your silence that means no, which makes you every bit as stupid for thinking you can actually come at me and walk away looking anything like you do now. So if you still want to be a ladies' man when this mission is over and Wraith is well out of your life, I'd think twice about it."

Maybe it was Dex's reference to Caleb being a ladies' man, or maybe it was the effortless way he spoke of Wraith leaving, but Caleb's emotions came down a notch. He closed his eyes, immediately pictured Wraith and Dex together, and opened them, a low growl in his throat. Several seconds passed before he looked once again at the were. "It's not like you to give fair warning, Dex. Why are you doing so now? You scared?"

Dex breathed out a ragged chuckle. "No, O'Flare. I'm not scared. I just figured I'd give you a little leeway since you're obviously suffering from the same thing Knox was not too long ago."

He scowled. "And what the hell is that?"

"A case of gotyouby."

"Gotyouby?" Caleb echoed.

"Yeah. As in, she's got you by the balls, man. And good luck, cuz it doesn't look like she's gonna let go anytime soon."

EIGHTEEN

Returning to Ramsey's nightclub now that it was dark outside was going to be a whole different experience than Wraith's earlier visit, but not until she was actually inside. She could barely hear the music blasting inside until the door was swept open by the doorman to welcome in a limo full of well-dressed patrons. As soon as the latest arrivals were inside, the parking lot was quiet again. The only clue that something interesting was happening inside was the presence of four solemn-faced, thick-necked men positioned two on either side of the door.

Ramsey's wasn't the type of joint where people waited outside in line to pay a cover charge at the door. To get inside, you either had to be a member or been invited by one. Surprise drop-ins were turned away with absolutely no exceptions.

At least, Wraith thought, until tonight.

She hadn't called ahead, and Ramsey didn't know she was coming, but she sure as hell wasn't going to let anyone turn her away from what she'd come for.

She was going to get a little of that forgetfulness she'd been seeking at Knox and Felicia's wedding. She was just going to have to get it in a different way than she'd been hoping. From a different man altogether.

Keeping her strides long and loose, her hips swaying, and her features set into arrogant lines that her unnecessary shades highlighted, she strode to the door just as another group of guests was being allowed inside. As she approached, the gazes of the four security guards honed in on her immediately, sweeping her from top to bottom, their facial expressions remaining stern and intimidating. She noticed one of the female patrons, a werecat with long, blond hair, check her out. The cat turned fully toward her, not bothering to hide her interest or the low purr in her throat.

The heavy attention didn't faze Wraith. Although she hadn't brought it up during the team's little powwow earlier, Dex had been right about what patrons would be expecting from Lucy at the nightclubs. Yes, they'd expect her to anticipate their touch, mostly because their skill and ability to pleasure her would be evaluated before she made her final choice. But what Dex hadn't said, whether it was due to ignorance or something else, was that most felines didn't limit their sexual activity to males. Most, like the werecat beside her, found females sexually stimulating. And the more unique and different their partners were, the better. In this case, Wraith was probably something new and novel, which meant she'd be all the more attractive to the female werecat.

That was something she could use.

Out of the corner of her eye, she saw the closest security guard move toward her. Smoothly, she turned her gaze on the female werecat and smiled. The cat's eyes widened before she returned Wraith's smile, prompting Wraith to walk up to her, close enough that their arms brushed.

"What's your name, wraith?" The way the security guard asked, it was apparent he was only covering his ass. Unless another wraith had been cleared for entry, he'd know she wasn't on the list, and while it was quite common for wraiths to frequent clubs like this one, their small numbers made it unlikely that one would be here tonight. The way he flexed his shoulders, as if preparing himself for battle, told her that, as well.

Instead of answering, she smiled once more at the female cat, whose nose crinkled in delight. The werecat gazed at the guard, looking him up and down like she couldn't wait to eat him up . . . as soon as she was through with Wraith. "It's okay,

Andre, she's with me. It was a . . . spontaneous invitation, and I didn't have time to call ahead . . ."

Andre was already shaking his head, a frown overtaking his features. "I'm sorry, Linea. No one gets in without being cleared, you know that."

With only minimal hesitation, Wraith reached out and placed her hand on Linea's bare shoulder. The cat's eyes widened and jumped back to Wraith's, then she licked her lips and pouted prettily at Andre. "Andre, darling, you know I'm a rule follower. Just this one time, can't you give me some slack?"

Andre smiled indulgently. "No," he said, the smile still on his lips.

With another glance at Wraith, Linea walked toward Andre so that Wraith's hand slipped off her shoulder. Instinctively, she knew the woman wasn't through trying to persuade the man to get what she wanted. No werecat would give up that easily.

Patiently, Wraith waited while the werecat rubbed her body against the guard, her left hand dropping to cup his dick through the placket of his pants. She whispered in his ear, and the longer she did so, the more flushed the man became. When she pulled away, she gave his dick a final squeeze that made a shudder run visibly through his body. He was breathing hard, his eyes glazed over, his mouth practically drooling. Casually, Linea turned and scanned the other three guards who were trying hard not to appear as if they were watching. Then she said the magic words, "And that goes for all of you. If you'll do me this one little favor. So how about it?"

The three men looked at Andre questioningly.

Several seconds passed. Wraith was beginning to wonder if she'd have to fight her way in after all, but then Andre nodded quickly. Linea beamed at him and patted his cheek. "Thank you, darling. I'll see you and your friends a little later." She looked at Wraith and waved her hand. "Shall we?"

Wraith preceded her into the club.

Even though she knew what to expect, even though she'd braced herself, it was a shock to her system. The pulsing music that repeatedly hit her body like a punch. The flash of bright lights only slightly dimmed by her sunglasses.

She took in the swarm of human flesh displayed in tight, shimmery spandex and soft leather. Many women wore see-through shirts with nothing on underneath. Bodies gyrated against one another in an undulating, primitive rhythm closely resembling sex. On the fringes of the dance floor, bodies were literally engaged in different acts. Different positions. Different pain thresholds.

Adding to Wraith's disorientation was the feel of Linea's hand caressing her back through her jacket and dropping to her ass. Swiftly but almost casually, Wraith grabbed her wrist and pulled the cat closer. "That was impressive. Thank you."

Linea smiled. "Don't thank me yet, darling. I'm expecting repayment."

"It's not going to be sexual repayment," Wraith said, bracing herself for the werecat's fangs and claws to make an appearance. Instead, the female shrugged so nonchalantly that Wraith, surprised, let go of her.

"Don't look so shocked, darling. Any idiot can tell you haven't been trained in the art of feminine love. Too bad. If you'd reconsider . . ."

Wraith narrowed her eyes at her. "Then, non-idiot that you obviously are, why'd you help me get in here?"

Linea snorted. "Because you looked like you'd make things interesting. I love Ramsey's, but I must admit, the past few times I've been here have proven to be a bit boring."

"And maybe you needed an excuse to get together with the security guard out back? And his friends, too?"

A flicker of surprise washed over Linea's face.

It was Wraith's turn to snort. "You like him. I could tell even before you checked me out." She also knew that while werecats were unapologetically sexual creatures, they were also very bound by societal expectations, and those expectations wouldn't approve of a high-class werecat like Linea sleeping with hired muscle. At least not without a reason.

"I'll back you up, of course," Wraith said. "If anyone asks. It always helps to have allies. Even a cat."

Linea nodded. "Yes, I could tell even when you touched me that it was a hard thing for you to do. Someday maybe we'll meet again, and you can tell me what you find so offensive about my kind."

"Maybe," Wraith simply said before turning away. When she did, there was Ramsey, waiting patiently for her, a small smile on his lips.

"Wraith," he said smoothly. Walking up to her, he bent low and whispered in her ear. "Naughty Wraith. Did you come to grill me about the feline rape again? I told you before, after you so delicately threatened to make this place the new Bureau hangout, that I thought you were being played."

Yes, that's what he'd told her. He'd also told her that the feline female who'd been allegedly raped after going out back to smoke a cigarette had been a regular, one who was careful about who she talked to and knew better than to wander outside by herself. But Wraith had seen the video from Ramsey's security camera, and it had showed her resisting her attacker—a tall, stocky man wearing dark clothes and a ski mask. Wraith had dismissed Ramsey's speculation that the feline raped in his club had fabricated the attack, but she still should have reported Ramsey's statement to Mahone. She hadn't. She'd told herself it was because, given the evidence, it would unnecessarily muddy the waters. But she also knew she'd done it to protect herself, because she hadn't wanted Mahone or anyone else on the team to think she or Ramsey, a man she had a history with, were making accusations against the felines because of her past. She hadn't wanted them to think Ramsey was a biased witness due to their history, but right now she was hoping he was indeed biased toward her. Or at the very least, that he wanted to repeat their history.

As Ramsey looked at her expectantly, Wraith shook her head. "I'm not here on business, Ramsey."

That seemed to give him pause. He glanced toward the front entrance and frowned. "How'd you get in, anyway? The cat helped you, perhaps?" He glanced meaningfully at Linea, who caught Wraith's gaze and waved flirtatiously at her.

Wraith shrugged. "It doesn't matter how I got in here, does it? It matters why I'm here. And what I want." She hesitated, then swallowed hard as she remembered the scene a few hours earlier with Lucy. With her whole team. Knowledge in every one of their eyes. Knowledge that she and Lucy wanted the same thing, and that, of the two of them, Lucy was the one who should have it. "What I want you to do to me. Or am I wrong, Ramsey?" she whispered, allowing herself to drop her defenses and let Ramsey, a man who'd once been her friend and protector, see how desperately she needed him. And how, for some measure in time, she needed to feel pain the way anyone would if touched a certain way. Pain in a certain context was appropriate. It was expected.

It was normal.

His eyes softened, and he shook his head. "No, Wraith. You're not wrong at all. Come with me."

Back at the hotel, Caleb had given up on pacing and had settled into bed. He tried shutting out his worry about Wraith, but it was going to take more than his own willpower to do that. Closing his eyes, he relaxed back into the fresh sheets and began the meditation ritual that would loosen his muscles and allow his mind to fall into a sleeping trance. The rest would give him more energy, and he'd come out of it refreshed, as if he'd actually slept through the night when he knew he probably wouldn't. Then he'd be better prepared to face Wraith.

When he slipped into peace, it was something he was completely aware of. It wasn't like losing consciousness, but rather like stepping into a place where his consciousness was heightened exponentially. The feel of the sheets on his skin was a heavy but pleasant weight, the sound of his breaths a deep, solid noise that surrounded him. He was even aware of the blood coursing through his veins, the way it felt and sounded and smelled.

It was like this when he was healing, too. His body ultra-receptive to sensation, both his own and any person he was linked with.

He'd never tranced himself during sex, at least not sex with someone else, although he'd heard the effect of doing so was mind-blowing. But he'd never given into the craving, not feeling comfortable with the idea that the moment he entered a woman's body, he would experience not only his own feelings, but also hers. He'd heard of shamans who'd gotten addicted to it. Abused their power. Used it so much that they lost touch of what was reality and what wasn't. Actually went crazy.

The vision came upon him before he could sense its approach. His instant thought was that he was glad he was alone in his hotel room, because while he was fully aware during a vision, just like he was in a trance, the difference was that he couldn't necessarily control his reaction to the vision. Whether it was physical or verbal—like the time he'd had the vision of

Felicia in Korea and had yelled out her name despite the armed guards they were trying to steer clear of—his ability to monitor himself lessened. Visions weren't innocuous. Sometimes they were confusing. Riddles. But when they involved danger, danger to someone he knew, his emotions became the primary thing he reacted to. With Felicia, he'd felt the need to shout out, to notify Knox that Felicia was in danger so he could get to her.

Quickly, he sensed this vision was about Wraith. He didn't know how, since he wasn't seeing her, but he knew. Her scent surrounded him, and all of his muscles tightened.

He saw a brick building. Heard music. Saw shadows of writhing bodies. He navigated by them unnoticed, like a wraith himself, carried by the hands of his ancestors. He knew some of what he saw wasn't an exact replica of reality, but it was good enough that he knew Wraith was at a club. Instinctively, he knew the club belonged to the man called Ramsey.

He reached farther for her with his mind and his speed picked up. Climbing stairs. Winding down a hallway where he passed several closed doors. As he did, he knew what was happening inside of them and his consciousness faltered, almost breaking the link as images of blood and bondage overwhelmed him, spurring his own memories from the War. Frantically, he called out to his ancestors for help, and they steadied him, bringing him to face a door.

He knew Wraith was inside. Even though he'd never been to this club, it was as if he had. As if his consciousness was burned with the same knowledge that had been burned into Wraith's when she'd walked to this room.

He willed the door open, but it wouldn't budge.

He asked for his ancestors' help once again, and still the door didn't budge.

Why? Why bring him this far only to deny him access?

Was his mind trying to protect him? Did his ancestors know there was something in the room he wasn't ready to see? That only made him more determined to get inside. More frantic when he couldn't.

Her name echoed around him and he knew his physical body was shouting her name.

He couldn't waste any more time trying to control the vision. It had given him what it felt he needed to know. Swiftly, he released control, and he was swept backward the way he'd come.

Conscious again, his body jerked, the sound of a shout dying in his throat.

He was sweating, the sheets twisted around him. Leaping out of bed, he grabbed his cell phone and punched in Mahone's number. Squeezing the phone between his cheek and shoulder, he swiftly stepped into his pants. He was dressed by the time Mahone picked up.

"Wraith's in trouble. I need the address to Ramsey Monroe's nightclub. Now."

Ramsey had Wraith stripped and strapped to a high velvet-covered table less than five minutes after they'd stepped into the small private room. It was their usual—"For old times' sake," Ramsey had teased—although the decor had been updated. It was still lined with the accoutrements that Ramsey preferred, although she saw that he'd picked up a new vice or two since she'd last been here.

"Ah," he said, obviously seeing where her gaze had gone. He picked up something that looked like a small pizza cutter with stainless steel spikes. "You familiar with this, Wraith?"

When she answered, she made sure to inject a note of boredom in her voice. Inside, however, she felt ready to crack. But she wouldn't. Not yet. Not when it didn't mean anything. "Can't say I am."

Ramsey smiled indulgently. "I picked it up off the Internet. It's actually designed based on a medical tool. Doctors used it to test nerves on the surface of the skin. Doctors know quite a lot about what the body can take, as well as the mind. In that way, they're like the mages who, I believe, you're far more familiar with."

The casualness with which he mentioned the mage didn't fool her. He looked angry. Angry that she'd spent her first few months of wraith life with him, then hadn't come to him for help after she'd escaped the mage? Or angry because of what had been done to her?

For the first time, she wondered just how deep Ramsey's feelings for her ran, but then she told herself she was being fool-ish. She'd provided Ramsey an outlet for his perverse sexual needs, that was all. He might've come to depend on her, but that wasn't the same thing as caring. "Been keeping tabs on me?"

"Actually, yes. It wasn't easy for me to let you go, especially when I knew you were with that drug-using vamp, Colt. Afterward . . . Unfortunately, my intel on you and your time with the mages was all hindsight. I apologize for that. If I'd known . . ."

Wraith laughed. "What? You would have come to rescue me? Please, Ramsey, no lies."

He looked troubled for a second, then shrugged, putting the tool with the nasty-looking spikes back in its resting place. "You're right, Wraith. No lies. That's always what's worked best with us. Total honesty. It's why we were together so long. Why you left. And why you're back tonight, isn't that right?"

"Yes. It is."

He stepped up to her and reached out, caressed the underside of her breast and flicked her nipple with the edge of his nail. The sight and touch should have been arousing, even with the pain that caused her to bite her lip. But it wasn't. And it didn't matter. She wasn't here for that. Unlike the pleasure she'd found with Colt, all she'd ever experienced with Ramsey was pain. Even so, she'd needed it. Been addicted to it. The more intense, the better. Someone else wouldn't understand, but wraiths were drawn to pain because they had no other choice. What they once feared and loathed became their comfort. Their reality. The only thing they had left of their human selves.

So she arched up and tried to force Ramsey to touch her again. To give her that jolt of pain as a prelude to what was going to come, but he pulled back and shook his head.

"Not so fast, Wraith. You've been gone a long time. We need to start slow."

She narrowed her eyes furiously. "Don't fuck around, Ramsey. I didn't ask you to ease me in. It's not what I need. I want you to work me over, and I want you to use your tools. All of them."

Sorrow was in his expression, making her feel real confusion. "We'll get to that part, Wraith. But right now, you don't know what you need."

I need Caleb, she thought, and she would have kicked herself if she could.

Even here, even now, even when she was asking, almost begging for what he would surely find abhorrent, she wanted him.

"*You* don't know what I need," she spat, and she began to struggle against her binds, hoping that it would incite Ramsey's need to contain her. Dominate her. "Besides, this has never been about what I need. That's what it was supposed to be, what you made me believe, but the truth was it was more about what you needed. The sick pleasure you take from people's pain. But I don't care about that anymore, Ramsey. Take your pleasure. Just give me the pain."

Her goading didn't work. Ramsey maintained his cool, through all her cursing and yelling, until she finally stopped, exhausted. Breathing heavily, she stared up at the ceiling and croaked. "Fine. Ease me into it, then," she said. "Just get started."

NINETEEN

Caleb bypassed the front entrance, which was being guarded by four pit bulls overseeing a steady stream of traffic. Instead, he decided to enter by the back, which was only being guarded by two. He wanted in and out as fast as possible, especially because he knew Wraith was going to fight leaving with him. That meant he needed the element of surprise, and it wouldn't serve his purpose if he got into a fight with the guards and it alerted her to his presence.

He took the drug-filled darts out of his back pocket and loaded them into his gun. They contained a tranquilizer that instantly knocked someone out when it pricked the skin. He'd have time to shoot both guards before the first even fell to the ground.

That's exactly what he did.

He swung down from the roof, rolled the bodies into the bushes, knocked on the door, and waited for someone on the kitchen staff to open it. Swiftly, he pulled the man out and knocked him unconscious, then stripped him of his kitchen uniform. The man was quite a bit heavier than Caleb, so he pulled the white uniform on over his regular clothes and stuffed his weapons into his waistband and the uniform's various pockets. Then he grabbed a dishrag and tray, kept his head down, and went after Wraith.

He'd persuaded Mahone to let him come alone. In fact, Mahone hadn't needed much persuasion. He knew as well as Caleb did that the chances of Wraith being here against her will were slim to none. No, she was here voluntarily, which was why Caleb hadn't asked Dex or Lucy to back him up. Instinctively, he'd known this was between him and Wraith. She wouldn't appreciate it if Dex or Lucy saw her in a compromised, weakened position. She'd hate him and would probably leave the team altogether. He wasn't taking the risk of humiliating her, but he was going to get her the hell out of this place. Then she was going to have to deal with the very thing that had sent her running here in the first place—him.

As soon as he got out of the kitchen, he found a secluded corner where a mage was humping a vamp and stepped out of the service-wear so he was back in his dark clothes. They didn't even look up at him.

Scanning the nightclub, Caleb got his bearings. He saw the layout of the room just as he had in his vision. With certainty, he headed up some stairs and in the direction of the room that contained Wraith. Just when he got to the beginning of the long hallway, however, a beefy hand clamped on his shoulder. Having expected some resistance, he maintained his control, turning as if he was an oblivious patron who'd simply taken a wrong turn.

"Hold on, man. Where's your pass?"

"My pass?"

The guy pointed at the sign: NO ADMITTANCE WITHOUT PASS.

"Oh." He shrugged. Scratched his head. "I want a room. Where do I get the pass?"

"Where do you think?" The guy jerked his head toward the bar and the cash register next to it, which was being manned by a young blond woman in a low-cut red sheath.

Caleb nodded and shrugged. Gave his charming, good-old-boy smile. "You want to join me?"

The man's lip curled and he gave Caleb a hard shove toward the woman in red, who gave him a seductive smile.

"Two thousand dollars," she said.

Caleb whistled. "Two thousand bucks? Man, that's a lot of money." He leaned in close. "You know, I don't usually do this kind of thing. But a buddy of mine told me about this place, and

I'm just curious. I'd like to see what goes on in there. How much would you charge me for that?"

The woman smiled tightly. "Two thousand dollars." She was obviously used to being sweet-talked.

"How about I give you a tip instead," he said, catching sight of the photo taped to her cash register. He reached into his pocket and took out his wallet, then flashed her his badge—discreetly, in case anyone else was looking. "You look like a regular working-class girl"—he looked down at her name tag—"Sheila. And I'm here looking for someone. All I want is to find her and get her out of here. If you let me go, let me do that, I'll make sure you're in the clear when my friends waiting outside come in and round everyone up. Do we have a deal?"

Sheila's eyes widened, and she studied him for several long seconds. He saw her gaze dart to the small picture he'd seen. It was of a little boy. Maybe five. One that had Sheila's nose and dimples.

Two minutes later, he flashed his admittance pass at the guy guarding the hallway and was directed to the eighth door down. Someone, he said, would join him shortly. He headed down, stopped in front of Wraith's door, and didn't bother to knock. He took out his gun, and with his grenade and gas canisters within easy reach, kicked in the door.

Ramsey had just gotten started, and Wraith hadn't allowed herself to scream. Then again, the small stuff he'd done to her barely warranted a whimper, let alone a scream, and it was seriously starting to piss her off. "Stop fucking around and just do it, Ramsey."

He pulled back his arm and hit her with the studded tails of the flogger, right across her stomach, and the impact caused her body to jerk up. He'd used some power this time, and a slight hiss had left her, but at the same time, tears had formed in her eyes. She could feel the damn moisture, and she wanted to spit.

It wasn't enough, she thought. For some reason, Ramsey was holding back. As if he'd changed. As if he could no longer dispense the pain she needed the way he had so easily years ago.

"Why? Why even start if you knew you wouldn't be able to do it?" Wraith whispered.

Ramsey's hand fell to his side, still lightly grasping the whip. "I don't know, Wraith," he said. "When I saw you, I could tell you were bad-off. I want to do it. I should be able to. But you're different now. This is different. It doesn't feel . . ."

They both heard the crash at the same time. The door to the room slammed open just before Caleb stalked in. Without glancing at her, Caleb kicked the door shut with his foot.

"What the . . ." Ramsey spun around, but before he completed the revolution, Caleb was on him.

Ramsey's head snapped back from the force of Caleb's punch, and he staggered until he fell against the table that Wraith was strapped to.

"Caleb!" Wraith yelled, but not to protect Ramsey, because she knew Ramsey to be a dirty fighter. Even so, when Ramsey pulled a knife out from under the table, Wraith reconsidered whether Caleb was the one she should really be worrying about. Caleb's face was set in a killing rage.

He didn't look at her or acknowledge her in any way. Instead, he wiggled his fingers at Ramsey, who'd regained his balance. "Come on," he ordered. "Let's see what damage you can do when your prey isn't tied up."

Ramsey wiggled his jaw and cocked a brow. "Happy to. But first, who are you to Wraith? Not a lover, of course."

Caleb scowled and inched closer. "Why the hell not a lover?"

Glancing at her, Ramsey taunted, "Because if you'd been lovers, you obviously weren't giving the bitch what she needed."

To her disbelief, Ramsey winked at her. Her shock made her hesitate, and the next thing she knew, Caleb roared and tackled Ramsey, his fists connecting to the man's face and body one after another. Despite the wink, Ramsey fought back, and the two men dragged each other around the room until they fell to the floor and Wraith lost sight of them. Flesh hit flesh. She saw Ramsey's arm rise and the glint of his knife more than once. At some point, the knife became covered with blood.

"Caleb. Ramsey. Stop! This is ridiculous," she repeated her words more than once even as she struggled against her damn wrist restraints. Finally, the room grew quiet.

Caleb rose to his feet, his fierce gaze locked on hers.

He was taking in deep breaths, not like he was exhausted, but like he was trying to control himself. Ramsey had cut his face in a shallow line that ran from the bottom of his nose into his ear. His lip was bloodied, too, and both eyes were already starting to swell.

His gaze ran over her, over her body, and she wanted to scream. Because he could see the scars on her body now. Long ago, he'd noticed the ones on her wrist. The ones on her throat. Maybe he'd even been anticipating the ones underneath her clothes. Because he didn't look surprised. He surveyed her body with dispassion—no desire, concern, or tenderness in his eyes. Stepping over Ramsey's body, he kicked the flogger out of his hand so it clattered against the floor. Then he picked it up.

The bastard had split her skin. He could tell, even though there was no open wound or blood in sight, but because of the light pink lashes around her torso and stomach that even now were fading. It should have calmed him down, the reminder that she was immortal. That she couldn't die. That any wound she suffered was only temporary. But Wraith's need for pain was obviously far from temporary, and that made him want to kill someone. Not her, but whoever and whatever had forced this upon her. So that the only thing she felt good enough for was this.

He hurled the whip across the room so it thudded against the far wall before falling to the ground. As he continued to stare at her, he had to give her props. She stared back. Even bent the knee of one unrestrained leg and cocked it so she looked sexually uninhibited and inviting.

"So you want in on the action yourself? You didn't have to knock him out, you know. Ramsey's used to sharing."

He glanced down at the were, barely resisting the urge to drive his boot into his face. He looked around, then caught sight of some leather rope. He tied the were's hands and feet until he was trussed like a pig, then grabbed a pillow off the bed, took off the case, and stuffed it in his mouth. With the other pillow-case, he shoved it over the were's head and secured it until he looked like a kidnapping victim out of a low-budget B movie. He tossed him in the corner, hard, out of his way, but not out of sight or mind.

"How'd you find me?" The thought that he wasn't alone must have just dawned on her because she suddenly looked frantic. "Are you here with—"

"They have no idea where you are. Mahone does, but he knows you're here on your own."

"So why didn't you listen to him? You're ruining my fun."

"Is that really what it is to you, Wraith? Because you didn't look like you were having much fun to me."

"You're wrong. If you didn't notice, Dex and I got into it pretty well. It confirmed I really have been out of commission for a while. I'm here to rectify that."

"This isn't the type of action you were giving to Dex. Or the type you were thinking of when you propositioned me at the wedding."

She turned her head away. "I told you. I was playing you. Now get the hell out of here."

"You're coming with me," he said, his tone resolute.

"No."

"You don't belong here, Wraith. You're worth more than this."

She still wouldn't look at him. "You don't know what you're talking about."

"Then tell me. Tell me what drove you here. What drove here before."

She remained stubbornly silent.

"I know you can feel pleasure. It comes with the pain, yes, but why this? You give yourself no chance whatsoever. Why not try to lose yourself in the pleasure instead of the pain?"

She looked at him then, her face twisted into a kind of grief she rarely let him see. "Because pleasure is as much a fantasy as everything else in this life. It's not real. It's not who I am or what I'm meant to be. Not anymore."

"So you're saying what? The pain is your destiny? What you're meant to experience?"

"That's obvious, isn't it?"

"That's bullshit." His flat statement seemed to take her by surprise. "You've got a condition, Wraith. Who the hell knows why? But you didn't ask for it, and you don't deserve it any more than the vampires asked to have to suck blood, or I asked for my visions, or someone asks to get cancer. Yeah, you have to live with it—but you don't just live with it, you relish it and then you even seek it out."

He thought, just for a second, that he might have gotten through to her. Her eyes seemed less filmy, and it must have been his imagination, because he thought they sparkled blue before she blinked and they got hazy again. She scowled at him. "I told you to get out."

They both glanced at the heap that was Ramsey as he began to shift and struggle.

Caleb sighed. "Fine. We need more privacy anyway."

"Yes, we can discuss this later—"

"No, Wraith. That's not what I meant."

"What do you—" She saw the syringe in his hand and stopped cold. "What the hell is that?"

"It's meprobamate. When we first formed the team, I did my research. It's one of the tranquilizers that works with wraiths. No side effects whatsoever."

She shook her head. "Don't—"

"I'd have preferred a pill if I'd known you'd take it, but this'll be fast, I promise."

She began to struggle in earnest now. "No, Caleb. You son of a bitch, stop. Don't!"

But he did. She was out within three seconds. It took far longer for him to get himself in control so he could dress her and get her out of there.

TWENTY

Lucy shut her phone and threw it on her bed so it bounced, then hit the floor. Neither Caleb nor Wraith were answering their cells. Not that she could blame them.

Furious with herself, she sat on the edge of the bed and dropped her face into her hands. What an idiot she'd been. It had been a brief moment of weakness that had prompted her to talk to Mahone about needing "special training" with Caleb. She'd realized it more than twenty-four hours earlier, but hadn't fully accepted it until right around the time Mahone had been meeting with the others in L.A. She'd hustled over there, hoping she could catch him before he mentioned it, but the instant she'd gotten to the room, she'd known. If she hadn't heard them talking about it, she would have known by the expression on Wraith's face.

Jealousy and longing and desperation all rolled into one, but they were capped off with something even worse—resolution. She'd known how Wraith would react to the suggestion, known she'd view it as yet another sign that she wasn't meant to have love, especially not in the form of Caleb O'Flare. In fact, that was exactly what Lucy had counted on.

The guilt ate away at her.

If she'd truly loved Caleb and thought he could feel the same way about her, she wouldn't have felt so bad. As part feline, she'd been taught to be sexually empowered, that she had a right to pleasure in all its forms including love. Her race's sexuality was a burden to her, but their capacity to love was something she'd always been proud of. Still, felines always knew when someone was interested in them or not.

Lucy had known Caleb would never love her, even believing her to be a full mage. And if she was really honest with herself, she'd questioned her feelings for him, as well. She was attracted to him, for sure. Respected him. Admired him. But was that love? A first crush, more likely. And for that, she'd become just another barrier Caleb was going to have to climb over in order to get Wraith to accept her feelings for him.

Lucy had no doubt that Caleb was going to try and climb those barriers. But there'd always been doubt that he'd be successful. How was she going to rectify what she'd done? After all, it wasn't as if love potions were real. She couldn't make someone fall in love . . .

Standing, Lucy practically squealed as a thought occurred to her. She had the ability to ease someone's pain, but it was usually a temporary measure and one most effective when she was in close proximity. That was how most of her magic worked. She'd never had much luck with spells; maybe it was worth another try.

But it wasn't like she carried around a spell book with her.

Frowning, she paced and told herself to think. To remember some of the generic spells she'd learned from her teachers. There were a few verses that kept coming into her head, but she had no idea what they meant. All she knew was that they were meant to bring someone something good, because those were the only spells she'd allowed herself to be taught.

Any kind of goodness would help Wraith, right?

Sitting on her bed cross-legged, Lucy closed her eyes and placed her palms together, prayer style. She concentrated on feeling her breaths entering and leaving her body, then murmured the verses, tying in Wraith's and Caleb's names, along with a few improvisational lines. She repeated the words over and over until she lost track of time.

Finally, she opened her eyes.

There. That was the best she could do. Maybe she'd been a bitch for not trying it sooner, but it wasn't as if she'd had much practice with these kinds of things. Or feelings.

Drained from the use of her powers and the events of the day, Lucy fell back on the bed and closed her eyes. She was just falling asleep when an intense cramp suddenly exploded in her abdomen and then lower. Biting her lip to keep her cries of pain in, she reached for the licorice in her drawer and chewed several down. They gave her some relief, but she knew the easing effect wouldn't last long.

She was going into heat, and the timing couldn't be worse.

The only way to stop the agony of the heat was to have sex, and since she had no intention of doing that, she was going to have to go into those clubs at a time when she was at her most vulnerable.

Curling into herself, she closed her eyes and waited. The fever took her first, then the shakes. When both eased, they were only to be replaced by a dull, aching throb throughout her body, one that made her feel empty, as if her body was caving in on itself without anything to support her. Caressing herself helped, but again only temporarily, and if she gave in to that urge, tried to reach orgasm herself, her pains would only get worse.

A couple of hours later, she was writhing on the bed, wishing she could somehow cast a spell to reduce her own pain. Or better yet, she thought hysterically, die. Death would be better than this. Better than being a mindless, sex-crazed creature who couldn't control her bodily urges. Nothing could be worse than that. Nothing.

Vaguely, she heard a knocking sound and shakily sat up.

Bleary-eyed, she stared at the door.

Then someone yelled her name.

Dex.

As he stared at the male in front of him, Isaac began to wonder if perhaps the vampire's natural tendency toward duty and honesty had started to screw with his priorities. The vamp had sworn that when Dante Prime had been taken into custody, nothing had changed. That he was determined to aid the Quorum in achieving separatism between humans and Otherborn. Now, his determination seemed to be wavering.

Or perhaps it was simply that the vamp had grown to admire his new sister-in-law and objected to hurting her specifically, no matter how worthy the cause.

"If I made a mistake in asking for your help, please forgive me. I indicated the Quorum's sole focus would be on the felines for a while, but this matter was only recently brought to my attention. I can certainly go elsewhere if—"

"No," Zeph Prime said before turning around. He was bulky with muscles, healthier than he'd been in a long time, almost as large as his half brother, the dharmire Knox Devereaux. When Zeph had worked with the Quorum to get the vamp antidote away from the Bureau, he'd ensured his anonymity by continuing to remain a victim of the vamp vaccine. Unlike his cousins, Lesander and Niles, he'd only occasionally drunk pure blood and only then when he felt his lack of strength was jeopardizing his cause. Accordingly, he'd always been gaunt and pale when Isaac had seen him. Now . . .

Zeph wasn't getting pure blood from the Quorum's supply. How he was getting the blood and from whom, Isaac didn't know, and Zeph would never tell him, but obviously it had to do with the Para-Ops team's return from Korea and the acquisition of the vamp antidote. Devereaux's scientists were either administering it to humans in order to feed vamps or had found a way to make a potent blood cocktail outside the human body. In any case, it wasn't just Zeph's strength, but the clarity and purpose in his gaze that made Isaac nervous.

Once again, he wondered if he'd made a huge mistake by seeking the vamp out, but how else was he going to get to the human female? He'd had a contact inside the Dome during the Devereaux wedding, but now that the guests had left and the Dome was once more secure, he needed someone on the inside, someone who was free to come and go as he pleased. He breathed a sigh of relief when Zeph grinned and slapped him on the back good-naturedly.

"I'm glad you came to me, Isaac. But I wish you'd done it sooner. Why didn't the Quorum act to stop the ceremony before the marriage was official? And they must have considered the fact that Felicia's a federal agent. One whose death won't be taken lightly. Do they really want that kind of heat jeopardizing all they're trying to accomplish?"

Isaac hesitated. Zeph Prime trusted Isaac because of his connection to the Quorum. If he knew Isaac was working outside the Quorum's authority, he wouldn't risk his neck or his objectives. Instead, he'd turn Isaac over to the Quorum on a silver platter, but probably not before he feasted on him first. Not for the first time, Isaac wondered whether staying in Athena's good graces was worth jeopardizing his position with the Quorum. At this point, however, he was well-caught in Athena's web. All he could do was forge ahead.

"The Quorum believes the risks are worth it. With Knox's father having successfully been turned by your mother, it's only a matter of time until Knox tries to turn his wife, as well. Do you agree?"

Zeph nodded. "Yes."

"It's an abomination. And besides, your brother would be risking his life. For a human. We thought for certain that would be something you'd want to avoid, but perhaps—"

"No," Zeph muttered. "You're right. Knox loves Felicia, and no matter what she says, he won't leave her to her human mortality for very long." He eyed Isaac. "But as for who would be blamed for the murder . . ."

"As I said, there are two choices. We'll leave the decision to you. The Quorum asks that the felines be blamed because that, of course, serves its objective of creating discord between the humans and the felines."

"It will also cause discord between vamps and felines, but I suppose that's a small price to pay in the grand scheme of things," Zeph said.

Isaac nodded and mentally laughed. He should have had more faith in Zeph Prime. Like father, like son, didn't they say? "Your other option is to blame another vampire. One who viewed the marriage as an insult to vampiric purity. Then the discord would be between human and vampire—"

"As it should be," Zeph interrupted yet again. He seemed to ponder the two options, then shrugged. "I'll think about it."

Isaac frowned. "Of course. But you'll need to let me know soon whether you'll accept the assignment or not. Because if you don't . . ."

With a sigh, Zeph shook his head. "No. You misunderstand

me, Isaac. Tell the Quorum I'll do what they want. But I'll think about who I want blamed for the murder. Because the individual blamed won't last a night once Knox has a name. My brother will kill him in as painful a way as possible." Zeph smirked. "Believe me, there are quite a few people I'd love to blame Felicia's murder on. It's only a matter of winnowing the names."

TWENTY-ONE

Caleb stared down at Wraith, awed by the way her unconscious state softened her features. Relaxed and tucked into her hotel bed, she looked vulnerable. Almost fragile. Her skin seemed less blue, and something about her hair looked different, although he couldn't pinpoint exactly what it was. No surprise, since images of her naked body kept flashing in his head, alternately making him hard or angry depending on whether he let himself remember the scars that had covered her.

He'd suspected it, but Wraith was as scarred on the outside as she was on the inside. If he made a wrong move now, he might as well take his knife and slash her skin into ribbons himself.

"Wraith," he whispered. When she didn't respond, he exhaled and swept a hand through his hair. Just walk away, he told himself. She's not ready for this and neither are you.

But even as he had the thought, he knew he wasn't walking away. This had been coming for a long time now, but especially since they'd returned from North Korea. Their mission had affected all of them, of course, but Wraith had come back different. Still prickly, but less mouthy. Less willing to react or to interact. Less . . . well, less Wraith. It was as if a part of her died on that mission. As if the regeneration of her body looked complete but really wasn't.

He'd let her have her space. Worried alongside Lucy whenever she locked herself inside her room. Let her walk away from him at Knox and Felicia's wedding, and then again when they first arrived at the hotel and after Lucy had dropped her bomb about touch therapy.

He knew how much the thought of him touching Lucy bothered Wraith. As much as the thought of Dex touching her had bothered him. But despite their mutual sense of possessiveness, it could never go anywhere. Never be anything that mattered.

Their bodies didn't care about that. Their bodies demanded relief, and every day they denied themselves, they were distracted. Prone to do things they normally wouldn't. That's why Wraith had gone to Ramsey Monroe. As a substitute for something she wasn't getting from Caleb or from anyone else, for that matter. When he'd seen her strapped to that table, surrounded by a collection of whips, masks, and toys, he'd finally gotten it through his head that Wraith needed to be touched, whether that touch came with a little pain or a whole hell of a lot. And although Caleb didn't want to hurt her, he needed to give her what *she* needed.

The second he'd brought Wraith back to the hotel, he'd known it was time. He'd convinced himself he could do it. That he could fuck her and that she could handle the pain he would cause her, just like she'd handled the whipping Ramsey had given her. But now, looking down at her, he knew he was going to hold back.

He didn't want her mind mixing him up with Ramsey or any other damn male she'd been with before. So although he was going to give her a little of what she needed, he wasn't going to cause her more pain than absolutely necessary. He'd rather cut off one of his body parts first.

The thought made him smile. When he told her what he was thinking, Wraith would probably be happy to do the cutting for him. He also knew which body part was going to be at the top of her list. In fact, she'd be so pissed that he'd drugged her that she probably would try it the instant she woke up. And sick bastard that he was, even that thought made him hard.

Wraith came to consciousness in full-blown panic. She knew instantly she'd been drugged, and to her, that meant she was helpless. Controlled. Weighed down. Just like when that mage had experimented on her.

The fact that she was in a hotel room and unrestrained should have calmed her down. It didn't.

The moment she saw Caleb, she went for his throat.

"You bastard! How dare you drug me!"

She kicked and punched at him, but he easily deflected her blows, proving to her he really was a badass. The whole time, he shushed her and asked her to stop. *Asked her*. She knew it was the gentle tone of his voice more than anything else that made her attempts to hurt him so feeble. Hearing his tone, the compassion and understanding there, made her picture how her body must have looked, spread out on that table, every inch riddled with scars.

Jerkily, she tried moving past him, gasping when he crowded her body with his, backed her against the wall, and caged her in by planting a palm on either side of her head. Immediately, she tried shoving him away, but froze when he shushed her.

"Shhhh. Don't. Relax, Wraith. Just relax."

Her body was shaking, but it settled well before she expected it to. With her face so close to his, his breath a light puff of air against her skin, Wraith stared into Caleb's eyes. The ones Lucy had said were green. She knew what Lucy had left out. That they were the most beautiful shade of green on earth. They had to be. But why in hell was she thinking that now? Her brow wrinkled with confusion, and she forced herself to stop from reaching out for him.

Perhaps sensing the fact that she was gathering her defenses, Caleb smiled somewhat wistfully. "Aren't you tired of fighting this thing between us, Wraith? Aren't you tired of fighting yourself? Don't you—for just fucking once—want to forget about what we should do and just do what we want?"

Before she could respond, he bent his head slightly, touching his nose to her ear.

She froze like a small animal caught in the shadow of a bird of prey. Without her brain's permission, the soft flesh between her thighs clenched. Her head was spinning. His touch and his closeness was an intimacy she could barely endure, his body so hot that, despite the inches that separated them, the heat managed to penetrate her through her clothes.

She closed her eyes to block him out and prepared to knee him in the nuts. Instead, the instant she closed her eyes, chaos exploded within her body. From a great distance, she heard herself whimper. Something thrummed to life in her chest, a slow, steady beat, a flutter of sensation like the gentlest ripple in a lake. Something inside her loosened in preparation for the next ripple. For the next beat to come. And then the next. And then the next.

A broken laugh escaped her and she shook her head.

It was a heartbeat. Slight and barely there, but it *was* there.

She had a heart. And this man was breaking it.

"Let me go. You can't give me what I need, Caleb. Not with your past. Not with who I am. You know that."

"And you think Ramsey can?"

She shrugged. "He did. Once. Why not again?"

"Because you're not the same. You've changed. That's why you left him in the first place, isn't it?"

She turned her head away, too aware of how persuasive he could be. "You don't know me."

"I know this—pain isn't what you need, Wraith. It's only what you think you need. What you've convinced yourself is the only thing you can have."

She smiled sadly. "It's who I am. I have to accept that. I live with pain every day of my life. It's the price I have to pay for pleasure."

"That's what you tell yourself to keep us apart. To keep yourself protected from me. Which is ridiculous, Wraith, because I'll die to keep anyone from hurting you. Don't you know that? The only way you were going to stay in that club with Ramsey was if he killed me first."

His quiet words, said so confidently, rang with truth, and Wraith bit her lip, wanting to believe him but also knowing it couldn't possibly be true.

"I—"

Before she could guess his intent, he swept her up so he cradled her in his arms. The world spun as he lowered her to the floor. He wasn't particularly gentle about it, either. She lunged and tried to slither away, but before she could, he covered her with the entire weight of his body. In seconds, he had her immobilized, with her wrists pinned to the ground on either side of her face. His fingers were on her bare wrists, lightly but still causing her pain. Far less pain than usual, however, and that made her frown and struggle against him again.

She didn't budge him.

And he didn't let her go.

"Now," he said. "Tell me you believe me. That you know I would protect you."

She bucked beneath him, trying to throw him off but barely moving him. "This is ridiculous, Caleb. You're showing me how much you want to protect me by using force? I don't know what you want but . . ."

He continued to stare at her as she swallowed her words.

He nodded, but his expression hardened. "That's right. You know exactly what I want, Wraith. And exactly how deep I want to be."

The innuendo in his voice made her freeze. The iron hard poker pressed against her thigh made her skin heat. Feeling her resolve slipping away completely, she made one last frantic grab for it. She renewed her struggles, pulling her head up and going for his throat with her teeth.

Placing both her wrists in one of his hands, he grabbed her jaw with the other, his fingers touching her bare flesh and forcing her jaw to remain open. The way he handled her, rough and without his normal concern, shocked her and made her moan with desire. "You know, I like the idea of you using your mouth," he said. "But how about we use it a little differently?"

Eyes sparking with intent, Caleb lowered his face to hers.

Wraith's eyes widened, and despite the pressure on her jaw, she managed to choke out, "Caleb, no. Don't." She made sure she sounded like he was hurting her, and he was—not her flesh, but her now-beating heart.

He paused, eyes narrowed, and released her jaw. "That's good. The little hitch there at the end was particularly inspired. Well, I promised you'd never have to fear me, Wraith, and I wasn't lying."

Releasing her completely, he stood and backed several feet away from her.

Slowly, she stood, as well. Swiftly, she moved toward the door, then stopped with her hand just over the door handle. Go! her mind screamed. But her body was shaking again, wanting to ignore what her brain was telling her and to go to him instead. To let him finish the kiss he'd been about to deliver.

"Caleb," she sighed. She turned toward him. "Caleb, I—"

He was right behind her and instantly took her in his arms. Lowering his head once more, he took her kiss. He was neither quick nor gentle. He ate at her mouth with a heated sucking motion, using his tongue to thoroughly penetrate her. He was a warrior determined to obtain her surrender, but one that fought with pleasure rather than pain. Despite her prior resolve to remain unmoved, unresponsive, she moaned when his tongue rubbed sinuously against hers, beckoning it to play. At the involuntary sound, his cock grew harder and pushed against the cradle of her legs.

Wrenching her mouth from his, she turned her face to the side and closed her eyes. "The others . . . We have to check in," she said, her voice harsh and raspy. It was a feeble excuse and she knew it.

"I've checked in with Dex. They don't need us back until tomorrow afternoon, when we'll get our final orders from Mahone. And you're not going anywhere, Wraith. Not until I show you that pleasure is inside you just as much as pain."

Wraith gaped at him. Masculine aggression emanated from him in waves, threatening to topple her over like a rag doll. He'd changed. Why? Because he'd seen her at Ramsey's? Had the idea of hurting her excited him? Given that he was touching her far more easily, and that he couldn't do so without hurting her, even though the pain was barely even there now, the idea wasn't wholly unpleasant. "So you're willing to hurt me? Because a lot of what you've done in this room has hurt me, Caleb." Deliberately, she raised her fingers to her jaw and saw him wince. "Caused me pain. You ready to give me more?"

Uncertainty flashed across his face, but only for a second. "I didn't say that."

She shook her head in confusion. "I don't understand."

"It just needs to be done, Wraith. We need to get it out of our systems. If not the normal way, then the abnormal way."

What the hell did that mean? For her, this was all abnormal. "Again, I'm not getting it, Caleb."

"You will. Let me show you. You're going to like what we do every bit as much as I will. I promise, I won't hurt you. There won't be any pain at all."

She saw the sincerity of his words in his expression and knew he'd worn her down. He couldn't possibly deliver on what he was promising, but she wanted it so badly, it hurt almost more than anything she'd ever experienced. She didn't just want what he was offering. She *craved* it. Blowing out a breath of defeat, she said, "Okay, fine. You win. No pain, huh? Go for it, Caleb. Show me how you can give me what no other man before you has."

Not cowered by her words, he stepped up to her. She expected him to kiss her. Instead, he reached down and slowly unfastened her pants and pushed them down until they stopped on her thighs. Just like that, the most vulnerable part of her body was exposed, but his gaze remained locked on hers. "Sit on the bed."

She did. Half of her was in shock. The other half was almost dizzy with anticipation.

"You're being so compliant." He ran his hand lightly up and down her arm, his fingers separated from her flesh by the cloth of her shirt. "Why?"

She struggled for a response and the right sarcastic tone. "Just waiting for you to spit out the punch line and leave."

"I think it's because you want what I'm offering. Because you know you deserve pleasure far more than you deserve pain." He leaned in and kissed her neck. "I'm not leaving, Wraith. Not until I give you a taste of what you've been needing."

She waited for him to do something like grab her jaw again. To show he was no longer afraid of touching her. To maybe even bite her. At the thought, Wraith barely failed to stifle the moan that rose in her throat. To do something like that, Caleb would have to be out of control, so taken over by lust that he didn't even know what he was doing to fulfill it.

He wasn't. And that was okay, too.

"I want to kiss you," he said. "I want to taste you. Put my tongue in your mouth. In your cunt. But I can't. Because I know that would hurt you. Even just a little bit. Right?"

Wraith swallowed hard.

"Right?"

She nodded and closed her eyes. "Right."

"Have you ever been licked to orgasm?"

Her eyes flew open when it became apparent he actually wanted her to answer his question. His face was close to hers, so close that she could see the pores of his face. Heat suffused her.

"Answer me."

"Yes."

"Did it feel good?"

Had it? Somewhat. "It hurt more." She said it as a challenge, lifting her chin defiantly, annoyed by all this talk and no action.

Instead of rising to the bait, he said, "I want to do it so bad, but tonight isn't about pain. Any pain at all, remember? It's only going to be about pleasure."

She laughed. "You've got something up your sleeve, maybe? A dildo? 'Cause I gotta tell you, Caleb, I'm really not in the mood for—"

"Not a dildo. Fingers. Yours."

Understanding washed over her. So she was right. He wasn't offering her a miracle, but he was offering her relief. Relief while he watched? "No . . ."

"Yes," he insisted. "I can feel your heat just standing here. You're slick and hot, aren't you? How much wetter—how much hotter would you get if I touched you?"

At his question, she imagined his fingers nestling into her folds. Imagined him inserting a long finger into her, then two, her inner muscles contracting around the stiff intruders, warm flesh and blood rather than plastic or glass. She groaned.

He lowered his head and blew against the tender curve of her shoulder. It made her reach to pull him down, closer, but he gently nudged her back with his body until the back of her knees hit the bed and she automatically sat down. Then he stepped back completely.

Without his heat to warm her, she crossed her arms around herself, hating the way her body instantly went cold. He moved away until the backs of his knees touched the small reading chair in the corner of her room. As Wraith watched, Caleb unbuttoned his pants and lowered his zipper, freeing his stiff member but immediately wrapping his fingers around it so she didn't get a true sense of its appearance. But she'd felt it pressed against her more than once. It was hard and it was big and her mind plugged in the details while her mouth began to water.

He slowly lowered himself into the chair and began stroking himself in a strong, steady rhythm. His gaze never left hers. Slouching down, he rested his free hand behind his head and pinned her with smoldering eyes. "So we've established you use dildos to get off. It doesn't hurt you?"

"N-no."

"Do you masturbate?"

Wraith sat motionless, speechless, her gaze unable to move from the sight of him pleasuring himself. What had he asked her?

"Answer me. Do you touch yourself?"

Her face burned. She thought of all the times she'd touched herself since meeting him. Always in the dark. Always under the covers. Embarrassment made her want to turn and run. Instead, she merely shook her head.

He tsked. "Now, now, Wraith. I thought you were going to be honest with me. You've never taken your fingers and dipped them into your heat, working yourself toward pleasure in the privacy of your room?"

Wraith refused to answer. What did he want from her? To admit that no matter how many times she'd sought release, she could never fill the ache of loneliness inside her? She wouldn't do that. Those moments were hers and hers alone. Even if they had always ended with ripples of pleasure that barely seemed worth the effort, there was no way she was going to reveal that to him.

"Well, I know one thing. You've never done it with me watching. That's about to change. Touch yourself."

Wraith knew he'd been leading up to this, but still, she inhaled sharply at his stark command. She shook her head, suddenly wondering if she could do this. Letting him touch her was one thing, regardless of the pain it came with. Letting him watch her while she . . . well, that was something altogether different.

"This is what I want, Wraith. It's what you need. We'll do it together and maybe this'll help us get the edge off." His voice was hypnotic. His offer both tempting and disconcerting. "Give us the push we need to find pleasure with someone else."

Someone else? Realization covered her like a bucket of ice water, breaking the spell he'd cast over her. That's what this was about. About him wanting to get over her and move on. Maybe he had the right idea. Maybe she should give him what he wanted. And get him the hell away from her. Because she couldn't afford to care if he stayed or not. Not if she wanted to remain emotionally intact. Not if she wanted to find out what his death mark meant and retain the ability to walk away once she knew he was safe.

Biting her lip, she slowly moved her hand down her body. When she tentatively touched herself between her legs—just with the tips of her fingers—heat exploded inside her with the force of a firecracker. She whimpered.

"Good. Spread your legs apart."

She moved as if she was in a trance, still refusing to look away from his stroking hand. He kept up his verbal assault, his deep voice vibrating into every nook and cranny of her body. He lifted his hand, sucked on his fingers, then wrapped them around his shaft once more. "I'm imagining your juices got my fingers wet. See how easily my hand is moving over myself? Feel how wet you are? Because I can see it for myself. On your pussy. Dripping onto your thighs."

Wraith resisted closing her eyes as she moved several fingers over herself. He was right. She was so wet she was dripping. The sight of his hand moving over his cock combined with the husky darkness of his voice increased her pleasure tenfold. A low, jagged moan escaped, the sound so prolonged that it sounded like she was singing.

"Put your finger inside yourself." Her eyes flew to his and her hand dropped away. She'd never done that before. Certainly not with anyone watching her. "No."

"Now, Wraith." His command brooked no resistance. "It won't be as satisfying, not for either of us, but a finger fuck will have to do. Do it."

Their gazes clashed for several long moments. He made no threat. No ultimatum. She knew he had chosen the raunchy words deliberately, to amp up her pleasure but also to remind her and himself that this was about sex, not more. She also knew if she continued to resist, he wouldn't force her. He'd leave instead.

She didn't want that. There was something about this human male. He got to her. More than any man ever had. He was light where she was dark, yet he still had darkness that called to her own and somehow seemed to bring out every traitorous softer emotion inside herself. She couldn't afford to be soft.

She moved her hand back toward her groin. His voice stopped her.

"Wait." Her hand froze at his words. "Lay on your side, prop yourself on your elbow and spread your legs apart."

There was no resistance left in her. Slowly, she did as he commanded. She felt entranced by him, and maybe she was. His heated gaze and his continual masturbation made her feel sexy. Desirable. His fist was moving faster now. Twisting. Pausing at the top of his shaft to smooth his palm over the head of his penis.

"Wider. Good. Now do it. Put your finger inside yourself."

Without taking her gaze from Caleb, Wraith obeyed him. "Oh . . . oh God," she moaned, barely aware she was speaking. She closed her eyes and imagined it was his cock that impaled her. Without him directing her to, she began to move her finger in and out. She vaguely heard the sound of Caleb shouting out as he stroked himself to completion. She wanted that, too. Wanted to feel the waves of pleasure engulf her. She pushed another finger into herself and moved them faster. Her hips shot up, the sensation pushing her higher, higher still, until she felt like a rocket, hurtling toward space at dizzying speed.

"Wait . . ." She said it breathlessly. Desperately.

She paused. Was about to pull her fingers out of her body when he said, "No. Don't you dare. Come on, Wraith. Let yourself go."

She tossed her head. Could barely get her eyes open. "I can't . . . Oh God it feels good, but . . . I . . . I . . . Oh God." She was scared. Terrified. Her control was gone. Shattered.

He cursed softly, moved toward her, then fell to his knees. Hovering over her, he pressed his lips close to her ear and began talking. About what he wanted to do to her. How long. How often. How deep. In between the raunchy descriptions, he crooned, "That's it. You can do it. Come on. Come on."

Her thighs began to tremble as small spasms of pleasure overtook her. Still, she wasn't quite there. Pressure climbed higher and higher. His mouth lingered next to her ear, his soft breaths caressing her lobe. His intent was silent, and though he was holding back, she knew what he was thinking.

"Do it," she begged. "Bite me . . ."

He pulled back, just a little. "The pain. I promised—"

"I don't care. Do it now, damn you!"

Instantly, he clamped his teeth around her earlobe, then sucked it into his mouth. That small pain coupled with the pleasure of her fingers sinking deep into her body pushed Wraith over the edge.

Wraith screamed as spasms of electricity worked their way mercilessly through her body. Her screams turned to moans. Then to gasps. Then for pleas of succor as Caleb continued to whisper in her ear. Finally, she fell back on the sheets, her limbs splaying out loosely.

Caleb rested his face on the bed beside her. They both breathed noisily in the silence of the room. Long moments passed, and Wraith blinked rapidly until the faint moisture in her eyes disappeared.

At that moment, he raised his head and looked at her. His piercing stare immediately had her on the defensive. "Well, that was a great effort, O'Flare. You . . . you almost proved your point. But in the end, it took pain to get me off. So what does that say about me now?"

The fire in his eyes immediately flashed out. He was quiet for a long time, then he straight-armed himself off the bed. He stood up, adjusted his pants, and slowly backed away. He moved for the door connecting their rooms, stopping before getting there. Over his shoulder, he said, "I guess it says I'm an idiot. Good night, Wraith."

Wraith watched him go with a leaden feeling of loss. She curled into herself on top of the mattress, turning around so her back was to the door. And even though she didn't allow herself to cry, she wanted to.

TWENTY-TWO

Caleb made sure he kept the door to their adjoining rooms open. Folding the pillow under his head, he stared up at the ceiling, listening to the sounds of Wraith tinkering around in her own room. At one point, he thought he heard the whisper of fabric against her skin as she undressed. Tension filled his chest. Ignoring it, he turned on his side, flipping the blanket over his head. He couldn't block out the sight of her playing with herself and giving herself pleasure. It had blown his mind, filled him with a sense of satisfaction, even as he'd been tormented by the knowledge that while she could have pleasure, he could never be the one to truly give it to her.

And then she'd dismissed it all. The pleasure she'd given herself. The pleasure he'd helped give her in the end. Hell, she'd dismissed him.

So he'd spoken the truth to her. He really had been an idiot, but all that was going to change. Tomorrow, things would be different. *He'd* be different. He just prayed sleep would come quickly.

A few hours later, he was dreaming of going down on Wraith while she moaned. But they weren't moans of pleasure. Far from it. She sounded scared. Jesus, didn't she know he would never hurt her?

The moaning got louder, jerking Caleb out of his dream so that for a moment he was disoriented. He wondered why he was sleeping in a strange hotel room with a straining erection. Just as he remembered where he was, Wraith screamed like someone had plunged a knife into her heart.

He jumped out of bed only to find the adjoining room closed and locked. He heard her scream again. Shit.

"Wraith!"

He pushed his shoulder against the door. Once. Twice. The third time he felt the door cave in against his weight. He expected the lights to be on and to see her struggling with someone or something. Instead, in the darkness of her bedroom, he could see her thrashing around on her bed, shaking her head and holding out her arms as if to ward off an oncoming threat.

Her eyes were closed and she actually looked asleep.

What the hell?

He raced to her bed, sat down, and grabbed her by the arms, wincing when she automatically tried to draw back. "Wake up. Wraith. Wake up! Now."

She fought him in her sleep. Reached out and slammed him in the head repeatedly with her clenched fists. God, she was strong. His ears rang and he felt a warm trickle on his face. She'd bloodied his nose.

Caleb grabbed her pummeling fists and pinned them to the bed, trying to get control of her struggling body. She kicked out, almost kneeing him in the nuts. He finally had to resort to lying fully on top of her, pinning her hands to her side, and squashing her into the mattress. He put his face close to her ear.

"Shhh. Wraith." He spoke firmly but softly. Trying to comfort her and pull her from sleep at the same time. "Wake up. You need to wake up."

Suddenly, her body went limp, sinking even farther into the mattress.

"Caleb?" The way she said his name almost broke his heart. Confused. And sad. And just a little grateful. Like she'd been in pain and he'd taken it away.

Before he could get off her, her chest started jerking in stuttering bursts. Small whimpers wrenched out of her despite her best efforts to contain them. He wrapped his arms around her, trying to comfort her, then realized what he was doing. How he must be hurting her. Swiftly, he pulled away from her until he was sitting beside her on the bed. Rather than easing her pain, his distance seemed to unleash a torrent of emotion in her. Her whimpers became louder until she was sobbing in the long guttural moans of someone in torturous pain. Her body started to shake, and feeling helpless, Caleb stroked her back over the fabric of her T-shirt and tried to make soothing sounds.

Minutes went by, and her voice became hoarse long before she started to calm down. Her body slowly stopped shaking, with only an occasional hiccup evidencing her still-raw emotions. Caleb smoothed his hands over her hair, knowing from experience that this kind of touch caused her very little pain, if any.

"Better?" he whispered.

She nodded her head, then let out a breathy sigh before burrowing closer to him.

"Was it the mage?"

She stiffened and tried to pull away, but Caleb wouldn't let her. Far more quickly than he would have thought possible, she gave in to him. He decided to push his luck. He knew about the mage who'd taken her. The experiments that had been conducted on her body. Hell, he'd seen the videos himself, and there was no way he'd make her talk about that.

But he'd had no clue how the mage had captured her. At least not until the day after Knox's wedding, when he'd been chasing her down and had a chance to think about things during his time on the road. To think about her obvious dislike for felines and her reaction to Mahone's news about their mission.

The only reason she'd harbor that kind of hatred for an entire race was if one of their kind had betrayed her and betrayed her bad.

"It was a feline who betrayed you to the mage, wasn't it?"

To his surprise, she didn't stiffen again or attempt to pull away. "You're a smart one, O'Flare." Her voice sounded drowsy—his mind was still boggled by the notion that she'd slept. Her defenses, for once, seemed to be down, and he vaguely wondered if it was fair to question her now. But with Wraith, he had to take every advantage he could.

"Who was it?"

She shrugged. "Just a female I'd befriended soon after my transitioning. I learned later that she'd brought him four others. They . . . they didn't make it."

Now it was he who stiffened. "What do you mean, they didn't make it? Wraiths are immortal."

He saw her mouth twist in a sneer of self-loathing. "I mean they went crazy. Lost their minds. Maybe I did, too," she whispered.

Now he pulled back and without thinking, hooked her chin to force her to look at him. "You're not crazy. You've dealt with more than anyone should have to, and you've done the best you can. And if you can't catch it yourself, that's admiration you hear in my voice, Wraith, not pity. I'm sorry you were betrayed, but you have the team now. You have me. I know that doesn't mean much to you, but—"

Before he could finish his thought, she reached out and pulled him down on top of her again. "It means more than you can know," she said.

All at once, he was aware that she wore nothing but a thin white T-shirt and a pair of panties. Which was more than the single pair of boxer shorts that he wore. At some point, her legs had opened so that she cradled his hips against the warmth of her body, and his erection was rock-hard against her.

He lifted his head and stared down into her face. Her eyes, which seemed less filmy than normal—again, he caught glimpses of blue—immediately focused on his mouth. When her pink tongue peeked out and licked her bottom lip, he groaned and tried to move off of her. "I need to get back—"

"No, Caleb. Don't leave me. Please."

He flipped on a lamp. She automatically flinched back from the light. This close up, her eyes were definitely blue, while her skin was less so. In fact, she had a pink flush on her cheeks. One that was duplicated on the visible parts of her body. What the fuck . . . ?

"What's going on, Wraith? Your eyes? Your skin? You look . . . you look—"

Human. Almost alive. He wanted to say it, but he didn't dare.

She'd been calm just a few minutes ago, but now she seemed jittery. Disoriented. She reached out for him. "Kiss me, Caleb," she breathed. "Please."

He shook his head. "Wraith—"

"Please, Caleb. You touched me a second ago . . . You

touched my chin. You touched me and it didn't hurt. I don't . . ." Her voice broke. "I don't know how. But it didn't hurt."

Her words were like a punch in the gut. Could it be true? Was she somehow changing back to her human form? Was that why she'd slept? Had the wraith's curse of pain left her body?

Slowly, he bent down and kissed her. The tender foray seemed more significant than intercourse. In fact, the gentle penetration of his tongue into her mouth felt like being welcomed home.

She opened her mouth immediately, sighing with relief as if she'd been waiting for him for a lifetime. He kissed her with long, smooth strokes of his tongue. She tasted sweet, like the cinnamon gum she preferred, but when he backed away he could taste the salty residue of her tears mingled with his blood. It jolted him enough that he let her arms go and tried to back away.

She wasn't herself. And hadn't he just sworn that he was through with this? With her?

"No." She murmured the word and wrapped her arms around his neck. "No. Don't go."

"You were dreaming, Wraith. Having a nightmare. You're obviously upset. You don't want this. You made that more than clear earlier."

She looked at him steadily. "I do want it, Caleb. Please. I know what I'm doing."

She leaned up and initiated another kiss. Hesitantly sought his tongue with hers. When he didn't respond, she backed away, looking hurt. "Don't you want me, Caleb?"

Caleb laughed and closed his eyes for several moments. Did he want her? More than his next breath. When he opened his eyes, she was still looking at him uncertainly. He reached down and cupped her breast, and she gasped in pleasure. But when he wrapped his hand around the back of her neck to pull her close, he saw her flinch and immediately thought he must be hurting her.

He pulled away. "I'm sorry, Wraith. I can't. Besides, we need to talk."

"Why talk when we can—"

"Wraith. Didn't you hear what I said about your eyes? And you were sleeping."

She stiffened. "No. I was just resting—"

"You were more than resting. You were asleep and having a nightmare."

"That's impossible."

"Is it?" He was watching her closely. Suspiciously.

"You think I lie about not being able to sleep, Caleb?"

"No, but what's going on?"

"I don't know. I guess it was a fluke. Or maybe a wraith needs to recharge every ten years or so. Who knows?" She stared at him as if seeking something in his expression. When she didn't find it, her expression hardened. "Thanks for waking me, but if we're not going to fuck, can you leave?"

Caleb clenched his teeth with fury and frustration, wondering why this kept happening to him. "Wraith, you know I want you, but I just can't . . ." As much as he wanted her, her sudden change of heart seemed unbelievable given the way she'd pushed him away earlier. Combined with the shock of knowing she'd slept, that she was changing, it troubled him. Told him to proceed cautiously.

"Yeah, I know. You don't want to hurt me, even though I told you the pain is gone. So why does it hurt when you're pulling away?"

He sucked in a breath. "We can talk—"

"Leave, Caleb. Please."

It was the way she said please that did it. She needed some space. So did he.

"We'll talk in the morning, Wraith."

TWENTY-THREE

It took Lucy several minutes and some bullshit about not being dressed to get herself composed. Now, standing in her hotel doorway, Dex looked at her with his moody hazel eyes, and she breathed a sigh of relief when she saw no judgment or recrimination in their depths. He had a stack of files tucked under his arm, which she assumed was the intel they needed on the clubs. She opened the door wider and motioned for him to come in. Even though her flesh was burning and the cramps were getting worse, she forced herself to act as if everything was normal. It wasn't that tough given that she'd had years of experience.

"Any word from Mahone?" she said.

"No. He's gone back to D.C. We're on our own."

She nodded her head at the files. "Are Caleb and Wraith on their way?"

"No."

Lucy paused and turned to look at him, confused. "Don't you think they should be? We all need to get up to speed."

"They can get up to speed on their own. Right now, we need to get a few things settled, Lucy."

She crossed her arms over her chest. "I don't know what you mean."

He looked at her chidingly. "Sure you do, sugar."

"Look, if this is about the one-on-one touch training I asked Mahone about—"

"As a matter of fact, it is. You know O'Flare isn't going to do it, Lucy. Even if he got it into his head to do it for your benefit and the mission's, Wraith wouldn't let it happen. She couldn't. The connection between those two is too strong, no matter what the other thinks."

"Wraith seemed to convince Caleb otherwise."

"Yeah, she's a trooper. We already know that. But then again, so are you."

The admiration in his voice made her even more ashamed. She was a liar, that's what she was. A liar and a slut, just like her mother. Just because she didn't act on her need for sexual release didn't mean she didn't crave it with every ounce of her being. When she was in heat, anyway. Which seemed like always. "What do you mean?"

"I know you . . . have feelings for Caleb, Lucy, but nothing would have made you do what you did without a greater reason. A reason that was making you desperate."

Fear made Lucy tense. Oh God. Had Dex guessed about her secret? If he had, she didn't know what she would do. She hated her body's weakness. How could he ever respect her if he knew what she was? Praying that he was just fishing, she said, "I just don't want to mess things up for the team because of my own inexperience."

"It's more than inexperience, isn't it?"

She said nothing.

"Lucy," he said softly. "I know."

No. No, no, no. "You know what?"

"I know you're a feline. That you're in heat. And that's the reason you think you're going to endanger the mission. Because if you don't get some kind of sexual release beforehand, that's all you're going to be able to think about."

"I don't know what . . ." She swallowed her words because looking at Dex's face told her they would be useless. Unable to look at him, she sat on her bed and stared at the carpet. "How do you know? Did Mahone . . ."

Dex walked up to her, crouched in front of her, and thumbed her chin up so she couldn't avoid looking at him. "I suspected right from the beginning. I'm a dog. We can sense a cat more strongly than others. Makes sense, right? You gonna be honest with me now?"

"You've got a good nose," she said bitterly.

"It's okay, Lucy. You're still the same mage I liked and respected the day I met you."

She pulled her chin away from his grasp and stepped around him. "The same whore, yes."

Dex snorted. "A virgin whore. That's a new one."

"Stop it. You know what I mean. What my destiny is!"

"What? Sexual pleasure? You've fought your nature for a long time, haven't you? Why?"

She whirled on him. "Because I don't want to be a prisoner to my sexuality, just like the rest of my race."

"It's part of you, Lucy, and it doesn't make you a whore."

"Just like being a were is part of you? Come on, Dex, if you could get rid of that part of you, be either fully human or fully were, wouldn't you do it? Instead, you're caught right in the middle, just like I am. Not wanted by either race because you're different."

"The felines don't want you?"

"Not as I am. Not when I'm a mage *and* I reject my sexual urges. They think it's unnatural. A rejection of what they are. And they're right."

He nodded. "Okay. So let me ask you this. You'd trust Caleb to touch you. Will you trust me?"

Stunned, she stared at him. "You can't mean . . . I wasn't going to ask Caleb to . . ."

He shrugged. "I'll admit it's a little weird. I know you don't feel that way about me, and I don't feel that way about you. But I care about you, little one. And I want to help. The only way you're going to keep others from guessing about your little problem and be able to do your job in those clubs tomorrow is to gain some physical release. I can do that for you."

Her confusion was genuine. "Why would you want to?"

Dex laughed long and hard. He actually wiped his eyes when he was done and shook his head. "Don't be ridiculous, Lucy. It might not be a romance between us, but you're incredibly beautiful."

Dex thought she was beautiful? "So you find me attractive?"

"Who wouldn't? How about you? Is the thought of being

touched by me unsavory? I'm not pretty like O'Flare. I'm rougher. With touch and words. Hell, I really am part dog . . ."

"Don't you dare put yourself down!" Lucy strode up to him until she was toe-to-toe with him, having to look up a long way to meet his gaze. "Not when you're being so generous with me, Dex. You're extremely attractive, and any female would be lucky to have that kind of gift from you. But I . . . I don't know. What about when you're gone? What if I become dependent on needing release? Then I could turn into the very thing that I hate . . ."

"I promise, little one, I'll always be here for you if you need me."

"You promise?" she whispered.

"Yes."

She looked at the bed, then back at him.

"Will you find your pleasure . . . ?"

He shook his head.

"Why not? I'd want you to. That would only be fair."

"I want this to be about giving you what you need. I'm not going to use you or take my pleasure from you when your heart isn't in it."

"You can make me want you. I know you can."

"Oh yeah. I will, you can count on that. And that's all you need to worry about."

She swallowed hard. "What are the ground rules?"

"You put yourself in my hands. You do everything I ask. You don't question me. Full trust not to hurt you. Full trust to teach you the pleasure I can bring you. Can you give me that, Lucy?"

She thought for a second of Caleb. She wanted it to be him saying those words to her, but she knew Dex was right. It was never going to happen that way. But she cared for Dex and knew he cared for her. Perhaps the way to beat her need was to accept it and work with it rather than against it. On her terms.

She nodded. "Okay. Everything you ask."

Dex narrowed his eyes at her, his expression edged with a heat that made her shiver. "Be sure you understand what you're saying. I can give you relief, Lucy, but I'm still going to be who I am. With sex, just as in every other aspect of my life, I need to dominate. That's how it is with weres. I need you to do what I say. If you challenge me, that's going to—going to bring out something in me that I don't want you to see, little one. You're not ready for it. Do you understand?"

He said it so calmly. So confidently. So she answered him just as calmly. Just as confidently. "I understand."

"Okay. Then strip."

Lucy's heart hammered against her chest and the prickles of heat that had taunted her all day exploded into an inferno. Doubt crawled up her spine, and she stepped back despite herself.

"If you can't even listen to me when I ask you to undress, Lucy, then this isn't going to work. Is that what you want? Do you want me to leave?"

Panic rose in her throat. Her heart was beating so fast that her body seemed to vibrate from the impact. She couldn't let him leave. She needed him. He was her best chance at controlling the heat that was overtaking her. Her best hope for doing what she needed to for her team.

She met his challenging stare. "No, I don't want you to leave."

She raised her hand to unbutton her shirt.

Dex forced his breathing to remain steady. He'd thought for sure that Lucy was going to bolt, but he'd underestimated her. And now his gaze was riveted to the sight of her small, elegant fingers slowly working her shirt buttons out of one hole and then the next. As each button loosened, a new patch of creamy skin was revealed.

Suddenly, despite his reluctance to make this offer, despite his doubts that he could actually have sex with a woman he cared for but didn't strongly desire, he was glad. Because his body didn't care what his mind didn't feel. It saw Lucy for what she was—a sexy, vulnerable female who'd never been with a man before but so clearly needed one now. He needed to give her what she needed, and that meant forgetting that he was her friend for now. He needed to treat her like a lover, and that's what he was going to do.

As she finished unbuttoning her blouse, his mind went blank with lust. She was no longer Lucy, but a sexy, warm, willing female willing to follow his every command for her own pleasure.

She removed her shirt, revealing small, rounded breasts encased in a utilitarian white sports bra. Her shoulders and arms looked smooth and creamy, her collarbone protruding delicately from one shoulder to the other.

He raised his gaze to hers and swallowed hard. Desire pooled in his belly, a heated simmer that slowly spread to his limbs, concentrating hotly between his legs. "Keep going."

She unbuttoned the fly to her jeans and pushed them down. Her legs were gorgeous. Not overly long but toned. She stepped out of her jeans and stood in front of him. Chin high. Back straight. Her body quivered and her face was flushed, telling him that she was starting to feel more than think, as well.

Good girl.

"Lose the bra."

She seemed to deflate before his eyes. For a second, she looked dazed, like a small animal caught in the beam of an oncoming semi. Dex refused to back down. If he was soft with her, tender, she'd associate this act with those emotions. He didn't want to take the risk of creating that kind of emotional bond between them. It was for her sake as much as for his. One thing was for sure; he was going to give her so much pleasure, she'd think she was going to die.

"Take it off, Lucy. Now."

She closed her eyes and took a deep breath. It gave him second thoughts. Maybe this wasn't what she needed. Hell, maybe she could find someone at the club tomorrow that attracted her. A stranger . . . He was just about to tell her to forget the whole thing when she raised her hands to her bra and pulled it over her head.

Her breasts were tidy. Sweet. They wouldn't fill his hands, but he bet they'd taste amazing. She held her arms stiffly to her sides, as if stopping herself from covering her chest only by sheer force of will.

"Now the panties."

"Dex . . ." she whispered.

He steeled himself against compassion. "We're almost there, Lucy. Take off your underwear and it's a done deal. You won't need to worry about not being yourself tomorrow or about writhing in pain because of the heat that you can't satisfy. Instead, you'll writhe with pleasure. Don't you want that?"

She looked at him, and her mouth formed the word even though she didn't utter a sound. "Yes."

She pushed down her panties.

TWENTY-FOUR

Wraith didn't sleep again, but the fact that she had before—and despite her denials to Caleb, she knew she had—troubled her for two reasons. First, it had to mean she was going to die soon—sooner than she'd thought. Second, it had resulted in something else that had never happened to her—a dream. She'd been dreaming when Caleb had shaken her awake. Or having a nightmare, more precisely. Flashes of the nightmare flickered in and out of her mind, but they were fuzzy. Didn't make any sense. Blond hair. A ballet slipper charm hanging on a gold chain. All innocuous objects. All filled her with a sense of fear and grief.

They were clues, she'd realized. Clues to who she was. Who she'd been before she'd been a wraith.

She'd desperately tried to fall asleep again, but couldn't. She kept thinking of Caleb. Replaying the way she'd jerked off in front of him. Then later . . .

She was too worried about what the morning was going to bring. That she was going to have to face Caleb, and that meant facing the fact that she'd practically begged him to take her and he'd declined. True, after what she'd said to him after he'd helped her come the first time, she couldn't blame him, but logic wasn't controlling her. Embarrassment was.

Finally accepting that morning had arrived, Wraith dressed quickly, then cautiously stepped into the opening of the doorway adjoining their rooms and peeked in. Caleb wasn't inside, but he'd left a note on the door.

"Gone to gym. Fourth floor. Come down if you want to let off some steam."

Despite herself, her mouth quirked.

Leave it to Caleb to know exactly what she'd need to get through the morning with her pride intact. Without bothering to change out of her leathers or heels, she made her way down to the fourth floor. The gym turned out to be behind a solid closed door with no transoms, as was often the case in hotels. She was expecting it to be a typical hotel gym with a wimpy weight bench and an outdated treadmill. It wasn't.

She opened the door and peeked inside.

Her mouth dropped open.

Across a large, cavernous space stood Caleb, his powerful chest and thickly muscled arms bare and on display. A pair of sweats rode low on his hips, the waistband drenched with sweat that was dripping from his temples, neck, and upper torso. He was alone, doing some fancy moves on the mat that looked like boxing punches combined with high kicks, lunges, and the occasional flip. As he changed position, a dark shadow on his right shoulder blade occasionally made an appearance before vanishing out of sight again.

It was a tattoo. A new one. One he hadn't had the last time he'd been bare-chested in front of her. But that damn death mark was still there, too.

Glancing down, she stared at the three dots on the back of her hand, faded but still visible, on the fleshy area between her thumb and forefinger. She'd noticed the markings for the first time this morning. At first she thought they were freckles or moles, but then she wondered if they were some kind of tattoo. She'd looked up the primitive design on the web. To her horror, it seemed to be associated with gang members, used throughout the world by Crips and Bloods alike, but with varying meanings. Sometimes, it stood for *mi vida loca*—my crazy life. Often it symbolized a gang triad: individual, set, gang. A gang member was expected to make a reputation as an individual to begin with, but only with the expectation of furthering that reputation for his set, the group he ran with, then his gang, the larger group to which he belonged.

Furthering one's reputation usually meant creating a direct link between your name and someone else's fear.

She hated it. Wondered if she'd hate herself completely if and when she ever did discover who she'd been. Maybe finding out her identity wasn't such a good idea after all. But then again, wouldn't it be better to know? Good or bad, the knowledge might bring her peace.

She moved closer, wanting to get a better look at Caleb's tattoo.

A punching sound, like someone was beating a bag, caught her attention and turned out to be exactly that. Caleb was kicking the shit out of a heavy duffel punching bag. For a moment, Wraith wanted to slip inside, take a seat somewhere on the floor, and just watch the show. Watching Caleb work out could be as addicting as—

"If you're going to come in, come in. Otherwise, you're letting in a draft."

Frowning, Wraith stepped inside. He'd stopped punching and swiped his arm across his forehead. She tried not to look at his bare chest, but that left his lower body or his face, both of which seemed too much for her to handle at the moment. She focused on his chin instead.

His gaze took in her clothes and the body beneath it.

"You really expect to work out in your leathers?"

"I do everything in my leathers, Caleb. You know that."

"You weren't in your leathers last night."

No, she hadn't been. As a result, she still felt the imprint of his hard body against hers. She also felt the small inklings of peace and satisfaction that had washed over her as he'd held her—just held her, soothing her and comforting her, asking her about her past as if he cared, *telling* her he and the team cared about her.

There was little evidence of that caring now, yet she knew instinctively it was still there. Without her quite realizing it, her eyes sought out the tattoo that even now was hidden from her.

He caught her looking. "What is it?"

She rubbed at the marking on her hand, then jerked her fingers away when she realized what she was doing. To cover, she used that hand to gesture to his shoulder. "You have a tattoo . . ."

He arched a brow then slowly turned until she could see it.

"It's a yin yang symbol."

Turning back to her, he nodded. "You familiar with what it means?"

"Two halves of one whole or something like that, right?"

His mouth tipped up. "Kind of. Chinese medicine focuses on the connection of mind and body to unite the yin and yang and to achieve a perfect exchange of energy."

"Uh-huh." Her voice was loaded with skepticism.

"You don't believe me?"

"Oh no, I believe you. I'm just wondering what a shaman is doing studying Chinese medicine."

His mouth stretched into a grin, one that made her eyes widen and her body tremble with desire. The man was lethal. "Earth People aren't held back when it comes to spirituality. I'm a healer, and that means I rely on everything and anything I can to heal myself and others, body, mind, and soul."

She felt almost mesmerized by his words. As if the intimacy they'd shared last night was wrapping around them even now, reminding them that they could never return to the place where they'd been. Distant. Hostile. No matter how hard she tried. Even as she fought that feeling, a small part of her was glad. "And how does the concept of yin and yang help you heal?"

He reached out and touched her cheek, testing, watching her closely to see if it hurt her. She shook her head slightly, telling him the touch hadn't hurt her.

"It's all about balance. The outer circle represents everything, while the black and white represents the interaction of yin and yang energy. Hot and cold. Male and female. Neither is absolute. Both are continuous. Illness is believed to be a disturbance in the balance of yin and yang. Sexuality is all about balancing the yin and yang between males and females."

"Re-really? That . . . that's interesting." His fingers were rubbing her scalp in slow, firm circles. His touch, combined with the deep murmur of his voice, caused jolts of pleasure to shoot through her groin.

"A female's genitals are internal yin, while a male's are external. Emotionally, however, the opposite is true. The female yang finds it easier to express herself, while the male yang is more internalized."

Caleb stopped the massage and pulled away, causing Wraith to groan in protest before she could stop herself. "That's how a man and woman complement each other. How they balance each other's energy. Sexually. Emotionally." Caleb shrugged his shoulders. "That's what I've read, anyway." He leaned down, kissed her lips lightly, then stepped back.

His expression pierced into her as if he was searching for something within her own gaze—understanding? But understanding of what? She realized she was leaning toward him, that she'd practically melted at his touch. At his words. What was wrong with her? Where was all this . . . this *human weakness* coming from?

She cleared her throat and stepped back. She forced herself to be as bitchy as she possibly could. "So I guess that tattoo of yours must be a tribute to all the females you've laid in an attempt to balance their *energy*, right? How big of you."

He just stared at her as if he saw right through her, making her avert her gaze. Instead of sounding snide or disgusted, she'd sounded exactly the way she'd felt. Defensive. Jealous. Fighting the connection between them with her last ounce of strength.

He jerked his chin toward the bag he'd been working. "You ever work on a bag?"

Her gaze jumped back to his in surprise. His expression told her he was letting her off the hook. For now. "No."

"Why not?"

She smiled slightly. "I've had enough practice on real individuals. Punching a bag seems like a waste of time."

He grinned and winked, causing her to narrow her eyes. "What?"

"Nothing. You wanted to blow off steam. You can either do that with me or the bag. I figured you'd choose the bag. Am I wrong?"

In response, she strode to the heavy bag and punched it. Then kicked it. Despite the power that made the bag swing on its chains, it felt foreign to her. She felt awkward. Incompetent. Weak.

That wasn't something she ever put up with.

She looked at Caleb. "Show me."

An hour later, Wraith was sweating, and her arms felt like they were going to fall off. More precisely, she wanted to cut them off; at least then she'd be in less pain. She was used to pain, but not the bodily exhaustion she was experiencing with it. Both were almost too much to handle.

"You ready to stop yet?" Caleb shouted to be heard.

Wraith shook her head and kept going.

She was on the last portion of a regimen Caleb had taught her. She didn't know if she could complete it, but damn it, she wasn't going to quit with him looking on.

First, she'd done a series of punch-out drills—short, rapid, successive straight-arm punches for sixty-second intervals, increasing intensity with each interval. Then she'd done four three-minute rounds of skill work, where she threw punches but had also integrated head movements, feints, combinations, and kicks. Next, punches in a variety of different combinations—left to right, right to left, hook, cross, and undercut. Finally, she got to what she was currently working on: varying her punches while hitting at full-out maximum power.

Her muscles were screaming, begging for mercy. Sweat was dripping into her eyes, stinging them. She wondered if at some point her body would simply get used to the pain and numb out. If so, she prayed that time came soon.

"Stop."

Even she knew her power was waning, but she had to keep going. She couldn't stop. She had to keep going.

Couldn't stop.

Had to keep going or she would lose.

Couldn't stop fighting or she would die.

"God damn it, I said stop!" Caleb grabbed her arms and roared in her face loudly enough to snap her out of her thoughts. He was panting hard, his eyes wild as he stared at her. His lip was also bloody and she . . .

Her eyes widened. "Did I . . . ?" No, she'd been hitting the bag, just like he'd shown her. She hadn't been hitting *him*. Had she?

"You didn't even know you were doing it, did you, Wraith? For all you knew, I could have been Doug or Emmett. Remember them? The two guys who attacked your friend Joanna? The two guys who were hired to snatch you? You were so zoned out you couldn't even tell foe from friend."

At the censure in his voice, she straightened, every muscle in her body and face stiff. "We're not friends, Caleb. We work together. You get on my nerves, but you're hot. Too bad you're not willing to inflict a little pain to give me a whole lot of pleasure. Or maybe your ability to give me pleasure was just a fantasy."

His face remained stiff and unreadable even at her jibe.

She stalked toward the door. "I need a shower."

"Not so fast, Wraith."

She froze.

"Look at me."

Bristling at the command in his voice, she turned, cocking her hip as she placed her hands on her hips. "What is it?"

"You're sweating."

He was right. She was. That was another thing that was new. "So. It's happened before," she lied.

"You're also tired, when I thought wraiths never tired."

"You were wrong again. Imagine that."

"So maybe I was wrong about other things."

She sucked in a breath at the heat in his eyes and the way he began circling her body like a lion going in for the kill.

"Like the fact I couldn't give you enough pleasure to make it worth it for me to touch you. You want to test it out, Wraith? If I can really give you what we've both been wanting?"

"Is that a rhetorical question? A threat?"

"What do you think?"

He began coming straight at her. She stepped back a few steps, not realizing what she was doing until she bumped up against the punching bag. "I think it's another tease. One that you're not going to follow through with, Caleb. You had your chance last night. I don't give second chances. Forget it."

"I can't." He raised his hand, tucking a strand of hair behind her ear. Immediately, she froze, her body trembling, her mind conflicted. She didn't want his touch because she was afraid he'd see right through her, see how much she still wanted him—no, *needed* him.

His fingers shifted, dipping into the hollows of her ear so that trembling turned into virtual shudders of delight. Desperate, she knocked his hand away, making him chuckle.

"Don't touch me. I don't want you to."

"That's okay. I'll change your mind."

"In your dreams."

"Always."

"Shut up, Caleb."

"What's the matter, Wraith? You didn't have a problem with intimacy yesterday. Why the sudden change?"

Why? He dared to ask her why? Even worse, to expect her to answer? To admit it had hurt, the knowledge that he could turn her away when all she could think of was being close to him, feeling his hands on her skin, feeling him loving her. When she'd already told him he wouldn't hurt her.

"Wraith?"

She frowned when he shifted closer, trying to keep him in her sights as he circled around her. "Maybe it was one rejection too many."

At first he looked confused. "Is that what you thought? That I was rejecting *you*? You know it's always been about me not wanting to hurt you, Wraith."

"I already told you . . ." She squeezed her eyes shut and shook her head violently for a moment. When she opened them, he was staring at her, his cheeks flushed, his expression determined. "Look, let's just go with that. Don't touch me. Don't hurt me, okay?" But he already had, simply by rejecting her, by pushing her back when she'd needed his warmth.

"It's too late—"

She shoved him in the chest, making him take a step back.

"Good. That's good. I love how strong you are."

Her eyes widened at his use of *that* word. She shoved him again, and Caleb grabbed her by the arms, kissing her. Her lips clung to his. Then she hooked her leg behind him and tripped him to the floor. She had to fight him, or he'd hurt her even more—not her body, but her heart. The heart she'd never thought she'd had but was just beginning to show signs of life inside her.

Caleb kept his hold on her as he fell back onto the gym floor, immediately flipping her over so that his large body pinned her to the ground. She struggled, trying to free her legs or her arms—which he'd pinned above her head—so that she could knee him in the nuts or do some serious damage to his face. So she could punish him for awakening this desire in her and then not fulfilling it.

He had to struggle to keep her in place, but he still managed to do so. She could feel the hard length of his arousal against her stomach. She wanted to surrender to it, to him. But her head fought her heart and won.

"Is that all you've got, Wraith? Come on, you're a badass, remember? You can do better than that."

Calling her a badass helped quiet that tiny voice in her heart that kept on telling her to give in. Narrowing her eyes, she met his challenge head-on. Literally. Raising her torso off the ground, she head-butted Caleb in the face.

"Shit!" His hands loosened momentarily, and she shoved him away, turned on her stomach, and tried to do a quick crawl away from him. She knew where this was going, and she had no intention of staying for it. She felt raw and jittery, incapable of controlling the emotions that Caleb brought out in her. Fear. Wildness. Desire. She needed to get out.

Caleb covered her body with his, grinding her breasts into the unforgiving concrete. He put his mouth to her neck, biting the vulnerable cord there, using none of the care that he normally took with her and forcing the fight from her body in a sudden rush of pleasure.

"I guess I asked for that. But you know what, Wraith? I'm strong. And I'm not afraid of your strength. I can handle it. Handle you. And you can handle me, too. That's where I've been going wrong, isn't it? Worrying about causing you pain when I know damn well you can take care of yourself. Hell, you could kick my ass if you really wanted to. *If* I was hurting you. So all I'm going to concern myself with is the pleasure I can give you. Do you want it?"

Wraith said nothing. Closed her eyes and relaxed her body so that her left cheek was resting on the ground. When he leaned down and kissed her mouth, she didn't fight him.

Caleb knew the instant she surrendered. She opened her mouth to his tongue, inviting it in with a prolonged groan that thrummed throughout his body. He ground his cock into her firm buttocks as he kissed her, running his hands along the length of her hips.

Lifting his body so she could turn onto her back, he caressed her breasts through her clothes. He tried to play with her nipples, but the thick fabric of her leathers hampered him. Growling with frustration, he unhooked and unzipped until he could pull the fabric away from her bare breasts. Lightly, he kissed his way down her throat, making a liar of himself as he watched for any sign that the pain was overriding the pleasure. From the way she was arching and grabbing his hair, it wasn't. He was about to cover a nipple with his mouth when she wrapped her right leg around his hip and twisted her body up and over. She grabbed his hands and immediately pinned them next to his head.

She stared into his face. "How does it feel? Having someone control you? Not so great, is it?"

He pushed his pelvis up into hers. "Actually, it feels pretty good to me."

That surprised a laugh out of her. She shook her head, then stared at him for a few more minutes. Slowly, she let go of his hands and sat up. He closed his eyes at the feel of her body shifting along his.

"So you think you want me? The real me? All right. You've got it."

With that, she shrugged off her leather jacket and undershirt completely. Caleb immediately sat up and buried his face in the lush valley of her breasts, inhaling the musky scent of female sweat. He grabbed her buttocks and encouraged her to arch into him, which she did.

"What do you want, Wraith?"

Instead of answering, she grabbed his hair and tried to push his face toward her nipples. Caleb wouldn't let her get away with that. He looked her in the eyes. "Full participation, Wraith. That's what I want. Now tell me what you want."

She bit her lip, and the vulnerable move, so foreign to how he thought of her, twisted at his heart.

"I want you . . . I want you to . . . kiss my breasts."

Caleb immediately did so, slipping first one nipple into his mouth for his attention before turning to the next. After several minutes, he lifted his head and studied the tight red nubs. Then he laid himself flat on the ground and put his hands behind his head.

"Take what you want from me."

For a moment she looked indecisive. Then determined. She raised herself up and to the side. Standing, she kicked off her heels and peeled herself out of her tight leather pants. Then, with the barest of hesitations, she reached down to remove his clothes. When they were both naked, she straightened but seemed to lose her nerve. She stared at his cock almost fearfully, which certainly wasn't what he wanted. He stood and reached around her, caressing her buttock. Wound his way around to her vagina and played with her soft folds. "What do you want, Wraith?"

She still didn't look away from his dick, and he felt himself getting harder.

"I . . . I want to kiss you."

"Then do it." As they both watched, a pearl of semen oozed out of the bulbous tip of his cock. Wraith met his gaze seductively and slowly lowered herself to her knees in front of him. Instead of covering him with her mouth, she flicked out her tongue and delicately licked the pearl of liquid off of him. He arched his hips and groaned in pain. Blissful, unbelievably pleasurable pain. It made him understand all the more that he'd been a fool for holding back simply because she'd experience some pain. He'd take much more pain himself if it meant he'd have the pleasure of being with her.

"You're going to make me come."

She lifted up her face, stared at him solemnly. "Isn't that the whole point?"

"No, this is about you. About you taking what you want, remember?"

"I want you to come."

He shook his head. "But you want to come more, don't you? Remember how it felt yesterday? How you touched yourself and struggled to get to the top, and then once you were there, you completely let yourself go? It felt like climbing a fucking mountain, didn't it?"

She nodded her head. "It did."

"So what do you want? My hands or my dick?"

His words seemed to shock her. Again. The fact that he could shock her just by talking dirty to her was a huge turn-on.

"Which one, Wraith?"

"Your . . . your dick . . ."

"Good. That's what I want, too. But first, I want to play a little more. Lie down."

TWENTY-FIVE

As if she were a robot obeying Caleb's every command, Wraith laid down on the hard floor. She couldn't take her eyes away from his erection. It thrust out aggressively, thick and hard, from between his thighs. Everything about the man was overblown, including his dick. He had the body of a warrior. Pumped up biceps. Hard pecs and rippled abs. Sturdy thighs with lean muscles layering his calves. Even his fingers looked strong. Capable. But her gaze kept returning to his crowning glory—his muscular shaft topped with a rounded, bulbous head. It quivered slightly, as if it was a horse waiting at the gate, ready for the race to begin.

To appear more confident than she was feeling, she stretched, pretending to preen beneath his gaze when part of her wanted to cover the bluish-hued skin that announced her as something different. Abnormal.

He knelt down and crouched over her, spread her thighs and moved between them. He was big and as hard as steel, and from the tightness of his features, she knew he wanted to plunge inside her rather than play. But instead of shoving himself into her body, he pushed her hair away from her face and bent down. Kissed her ear. Then her neck. Pain was the furthest thing she felt. She let out a soft sound of pleasure.

Caleb trailed his hand down her face and neck to her chest and gently cupped the weight of one breast in his hand. He massaged it slowly. He then trailed his mouth down her throat to her chest, not quite kissing her, but definitely taking his time. When he reached the breast he held, he cupped it tighter in his hand and lifted it to his mouth, opening his mouth over the nipple and sucking it gently inside.

The warm suction caused tremors to explode between Wraith's thighs, and she moaned softly. At the sound, he increased the pressure of his mouth, then released her nipple with a soft pop. He bit down softly on the tip.

Pleasure shot through her like a jolt of electricity. Her body arched up. For one moment, she wanted to wrap her legs around his waist and rake her fingers down his back. That scared her so much she tried pushing him away. Physically and emotionally. She shoved against his shoulders, but he didn't budge. "I thought this was about showing me some pleasure, O'Flare, not lulling me to sleep."

Caleb raised his head and looked at her. His eyes had darkened so much, they seemed almost black. He grabbed her wrists and lowered her hands to her side, then trailed his hand down to her crotch. "Don't worry. I'll keep you awake." He used his own legs to push hers farther apart. "Bend your knees."

Wraith complied and he pushed one thigh toward the ground, opening her wide for his gaze and touch. Before she could move, he spread her apart and inserted a long finger into her. Wraith bit her lip to keep from moaning out loud as he circled it slowly inside of her, testing the muscles that hugged him.

"Does this hurt? Too much?"

She barely heard him. Spasms of pleasure wracked her body, threatening to obliterate all thought.

"You're so tight." He pulled his finger out of her slowly, and then pushed it back in, even deeper than before.

Wraith's hips involuntarily lifted as her body and mind tried to absorb each new sensation shivering through her. She kept her voice calm but wondered if he could detect the breathless huskiness that had altered it. "It . . . it doesn't hurt. Not at all."

She wasn't lying, either. Whatever pain there was—and yes, she suspected it was there—was washed out by the pleasure of his touch.

Caleb didn't react to that statement. He seemed fascinated

by the sight of his finger moving in and out of her. By the contrast of his strong, tanned wrist and the soft dusting of platinum hair covering her pale flesh. As she watched, he withdrew his hand, and she was mesmerized by the slick shine on his finger. It was wet. From her.

He lifted his finger to his mouth and licked, filling her with combined terror and desire. Her legs shifted restlessly, and he focused on her core, pinning her in place with hot eyes. "I've got to taste you."

"Wait . . ."

Before she could say more, he bent down, pushed her legs apart, and crowded his shoulders into the cradle of her body. He inserted his finger into her again and flicked his tongue over her clitoris. The pleasure was staggering, and she moaned, a raw, desperate sound of need. He removed his finger and replaced it with his tongue, stabbing it in and out of her.

The pleasure built until she thought she was going to explode. Her body's response stunned her, making her realize that the release she'd gotten from Cole with the drugs, or from Ramsey with the pain, had been child's play. She closed her eyes and clasped Caleb's head, sighing when the smooth strands of his hair tangled in her fingers. She felt him stiffen at her touch and almost cried out when he pulled away with one last lingering swipe of his tongue.

He grabbed her by the back of her bent knees and spread them wide. Prepared to enter her. "I'm sorry, I don't think I can hold off very long. I'll probably come as soon as I get inside you. But we've got all day. Right?"

Wraith's breath was barreling in and out of her so hard that she was shaking. He let go of one knee and gripped his shaft, rubbed it against her clit in tight dragging circles. Then pushed it against her opening. She moaned. "Right, Wraith?" His narrowed eyes bore into her as he rubbed even harder. "Right?"

She nodded her head. "Caleb . . ." She stopped talking as the broad tip of his cock prodded at her. When he slipped it in just the slightest inch, he groaned.

She couldn't look away from him. His face was contorted as if in pain. She felt a thrill at the thought that she was pleasuring him. When she felt him push another inch into her, the thrill was overcome by panic.

Memories washed over her. Memories of being invaded—by

the mage. Ramsey. Even Colt, the vampire who thought he'd been saving her from Ramsey. Others. Although Colt hadn't wanted to cause her pain, he still had, but only at the moment he entered her. The drugs had numbed everything else, but whenever Colt entered her—anyone had entered her—the pain had been devastating.

Now Caleb was pushing inside her, bigger than anyone she'd ever taken.

He felt huge, stretching her beyond capacity. And he'd only just started.

"God, you are so fucking tight." Caleb tried to push in another inch, but stopped when her body resisted.

Wraith's immediate thought was that she'd kill him. She'd kill him if he stopped now.

What the hell? Caleb stiffened his muscles, fighting the urge to keep going. But Wraith's tight muscles had swallowed the tip of him, surrounding him with such incredible heat that he was a hairbreadth from losing it. Sweat dripped down his forehead and his body trembled with the effort of holding still. The only thing that kept him from pushing farther into her was the look in her eyes. That pain had come close to overriding pleasure was clear on her face.

Wraith was a virgin.

Equal parts shock and shame filled him, tempering his lust, but by no means extinguishing it. He'd known she was more than she appeared. That she had a good heart despite her cocky, mouthy demeanor. But to know that no other man had been inside her? That she'd trusted him with that when she'd never trusted anyone else?

He shifted, ready to move off her but freezing when she grasped his hips and moaned. The deep, throaty sound was tinged unmistakably with the sound of pleasure. A tremor went through her, making the muscles of her pussy contract around him. She arched upward. He hissed and closed his eyes, grabbing her hips and pinning them down on the ground. He took several deep breaths and then opened his eyes. She stared back at him, a slight furrow between her eyes.

"Come on. Do it." She tried shifting her hips in his grasp, but he held firm.

Caleb told himself to pull out of her. But he couldn't. Even only partially inside her, even swamped by a tangled mess of emotions, he felt more alive than he ever had. He cleared his throat. "You're a virgin?"

Unbelievably, she shook her head. He let out a disbelieving snort and pushed against her. The head of his dick butted up against an unmistakable barrier, pulling another gasp from her.

"Don't lie. If you weren't, I'd be all the way inside you right now."

Her lips firmed, and she moved her hands from his hips to his shoulders. "I already told you. I've been fucked before, Caleb. Only I'm a wraith. My body regenerates itself. Get it?"

He blinked. Yeah, he got it. He should have guessed, of course, but he hadn't. The idea of her body maintaining a barrier against him, a way to shield herself from his lustful invasion, shocked every doubt he'd harbored about this moment back to life.

She pushed against him, but he resisted, countering her movement with muscles honed from years of battle. She growled in frustration.

She gripped his wrists, trying to get him to release her hips. Again, he didn't budge.

"Look, I didn't realize your offer was dependent on my expertise. Apparently, you don't believe me, or me having a hymen is a total turn-off for you. So just get off." When he didn't, she pushed once more against his chest. She was strong, but he was stronger. An immovable force.

He grabbed her hands, and this time he pinned them on either side of her face. The movement dropped his weight so that her luscious tits cushioned his chest, and her thighs involuntarily spread wider. Her hips shimmied, sending a sizzle of pleasure through him. He groaned, dropping his forehead onto hers and trying to make her understand. "It's not that . . . It's just . . . Am I really what you want?"

She frowned. "Wanted. Past tense." Once more, she tried to shove him away.

"Because you're what I want, Wraith. I'd give my soul to fuck you right now."

Her eyes were huge. Her breath thready. Just when he thought she was going to tell him to go to hell, he felt the soft caress of her legs as she brought them up and around his waist. "Then do it," she whispered.

The husky command made his hips involuntarily jerk. A haze of lust blurred his vision, and suddenly he was moving. Growling. He pistoned himself into her in short, shallow thrusts, not deep enough to break through the barrier of her virginity but enough to rub against her sensitive nerves. He saw the minute pleasure began to annihilate her control.

She closed her eyes, biting her lip to keep in her moans. But he didn't need to hear her to sense her pleasure. He could see it in her face. Feel it in the way her muscles contracted around him.

He released one of her hands and squeezed his between them, searching for her clit through her moist folds. She gasped when he hit the right spot and he continued his shallow thrusts. She raised her hips and slid herself back and forth over his cock.

He closed his eyes, blocking out her innocence. Blocking out his conscience. He concentrated on his own pleasure. On the gasps of pleasure that he was drawing from her. And soon his body was tightening, preparing itself to send a stream of come straight into her body. Unrestrained. Unfettered. Unsheathed. In one corner of his mind, he suddenly realized he wasn't wearing a condom. "Shit, Wraith, stop . . ."

"Don't stop," she breathed, tossing her head back and forth, working herself on him frantically.

Caleb threw back his head and closed his eyes, absorbing every shimmer of sensation. "I can't . . ." He released her wrist and straightened, searching for the strength to pull out of her.

"Stop. Don't stop," she whimpered. She grasped at him, but he lurched back, groaning as he slipped out of her.

"I'm sorry. Don't worry, I'll . . ." He was about to say he would take care of her. That he wouldn't leave her without pleasuring her. But she suddenly raised herself to her knees and went after him, grabbing hold of his dick, wrapping her long, cool fingers around him, jerking him off. Against his will, he covered her hand, guiding her movements with his own and showing her what he liked. Soon, the world seemed to fade and a buzzing sounded in his ears. He felt his sperm building. Gathering inside him until he was ready to explode.

"Caleb . . ."

He spoke through gritted teeth. "Please. Keep doing that."

Caleb's eyes flew open to see her gaze on his face. As he

continued to work her grip over him, he didn't look away. The muscles in his jaw tightened, and his entire body shook. Sweat dotted his forehead.

Caleb stilled her hand and squeezed it tightly around his cock. He shouted as he came, and semen shot out of him in violent bursts, covering her hand and her belly. They knelt that way for several moments as tremors racked him. Suddenly, he collapsed forward, taking her down to the ground.

Wraith curled up into a ball, the small distance between her and Caleb seeming like a deep, cavernous abyss.

He'd come. She'd pleased him. That tempered some of her disappointment. But to know that he'd held back, that he hadn't taken her when that's what she'd wanted . . . She'd begged him, and he'd rejected her yet again.

She dragged herself up, determined to get away, but he grabbed her arm and pulled her toward him.

She wildly resisted, needing to get away. "Let go, you bastard!"

He wrestled her around until she was on her back and he was kneeling over her. "You deliberately didn't tell me you were physically a virgin. Why?"

"Because I knew you and your overblown conscience would get cold feet again. Hell, it took you so long to touch me because you thought it would hurt me, what more if you realized I was technically a virgin, even if it was for the fifth or tenth time of my life?"

"It's a real concern, Wraith, me ripping through your body . . ."

"I've survived it before. Multiple times," she sneered. "You didn't have to pull out, but maybe it wasn't me you were concerned about. Maybe you suddenly just couldn't stomach shoving yourself all the way inside something dead. Isn't that right, Caleb?"

"You're wrong. I pulled out because I wasn't wearing protection. I don't even know if you can get pregnant but—"

"But why risk creating a half-breed Indian-Irish-Who-Knows-What-the-Hell-I-Am child," she said flatly. "Well, let me reassure you, Caleb. I can't. Get pregnant. But apparently the possibility was such a turn-off for you—"

Narrowing his eyes, he lowered his face until their noses brushed. "Did I seem turned off when you jerked me off and I spilled all over you?" He dragged one of her palms to his erection, still impressive. Still apparently eager. "Do I seem turned off now?"

Without thought, she curled her fingers around him, quivering when he closed his eyes and groaned. "Then . . . then why didn't you come all the way inside me? Before you—"

"Because I need you to be sure."

"I was sure!" she whispered.

"No, you don't understand. I need you to show that to me, when pleasure isn't clouding your judgment."

"You're not making any sense."

"I can't take your virginity, Wraith, even if it's just a piece of skin. You need to give it to me. *You* need to take *me*."

It stunned her, the firmness and finality in his voice. Obviously, this was something he was taking very seriously. "So aside from your concern about protection, your restraint wasn't about you suddenly realizing I was dead and not wanting—not wanting to . . . ?" Her voice broke and she cursed her weakness.

"No, Wraith." He smoothed back her hair. "Not at all. But since protection isn't an issue. . ." He released her, and she watched as he lay back on the floor. "If you're sure. If you want me, Wraith. Take me."

As she stared down into Caleb's beautiful eyes, Wraith suddenly realized what he was giving her. Not just sexual satisfaction, but sexual empowerment. Apparently he'd sensed how vulnerable she'd been feeling. And instead of taking further advantage of that, he was giving her control. Making her take what she wanted.

When she moved to straddle him, he lightly clasped her hips, helping her to kneel above him so that his penis nudged at the entrance of her opening.

Caleb relaxed back and watched her, his eyes narrowing when she cupped her breasts with her hands and tweaked her own nipples. He forced himself not to reach out for her, although he couldn't help arching his hips so that his cock dragged against her mound. She was so wet he could feel her lube slicking over his cock.

He crossed his arms behind his head, striving to appear casual but knowing if he didn't restrain his hands he'd be pulling at her. Overwhelming her. Ravaging her. And he didn't want to ravage her. Not now. He wanted her to take him, just as he'd said. "Show me. Show me what you want."

She hesitated, then moved off him. Kissed him gently. Her tongue moved tentatively over his lips, becoming more assertive when he opened his mouth eagerly. She pulled away and showered kisses down his throat and over his chest. Then his abdomen. Her fingers moved lower, caressing his quivering muscles until he thought he would die from frustration. Then she dipped them even lower and cupped him in her hand.

His breath exhaled in a ragged moan of pleasure. She squeezed him tighter, moving her hand up and down the entire length of him. His hands left his head and grabbed her hair, pulling her down for a kiss.

He could feel her passion spike along with his. She pulled away and knelt over him, her face within a hairbreadth of his cock. She grasped him with both of her hands, running them up and down him like a favorite new toy. He felt his balls tighten in preparation for an explosive orgasm.

"Please!" The word exploded from him.

She looked up at him seductively. "Please what?"

"Suck me, Wraith."

Her gaze shot to his, then back down. Despite his calm words, his dick was fairly vibrating in anticipation. She licked her lips and slowly bent forward. When she awkwardly closed her mouth around the tip of him, he couldn't tear his eyes away.

She'd obviously never given a blow job before. She moved her mouth awkwardly, catching him a couple of times with the edge of her teeth. It didn't matter. She caught on fast, taking encouragement from his groans of pleasure to use her hand in sync with her mouth. With her hand gently cupping his balls and her tongue swirling around the length of him, she drove him quickly toward climax until he had to yell for her to stop.

He reached down and moved her head away, dragging her up his body until she was straddling him. He reached down. She was so primed for him that his fingers slid easily into her. He hooked his fingers and pushed against her hot spot, at the same time rubbing his thumb aggressively against her clit.

She was the one screaming now. He waited until the spasms turned into ripples before making his next request.

"Now fuck me."

She looked shocked again. He removed his hand and reached up, rubbing his fingers against her lips, forcing her to taste how ready she was for him.

"I want to be inside you, Wraith. Now. Fuck me." He smiled wickedly at her. "Please."

She reached for his cock and slowly guided him to the entrance of her body. He grabbed her hips lightly, not controlling her movements but offering support if she needed it. She slowly lowered herself onto him. She bit her lip and moaned.

Caleb couldn't take his eyes off her. She was amazing. Sexy. Gorgeous. He wanted so badly to take control. Flip her over and thrust and pound and grind into her until his semen burst out of him in shocking waves of pleasure. But he could feel the tightness of her body. The hymen that even now was denying him access to her. This was for her.

Wraith felt dizzy with pleasure. She flattened her palms against the tense muscles of Caleb's chest, marveling that as hard as his pecs were, his cock was even harder inside of her. His jaw was clenched as he visibly tried to restrain himself and she knew she should do it, thrust herself down onto him. She wanted to. Wanted to feel him completely invade her. But suddenly, she was scared. Not of the physical pain. Afraid that once she gave herself to him, there'd be nothing left but a limp quivering bundle of flesh, stripped raw of all defenses.

Unbelievably, the words, "I'm scared," came out of her mouth.

He looked up at her and cupped her face. "I know, baby. But believe me. It'll be worth the pain. Come on. Do it."

She shook her head, trying to tell him she wasn't scared of the pain. Trying to explain that he made her feel vulnerable in a way that no one ever had before. He made her want things. Silly things. Things that could never be hers. A little house with a vegetable garden in the back. Nights cuddled up close to a fire, drinking wine and playing strip poker. A minivan packed with kids to chauffeur back and forth to school. The chance to make love with him every day for the rest of her life. How could she tell him that's what she wanted when it was such a ridiculous notion?

She couldn't. She wouldn't. It was impossible. It was nothing he wanted. Nothing he could give her.

She tried concentrating again on the moment. On the feel of his body under hers. On the intense desire she saw burning in his eyes. This was enough, she told herself. He was giving her what she needed. For just a moment. She could give that to him, as well.

She slowly lowered herself down another inch. Felt the barrier of her hymen break with absolutely no pain.

"You okay?" he breathed harshly.

She simply nodded, biting her lip to keep from moaning, but didn't succeed. Neither did Caleb. Their moans melted together as one, melodic and harmonious. She pushed down even farther.

Caleb stared at her. "That's the way. Go deeper."

She kept going until he was almost fully inside her. Swiveling her hips at the last moment, she lifted herself off him. He groaned with frustration. She immediately sunk down, pushing hard until he was all the way inside.

Caleb reached down and rubbed her clitoris with his thumb. The jolt of pleasure caused her to moan and arch her hips. Her moan went up several octaves at the sensations that movement caused inside of her. Going on autopilot, she raised herself on and off him repeatedly, enjoying the drag of her sensitive skin against the hardness of his shaft. She was oblivious to how much time went by as she rode him. Seconds. Minutes. Hours. She was lost in sensation. Aware of nothing else. Until his fingers dug deeply into her hips and she heard him begging.

For a moment, she hesitated, but he wouldn't let her back away. He reached down and played with her clit, relentlessly forcing her toward pleasure again until she screamed.

"Oh my God. I'm going to come. Come on, baby. Move faster. You've got to move faster."

His words spurred her on until she was fairly bouncing on him, her breasts rocking in time to her movements. Her release was just out of reach and she wasn't sure what she needed to do to grab it.

Caleb leaned up and gently bit one of her nipples. The shock of pain and pleasure made her scream, and caused her uterus to contract violently around him. Suddenly, she was there, hurtling herself over the side of the mountain with abandon, relishing the feeling of flying with each spasm of pleasure that racked her body. She could hear Caleb groaning as he flew with her.

When she landed, Caleb was lying back on the floor with his arms around her. Her head was resting on his chest, which rose and fell with each labored breath he took. His heartbeat thumped powerfully in her ear. She enjoyed the rhythm and closed her eyes, wondering if she could fall asleep like this.

Caleb's cock, still lodged firmly inside her, had other ideas. It twitched and started to swell, growing inside her until she felt full to bursting. She leaned up and looked down at him.

He pushed her hair out of her eyes. "Ready for another round?"

"Don't you need to rest?"

"Didn't I tell you? In addition to being psychic, my ancestors blessed me with amazing stamina. I can go longer than any human ever could, Wraith. And with you, I'm betting I could outlast any Otherborn, too."

"Really?" She trailed a hand down to his cock and caressed him until he shuddered. "Next time you have one of your visions, be sure to thank your ancestors for me," she purred.

Wraith didn't have any idea how many rounds made up a boxing match, but as time passed, she was fairly certain she and Caleb got close. The third time they made love he pinned her down and drove her crazy with his body and tongue, refusing to give in to her demands for release until he was ready. She'd been acutely aware of the fact that, despite her strength, he was even stronger. It was nothing she'd admit, but she wasn't going to beat herself up about it, either.

They worked their way back to her hotel room between rounds three and four and kept going until hunger had finally forced Caleb away from her to grab some food.

His distance gave her the time she needed to think. It had been amazing, surrendering to her sexuality and allowing herself to feel pleasure without any kind of drug. The pain had been there, but at no time had it ever overwhelmed the pleasure Caleb had given her. That had never happened before, and she wondered if Caleb had some special ability to take away her pain as part of being a healer.

She'd have to ask him about that.

As she waited, she found her eyes getting heavier with what could only be sleep. Even as amazement tickled her mind, the darkness came over her.

When Wraith woke, she was alone in her bed. She was still naked, the flesh between her thighs aching and covered with dried semen. She heard water running in her bathroom and immediately rolled onto her side and closed her eyes before Caleb walked back in.

She was silent, aware that he was standing there looking at her. She didn't know how long she'd been asleep or when he'd come back, but she expected him to leave and go back to his own room. Instead, he climbed under the covers, pulled her back into his chest, and wrapped his arms around her. "We need to talk, Wraith. I need to know what's going on. Your appearance is changing. You're sleeping. You don't feel pain when I touch you. And your virginity. The second time—your hymen didn't repair itself . . . not with me."

She barely managed to choke out, "I don't know . . ." Dear Essenia, she hadn't even thought about that. "Shhh," he said, stroking her hair. "I said we have to talk. But not now. Tonight, you just need to relax."

She didn't move at his words, but her mind raced, and tears came to her eyes. He sounded so reassuring. She could almost forget everything else. She remembered one thing, however— their conversation yesterday about the feline who'd betrayed her. Talking about Maria had somehow felt right to her. It hadn't brought the pain the memories normally brought her, either. It had been as if Caleb's mere presence had insulated her from the pain of the past. She wondered if somehow she could do that for him.

Tentatively, she said, "The feline who betrayed me?" The hand stroking her hair stilled and she felt the way he held his breath. "Her name was Maria. The mage said she did it to escape the feline heat. She wanted a cure. Hated the way it made her dependent on males day after day. The mage gave it to her. In exchange for . . ."

As her voice dropped, Caleb began stroking her hair again and finished for her. "In exchange for betraying you and other wraiths. She traded her own pain for the pain of others."

"It's what people have been doing since the beginning of time, I suppose," she said. "It's what . . . it's what you're doing, too, Caleb."

He pulled away from her and sat up, the frown on his face as dark as his tone. "What does that mean? You think I'm causing someone pain in order to—"

She shook her head. Wrapped her arms around her bent knees. "No, that came out wrong. I just meant you're using pain to balance things out, too. You feel responsible for Elijah's death, and you've been torturing yourself over it. I know perfectly well that your service on this team is some kind of penance, just like I know Mahone manipulated your past to get you here. Just like he did to the rest of us. But I've read the reports, Caleb. I know why you refused to help the army interrogate Elijah, and it wasn't because you didn't care. You didn't believe in what they were doing. They were torturing prisoners of war for information . . ."

"And in the end, what does that matter, Wraith? If I could have stopped your pain by helping that mage get the information he wanted—the secret to your immortality—wouldn't you have wanted me to? Wouldn't you have blamed me for any pain you suffered after I refused?"

His reasoning stopped her. Almost made her agree with him. But then she allowed herself to imagine that exact scenario, and she shook her head. "Someone who could do that to me for information wouldn't do good things once he had it. He'd have wielded the knowledge of immortality for his own gain, regardless of how he hurt others. So would I blame you for letting me suffer because you didn't want that to happen? No, Caleb. I wouldn't. I'd hate the pain, but I wouldn't hate you. And if Elijah was any kind of friend to you, he would have understood that. You didn't kill him. His interrogator did."

Caleb's lips parted, and she saw the realization spark in his eyes, but only for a moment. The stubborn man, obviously too used to living with his guilt, pushed her words away. Reaching out, he pulled her to his chest again until they were spooning. His closeness felt so good, she remained quiet. He'd think about what she'd told him. That was enough for now.

Reaching out, he cradled her hand, his thumb smoothing over the three dots she'd noticed earlier. "What are these? Freckles?"

"I . . . I don't know," she whispered, but she immediately began thinking of her past again. Whether the dots were the gang symbol she thought they were. What that said about who she really was.

"Stop thinking. Go to sleep, Wraith. Everything's going to be fine."

She tried. She really did. But she couldn't. Her mind was awash with worries. About their mission. The men who'd come after them. Her future, and if she even had one. Caleb's future, if *he* had one, and whether he'd someday release the guilt that bound him in order to let himself be happy. Whether that happiness would include a female . . .

He sighed behind her. Nudged her legs apart with his thigh, interrupting her thoughts like a runaway train appearing out of nowhere. He nudged his cock inside her, and she winced slightly at the slow, insistent invasion. He didn't stop until he was seated inside her fully. He cupped her breast with his right hand and nudged her hair away from her ear, kissing her gently. "I promise, Wraith. It's going to be fine. Now go to sleep."

After several stunned moments, Wraith realized he actually meant it. He was hard as a rock inside of her, but he made no move to satisfy himself. He actually expected her to accept his reassurances and go to sleep. It was so ridiculous that it actually worked. Filled up with him, she didn't have the energy to think of anything else. She closed her eyes. Listened to him breathing. Felt the pulse of his heartbeat seep into her.

And fell asleep.

TWENTY-SIX

Knox stared at his brother for three seconds before he went for his throat.

Zeph didn't try to dodge his grasp, even when Knox threw him against a wall and started to transform into a bigger, badder version of himself. Instead, Zeph watched the change quietly, his entire body indicating a quiet and calm acceptance of Knox's wrath.

"Zeph," their mother whispered from behind them. "How could you? How . . . ?" Her voice broke, and her loud sobs seemed suddenly muted.

Knox knew she'd turned her head into his father's barrel chest, instinctively seeking her husband's comfort after decades of having to do without it. Knox breathed in deep, trying to reconcile what his brother had just told him with the fear that was even now threatening to dismantle his control.

Where was Felicia? He'd sent the guards after her the instant Zeph—

"Knox? What's going on?"

When he heard her voice, the relief he felt almost drove him to his knees. His security team had been going over the security footage from the night of the wedding reception, but the Dome was a huge place and it was taking a significant amount of time. They were about halfway through the film, but other than Wraith's brief wrestling match with Joanna's boyfriend in the garden, nothing troubling had revealed itself. Certainly nothing to warn Knox about what his brother was mixed up in.

The entire room, Zeph included, sighed as one. Releasing his brother, Knox dove for his wife, encircling her in his arms so tightly, she gasped. Then she wrapped her arms around him and hugged him as tightly as she could.

"Shhh," she said before threading her hands through his hair, trying to calm him. "I'm here, Knox. Now tell me what's wrong."

With his face buried in the crook of her neck, Knox shook his head. Not yet, he thought. He couldn't release her yet . . .

"Felicia," Zeph began, "I was just telling Knox about an assignment I'd received."

"Assignment?" Felicia asked over Knox's head.

"Yes. An assignment to—"

Knox raised his head abruptly and whirled on his brother. "Stop! You're not just going to blurt it out again."

Zeph pressed his lips together, his expression no longer calm but angry. Knox stared at his brother, at the grimness of his expression, and couldn't believe how thoroughly he'd deceived them all.

He felt Felicia's hand on his arm. "Knox, it's okay," she said firmly. "Let Zeph speak." When she raised her hand to cup his face and turn it toward hers, Knox grabbed it and kissed it. Then he glared at Zeph but said nothing more.

"I was approached," Zeph began again, "about a contract on your life, Felicia. One put out by an organization that views your marriage to Knox as an abomination to humanity."

Felicia's eyes widened and jerked to Knox's. He felt her confusion and fear, and it made him sick. That her life was in danger because she loved him . . .

She shook her head furiously. "Don't you dare, Knox. Don't you dare think what you're thinking. I love you and there's nothing wrong with that, and it's not your fault that others think there is. There will always be people who hate, but I'm not afraid of them. I'm not afraid," she emphasized as she turned back to Zeph. "Just how do you know about this organization, Zeph?"

Knox couldn't keep himself from speaking up this time.

It still blew his mind that his brother had been working with these people behind their backs. "Zeph's been working as a double agent for an organization called the Quorum. They recruited Dante Prime, and he, in turn, recruited Zeph. But Zeph only went along with Prime's machinations because he's hoping to bring the Quorum down. With Mahone's help."

Felicia's mouth dropped open. "Mahone . . ."

Knox nodded. "Mahone suspected Prime had stolen the antidote and given it to North Korea. So did Zeph. But Zeph only discovered who Prime was working for, a group of humans calling themselves the Quorum, when Mahone was captured. Zeph was there, trying to figure out a way to get Mahone out without blowing his cover, when Caleb and Team Blue arrived. Zeph maintained his cover, and he and Mahone decided not to tell the rest of us about the Quorum because of some bullshit—"

"It's not bullshit, Knox," Zeph gritted out. "It's just not your mission to bring them down. You can't be everywhere at once. The Para-Ops team's role is to deal with the shit the Quorum and other scum—human or Otherborn—cause, not with the Quorum itself. You're needed on the streets, in the action, and if the Quorum gets wind that you're after them, they'll go to ground fast. By keeping the hunt for the Quorum leaders separate from the Para-Ops team's role in maintaining peace between the races, Mahone was doing what he thought was best for everyone."

"So you and Mahone are buddies now?" Knox questioned in disbelief. "Swapping secrets and keeping them from your family? From *me*, Zeph?" Damn Mahone. The man was proving to be full of deception. First, he'd pitted Caleb against Wraith. Now Zeph against Knox. What would he do next?

"I understand Mahone's reasoning," Bianca said quietly.

Shocked, Knox jerked his head toward her. "Mother, how can you condone what they've done? It's always better to know the existence of one's enemy."

Stepping out of her husband's protective embrace, Bianca smiled. "But you already knew someone else was pulling Dante Prime's strings. And Zeph's right—you can't be everything to everyone, and you can't be everywhere at once. You had to lead this clan by yourself for so long, but you no longer have to. You also don't have to fight the Quorum alone, and I'm grateful for that."

"That's ridiculous. I would never turn away help, but—"

"Knox, how hard was it for you to take this time for you and Felicia to be together, away from your team? For both of you? We had to practically threaten to tie you down before you'd agree to it."

Knox glanced at Felicia, who had flushed guiltily. They'd relished this time together, but their first instinct had been to go right back to work . . .

"The things Kyle Mahone is asking of your team involve stopping the crimes that the Quorum have set in motion. The Quorum is the source and provides the funds, but the cancer they wield is imbedded within the communities of this nation. You can't be in the trenches while trying to fight the corrupt politicians, as well. It would fracture the team's focus and unnecessarily. Especially when they have others, like Zeph, who are willing to carry the other half of the load." Bianca turned her narrowed gaze on Zeph. "That, however, does not excuse the fact that Zeph failed to tell his mother and his Queen how he was occupying his time. And you can bet Mr. Mahone will be hearing from me about that."

The room went silent. Knox heard his mother's words and knew she was right, but he didn't say so. He didn't look at his brother. He couldn't.

With a curse, Zeph left the room.

Felicia took Knox's hand and squeezed. With a sigh, he squeezed back. He was about to lead her from the room when he felt a heavy hand on his shoulder and turned.

His father, Jacques Devereaux, the human-turned-vampire whom Knox had only recently been reunited with, looked at him with unflinching directness. "Your brother came to you as soon as he knew Felicia's life was in jeopardy. He didn't even talk to Mahone about it first. Because his family, of which Felicia is now a part, is his main priority. He learned of the Quorum's plan because he deceived you, Knox. Because the Quorum believes he's still of use to them. You and he and Mahone can fight all you want about whether keeping certain information from one another was justified, but you'll do it later. After you take care of what needs to be taken care of. Understood?"

At his father's words, Knox, who'd led the vamp clan for years during his father's absence and his mother's illness, instinctively bristled at his father's calm, commanding tone. But that lasted only a moment. Then he remembered how grateful he was to no longer be the only one leading the clan. He had help now. Support. Others who would not only help him protect the clan, but would die with him in order to protect his wife.

Knox nodded. "I understand." He turned to Felicia and met her eyes. "Let's go find Zeph and figure out what we're going to do."

TWENTY-SEVEN

When morning came, Caleb wasn't even fully awake before he knew Wraith had retreated from him. Beside him, she sat up, the sheet pulled around her. "Playtime's over, Romeo. We need to get going."

Despite her calculated words, her voice trembled. She was troubled, but she was also probably still turned on. He'd bet anything that if he cupped her with his hand, she'd be dripping wet. It made him want to go down on her again. Making her come like that would be the highlight of his year. Feeling her juices on his face. In his throat. If she hadn't yet learned to enjoy it, too damn bad. He'd give her so much pleasure, she'd let him do anything to her. Everything.

He pressed his lips to her shoulder, following an intriguing trail of freckles just visible under her skin. He narrowed his eyes, thinking her skin had hardly any blue left to it. Listing all the changes she'd undergone in his mind, he lightly caressed her other arm with the tips of his fingers. "Are you in a hurry?" he murmured.

"Lucy and Dex—"

"Don't need us right now. The clubs aren't open until tonight, you know."

She stiffened as his lips trailed close to the rise of one breast, putting her hands on his chest as if to push him away. He tilted his head up slightly to look at her, feeling her fingers flex against him. But she didn't apply any pressure. Simply rested her fingers against him, their warm weight an erotic pressure against his nipples.

She licked her lips and he almost growled, wanting to chase her tongue as it disappeared back into her mouth. "I know, but . . ."

He moved his hand, rubbing his thumb against one nipple so her body jerked in surprise. Her teeth were white against the softness of her lips as she bit down, trying to stifle a gasp but not quite succeeding. God, she was responsive. He moved his thumb in tight circles and resumed kissing her fragrant skin. "Besides, I haven't gotten enough of you. I want more."

She swallowed audibly. "Fine."

"Fine?"

"Yes, that's fine. But one more time. That's it. Then we've got to go."

He laughed darkly, his throat scratching at the almost forgotten sensation. "All right. One more." Suddenly, he couldn't wait any longer. He needed her. Now.

While they made love, she was silent, except for a moment when he thought he heard her whisper, "One more."

When he woke again, Wraith was gone. And he knew, if Wraith got her way, the time they'd spent together had truly ended.

Later that evening, four of the Para-Ops team's six members were mingling with over a hundred people looking to get drunk, high, and laid. Wraith had never craved alcohol, but she knew Caleb had struggled with an addiction in the past. Nonetheless, she wasn't surprised that he was nursing a real beer because ordering anything without alcohol would call attention to him, and that was the last thing he wanted. Even so, he drank slowly, pacing himself and keeping his attention focused on what was going on around him.

At the same time, Wraith struggled with her own cover. To appear unaffected by who she really was and what it was she really wanted. Because in just a few hours, she'd discovered she was addicted to Caleb and his unique brand of sex. So addicted, in fact, she'd thought about him all day, like a junkie going through withdrawals, even as she'd avoided him and pretended to be thoroughly engrossed with preparing for their mission.

Only, pretending she didn't know Lucy, Dex, and Caleb while asking questions in a nightclub really didn't require that much preparation. She knew it and so did Caleb. Thankfully, he seemed amenable to letting her dodge him, and she only hoped that continued. Because she wasn't ready to face what it was they'd done together—to each other—and she wasn't sure if she ever would be.

At least Dex seemed relaxed and appeared to have put aside his concerns about Lucy. She could see why. As Wraith scanned the bar, not allowing her gaze to linger on Lucy more than any other person, she couldn't deny it—Lucy looked fuckable.

In fact, none of them should have worried about her ability to pass herself off as a feline on the prowl. If she didn't know better, Wraith would have sworn Lucy was part feline, but more importantly, that she'd spent the past two days getting the sexual experience she lacked from Caleb—but of course, that was impossible.

Because that's what Wraith had been doing.

She shivered when she recalled how many times and how many different ways she'd had him.

Now, from across the room, it was as if none of it had ever happened.

They were all playing their parts.

After a short briefing over the phone with Mahone, they'd decided against her playing at being Lucy's friend. After all, she scared most people, anyway, and she didn't want that to affect whether people approached Lucy. Dex and Caleb would keep their eyes on her. Wraith's job was to mix and mingle and try to get information on the drug rapes.

So far, she wasn't having any luck.

She loitered around the bar until a hard-looking woman, the kind that looked like she'd started smoking early and had never stopped, sat down beside her.

"Hey. I'm Wilma. What the hell are you?"

Wraith liked her instantly. "I'm a ghost. I'm called Wraith."

"No shit?"

"Uh, no," Wraith said. "I mean, yes. No shit. Haven't you heard of wraiths before?"

"I've heard of them but I never met one in person."

Wraith plastered a look of unease on her face and pretended to scan the bar before saying sotto voce, "Yes, well, I hope it doesn't make people uncomfortable. I've heard the felines have been getting some flack in these clubs lately. I don't want to attract the perverts who've been drugging and raping them."

Wilma patted her arm and said, "You don't have anything to worry about, hon."

"Why's that?"

"Like you said, it's only felines that have been hit."

Had that been approval in Wilma's voice? Going with her instincts, Wraith nodded and responded in a whisper. "Yeah, and they sure ask for it, don't you think? They're so damn loose. Will sleep with anyone or anything. But who knows when their attackers will look for fresh meat. Aren't you scared someone will slip something into your drink and—"

Wilma laughed. "No."

"Why not?" Wraith tried to sound more surprised than interested.

"One, I'm careful. I don't drink much, and when I do, I don't let anyone near my drink. Two, I've got other ways of protecting myself from pervs."

"Like?" She expected Wilma to say she had a gun. Or a can of Mace. Or a Taser.

Instead, she said, "I've got a dick. And if they try anything, I'm not afraid to use it."

Wraith choked on her drink and laughed her ass off. "I knew there was a reason I liked you," she said.

Wilma snorted. "Stick with me, Wraith. They might think we're freaks, but we know different, right?"

Wraith hummed in agreement, not realizing her gaze had unconsciously moved toward Caleb until Wilma said, "He's hot, but not as hot as the were next to him. Hon, if I could get a dog like that to bang me, I might even consider getting some surgery done, if you get my meaning."

Disconcerted by the brief, heated look Caleb shot her, Wraith shook her head. "Don't do it. Any male worth taking to bed should accept you for exactly who you are, right?"

"You've got a lot to learn about males, Wraith. It's not about who's genuine when they take someone to bed, it's about who's available. And luckily, sometimes that includes me."

"Of course it does, Will. You're definitely worth switching sides for."

They both laughed. And the whole time they talked, Wraith kept her eye on Lucy. Men were crowding around her and she was handling them with ease. In fact, she actually looked like she was enjoying all the attention, which included a whole lot of fondling.

Imagine that. Looked like they were both learning something about themselves on this mission. What exactly that was, she still didn't quite know.

"Lucy's holding her own," Caleb murmured.

"Yes, she is," Dex replied even as he scanned the club.

"You wouldn't have anything to do with that, would you?"

Dex scoffed. "That was supposed to be your job, remember? If you and Wraith had been around, that is. Did Wraith squirrel you away to make sure that didn't happen?"

"We didn't even see each other until tonight."

Dex nodded, then caught Caleb's gaze and held it. "Same with Lucy and me."

"Got it." And he got it, all right.

"Wraith looks like she's having a good time, doesn't she? In fact, she looks quite at home."

Caleb didn't glance at Wraith. He didn't have to. He'd kept tabs on her from the second they'd entered the club. At first, it had surprised him, how comfortable she'd seemed hanging out and chatting it up with strangers. She'd seemed to drop her natural defensiveness in favor of a laid-back attitude. She seemed more natural with the transsexual sitting next to her than she did with her own team, and that kind of pissed him off, especially given how thoroughly she'd been ignoring him. But then he'd reminded himself that she was doing a job, and Wraith was only doing what she needed to. Glancing at Dex, aware he hadn't responded to the were's comment, Caleb murmured, "I don't know if Wraith's ever had a place to call home."

Dex took a drink of his beer. "Sometimes that's a good thing, O'Flare."

Remembering the reservation and the comfort his people

had brought him, even despite the hardships, he wasn't sure he could agree. But he knew his life was far from what Wraith or Dex had experienced.

"So you never told me what Mahone is paying you for joining the . . . basketball team," Dex finished with a grin, despite the way Caleb had started to glare at him.

"Funny. I was just about to say the same thing to you."

Dex shrugged. "I'm not shy about what I want. It's something I'm going to do myself, but Mahone's assured me that he and others will be looking the other way when it happens."

"Ah," Caleb murmured as he nodded. He forced himself not to look at Wraith even though he wanted to. "I get it. Tough thing about that, though: When everyone's looking the other way, no one can be watching your back."

Dex didn't say anything, and when several minutes went by, Caleb couldn't help himself. He checked to make sure Wraith was still sitting at the bar.

Laughing, Dex leaned back farther in his chair. "What's going on with you two? If I didn't know better, I'd say you guys finally did the wild thing, but you're avoiding each other more than ever."

"Shut the . . ." Caleb spotted something from the corner of his eye and suddenly straightened. "Shit," he breathed, feeling his stomach drop.

The were went on high alert. "What is it?"

Caleb just shook his head, forcing Dex to follow his line of sight.

"Oh yeah. I'd say that's beyond a shit and more like a holy-mother-fucking hell."

Not about to disagree with him, Caleb watched as Princess Natia wound her way through the crowded nightclub and made her way not toward Caleb and Dex, but toward Wraith.

Caleb was on his feet and had grabbed her arm before she'd taken another two steps. "Natia . . ."

Eyes rounded with mock surprise, Natia smiled and threw herself into Caleb's arms. Then she kissed him.

TWENTY-EIGHT

"I need you to get me out of here, Isaac. Now!"

The voice that spoke the urgent command was a familiar one—Zeph Prime's.

Looking around the five-star French restaurant, Isaac spotted a private corner and excused himself from his date. Holding his cell phone to his ear, he didn't speak until he was convinced no one could hear him.

"What are you talking about?"

"I'm talking about the fact my damn brother had already started to turn Felicia and I didn't know it. And now, thanks to you, everyone in my whole damn clan knows I tried to kill her and that she kicked my ass in the process. I'm talking about the fact that I'm now friendless and family-less and if you don't get to me and get me someplace safe real fast, I'm gonna start talking about you and the twelve Greek Gods you're working—"

"All right," Isaac said. "Calm down. I'll take care of the situation. Where are you?"

"I teleported to Nevada. I'm at the Bellagio. How long will it take for you to get to me?"

"I'll send someone—"

"No way," Zeph snapped. "I don't know who to trust, but

you're the devil I know. It's either you or no one. In fact, that's starting to sound more and more appealing to me, now that I think of it."

"Fine. I'll come for you myself. I'll be there in an hour." Gritting his teeth, Isaac terminated their connection and pocketed his cell phone.

This was not good. Now one of the Quorum's key agents was on the run because Isaac had sent him to kill the vampire prince's human mate. Something the Quorum as a whole would be surprised to hear. And if he tried to explain that he'd been acting under orders . . .

Isaac shuddered as he imagined what the scarred one would do to him, but only after he let the female have her fun first.

Damn Athena and the one called Ares. If they hadn't set the damn assassination attempt in motion, Isaac would be enjoying a meal with a Playboy bunny and anticipating what—or rather *who*—was to come later that night. Instead, he had to pick up Zeph Prime and either convince the vamp to keep quiet or find a way to eliminate him. Of course, since Isaac had no hopes of overpowering the vamp himself, eliminating him would mean involving yet more individuals in this mess, which would leave another trail when there was already one far too long for Isaac's comfort.

He considered his options, then dialed a number he'd never thought he'd use while in public.

"What is it?" a voice answered.

"I've run into trouble," Isaac said.

"And this concerns me how?"

"Because my trouble is your trouble. Our objective hit a wall. One that turned out to be *sharper* than we thought."

One thing about Athena: She was a bitch, but she caught on fast. "Locke's been turned?"

"According to my source, yes."

"And you trust him?"

Isaac thought about it. Did he? Yes. Zeph Prime had sounded genuinely pissed on the phone. And he'd proven himself very valuable in the past. But what really convinced Isaac was the common knowledge that it was biologically impossible for vampires to lie. "I trust him," he said.

"Then bring him to me. I want to assess this vampire for myself."

"What about Felicia Locke? And Ares?"

"Leave Ares to me. Once he learns his daughter has been turned, he'll probably urge the Quorum to go after the vamps with guns blazing. After all, he'd considered her death more merciful than a life with vamps, even as a human. Imagine how he'll feel once he discovers she is one. The Quorum, however, will see the folly in such a move and refuse. I'll make sure of that."

"But he'll be furious with you . . ."

Isaac felt the chill across the line even before he heard it in her voice. "No," she said softly. "He'll be furious with you, Isaac. And he'll demand you fix the situation. How you choose to do that is up to you. As far as I'm concerned, you should never have acted without the Quorum's full authority by giving in to Ares' demands."

Dumbfounded, Isaac sputtered, "But you—"

"I what?" Athena asked silkily, her voice edged with challenge.

Isaac swallowed hard. He wanted to choke the life out of the human female, but even though the other Quorum members didn't know her identity, Isaac did. If she chose, she could wield more power than he, Ares, and all the other Quorum members combined. "I apologize. I . . . I lost my head for a moment."

"Do it again, and you'll lose more than your head, Isaac. Now bring the vampire to me. Once I talk to him, I'll meet with the Quorum and let them know we've lost another human to the Otherborn."

She hung up, leaving Isaac to shut the cell phone and make his excuses to his date. As he did so, however, he was also weighing his options. He'd allowed Athena and Ares to sway him from the Quorum's course out of greed. That was perfectly understandable. He wasn't a fool, however. He didn't appreciate Athena's threats, and while he didn't have any hope of bringing her down, Ares was a different matter altogether. If he became a threat to Isaac—if he chose to wield his power against him—Isaac would tell Zeph Prime the identity of the individual who wanted Felicia dead: her father. The human she thought had died along with her mother, but really was the person responsible for her mother's death.

* * *

Knox stared at his brother as Zeph ended the call with the one called Isaac. Around them, the sounds of the Bellagio acted as background noise, irritating Knox's already jagged nerves.

"So apparently you've discovered a way to lie and haven't bothered to tell me that, either. Is that Mahone's doing, as well?"

Zeph simply looked at him, making Knox laugh bitterly.

"At least tell me this. Is the antidote real? Is the testing we're doing warranted, or are we wasting time on a false hope that may or may not lead to my wife's death? To the death of the humans who've chosen to take the antidote in order to give our clan a chance to survive?"

Sighing, Zeph rubbed the back of his neck. "It's real," he said quietly. "But we don't know what the lasting side effects are. So the testing is warranted but . . ."

"But inconclusive," Knox finished. "And even though Felicia must now pretend to be a vampire to increase her chances of survival, she's even more adamant about not being turned."

"I agree with her. She knows how valuable you are to the clan—"

"If she dies, I'll have no value. I'll die, too. In spirit, if not in body. Can't you understand that?"

Zeph opened his mouth, but before he could answer, Knox sliced his hand in the air, silencing him. "Of course you can't. You've never loved a woman, Zeph, have you? You can't understand what kind of pain would come from being separated from her."

"No," he agreed. "But I love my family. And I think I understand a little about the pain of separation." He glanced at his watch, then back at Knox. "It's time for you to leave. Tell Mother I'm sorry I didn't say good-bye, but this is for the best. This way, I can work the Quorum from the inside—"

"Yes, you're good at that. Deceiving people from the inside, I mean."

Knox cursed himself when he saw the flash of pain that traveled across his brother's face. But damn it, Zeph wasn't a little boy anymore. He'd been working with Mahone for a long time now, taking care of himself and doing what he could for the clan. Knox understood why, but logic didn't temper the hurt or sense of betrayal he felt that his own brother had lied to him over and over again.

With a curse, Knox turned and walked a few feet away. He stopped when Zeph spoke.

"You've been checking the surveillance tapes from the night of your reception."

Slowly, Knox turned back to his brother. "And?"

"And have your men reported any film showing that the mage on your team was suffering from pain on that night?"

Frowning, Knox took a step closer. It was plain from Zeph's tone that he knew something, but what? And why bring Lucy up now? "Lucy suffers from an ailment that rears its head occasionally. If you saw her experiencing discomfort, you should've said something to me that night. Certainly well before today."

"Why? So you could deny what she is? A feline?"

Despite the automatic questions that came to his mind, Knox asked, "Why would I deny anything?" It wasn't a lie, but it was evasion, plain and simple. He knew it even as he said it, but he couldn't confirm Zeph's suspicion, either.

"Ah, that's right, Knox. Don't answer directly. I understand." When Knox remained quiet, Zeph nodded. "You're doing what you believe is right. I was doing the same when I kept my role with Mahone from you. And it's why I'm going to tell you what I am now, even though it's pure speculation on my part."

"So tell me," Knox snapped, not allowing himself to show any softening toward his brother. He understood what Zeph was saying, but logic didn't sway him at the moment—only the belief that his brother's secrecy had somehow endangered Felicia controlled him. That wasn't something he could easily forgive or forget.

"You said yourself Lucy has to live with the affliction of being in heat. So does every female feline in this world. Imagine how difficult that would be. What one might barter in order to get rid of it."

"Are you implying Lucy has done something dishonorable in order to obtain relief from the heat? When sexual activity would bring her not only relief, but pleasure?"

"Even pleasure, when you're given no choice in accepting it, can lose its appeal, Knox. And no, I'm not accusing Lucy of anything. But she wasn't the only feline at the Dome the night you married, Brother."

Knox's eyes widened as mental links connected. The attack on Wraith. A feline who'd been in his home with a past attachment to Caleb O'Flare and a possible motive to want the wraith out of the way. "Princess Natia ordered an attack on Wraith? When the team is trying to find the bastards raping her people? Her own sister? That makes no sense, Zeph."

"I know of no attack on the wraith. But pain and jealousy can drive people to do horrible things. To betray their clan or betray others in order to help it. Perhaps you need to look into exactly what Natia would be willing to do." Zeph shrugged. "But like I said, it's just something I've been thinking about. I could be completely wrong."

"You could be," Knox murmured, but already he was planning to go to his security team. To focus on the security footage from Princess Natia's guest quarters himself.

He cast a final glance at his brother and nodded. "Thank you for sharing this information." He didn't forgive his brother. He didn't embrace him. But as he prepared to teleport, he gave his brother what he could. "Lucy's secrets are not my own, Zeph. It's not my place to expose them. I have always opened myself to you and thought you gave the same. I hope Essenia watches over you, Zeph. Return soon, but only when you can look me in the eye and tell me the full truth again."

TWENTY-NINE

Wilma was clearly intoxicated, and Wraith figured it wouldn't be too long before she let something slip about the feline rapes. If she knew anything, of course, but Wilma was too savvy and connected not to know a bit more than she was letting on.

Right now, however, what Wilma wanted was for Wraith to come to the bathroom with her. That was perfect. A little girl talk in the potty could only make Wilma feel more secure. Subtly, Wraith glanced toward Caleb, wanting to let him know where she was going. What she saw, however, made her mouth almost drop open.

Although Dex lounged at the high top table, chatting it up with a slender vamp and pretending to be drunk, Caleb was just walking back to the table with his arm around a small female. When they turned, she gasped. It was the same small female he'd been dancing with at Knox's wedding. His ex-girlfriend, the feline princess Natia.

Natia shook her head and stopped walking to press a hand to Caleb's chest. She said something and caressed his cheek with the back of her fingers. Instead of freezing her out with a scowl as Wraith expected, Caleb laughed and leaned down toward the feline. When she pulled his head down for a kiss, he didn't resist. In fact, he gave as good as he got.

Feeling like she'd been hit by a sledgehammer, Wraith turned and followed Wilma to the bathroom. When she got there, she had the immediate urge to go back out and rip that feline to shreds. It was only through pure force of will that she avoided doing so. So when Wilma said she'd forgotten her purse and would be right back, Wraith said she'd wait for her. She didn't trust herself to go back out there and not make a scene. Dex and Caleb were there to protect Lucy, and she wasn't going to do anything to jeopardize that task.

When another feline walked in and smiled at her, Wraith went into a stall and sat down just to have a little privacy. She took a moment to examine herself. The changes were coming faster now. While most people wouldn't see it unless they were looking for it, Wraith felt the biggest changes inside her. In the way her heartbeat was getting stronger. Her lungs filling more and more with air. Her body responding to touch with very little pain now, if any at all. Part of her wondered if it was her age or Caleb's touch that had quickened all the changes inside her.

Only, even if the answer was yes, that Caleb's touch had made her change, what was she supposed to do with that information? She'd managed to avoid him under the guise of the mission. But she knew he'd only given her a temporary reprieve. Soon, whatever was happening between them was going to come out in the open and she had no idea what to expect. Because even as she wanted to cling to every experience that Caleb had given her in the past few days, she wanted to run from them just as much. Now she knew exactly what she was going to be missing when she died, and she was almost willing to end everything right now just to avoid that feeling.

She heard female laughter, and the bathroom door opened and closed. "Wraith?"

It was Wilma. Closing her eyes, Wraith took several breaths—relishing every single one of them—and focused her mind. Mission. Date rape drug. Lucy as bait.

She had purpose. For a short time longer, anyway.

Wraith exited the stall and walked out, blinking when the lights went out. She heard a faint scrape just before something grabbed her by the back of the head and slammed her face-first into the stall doors, knocking her semi-unconscious. A prick on her arm followed, and she immediately felt the infusion of liquid into her body. Every muscle in her body went slack.

Caleb raised his mouth from Natia's, hoping like hell that Wraith had missed that little display.

Of course, what were the chances of that?

"You've got to get out of here, Natia. It's too dangerous for you."

"She's my sister, Caleb, and some bastard raped her. If that *wraith* can help—"

"That *wraith* has been trained in military warfare and surveillance, Natia. And you . . ." Natia had been protected. Sheltered and pampered. She'd been kept far away from the horrors of the War, something Caleb had always been grateful for, but it made her presence extremely dangerous to them all. If she said the wrong thing and it was overheard, she would endanger not only their mission but their lives. That's why he was cajoling rather than yelling at her the way he wanted to. The surest way to get Natia to do anything was to soften her up; the instant she felt like she was being controlled or condescended to, she'd dig her feet in all the more.

Now, who did that remind him of?

"I'm older now, Caleb. I can help. I *want* to help."

"O'Flare."

Turning to Dex, Caleb saw he was still maintaining his cover, only he didn't look as laid-back as he had before. Of course not. With Natia's foolish behavior, this mission was turning into a three-ring circus. Who knew maintaining cover in a sex club would be more difficult than dropping undetected into North Korea via spy plane?

"We've got trouble," Dex said.

Immediately, Caleb's eyes went to Lucy. She was talking to Wraith, a sappy smile on her face as they hugged. It wasn't consistent with what they'd planned, but Caleb assumed they'd decided to kiss and make up. Wraith wrapped an arm around Lucy and began to lead her toward the front door. But as she did so, something strange happened. Lucy stumbled, then weaved. Almost as if she was drunk.

Without hesitating, Caleb thrust Natia into Dex's lap. "Get her out of here."

Vaguely, he heard Dex curse and say to someone, "Get her in a cab."

Making a beeline for Lucy and Wraith, he stepped in front of them, blocking the door.

"You feeling okay? Anything I can help you with?" he said for the benefit of those around him.

Lucy smiled and wriggled her fingers at him. "Hey, Caleb. Wraith was just giving me a hand here."

Wraith was staring at him from behind those damn sunglasses again, her face as impassive as ever.

"A hand with what?" Caleb murmured.

Wraith shrugged. "She's had a little too much to drink. Was feeling light-headed. I thought she could use some fresh air."

Right. Pushing down the urgency that was urging him to separate the two females, Caleb nodded and swept his arm toward the door. "I think you're right."

Lucy smiled and waved again. The two of them walked through the door and as the air from outside filtered past them, Caleb smelled it.

Roses.

Shape-shifter.

As Wraith and Lucy walked out into the parking lot, Caleb was right behind them. With a light shove, he pushed Lucy out of the way, grabbed Wraith, and shoved her against the door, knocking off her sunglasses. Bracing his forearm against her throat, he applied enough pressure to cut off her airway. Wraith choked and tried to pry his arm away. "Can't . . . breathe . . ." she gasped.

Lucy screamed and jumped on his back, asking him what the hell he was doing. "You're hurting her, Caleb." He saw her bracing herself, probably preparing to use a spell on him, so he gave her another light shove. It sent her tumbling back and into Dex's waiting arms. He and Dex locked eyes, their mutual understanding evident.

Turning back to the wraith, Caleb said, "The thing is, Lucy doesn't drink alcohol. She can't because it's toxic to mages; dilutes their power. Most people don't know that, but Wraith sure as hell does. That tells me you drugged her. Isn't that right?"

"You're crazy. I'm her friend. Why would I—" The wraith wheezed as Caleb pressed even harder against her throat.

"Wraiths don't have to breathe, so I can't be choking the

breath out of you. Not if you're really Wraith, that is. Now where is she?"

Through waves of pain, Wraith felt her body fall and her head hit the floor, the movement causing the pain in her already sore head to intensify sharply. She moaned.

"Shut up, bitch. We're gonna have some fun."

Her attacker's voice was deep and male. He picked her up like she was a small animal and—*ooomph*! He flung her back to the ground like a horseshoe, causing her to skid a few feet on the linoleum before landing on her stomach. Her face scraped against the ridges in the floor.

She immediately tried to raise herself on all fours and get to her gun, but her assailant pushed her down with one foot on her back.

"Don't even think it, bitch! You're right where I want you. God, you're hot. I've been wanting a taste of one of your kind for a long, long time. Now that my orders have changed, I can finally do what I want with you."

She couldn't move. Why was her mind so fuzzy? What had he given her? She'd taken hits like the one he'd given her and been on her feet within seconds.

Wraith opened her mouth to scream just before he slammed her head into the floor again. Liquid spurted in her throat, choking her. With horror, she realized it was her own blood. When she felt the man's weight on her and his heavy grasp between her legs, a long, guttural moan escaped her. She writhed back and forth, up and down, in an effort to shake him off her.

"Giddy up, giddy up." The man laughed villainously. "Shit, you had to wear pants, huh? Stupid cunt. Feminist bitch." The man grabbed Wraith by the shoulders and flipped her over. She tried to get a look at him, but it was too dark. How could he see her? Something, most likely the man's fist, crashed into the side of her face, causing her to collapse back limply.

Her thoughts immediately went to Caleb. Her heart constricted with sorrow. Oh, Caleb.

"No more screwing around. No more getting you out of the way while minimizing the damage. She's paying me to kill you now. But shit, I think I'd do this for free, you know? Plus, she's good with her mouth. What about you, huh? You good with your mouth? I might as well get something else for my trouble, doncha think?"

The man ripped open her leathers, then unzipped his pants, pulled out his penis, and rubbed himself across Wraith's naked breasts. She shuddered in horror, feeling helpless. Just as she had with that mage. She'd sworn she'd never feel that way again, damn it. She wouldn't let this happen.

"I'd have you suck it, but you'd just bite it off, huh? Yeah, that's what I thought." He slapped her again. She barely felt it.

"Well, let's see what you do with a real man. Yeah. Show you some pleasure before you die."

He started working at the fastening of her pants. Out of necessity, he let go of one of her hands and tried to contain both of her hands in one of his. When Wraith felt his hand slip, she acted on sheer instinct. Yanking with all her might, she freed her hand, tensed it into a half-claw, and jabbed him in the middle of his neck with her fingertips.

The man gagged and let go of her completely in order to grab his throat. Wraith immediately sat up and went for his eyes, clawing like a lioness. Screaming like a madwoman. Her fists flew, inflicting damage that caused the man to gasp and moan. Until he managed to choke out a name.

"Foster."

The name slammed into Wraith and instantly triggered her memory even as it caused her body to freeze. Foster. The little boy with the distinctive name who'd given her his kitten for safekeeping. Her hesitation cost her.

The man grabbed her shoulders, slammed her back down to the ground, and slapped her again. Several times. She responded by rearing up and biting his throat as if she was Dex. The man screamed and pulled away, giving her time to go for her weapon. But the press of cold metal against her temples told her he'd gotten to his first.

She froze, but spit out, "Why did you say that name? Foster? Why?"

He caressed her skin with the barrel of the gun. "It was my safety measure. You seemed to really like the little tyke at the bus station. Doug pointed it out to me. You even took his little kitten, didn't you?"

Doug. Of course. The man she'd chased down in Wyoming while Caleb had subdued his friend. What had been his name?

Emerson? No. Emmett.

So they'd been watching her at the bus station, too. Had probably been getting ready to jump her before Caleb had shown up. "Did you hurt the little boy?" she asked, her voice a low growl that dripped with menace. She pictured Foster's face. The purity of innocence in his eyes. Had those eyes gone dim because of her?

Amazingly, the man sounded insulted. "I don't kill little kids. Especially human kids. We're already being overtaken by you freaks. Someday he'll know to fight you, not make friends with you. As for me? I shoulda just shot you the first time I had a chance, but I can fix that now."

She'd never felt relief at discovering someone's bigotry before but she felt it now. If it helped save an innocent life like Foster, she'd deal with the other repercussions any day of the week. "Wraiths don't die, you idiot. Whoever sent you here is playing you. You can't hurt me, and if you try, I'll just come back and make it worse for you."

"Ahhh. Wraiths can't die, but I know you happened to have a particularly important birthday a few months ago. That changes things, right? And from the looks of you, your body isn't up to regenerating. I wonder why? Did you use up all your energy fucking the pretty boy outside?"

"How . . . ?" Wraith blinked, straining to see. How did he know about her birthday? That she and Caleb had been intimate?

"Any last words before you die?"

THIRTY

When the shape-shifter didn't answer him, Caleb turned swiftly to Dex. "When was the last time you saw her?"

"She was at the bar chatting it up with a tall human. I didn't see her again, not until we saw . . ."

Shit, Caleb thought. No, of course they hadn't seen her. Caleb had been so intent on intercepting Natia before she reached Wraith, and Dex had been talking to the vampire at the table, pretending to be drunk while keeping his eye on Lucy. They'd been sloppy, and even though they hadn't thought there was any reason for Wraith to be studiously watched, they should have kept tabs on her. Hell, that was twice as true given the fact someone was gunning for her—something Dex didn't know, but Caleb certainly did because of their run-in with Doug and Emmett.

And what about Wraith? She knew better than to leave without giving them a heads-up, which meant she probably hadn't left on her own.

"Where is she?" Caleb spat as he leaned harder on the shifter's throat. Her lids fluttered as she struggled to hold on to consciousness, but Caleb refused to give her any air. Her mouth—what seemed to be Wraith's mouth—moved in an effort to speak, but no sound came out. A whimper escaped her, one so pathetic, he almost automatically backed away.

Caleb had to remind himself that this wasn't really Wraith, but it was harder than he would have thought. He knew Wraith's body intimately now, and this shifter *looked* like her, right down to the recent sparks of blue in her eyes. How the hell was that possible?

Her mouth moved again, and Caleb eased back on his hold, but just slightly.

"Can't breathe—"

"Tell me where she is!"

"Can't—"

Caleb immediately put more pressure on her throat, and the shifter's eyes rolled back in her head.

"O'Flare," Dex said from behind him. "Back off. You have to let her go."

Caleb's mind was spinning. His body felt too hot and he knew his rage was controlling him. He was out of control.

"—let her get some air into her first. O'Flare! Think of Wraith!"

Think of Wraith. He did, and that gave him the measure of restraint he needed.

He hesitated only a moment before backing off.

The shifter took in great gulps of air. Her body shimmered back into her alien-like form, and a rose-scented cloud wafted around them.

He was beginning to hate the smell of roses.

"Thank you," the shifter said, its voice gravelly. It was hard to tell a female shifter from a male, except when they talked. This one's voice was low and masculine.

"Where is the wraith?" He spaced the words concisely and thought of the way she'd questioned Doug, the man they'd caught in Wyoming. The way she'd pulled out her knife, prepared to use it to get her information. He wouldn't need a knife to rip this shifter apart if he didn't start talking.

"I saw her go in the bathroom. I took the opportunity to . . ."

Caleb glanced at Dex. He struggled to keep hold of Lucy, who alternately fought him and swayed as if about to lose consciousness. God damn it, how were they—

The door to the club suddenly swung open, bumping against the shifter. "Hunt, you gonna let me out of here?" a cross voice inquired.

Cursing, Caleb grabbed the shifter and pulled him out of the way. The female who'd spoken slipped outside and closed the door. It was the vamp Dex had been talking to. She took them all in, including the shape-shifter, with calm eyes. "You need help?" she asked silkily.

Dex cocked a brow. "You willing to take care of my friend here?" he asked, tipping his eyes toward Lucy, who seemed to have fallen asleep.

The vamp quirked her lips. "Depends. How good a friend is she?"

Narrowing his eyes, Dex said, "A good friend. Very good. Meaning, if anything happens to her while she's in your care, I'm gonna make you really sorry you decided to stop at my table to flirt with me."

Instead of taking offense, the vamp simply laughed and nodded. "In that case, since you asked so nicely, yes." She reached out, eased Lucy away from Dex, and easily swung Lucy into her arms, cradling her like a baby. "But there's something I need to tell you. About the feline who left out the back. She—"

"Not now," Caleb snapped, mad as hell that Natia's presence had distracted him for even a split second from Wraith.

Instantly, Dex strode toward the shape-shifter and nodded to Caleb. "Go."

Wraith heard the sound of a gun cocking and shut her eyes. Not because it would hide anything, but because she wanted her last images to be of Caleb, untainted by this horror. "Do it," she said, knowing this could be the moment her immortality failed her.

It was as good a time as any, she supposed. She'd just experienced the pleasure that was possible in life. Why not kill her when she'd regret it the most?

"Wraith!" She heard Caleb's voice over the din outside. Her attacker's body jerked, indicating he'd heard, as well.

A surge of hope raced through Wraith's body, bringing with it a jolt of adrenaline and energy. Her mind cleared. Her attacker was distracted. His body open and vulnerable. And sometimes the most obvious choice was the only choice.

Wraith raised her knee into the man's groin. He doubled over in pain, and she threw him off, quickly curling her body into a crouch. With a primal scream, she propelled herself toward him . . .

She felt the pain an instant before she registered the cracking sound of a gun going off. The impact of the bullet flung her backward until she hit the ground. Surrounded by darkness, fire traveled from her abdomen, sizzling through her veins and into her extremities.

It wasn't that bad, she realized, being shot.

Compared to everything she'd experienced over the past ten years, it wasn't that bad.

Tentatively, she touched her belly, then jerked when she felt the warm, sticky wetness covering it. Blood. Warm.

She smiled, but it wasn't with relief. It figures, she thought again.

The door to the bathroom flew open. "Wraith!" The lights sprang on.

She registered the shock on Caleb's face the instant he saw her. Her attacker's back was to her and she whimpered, trying to call a warning as she saw his arm rising. With a roar, Caleb flew at him.

Wraith struggled to get up, falling back when fingers of pain twisted inside her, yanking her organs out one by one. Her vision wavered and darkness descended. Just before she passed out, she heard the reverberation of another gun going off.

Caleb.

THIRTY-ONE

Caleb heard a gunshot reverberate just before something hit him in the side.

It was like being bitten by a gnat. Insignificant. His entire focus was on the bearded man whose eyes were filled with fear—on the need to kill him, quickly and efficiently so he could get to Wraith, who was lying in a heap on the floor, eyes closed, her body bleeding out on the bathroom tile even though she wasn't supposed to bleed.

Emmett, the same man he'd chased down outside that restaurant in Evanston, tried backing away, but Caleb wrapped his arms around him, his forward momentum slamming them into the opposite wall hard enough that the impact shuddered through both of them.

He didn't take the time to disarm him or question him, not even about how he'd managed to get away from the police. He didn't even take the time to ensure the man knew what was coming so he'd feel that wild, vicious fear in the few seconds before he died.

Grabbing Emmett on either side of his face, Caleb twisted his neck and instantly heard bone snap. Dropping the man's body to the floor, Caleb rushed to Wraith.

The blood—her blood—was everywhere.

He laid his hands gently on her chest, getting yet another shock when he felt the strong, frantic beat of her heart. Damn it, he'd known she was changing, but not to this degree. Not to the point where she could die. Why hadn't she told him?

Shutting his eyes, he waited for his ancestors to infuse him with their healing power. Only it didn't happen.

"Damn it," Caleb gritted out. "Help me! Please."

But despite his plea, no one answered.

Swiftly, Caleb spread her jacket open, wincing when he saw the damage to her flesh. Rising, he lunged for the basket of white hand towels by the sink, then methodically covered Wraith's wound with a makeshift compress and applied pressure. Memories of his time on the battlefield crashed through him, of soldiers, human and Otherborn, moaning and writhing as they fought death.

Wraith was doing neither, but it was because she was unconscious, not because she was giving up. He wasn't letting her give up.

"Get back, damn it!"

Caleb's head swung around at the sound of Dex's voice. Only then did he see the crowd gathered at the doorway.

"Move away from the door and let me the fuck through!" Dex pushed his way past the nearest gatherers. "Damn it," he whispered. His gaze landed on Emmett then Wraith before meeting Caleb's eyes.

Caleb shook his head. "I tried healing her . . . it won't . . . she won't . . ." Was that trembling voice really his, Caleb vaguely thought, or was it a voice from the crowd?

He didn't recognize it.

Turning back to Wraith, he felt moisture gather in his eyes. She looked paler than normal, and unbelievably, her mouth was tilted up on one end in what could only be seen as a smirk. A twisted recognition that she was finally getting what she'd wanted. An end to her pain.

Pressing his lips together, Caleb shook his head. "No. You don't need that now. You're not alone, damn it, so don't you dare leave."

But when he checked, her pulse was thready. His own heart almost stopped when hers did. "Dex!"

Dex swiftly kneeled by Caleb's side.

"Keep your hands on the compresses," he snapped. "Tight."

The were's hands replaced his, and Caleb immediately moved to straddle Wraith. He positioned his hands over her heart and began pumping the organ for her. "I'm not letting you go, Wraith. Do you hear me? You're not alone. You have me. You have the team. So stay with me, damn it. Stay with me."

Grim, Dex watched O'Flare work on Wraith.

With her blood oozing through the cloth and through his fingers, Dex held no hope that Caleb would be bringing her back. The bullet had hit her vital organs, and somehow she'd obviously acquired not only the ability to bleed, but to die.

Vaguely, he wondered if Caleb had known. If he had, he knew exactly how Caleb would feel once he accepted Wraith was gone. He could see the terror and grief and guilt on the human's face quite well.

Instinctively, Dex looked away, the emotion on O'Flare's face too intense for comfort. He could still hear him, though, and the words that alternated between strong and angry, soft and pleading.

"Damn you, Wraith. Come on. You're too big a bitch to give up. Come on, damn you. Please, come on."

The crowd at the door shifted until, suddenly, the female vampire was there, her arms supporting Lucy, whose eyes were open now, but watching them with a blank expression that made Dex wonder how much she actually saw or understood. He didn't have to wonder that about the vampire. Her beautiful features were set into a grave expression as she stared, not at his teammates, but at *him*. The knowledge of Wraith's death was there, mirroring his own thoughts. And for once in his life, Dex hoped like hell his instincts were wrong.

THIRTY-TWO

Pain surrounded Wraith. Although she tried to escape, to move physically away or to slip into her own mind and disappear, something was stopping her. Hands held her body down and a voice talked to her, refusing to give her the quiet she needed to slip away. It was the mage, she realized. Somehow he'd gotten her back.

Or maybe he'd never lost her.

Maybe the life she'd imagined in the past few years had all been a dream. A way for her body to cope with what he was doing with his knives and needles and hammers.

She'd never fought in the War.

She'd never been on the Para-Ops team.

She'd never met Caleb or been touched by him.

Loved by him.

A pathetic whimper escaped from her mouth, and she couldn't even chastise herself.

He'd never said the words, but that's what Caleb had made her feel like when he'd touched her. Like she was being loved. And it had all been her imagination. The thought hurt more than what the mage was doing to her.

"Wraith . . ."

She frowned when she heard the voice because it didn't sound like the mage. It sounded like Caleb.

"Don't leave me, Wraith. Stay with us. We need you. I need you."

The words gave her the strength to try and open her eyes again. This time, when she did, she felt something jerk in her chest.

"Yes . . ." Caleb breathed. "That's it, that's it."

Her lids flickered and she glimpsed light. Shadows hovering over her. Her vision cleared until she saw it. Her very own dark angel.

Caleb.

Then the darkness overtook her again.

THIRTY-THREE

As soon as Caleb got Wraith's heart beating again and saw her eyes flicker with life, Dex had shown the club owner their IDs and cleared the place. Now the were glowered at Caleb, who'd gone back to kneeling next to Wraith on the bathroom floor.

"What do you mean, you're not going to call Mahone?" Dex yelled. "Have you fucking lost your mind?"

Caleb glared up at Dex. "I'm telling you, it's the best way. We pretend she died. That we both did . . ."

"That might not be too difficult given the way you're bleeding out."

He didn't bother glancing down at the wound he couldn't even feel. "It's shallow. Hell, I can treat it myself. But listen to me, Dex. You've seen for yourself how Wraith has changed. She wasn't letting anyone know and there must be a reason for that. And we don't know what Mahone would do with her or the information. We need to talk to her first."

"You and Wraith saved Mahone's life, and you don't trust him enough with this?"

"No," he said calmly. "I don't."

They stared at each other for several seconds before Dex

shook his head. "We need to get her to a hospital. You revived her, but her wounds aren't closing."

The were was right, but Caleb was a doctor and he *cared* about Wraith. He wouldn't let anything happen to her. He knew what she'd want—time—and he was going to give it to her. "I know that, Dex."

"Yeah. Did you know she was changing?"

Caleb pressed his lips together before reluctantly answering. "I saw the clues. I asked her about it but . . ." His voice trailed off when Dex laughed.

"Let me guess? You got distracted? Because maybe another thing had changed, too? Her ability to feel pain? So you fucked her instead of figuring out what the hell is going on with her?"

If he wasn't so concerned about Wraith, Caleb would have met the were toe-to-toe. As it was, he snapped, "Back off, Dex. Now."

"I'll back off when you admit your dick led you someplace your head wouldn't have."

"And yours didn't?" Caleb looked pointedly at Lucy, who was sitting next to the female vampire. The two of them were talking softly. A minute earlier, Caleb had checked Lucy and her vitals were normal. Her body was reacting as if she'd had a little too much to drink but was recovering.

"I did what I needed to do to help Lucy. What's your excuse?"

"I'll take Wraith back to another hotel. Make sure we aren't followed. I can treat her there—"

"Had much experience treating wraiths? 'Cause I think—"

The vampire female cleared her throat, making both their heads jerk around. "As entertaining as this bickering is, it's obvious neither of you knows what's happening here. Let me enlighten you. The wraith is turning, but she hasn't reached the point of no return. Not yet. Her body is simply taking longer to rejuvenate. Look, her wounds are starting to heal right now."

Both Dex and Caleb dropped their gazes to Wraith's body. Caleb swiped away some of the blood staining her skin. It was subtle, but the vampire was right. Wraith's wounds had started to heal.

"You know what's happening to her?" Caleb asked.

"She's dying," the vampire confirmed softly.

"But you just said her wounds—"

She shook her head. "Not now. Maybe not for a few months. But she's ten, and before she's eleven, she's going to die."

"How the hell do you know that?" Dex asked when Caleb clearly wasn't able to speak.

"I knew a wraith once. She was . . . a friend."

The way she said "friend" made Caleb immediately think they'd been lovers. "Did you know the wraith before her tenth year or only after?"

"After. I knew her only a month before it happened."

"I've never heard—"

"It's a closely guarded secret among wraiths. For obvious reasons."

"Do you think she knew? What was coming, I mean?"

"She knew."

Caleb glanced at Dex. "What if she knew in Korea? And before starting this mission? Why would she—"

"What else was she going to do?" Dex said. "Sit around and twiddle her thumbs?"

Lucy moaned and shifted. With effort, she sat up and raised a shaky hand to her head. "Dex . . .?"

Dex immediately moved to her side. The vampire smiled and rose. "You should sit with her."

In a flash, Dex's hand whipped out, and his fingers wrapped around the vampire's wrist. "You're not . . . I mean . . ." He coughed. "You're leaving?"

With an arched brow, the vampire stared at the were's fingers. "You don't need me for anything else," she said lightly. "Do you?"

Dex opened his mouth as if to protest, then slowly released her. She continued toward the door, then turned to Caleb. "Has she told you anything about who she is? Any memories that she's had about her human life?"

"No. Does memory return in a wraith's tenth year, as well?"

"I don't know the answer to that question. But my friend, she was obsessed with finding out who she was. Became more and more so as the days went on. Is your wraith the same way?"

Caleb remembered how upset Wraith had been with Mahone when he'd changed the mission on her. "Yes, only I wouldn't say she was becoming more obsessed with time . . ." In fact, now that he thought about it, Wraith had seemed to become *less* obsessed with that goal. She hadn't even mentioned it again since he'd found her at the bus station, but that could simply be because she'd agreed to finish the mission.

What if finding out her identity had been more important than any of them had realized? What if, by dragging her to Los Angeles, he'd somehow turned her from a course that might have saved her?

He cursed even as the vampire seemed to read his thoughts. And maybe, despite the fact that it would be breaking a whole host of rules, she actually did. "It's what all wraiths are obsessed with. Becoming more obsessed at the end of their lives makes sense. If they became wraiths because of something that happened in their human lives, then—"

"Why not link their deaths to the same thing, as well?" Caleb finished for her. "So what you're saying is that not finding out what killed them as humans is probably what kills them as wraiths, too? That if they did know and resolved something in their lives, that might somehow stop the turnings and their eventual deaths?"

"It's just a theory," she murmured sadly. "I never had anyone to talk it out with before. No one who'd cared for a wraith the way I had. But you care about her. That's obvious."

Caleb was aware of Dex listening, his gaze still on the vampire. The were's presence didn't impede the swiftness of Caleb's answer. "I care about her. More than anyone or anything," he said.

The vampire's smile radiated both pity and compassion. "Then you need to find out who she is. Fast."

THIRTY-FOUR

Wraith awoke in a comfortable bed with down pillows and a plush white comforter that smelled of lavender. The grittiness in her eyes and the fogginess in her brain made her think she must have slept again, but her body was achy and her head throbbed. If she'd slept, she should feel refreshed, not like she'd just been run over—if not by a semitruck, then at the very least a golf cart or an ATV.

She scanned the room until her gaze landed on Caleb, sitting in a chair near the foot of her bed. His expression was grim.

"Why didn't you tell me, Wraith?"

She blinked at the anger in his voice. Instinctively got her defenses in place. "Tell you what?"

"You're dying."

Those two simple words knocked her defenses down with ease. Her eyes widened. "How did you—"

"Dex met a vampire with a certain degree of knowledge about your kind. Do you even remember last night?"

She struggled to get her mind working. Of course she remembered last night. They'd begun their surveillance at the club. She'd been talking to someone . . . Willie . . . no, Wilma . . . and she'd gone to the bathroom with her, right after she'd seen

Caleb with the feline. Anger at the princess—at Caleb—made her hand itch to slap him, but then . . .

She jerked to a sitting position, wincing at the fire that flamed across her ribs. Falling back against the pillows, she took quick breaths of air (even as part of her still marveled that she could), trying to work through the pain so she could talk. "The . . . the bathroom . . . Someone attacked me!"

Caleb nodded grimly. "Emmett. The man I chased down at the restaurant. I should've killed him then, but don't worry, I didn't make the same mistake."

She swallowed hard. She knew Caleb didn't take killing lightly. The fact that his eyes held no remorse told her he'd kill Emmett again and again if he had the chance, each time using a method more painful than the last. That, as well as his touch, told her he cared about her. Told her that kissing the little cat at the nightclub had been more about protecting the mission and Wraith than about getting his rocks off. Even as that realization spread through her like warm honey, she forced herself to think about the attack. The mission. The things that, unlike her feelings for Caleb, could be analyzed and worked and controlled, given enough information.

"You said you talked to a vampire. Someone who knows about wraiths?"

"She befriended a wraith right before she died. But I want to know why you didn't tell us what was happening. About how extensively and quickly the changes were happening."

She plucked at the sheets on the bed, then folded her hands in her lap. "What does it matter? It was happening, and there was nothing any of us could do about it."

He stood, pushing his chair back so hard it toppled over. "You can't be serious. Resignation. That's your response? You're just going to let it happen? You? Because I know what comes when this change of yours is complete, Wraith, and I'm almost certain you do, too. In case you don't, though, let me lay it out for you—death!"

"I'm already dead," she said tonelessly.

"Damn it, do not play that card now. I'm talking about the end, Wraith. Your end!"

"And exactly what do you think I can do about that?" she snapped, wanting to cover her ears and hum to drown out his words. He was basically accusing her of being a coward, just as he had before. But it wasn't cowardice to accept one's fate. To give in gracefully and maybe—just maybe—even look forward to some peace. Was it?

"How about fight? Search for answers? Find out who you are? How you died? Ask. For. Fucking. Help. From the people who care most about you."

Wraith snorted. "I tried that already, remember? This mission was more important."

"It was more important given the information you gave us, but you left a little something out, didn't you? Did you really think I'd let this mission get in the way of saving your life?"

He said it with such conviction. As if helping her wouldn't have given him a moment's pause, even if it meant abandoning his former girlfriend or risking the felines declaring war again. For what? For *her*? A female who was already *dead*? He was fooling himself, but he couldn't fool her. "I don't have a life, Caleb. I'm *dead*. Why can't you get that through your head? Dead, dead, dead, dead—"

His face flushed, and he looked angry enough to kill her himself. "Stop! That's not true and you know it. I had your fucking blood all over my hands when your heart stopped, and it was still there when I got your heart pumping again, so don't try that bullshit on me, Wraith!" His breaths were noisy, his eyes wild, his nostrils flaring.

So she *had* died. And he'd brought her back. She shook her head. "I don't know what you want me to say," she said quietly. "We . . ." She swallowed and instinctively replaced the words she wanted to say with ones she was more familiar with. "We *fucked*, O'Flare. And yeah, it felt good. Thank you, and I mean that from the bottom of my recently revived heart. But nothing has changed. You're alive. I'm dead. I'm probably going to die again really soon, no matter what you did to prevent it from happening in that bathroom, but we'll get this mission done. Afterward, I'll see what I can do about—"

He laughed, a caustic sound that took the words right out of her mouth. His eyes narrow slits in his handsome face, he moved closer until he loomed over her. "You seriously think this mission's still viable? That even if it was, you'd work it? The mission's over. We blew our cover last night. Someone else is going to handle it."

It took her a second to comprehend what he was saying. The

mission was over? Because of her and the damn man who'd gotten the better of her in the bathroom? Failure was a heavy weight on her shoulders as she said, "Then I guess it's time for me to go."

Throwing off her blankets, she sat up, wincing as she did, but she breathed deep until she managed to get to her feet. To her utter amazement, Caleb calmly walked up to her and lightly pushed her chest so she fell back onto the bed.

"Do not piss me off any more than you already have, Wraith."

She narrowed her eyes. "Don't think because you've given me an orgasm or two that I'll even hesitate to take you down, Caleb."

He flashed his strong, white teeth in a feral grin. "Go for it."

They glared at each other, and she really tried to muster the strength to pop him in the face, but she couldn't even make it to her feet again. To cover for her weakness, feeble as the attempt was, she said, "Did Lucy get any takers last night?"

The way Caleb blinked instantly told Wraith something had happened to the mage. Her chest filled with dread. "What happened, Caleb?"

When he told her, she shook her head. "Where's the shape-shifter?"

"Last I saw, Dex had him tied up and had called the Bureau to pick him up."

"We need to talk to him. Find out who he's working for."

Caleb looked ready to throttle her again. "Didn't you hear anything I said, Wraith? Let the next team handle it. Hell, Dex and Lucy can work the mission in some way, but you and I need to concentrate on you. On finding out who you are."

"Talking to the shape-shifter *will* be concentrating on me, Caleb. Because how do you think the shape-shifter took my form in the first place? He had to have my DNA."

"He could have lifted that from your glass at the bar. Or rubbed against you when he was walking by. We wouldn't have known because he could have adopted twenty other identities while he was doing it."

"But why would he have counted on chance? Emmett was there to get me, and he got his orders from someone who knew I would be at Knox's wedding reception. Maybe he and the shifter were working together, and the shifter had my DNA before he walked into the club, in which case he might know something about me that I don't."

She could tell she'd said what she needed to convince him. She didn't believe it herself, but if it got Caleb off her back and to the shape-shifter sooner, so be it.

Suddenly, it occurred to her what she was doing. She was resisting his attempts to find out who she was. Because she really no longer cared.

The realization floored her, and she had to brace her palms on the bed to keep from crumpling. Seeing Caleb in the bar with the feline princess and then getting attacked in the bathroom, facing her impending death—it had all changed something inside her. Or maybe she'd changed before that, when Caleb had taught her the meaning of pleasure and intimacy. She no longer cared who she'd been, she realized.

She was Wraith. A member of the world's first Para-Ops team. She belonged in this world, and so what if she'd been betrayed by a friend or two? Big deal if she was going to die like every other human. She'd packed decades into the past ten years, and she needed to stop worrying about the past and the future. She needed to do what she was meant to. Hunt the bad guys. Stop them from hurting felines.

And spend as much time with Caleb O'Flare as she could before she exited this life with some dignity.

Caleb had no clue what she was thinking. He was obviously still focused on her statement about the shape-shifter having come to the club with her DNA. "Who would have DNA from you?"

She almost smiled but stopped herself, knowing he'd view it as her mocking him, when it was really about her knowing him. Maybe even better than she knew herself. And what she knew of him, she liked.

More than liked.

She licked her lips and answered, even though her gaze had focused on his mouth, and in her mind she was already kissing him. "Colt, Ramsey, Mahone. And the mage who experimented on me."

"It wasn't the mage."

He said the words with such confidence, such finality, that Wraith blinked. "How . . . how can you know that?" When

Caleb didn't immediately answer, she narrowed her eyes. "Caleb?"

"What did you think I'd do after I saw those videos of him torturing you, Wraith? How did you think Mahone got me to play his stooge? Did you really think it was because he asked nicely?"

"You found the mage?" Wraith whispered, the notion that Caleb had gotten even remotely close to that kind of evil making her shiver.

But Caleb shook his head. "He was already in federal custody. Had been for years. He was a mage leader, however, with a lot of money and influence. He'd built a strong defense team around him, and that team had filed enough paperwork to guarantee the mage would die in prison before he was executed for his crimes."

"And you made sure that didn't happen? You killed him? For me?" Even as she felt horror at the thought—that Caleb would have to live with the stain from a cold-blooded execution on his hands—he shook his head. Her brow furrowed in confusion.

"I made sure he died slowly and painfully, Wraith, but I didn't actually kill him. I wanted to. Desperately. But I . . ." He swallowed hard and Wraith stood, a sudden strength thrumming through her body.

"But what?" she prompted.

"I didn't want to touch him. If you touched me, if you looked at me, I didn't want you to even think about the fact that I'd touched a man who'd caused you so much pain. Is that stupid?"

Moving purely on instinct, she walked closer to him. She lifted her fingers to his lips and covered them. They felt soft and hard, warm and cool, as complex in nature as the man they belonged to.

"Caleb . . ." she said softly.

His eyes blazed above her fingers.

"I don't find that stupid at all. I'd heard he was captured sometime during the War, but I . . . but I never knew for sure. Thank you for telling me. For caring enough to avenge me. For bringing me back from the dead." She skimmed her fingers over his mouth and across his cheeks. His throat. "Now kiss me."

*　　*　　*

Caleb felt like someone had suddenly pushed his head under water and was holding him down so he couldn't breathe. The blue sparks in Wraith's eyes had expanded as he looked at her, until the blue had spread throughout her irises. The color glowed and sparkled like a million tiny sapphires, urging him to stay in their cool, crystalline depths.

Wraith slipped her fingers off his lips, but otherwise remained still. Watchful. Waiting.

He licked his lips and slowly, so slowly because he was reluctant to look away from her gaze, he lowered his head. His eyes closed the instant his lips touched hers.

She sighed. Melted into him as if she'd gone boneless. Her body conformed its shape to his, and he gently cradled her, ever mindful of the wound in her side. Her lips sipped at his, retreating and then coming back for more. His tongue followed, tracing her lips with a reverent skim until he realized she was smiling.

As if she was happy.

It almost brought him to his knees.

Because he knew what she was doing. She wasn't kissing him off. She was saying good-bye. Not because she intended to go anywhere, necessarily, but because she was no longer fighting what she was or what was going to happen to her. More than anything, her acceptance scared him.

He pulled back, wanting to argue with her and shake her until she agreed to fight. To try something instead of just waiting for death to claim her. But her expression was one of utter contentment, and he choked back his words, knowing how precious that must be to her.

Lifting his hands, he threaded his fingers through her hair. It was still predominantly white, with chocolate brown roots. She closed her eyes as if savoring his touch and tilted her head back, exposing the long, graceful arch of her neck. Her skin had only the slightest blue tinge to it now, and when he bent down to kiss the corner of her mouth, he felt the slight puffs of air as she breathed out. In. Out. In . . .

"What do you want, Wraith?" he asked, suddenly wanting to give her everything. "If I could give you one thing, anything in the world, what would you ask for?"

Her eyelids drooped, as if they were weighed down, and he felt his own lids getting heavy. Her hand caressed his face, drifted down his chest, then moved to his groin. He sucked in a breath when she cupped him through his pants.

"I want you to make love to me, Caleb. Tenderly. Slowly. With all the patience in the world. Not because you're afraid of hurting me, but because you never want the moment to end. Just like me."

Her tone, her words, her meaning—they all slammed into him like an out-of-control locomotive.

Without further thought, he picked her up, still mindful of her wound. Sighing, she wrapped her arms around his neck and laid her hand on his shoulder. As she stared at him with her beautiful blue eyes, Caleb couldn't help thinking this must be a dream, and he prayed he'd never wake up. That he could keep her here with him, lost in this moment for an eternity.

Without taking another step, he kissed her again, using his lips and tongue to give her what she wanted, exactly how she'd asked for it. Tenderly. Slowly.

But he found he couldn't maintain his patience for very long.

He wanted her naked, her flesh against his, her hands on his body. Sliding and sucking and nibbling each other for hours until they were both exhausted but still unable to stop. Putting her down on the bed, he slipped her out of the loose sweats and T-shirt he'd dressed her in. Keeping his palms flat, he started at her shoulders and smoothed his hands along her body in ever-expanding circles. Over her breasts. Her stomach. Her hips and thighs and calves. They were still riddled with scars, but he barely noticed them. They were normal. They were . . . Wraith.

Soon, his mouth hovered over her soft, warm core and he buried his face there, breathing her in. Her fingers tangled in his hair, but she didn't rush him. Now it was his tongue he used to pleasure her. Flicking and curling around her pink, dewy flesh so slowly he wondered if he was trying to drive himself insane. The thought led to another, and rather than feeling an ounce of apprehension, he savored the rightness of it.

Pushing himself up and over her, he straddled her with his knees on either side of her hips. She looked up at him with the same small smile on her lips, although her eyes were mere slits now, her eyelashes fluttering as she struggled to keep them open.

"Do you trust me, Wraith?" he asked.

She hesitated, then breathed, "More than anyone or anything."

"Then will you let me have you? In a way I've never had another female before?"

In response, she shifted until he no longer hemmed her in, spread her thighs wide and lightly clasped his sides to pull him in close.

The tip of his dick unerringly found her, and he hissed at the first contact of turgid flesh with moist fire. She bit her lip and finally closed her eyes, her face going taut as he pushed himself into her, past the muscles that hugged him, a little at a time. He took her so slowly, so carefully, that by the time he was fully seated inside her, he was sweating bullets and his arms were shaking. Carefully, he bent his arms until he was lying fully on top of her, his face close to hers.

He didn't move. Her eyes were closed now, her expression tight with pleasure. He closed his eyes, too, and then he tranced himself. He opened himself, everything he was and ever wanted to be, to the female lying in his arms.

He felt the peace first. The silent lull of time, as if he was being rocked to sleep by the arms of his ancestors. They were silent now, and all he heard was the light breeze of the Otherworld around him. They were alone in that middle place, with only each other to keep themselves anchored. Slowly, his skin began to tingle, and he savored the familiar pleasure of being inside her, this female who was so strong yet so needy at the same time. Needy for *him*.

He waited. Waited. Then he began rocking his hips softly. Withdrawing just slightly before pushing back into her. Doing it again and again, with each thrust pulling back farther and farther and returning deeper and deeper.

Soon, he felt his pleasure spike. Knew when Wraith's did, too, by the way her body suddenly bowed beneath his. He opened his eyes and stared at her. Her mouth opened, and he heard her labored pants for air, as well as the tiny sound of fear she made.

"Caleb!"

"It's okay, Wraith," he soothed. "It's just us. Sharing the pleasure we're feeling. Heightening each other's as well as our—" He bit back his words as his hips moved forward, driving his cock deeper than he'd ever been inside her. Lava began to flow through his veins, burning him up inside with enough pleasure that he welcomed the fire and knew she did, too. Because he was feeling exactly what she was feeling, and she was feeling what he was. "Oh . . . God . . ." he groaned.

"It's too good. Oh God, Caleb, too . . ." she moaned.

He blinked and tried to focus on Wraith. He didn't want her to be afraid, but his hips moved faster, and the sensations built on one another until he knew he was pounding her into the mattress, and he didn't want to stop . . . didn't want to stop . . .

". . . stop! Don't stop, Caleb." It was Wraith's voice, and he suddenly became aware that as heavy as his thrusts were, she was countering them, moving her hips, pushing up toward him, keeping pace without faltering. The smile was back on her face, dazzling him with its intensity, and when the world exploded, taking the sun and stars with it, all he could think was, "I can't live without this. I can't live without her."

He didn't know how much time passed before he finally roused himself enough to prop up on one elbow. Immediately, he saw the blood staining the sheets, her side, and his own. "Oh shit!" He leaped up, horrified, and got down on his knees to check her injury. "I'm so sorry. I completely forgot about—"

Wraith's eyes were closed, and her head turned to the side when she muttered, "If you apologize again, you're going to really piss me off, Caleb." She yawned. "And since I really want you to do that again soon, I'd rather sleep than get mad, okay?"

He shook his head, then couldn't believe it when she actually did fall asleep. He finished tending to her wound, cursing the whole time, then covered her with a sheet. Stalking to the bathroom, he washed his hands and braced his arms on the sink to stare at his reflection in the mirror.

That had been life-altering, and he knew exactly why. He'd given Wraith what she'd wanted and what he'd wanted, as well. He'd made *love* to her.

He loved her, damn it. And what did he do now? There was no treatment for what ailed her. No medicine. No one to beg, bribe, or threaten to ensure her safety. Except . . .

The Goddess Essenia, he thought. He'd prayed to her just like everyone else had on occasion, but he'd never tried to seek her out. Didn't even know if that was possible. But he of all people believed in the spirits of the Otherworld, the place Essenia was thought to inhabit. If he could journey there, somehow meet the Goddess with his ancestors' help, maybe he could do what he'd always been meant to.

Heal.

Heal Wraith, and in doing so, heal her body and her soul, and fulfill whatever purpose the earth had contemplated when it had birthed her just over ten years ago.

He returned to the bedroom to check on Wraith and saw she was still sleeping. He hesitated, wondering if he should tell her about his hopes or not. Then he heard the heavy knocks at his door.

Cursing, he swiftly exited the bedroom and closed the door. Even before he could reach the front door, however, he heard Dex. "O'Flare. Wraith. Open up! Please!"

Caleb's brows shot up. *Please?* From Dex Hunt? Something was seriously wrong.

Throwing open the door, Caleb didn't bother asking questions, but simply waited for Dex's words. He knew from the look on the were's face that it was going to be bad, but he couldn't have anticipated how bad.

"We've got trouble. Mahone called. Knox and Felicia were attacked."

"Shit," Caleb thought, but he took comfort in Dex's words. Attacked, not *killed*.

"That's not all, O'Flare," Dex warned. "According to Knox's brother, your ex, the feline princess, isn't to be trusted. Zeph implied that she might have something to do with the attack on Wraith. That something might be bogus about this whole mission. Her showing up last night seems to weigh heavily in that direction."

Caleb didn't bother arguing with Dex. He had no reason to doubt his words, and he'd determine for himself whether Natia had anything to do with the attack on Wraith. If she had . . . His fury wasn't a slow burn, but a hot flash that engulfed him. He'd always felt affection for Natia, but nothing would keep him from exacting vengeance if the feline had knowingly placed Wraith in jeopardy.

Through his dark thoughts, Dex's words continued to bleed through.

". . . that happened last night, I took Lucy to another hotel, as well. Just to be safe. I put her to bed. And then I slept out on the couch. When I . . . when I woke up this morning to check on her . . ." The were covered his face with his hands and rubbed at his eyes. He was shaking. Being eaten alive by emotions that he plainly wore on his sleeve, when just yesterday, Dex would rather have died than admit he felt them at all.

Caleb grabbed his arm and shook him, foregoing compassion in favor of need. "Where's Lucy, Dex?"

Dex dropped his hands, the grief on his face so raw he might as well have been bleeding from his eyes the way Mahone had been in that warehouse. "She's gone." As Caleb watched, the grief etching Dex's features gradually morphed into something darker. Something violent. "She's gone and I have no idea how she got out or who took her. Lucy's gone."

A scream erupted behind Caleb, but it was muffled by the bedroom door.

Wraith.

Throwing off the shock of Dex's words, Caleb bolted for the bedroom door and threw it open. The bed was empty, the sheets still stained with remnants of Wraith's blood. He sensed Dex behind him.

The were muttered, "What the . . ."

Another scream pierced his ears. Swiftly, Caleb ran to the bathroom and came to an abrupt stop in the doorway. Wraith was standing naked in front of the mirror. The sheet she had wrapped around herself was pooled at her feet. In the mirror, her expression was one of complete and utter horror. Her eyes met Caleb's, but he couldn't tell what she was feeling based on her expression.

He didn't have to.

The blue in her eyes was gone and the film that had once covered them was back.

And that wasn't the only thing that had changed. Her hair. Her skin. All the traces of humanity she'd been slowly acquiring over the past few days had disappeared.

Wraith was back.

And right now, she didn't look like she wanted to kill herself.

She looked like she wanted to kill everyone in the entire world, him and Dex included.

THIRTY-FIVE

As Lucy stood in the alley behind a small medical clinic, gasping from the painful aftereffects of teleportation, she glanced at the vampire, Jesmina, beside her. "Thank you for your help. I think."

Jesmina shrugged. "You won't be thanking me once the were finds out how you tricked him."

The thought of Dex's anger when he found her gone made her straighten, then shiver, but she tried to push past it. "You mean, how *we* tricked him. You told me what room to ask for, then teleported in to get me, remember? And Dex isn't my keeper."

"But he's your lover?"

Stiffening, Lucy studied Jesmina closely, but her expression was blank. So blank she knew the vamp's question was based on anything but idle curiosity. "Only because he was being nice."

Jesmina looked stunned, then laughed so long and so hard that Lucy flushed. "I mean . . . we aren't . . . Oh, you know perfectly well what I meant! You know what the feline heat can drive felines to do, after all."

"Yes. Far more than taking a were for a lover when you normally wouldn't. But I told you that based on the information

I uncovered from my friend. With respect to the feline rapes, you're the one who assumed I was right."

"My assumption is logical," Lucy said. "You recognized Natia as someone who's had contact with your friend. If you're right about what he's been doing, what *they've* been doing, then the felines are faking being raped." She shook her head. "I can't say which would be worse, you being right or wrong. As part feline, I'd like to think I wouldn't fake being raped, but if that meant freedom from the heat . . ." Lucy shrugged. Inside, however, she cringed. Despite the drugs she'd been given, she remembered everything that had happened earlier, including how wasted and out of control she'd been. It had been like she was two people—the one stumbling and stammering, oblivious that anything was wrong. And the one watching from the side-lines, knowing she was going to hate herself when the drugs wore off.

That had begun happening just as Dex had been dealing with the shape-shifter outside. She'd heard the vampire try to talk to Dex about Natia before Caleb had cut her off. Had remembered that fact as they'd sat in the bathroom while Dex and Caleb argued about what to do about Wraith. Lucy had questioned the vampire about Natia, and the vampire had told her she believed the feline rapes weren't rapes at all, but a desperate last resort by feline females to gain control over their own bodies. Stunned, Lucy had extracted her promise not to tell the others, and for her own reasons, the vampire had decided to play along. They'd devised a plan for her to get Lucy away from Dex sometime after Caleb had brought Wraith back to life.

Once they'd checked in to the appropriate room, Dex had tucked her into bed, and tears had filled her eyes when he'd gently kissed her good night. Because she'd been relieved but still worried about Wraith, she'd lain awake but had almost forgotten their plans until the vamp had teleported inside her hotel room, scaring the crap out of her. Now, Lucy could only hope the vampire wasn't lying about the felines and that she hadn't laid a trap for her.

The vampire was watching her with a somber expression. "I know a little about desperation myself. Another friend of mine . . . she needed information to save herself but could never get it. Just like you, in some ways."

At the vamp's words, Lucy paused with curiosity and sympathy, but she didn't have time to draw the vampire's feelings out. Not right now, anyway. "So this person you were telling me about . . . the one who performs the surgeries . . . ?"

The vampire sighed. "Alton Maddox. He's a good man. I've known him for years, but he has an unfortunate tendency to talk too much when he drinks. Like you. A few weeks ago, he mentioned he'd been doing some work for the felines. Something that will allow them to have more control over their bodies while at the same time giving him some extra cash for the clinic. I see him with felines all the time. They are his primary patients. But the one in the club, she stood out. Had an air that was different from the others."

"The air of royalty, replete with arrogance to spare," Lucy muttered.

The vampire laughed. "Not all royals are that arrogant, but I suppose more are than not. Anyway, I was curious, but he wouldn't say more. Only he had me over for dinner the day after the first rape occurred. When the story came on the telly, I could tell something was wrong. He was acting so strangely that I, well . . . I snuck a peek into his mind, just for a few seconds"— she rushed to explain, obviously aware that mind reading was prohibited by the Humanity Treaty—"but long enough to hear his thoughts. He was thinking that rape was the price she'd had to pay to gain her freedom. That was all I got before he sensed me and . . ." She shrugged. "He's refused to see me since."

"You didn't go to the police. Why?"

"I don't like the police as a general rule. I certainly wouldn't go to them without more information than that. I think the more relevant questions here are why you didn't tell your friend what I told you or where you were going tonight."

Lucy hesitated. She knew Dex would be worried when he woke and found her gone, but that couldn't be helped. If it turned out Jesmina was right, the Para-Ops team and Mahone would need to know, if only because the Bureau was spending valuable time and resources investigating crimes that weren't real. Not to mention the fact that falsely reporting a crime was a felony in itself.

The only problem was, if Jesmina was right, and the felines were lying in order to explain what they were doing to their own bodies, telling Mahone could prove disastrous not just to the felines involved, but to all felines. Because even without speaking to Alton Maddox, Lucy could guess what surgery he was performing on the felines—sterilization. A feline's sexual heat—which lasted seven days and then returned after another seven days—was nature's way of ensuring that the feline race flourished through procreation. That nature had gone a little overboard didn't matter. The felines worshipped their females' sexuality and ability to procreate. Any feline who voluntarily sterilized herself in order to be free of the heat would be a social outcast, rejected as a veritable heathen. That one of those felines was a royal princess would cause a scandal that wouldn't die for generations to come. Lucy assumed the rapes were a way to explain away infertility should it be discovered—the felines could always claim their attacker had rendered them infertile during the rapes, either deliberately or not. Lucy wasn't so sure that outing the feline's falsity was the right thing to do.

Then, of course, there was her personal reason for wanting to talk to Maddox alone.

She'd had sex with Dex, something she never would have done but for the heat and her desperation to do her job in spite of it. Even so, it was only a temporary cure. She could already feel her body beginning to cramp with the renewed need to be filled. Dex's touch had been incredible, but it still had felt wrong because she'd seen it for exactly what it was—a pity fuck. As much as she wanted to be strong, she wasn't certain she could be as strong as she needed to be, not when she had years of life still ahead of her. Unlike the others, she didn't need to be accepted by the feline society, so being sterilized sounded like a viable option . . . especially since she had no plans to ever mate or have a family.

Her mother had mated and procreated enough for both of them.

"I'll call as soon as I've spoken to Maddox and decided what to do," Lucy said. "But right now, I have to think about the felines first."

Jesmina nodded. "I'll wait here. But if you need me, yell. I . . . I won't like it, but if you feel it's necessary, I can use persuasion to get the information you need."

Lucy tilted her head. "Hopefully that won't be necessary. Mr. Maddox sounds like he's got a good heart. Let's just hope he trusts me, and that no matter what he says, we can think of a way to help."

Wraith sat on the couch in her hotel room and listened to Caleb and Dex talking in hushed tones, as if they were afraid the news of Lucy or Felicia would send her over the edge and into a void of insanity. For some reason, she found the notion hilarious. A laugh escaped her as she thought, Too late. I've been there for over ten years.

While she was worried for her friends, she was far more concerned with herself at the moment, and that was just pathetic. Felicia and Lucy had long, full futures ahead of them. *She* was a ticking time bomb that had already gone off multiple times. Instinctively, she knew it would only take one more detonation to kill her.

This time, she giggled, the sound rife with hysteria. Caleb broke away from Dex to crouch in front of her. He reached for her hands, but pulled back before he touched her. Wraith smirked.

Everything was back to normal, apparently.

"Wraith, Dex called Mahone. He said Felicia is fine. She was never assaulted. The report of an assault was a cover— they've spread news of it for a reason, but he'll fill us in on what happened when he sees us in person. Right now, we need to concentrate on finding Lucy, but based on the evidence, it doesn't appear she was taken against her will. She must have used her powers to enchant Dex or used a silencing spell so she could leave the hotel room undetected. The only question is why, and with whom? Can you think of anywhere she'd go?"

Wraith stared at Caleb and felt a rush of regret. He had the purest heart of anyone she'd ever known. Not perfect, but loyal and honorable. She knew he wouldn't rest until he found Lucy, and then he'd commit himself to finding out Wraith's identity, thinking that would save her somehow. Her longing to be saved, after everything she'd been through, made her angry, angry enough to say, "Maybe she had second thoughts about screwing Dex just so she could do her job."

Stunned silence followed Wraith's statement.

Flicking her gaze to the were, she asked, "Nothing to say,

Dex? Because I bet you were plenty persuasive when you asked her to take one for the good of the team."

The were didn't so much as flinch. "What do you want me to say? That could be exactly why she left."

Caleb straightened and cursed. "I kidded you about that in the bar, but how . . . ?" He turned to Wraith. "How did you know?"

"One of her admirers got fresh last night. Unbuttoned her shirt and pushed it aside like he wanted to mark her neck. Only, someone already had. She had whisker burns and bite marks. Wolf, not vampire." She glanced sideways at Dex. Part of her tried to hold back the words that were on the tip of her tongue, but the other part of her relished saying them. "So how was she? Did she know anything, or did you have to hold her hand the whole time?"

Dex finally started to look pissed. "Don't go there, Wraith, because you won't like where it leads us, I promise. Neither of you will."

She caught his meaning immediately and quickly glanced away. Thoughts of Caleb "holding her hand" played through her mind, taunting her with what she'd been given a small taste of. Then she thought of the horrified glances she and Caleb had shared in the bathroom mirror twenty minutes earlier, when they'd both realized she'd become full wraith again. As it had then, her stomach clenched, and her chest felt hollow and empty, devoid of life and purpose.

"Wraith, what about your friend Colt? The vampire you were dancing with at Knox's wedding? Did you see him talk to Lucy that night? Do you think she'd have any reason to trust him?"

Her gaze slowly catching Caleb's, Wraith struggled with confusion. Why was he asking her about Colt? What could the vamp possibly have to do with Lucy's disappearance?

"Lucy could have gotten out of her room without Dex knowing about it if someone teleported her out. A vampire," Caleb explained.

"And why would you think that vampire would be Colt?" she choked out.

Caleb and Dex briefly met gazes before Dex nodded, his features grim. Caleb turned to her. "I told Knox about the two men sent after you. He started looking at security footage from the night of the reception. After a time, he focused on Natia because of something his brother had said."

"Natia. I knew something was off with that one," Wraith interrupted, but she gleaned no satisfaction from being right. Regardless of what the feline had done, Caleb had been close to her at one time. Cared for her. Her betrayal was clearly hurting him. Just as Wraith knew his next words were going to make her hurt, as well. "So what does this have to do with Colt?"

"Knox discovered footage of the two of them talking. Money exchanged hands, and then Colt made some calls. Less than five hours later, your friend Joanna was attacked by two men. The same men who came after us."

"Circumstantial evidence," she muttered, but she knew it was enough. As much as she'd hated the drugs Colt had used to give her sexual relief, she'd never hated him. A part of her had always been grateful to him, but obviously he'd had no problem selling her out to the highest bidder. Vaguely, she wondered if she'd at least been worth more to him than the five hundred dollars Doug and Emmett had accepted.

"I'm sorry, Wraith. We can't know what Colt's involvement is, but if there's any chance he got to Lucy . . ."

"I never saw them together. Not once." Unable to bear the men's scrutiny for a second longer, Wraith stood up, strode into the bedroom, and slammed the door shut behind her. Helplessly, she looked at the bed, the sheets still rumpled from when she and Caleb had made love. Tentatively, she reached out and smoothed her hand over them. Then, firming her jaw, she snatched up her clothes and began to dress.

She's barely holding it together, Caleb thought, but unfortunately he didn't have time to coddle Wraith. He wanted to. He wanted to cradle her on his lap and comfort her and tell her she'd be okay no matter what she looked like or what she was, but he knew just how little she'd appreciate that. Plus, he wasn't at all certain he'd be telling her the truth. Regardless, they had other things they needed to deal with right now. Caleb ran his hands through his hair before looking at Dex.

"You really think you're the reason Lucy left? Or that she

would've gone anywhere with a strange male, even a vampire that Wraith had once known?"

He hesitated, then shook his head. "No. She was fine with what happened. And I don't think she'd go anywhere with this Colt. She doesn't seem to trust males in general, except for Mahone, Knox, you, and me. But I never thought she'd use her powers to sneak out on me, either. Not unless she'd learned something critical in the last few hours, and she was drugged up most of that time. Besides us, she didn't talk to anyone . . ." A stunned expression transformed Dex's face. He smacked his fist into his palm. "A vampire," he growled. "Not Colt. Not a male. But how about a female? The one who held her while I helped contain the shape-shifter? She must have convinced Lucy something was wrong and that she couldn't confide in us for some reason."

Caleb immediately understood where he was going. "The vamp said something about Natia. That she wanted to talk to us about it. I was so concerned about Wraith, I cut her off. But she and Lucy, they had time to talk before you left. Who chose the hotel you stayed at?"

"Lucy," Dex said grimly. "She said she'd read about it on-line and wanted to check it out."

"And did she ask for a particular room?"

"I don't know. She checked us in while I was on the phone with Mahone. Shit!"

"So the vampire teleported in and out with Lucy?" Caleb asked.

"It's as good an explanation as any," Dex said.

"Did you get the vampire's name?"

At the sound of Wraith's voice, they both looked over. She'd gotten dressed in her leathers and even had her sunglasses on. She looked ready to kick some serious butt, and Caleb couldn't help thinking how different she looked from the vulnerable female who'd been in his bed less than an hour earlier.

"Jesmina Martin."

The name rolled off Dex's tongue so swiftly that Wraith's mouth twitched upward. "Made an impression, did she? Do you think you did the same for her?"

Dex shook his head. "Not yet. But if she's hurt Lucy, I'll leave more than an impression on her. I'll have her begging for mercy."

"On the bright side, if Lucy is well and happy, maybe you can still make an impression on the vamp—"

"Don't." Wraith glared at Caleb. "I just lost my humanity again, and who knows where Lucy is. Jokes about threesomes are not allowed."

Even so, he caught the small spark of amusement in her voice and thought, You see. You're not completely lost to me, Wraith. Not yet. And while he hadn't forgotten Jesmina's revelation that Wraith was probably going to die unless she found out her human identity soon, he couldn't help thinking things might have changed. The human traits had left her, and maybe that meant she'd been given a reprieve. Even so, she wasn't who she wanted to be, and that, more than anything, including the pain she'd no doubt feel when he touched her now, was what would keep them apart.

THIRTY-SIX

Wraith stared at the shape-shifter who'd been brought into the Bureau interrogation room over fifteen minutes ago. They'd cajoled, questioned, and threatened him and he'd yet to say a word to them. Now, sitting on the long table next to him, one leg crossed over the other, she swung her foot and loudly chewed her gum. Every time she cracked it, the shape-shifter looked annoyed, so she kept right on doing it.

She couldn't help but wish there was a vampire handy to read the creature's mind. Sure, it would constitute a violation of his constitutional rights, but Dex looked about ready to call it quits and start pummeling the shifter. The only thing that was probably stopping him was the camera in the room, but even that would fail to control him if the shifter didn't talk soon. And she'd be waiting in line to get her punches in, as well.

"Your friend would have been grateful to me, you know."

The shape-shifter's words made Wraith jerk in surprise. She glanced at Caleb and Dex, who immediately took their seats and leaned forward, waiting for the shifter to say more. Wraith saw the way he immediately closed up.

She turned to them. "Get out."

Dex snorted. "Get real."

Wraith locked eyes with Caleb. He hesitated, then got to his feet. "Come on, Dex. I need some coffee."

Dex's expression became mutinous. After knocking his knuckles on the table about ten times, he finally nodded. Standing, he planted his palms on the metal surface and leaned forward threateningly. "Don't screw around with me. You aren't the only thing in this room that can shift. If I do it, it'll be for one reason and one reason only. To rip your throat out. I'd talk fast if I were you."

"Come on, Dex. Now." Caleb pulled Dex toward the door. The were left, albeit he dragged his feet and glared at the shifter the whole time.

Wraith popped her gum and threw her hands up in a gesture that seemed to say, "What are you going to do? We just can't seem to control the wolf." "Sorry about that," Wraith said. "But you see . . . Dex and Lucy are particularly close, if you get my meaning, and he's worried about her."

"She used him to ease her heat, just like most felines use men. Or, should I say, let themselves be used." He didn't say the words disdainfully, the way someone like Harry Jenkins, the televangelist Otherborn-hater, would have, but rather, he seemed to hold a great deal of compassion for the felines. He'd obviously fallen for Lucy's feline act just like they'd wanted.

"I'm not sure what you meant earlier, but if Lucy was going to appreciate what you planned to do to her, why'd you have to drug her first?"

He looked affronted. "I couldn't do it to her otherwise. The procedure would have been too painful if she was fully sober."

Procedure? "Enlighten me. Please."

"Sterilizing a feline is major surgery. Ideally, she'd be in a hospital and put under. But given the circumstances, I do the best I can for them."

What the . . . *Sterilizing* a feline? She struggled for words and finally said, "So you think you're helping the felines? By sterilizing them?"

"Of course. It's what they want. What they'd choose if they felt they had the option."

"Says who?"

"They do," the shifter said gently. "When they come to the clinic I work at. Every day, they beg us for meds to ease the heat.

To give them some modicum of control. They complain about their partners or how they don't want to have more kids, but they don't have any choice, not when the heat controls them half the time. Did you know that while licorice can help ease their heat, it's only a temporary fix?"

"Uh, no. I didn't know that." Wraith thought of what Ramsey had told her. That the feline rapes weren't rapes at all. Despite his warning, despite how great she was with riddles, she hadn't put two and two together, not even given her past experiences.

Maria had betrayed her and turned her over to the mage, ostensibly in exchange for some kind of relief from the heat, but Wraith hadn't really believed it. Wraith had known many felines who enjoyed their sexual natures, adored their children, lived happy, full lives. She'd convinced herself that Maria's motivation must have been something else. Something more universal. Money. Power. Love. Had she really been that wrong? "Lucy didn't want to be sterilized," she pointed out. "She's not even a feline."

The shape-shifter pursed his lips. "What planet are you living on?"

That made her mad. She scooted off the table, stood threateningly close to the shifter, and rested her hands on her hips. "Meaning?"

"Meaning she's part feline. The were knows it. He helped her because she wanted an end to the heat. She wanted to break its control on her."

Lucy was part feline? Wraith's first instinct was to feel betrayed all over again. But she quickly pushed the feeling away. Lucy was her friend. A true friend. She'd kept her secrets, just as Wraith had kept Lucy's. She hadn't done a thing to hurt Wraith, not the way Maria had.

But how could she not have known she was feline? It hadn't been in Mahone's files, but did . . . ? She scowled. Of course Mahone knew. The bastard's machinations were really starting to piss her off. "How did you know . . . ?"

The shape-shifter just smiled secretively, causing her to narrow her eyes. Fine.

"How did you get my DNA to impersonate me? Did someone give it to you?"

Now the shape-shifter looked confused. "Who would give it to me? I just waited until the bartender took your empty drink.

Then, when I got my chance, I grabbed the glass before it went into the kitchen. I licked the rim, and presto!"

Wraith grimaced at the visual. "Yeah. Presto, change-o. You're a wraith. Lucky you."

"Don't be so hard on yourself. It won't be long now. You'll have your chance at peace."

Whoa. Were all shape-shifters so woo-woo? "What do you know about it?"

"Only what you do. What you feel. I know you're close to the end, though I'm not sure why you regained your wraith appearance. It's rather exciting, if you think about it."

"So when you take someone's form, you also pick up their thoughts? Their feelings?"

He shook his head. "I can pick up emotions and feelings simply by touching someone. I don't have to take the person's form."

"And you picked up on my 'feeling' that my end is near?"

"I feel your sadness. Your longing. Your regret. Major bummer."

Well, crap. "Sorry I couldn't be more cheery for you," she snapped.

"Don't be. Your emotions are what they are. They're part of you, so they should be appreciated. Valued. Interestingly, what I picked up most from you was resignation. You've already given up, you know. I never would have suspected, but then most people wouldn't, would they? That's the bitch about being a wraith."

Unconsciously, she took a step away from the shifter. Resigned. Was that really such a bad thing? Why fight for something when all hope was obviously lost? Wasn't it better to die with dignity? Aware that he was distracting her, she tried to steer the conversation back on track. "Let's get back to Lucy. You said my friend wanted an end to the heat and you wanted to help her. Have you helped others?" He glanced away, but not before she saw the confirmation in his eyes. "You have, haven't you? You raped those felines."

His eyes rounded. "Certainly not. I merely gave them what they asked of me. They chose how to characterize it to others for their own purposes."

"You sterilized them, and they cried rape?"

"It's the only way they felt they'd be accepted—by claiming

that somehow the rapes were connected with their future inability to have children. I didn't think I could pity them more, but there you have it. Dr. Maddox warned me how extreme felines could be, but I didn't listen. Not until I saw it for myself."

"Dr. Maddox?"

"Dr. Alton Maddox. He's a doctor. My mentor. He does much for Otherborn. He even helped them during the War."

"So he's okay with helping felines report false crimes? So long as it helps them? Sounds like Dr. Maddox is an 'ends justifies the means' kind of guy."

"I'd say you're right. Just like me. So tell your friend she can come see me. After I'm out of here, of course. Just look up Dr. Maddox's clinic, and he'll get us in touch."

"Oh, I will. But tell me something first."

The shape-shifter looked at her expectantly.

"Why are you telling me all this?"

The shifter smiled. "Believe me, you don't want to know."

She grinned, showing her teeth. "Believe me, I do."

"Fine, but don't say I didn't warn you. It's because I can feel your pain. You genuinely care about the girl. So do your friends." His mouth tilted in a mocking smile. "I felt how much they cared when they were choking the life out of me."

"And?" Wraith prompted.

"What makes you think there's more?"

She simply stared at him.

He shrugged. "And . . . well, honey, believe it or not, I feel sorry for you. We shape-shifters look like aliens, and we spend our whole lives pretending to be someone else. You don't get that benefit. I wouldn't want to be you for anything on this earth. Plus, you're dying. I guess you can look at this as a farewell gift. One outcast to another."

THIRTY-SEVEN

Caleb and Dex were waiting just outside, nursing some coffee, when Caleb saw Wraith. He stood as Wraith approached them.

"Well?" Dex growled.

She looked shaken but tried to hide it. "We need the address for a Dr. Alton Maddox."

"Who's he?"

"He and the shape-shifter have apparently been sterilizing felines. Most with their consent. Some with what they assumed would be consent."

"Sterilizing, not raping . . ." Caleb froze. "You're saying the felines *faked* the rapes? We suspected Natia, but Morgana . . . A feline princess lied to the police about being raped?"

"What? You think your ex-girlfriend is capable of hiring goons to come after me, but you don't think she'd be capable of crying rape on behalf of her sister? And in all likelihood, on behalf of herself eventually?"

"Damn it, Wraith, stop twisting my words," he snarled.

"Who reported the rapes?" Dex snapped.

Reluctantly, Caleb turned to the were. "I assumed the victims did, but . . ." Caleb shrugged. "Let's check it out right now."

The three of them converged on the records clerk and had

the files they needed in under five minutes. Each of the rapes had been reported by a Dr. Alton Maddox, after the felines had been brought to his clinic for sexual assault. He'd done an examination first, confirmed sexual assault, then signed off on the paperwork.

"I can't believe we overlooked it."

"I can. He's the doctor who treated them. He regularly treats felines. We had no cause to be suspicious," Wraith said. "We've got the address to his clinic right here. We can—"

A cell phone rang. Dex's.

He checked the screen. "It's Lucy." Swiftly, he flipped the phone open. "Lucy," he said. He looked at Wraith and Caleb and nodded. Caleb felt Wraith relax just as much as he did. "Yeah, we figured that out on our own. Is the vampire with you?" Dex scowled. "You know damn well who I'm talking about, Lucy. Is Jesmina Martin, the vampire who was at the club, with you? Oh really? All right, we're coming to get you. Do not leave. And Lucy? I'm pissed, so I wouldn't try anything else stupid tonight, all right? Do not warn the vampire that I'm coming."

Dex flipped his phone shut. "She's at Maddox's clinic. She went there to talk to him after the vampire tipped her off about the sterilizations."

"Why?" Wraith said. "Why wouldn't she have come to us?"

"Who knows," Dex growled. "Maybe she was embarrassed. Pissed off at you two for what went down in front of Mahone. Pissed off at me for . . ." He shook his head. "Hell, it could be a hundred different reasons."

"Yeah, and that reminds me . . ." Wraith turned on Dex. "Did you know Lucy is a feline?"

"What?" Caleb exclaimed. Wraith glanced at him, then back at Dex.

"I figured it out a couple of days ago. It was the main reason I—"

"I'll bet Mahone knew and chose to keep it from us," Wraith said. "And Lucy let him! Here I am, giving everything I've got to this team and Lucy holds something like that back."

"Everything you've got, huh? Like telling us you were turning human? I'm sorry, but that would've been nice to know before I relied on you as my backup, don't you think?"

"Screw you, Dex! I—"

"Stop it!" Caleb yelled. "We've all got our secrets. Every

single one of us. Lucy wanted to keep hers, fine. We need to get to her and figure out what we're going to do about this whole damn mess." He turned to Dex. "What else did she tell you?" Caleb asked gruffly, still reeling from the idea that the felines had made up something as serious as rape.

"When she got there, Maddox was dead. His throat slit. Lucy called on her cell from his office and is meeting the vampire outside."

Wraith cursed and Caleb immediately knew what she was thinking. "Dex, we don't know anything about the vampire. How do we know she didn't kill Maddox? How do we know she didn't set Lucy up?"

Dex looked confused for a second, then fire blazed in his eyes. "No. I talked to the vamp—I would've known if she . . ." Dex closed his eyes. When he opened them, his expression was shuttered. On him, it was the same as deadly. "Let's go."

From the shadows of the clinic entrance, Lucy stared at Jesmina Martin, the vampire who'd led her to Dr. Alton Maddox's clinic. She was standing under a streetlight several feet away, her long, silver hair gleaming. Maddox hadn't died pretty, and Lucy couldn't help wondering if accompanying the vampire had been a huge mistake.

Oh, she'd told the truth about Maddox. After Lucy had discovered his body inside, she'd searched through his files. She'd found the ones on the felines inside his locked safe, which she'd easily opened with an entry spell. He and his assistant, a shapeshifter, had indeed sterilized the three felines at their request, then helped them cover for the surgery with reports of rape, rape and deliberate or consequential sterilization—either one would do—so they wouldn't be shunned by their clan. However, according to the files, Maddox had sterilized other felines. He'd called what he'd been doing feline liberation, regardless of whether his patients had sought his help or not. The ironic thing was that Maddox and his assistant had drugged those felines, but afterward, the felines hadn't remembered enough to realize what had happened. Either that, or they'd been convinced not to talk. The only proof of what had been done to them was in Maddox's files.

And Maddox's suspiciously timed death was also something to consider.

After all, it was highly likely that at least one of Maddox's so-called liberated felines had found out what he'd done and shown him just how much she *hadn't* wanted his help.

The thing was, Lucy regretted bringing the vampire with her now that Dex was on his way. Despite their short acquaintance, something was going on between the two and—

Jesmina turned with a sigh and called out to her. "I can read your thoughts from here, Lucy. Stop worrying. I'm not afraid of Dex. Did you talk to Maddox?"

Lucy bit her lip, wanting to break the news gently because she knew Maddox had been Jesmina's friend. She needn't have bothered. Jesmina took one look at her face and smiled sadly. "Poor Alton. Was it someone he helped who killed him?"

"More likely someone he helped who didn't want to be helped."

That seemed to surprise Jesmina. She tried to speak but couldn't until she'd taken several breaths. "My record's holding firm." She smiled at Lucy's confused look. "I have horrible judgment when it comes to men. That's why I try to stay away from them."

"Dex is on his way," Lucy said, feeling it was only fair to warn her.

"Thank you," Jesmina said. "I'd stay and help you explain, but I'm afraid I'm a little tired. If you don't need me, I'll be going."

Lucy nodded. "Thanks again for your help."

"Sure." She took several steps away from her, then stopped. "Lucy," she called over her shoulder. "Always remember that who we are might not be who we want to be, but in the end, we'd better be willing to fight for what we have. Tell that to the wraith, would you? And tell Dex good-bye for me."

THIRTY-EIGHT

What idiots we were, Elijah. Or did you know? Did you
know when you died that someone you trusted with all
your heart and soul had been your true executioner?

Caleb tried to harness his thoughts into something useful.
Something besides the mass of shock and self-castigation that
warred with regret and grief. It was as if his friend had *just*
died—that's how intense the sting of loss and betrayal felt. He
wanted to get plastered. To drown himself in a bottle of whiskey until he floated to another world where such horrors never
occurred. He wanted to reject the information he'd received,
reject it all, but he couldn't.

The papers Lucy had retrieved from Maddox's safe told
Caleb in black-and-white that he'd been a blind fool. Wraith
had once accused him of not wanting to shove his dick in something dead, but truth was he'd done that a long time ago, long
before he'd ever met her.

Because Princess Natia, Caleb's former lover, had been dead
inside when he'd made love to her, her outward beauty disguis-
ing her blackened, shriveled heart, fooling not only Caleb but
many others.

Elijah.

Her mother and the rest of the royal family.

And Alton Maddox.

Yes, Maddox. Because lo and behold, Maddox had worked for the U.S. government as a military doctor before he'd started his own practice, and somehow Natia had convinced the doctor to pay a visit to a certain prisoner of war just before he'd died. Maddox had killed Natia's brother, and Caleb knew he wouldn't have done it unless Natia had given him a very good reason. But what had it been? That was a detail Maddox hadn't included in the records spread out in front of Caleb.

Wearily, Caleb rubbed his hands over his face. He jerked when he felt a heavy hand on his shoulder. He turned and saw Dex.

"You're not looking so hot, Romeo."

Caleb looked away to stare once more at the mess of papers before him. "You wouldn't either if you'd just discovered you'd dated a woman evil enough to mastermind her own brother's murder. Not to mention let you carry the burden of guilt for his death for years."

"From murdering bitch to dead bitch. Way to pick 'em, O'Flare."

Fury incinerated the misery he'd been feeling. Springing out of his chair, Caleb was on the were in an instant, grabbing him by his shirt and shoving him up against a wall. "Don't fucking talk about Wraith that way. She's not a bitch and she's not dead. Not really. Not—not—"

As his voice cracked, Caleb released Hunt and turned away, breathing in hard and blinking his eyes in an attempt to clear them of the sting of moisture that had collected.

"Not yet," Hunt finished quietly.

Caleb turned and pointed an accusatory finger at him. "Don't. Go. There. Wraith isn't going to die. I won't allow it."

Hunt's gaze didn't waver. "I know you won't, man. I was just shaking you out of the little pity fest you were mired in. So Natia killed her brother. *You* didn't. You're here. You can avenge him. You can save someone else."

"Yeah, it's so easy to say. Avenge him when I have no idea why Natia killed. Save Wraith when I don't know how. When I don't know when—" With a bellow edged with fury and helplessness, he swept everything off the table he'd vacated: Maddox's files, the research he'd printed out on wraiths, the lamp that shattered into several large, jagged shards.

"Feel better now?" Hunt drawled.

Caleb glanced up and, to his surprise, managed to laugh. "Actually, I do."

"Good. So what now? You going to pay your ex a little visit?"

He pictured Natia. How she'd looked and felt when he'd danced with her at Knox's wedding. How she'd sounded and smelled when she'd greeted him and kissed him in the same bar where he'd found Wraith, bloodied and dying on the bathroom floor. The need to avenge his friend—to avenge himself—burned bright for a heady second, then faded. He shook his head, noting Hunt's look of surprise.

"Maybe there's something good that can come from all this. Something I'm meant to teach you."

Hunt glared at him. "Enlighten me."

"There are more important things than revenge, Hunt. I'm not going to waste any more time on the past than I already have. No matter what Natia has done, she introduced me to Elijah. A man who was my true friend. He'd understand what I need to do. He'd want me to do it."

"And what's that?"

"Choose. Choose hope over despair. Choose the future over the past. Choose love over revenge. And that's what I'm gonna do. I choose Wraith. The question is, what will you choose?"

Back at Wraith's hotel room, Wraith stared at Lucy as the mage delivered the vampire's message. "I didn't want to tell you earlier. Not with Dex and Caleb around. Even if Dex had given me a chance to talk, which of course you know he didn't."

"He was worried," Wraith said. "We all were."

"I know. And that's why I let him rant at me. But I had my reasons for meeting the vamp alone."

"I know you did, Lucy. And so does he. We were worried about that, too. If you'd told us you're part feline . . . If you'd told us about the heat . . ."

"What? You could have helped?" Lucy shook her head. "I see how you stay away from felines, Wraith. Obviously there's something in your past that makes you suspicious of them, and I didn't want to be stuck with that particular label. Besides, I didn't tell you about the heat for the same reason you didn't tell us about your momentous birthday—it wouldn't have changed anything, and we didn't want to be the objects of anyone's pity."

"You're totally right. But now that I know, I don't pity you, Lucy. Because the heat might be a pain right now, but when you find the man you're meant to be with, who knows? At least you'll get the chance to find out."

They stared at each other, and Wraith suddenly felt foolish. Had she really talked of Lucy meeting a man with wistfulness lacing her words?

"Wraith, the vamp's message . . ."

"Thanks for delivering it," Wraith said with a brittle smile. "I'll be sure to keep her wisdom in mind, right along with all the other new age stuff that shape-shifter told me. Right now, however, I need to pack." She started to walk into the bedroom but stopped before she reached the doorway. Over her shoulder, she said, "That reminds me, the shifter had a message for you, as well. He said he can help you, if you want. If you're still considering . . ."

Lucy hesitated, then shook her head. "No. Not right now, anyway. But Wraith . . . we never had a chance to . . . I mean, can you forgive me for what I wanted . . . with Caleb?"

"There's nothing to forgive, Lucy. You wanted him, and let's face it—you're a way better choice for him than I'll ever be."

"But he wants you, Wraith, not me. And I've known that all along."

It shouldn't have comforted her so much, but it did. Caleb had wanted *her*. He might not want her anymore, but that didn't change the fact that he once had. "Yeah, well, what's that Stones song about not getting what you want? If you try sometimes . . ." She shrugged, then laughed. "Well, I tried and I failed. But Caleb can still get what he wants." Especially now, she thought. Because although she still didn't know why, the death mark he'd worn the entire time they'd been in Los Angeles had finally disappeared. Right about the time they'd picked up Lucy outside Alton Maddox's office. So while she was still dying, Caleb was safe. In the end, that's what truly mattered. "He'll get what he wants when I'm gone," she said firmly.

"I don't believe that," Lucy whispered. "And neither does Caleb."

"Sometimes Caleb doesn't know what's good for him."

"But you know what is?"

Wraith smiled. "Yeah. The best thing for everybody is to stay as far away from me as possible. Even when I'm being impersonated, I'm a danger to you, Lucy."

"You can't blame yourself for the shape-shifter trying to take me, Wraith!"

"Didn't you know, Lucy?" They both gasped when they heard Caleb's voice. "Wraith blames herself for everything. Why not that, too?"

Wraith didn't turn around, but Caleb just moved until he stood in front of her. "It's not like she'll let Dex or me claim our lion's share of the guilt, considering we were the ones supposed to be keeping an eye on you. Wraith's a plain old misery hog, aren't you, Wraith?"

She refused to answer.

"Look at me," he said.

She didn't want to, but now that he'd said the words, she couldn't resist. It was as if he'd borrowed some of Knox's persuasion powers. She met his gaze and gasped. Rather than the anger or disdain she'd expected, his expression was one of sheer weariness.

"You're not the only person who brings trouble to those around you, Wraith. I reviewed the files that Lucy retrieved from Maddox's office. He was sterilizing felines, some by their choice and some by his choice alone. But all the procedures had one thing in common—they were funded by the same person. The same person who paid Maddox to kill Prince Elijah. The same person who hired Doug and Emmett to come after you. Natia. I trusted her, Wraith. Danced with her at Knox's wedding, and she—"

Hesitantly, Wraith shook her head, not in denial, but to stop his words. His voice emanated pain. "Stop. Don't do this to yourself, Caleb. Don't take on more guilt. You've had enough, and I don't want you to carry any more."

"I know. The question is, why?"

"Because it's hurting you," she whispered. Vaguely, she was aware that Lucy had left the hotel room, shutting the door behind her so it was just her and Caleb. Together. Alone.

"Sometimes we need to live with the pain. Isn't that what

you've tried to tell me all along, Wraith? That to be truly free, to get where we need to be, we have to be willing to feel everything, the good and the bad?"

"That's true for me. Not for you. I don't want you to have to live with that kind of pain."

"And yet I'm going to, whether you want it for me or not. And you just denying it or pushing me away makes me hurt more. Especially when I know why you're doing it. Especially since I did the same stupid thing to you." He lifted his hand and let it hover near her temple, but he didn't touch her. "Tell me, Wraith. Why would you spare me that pain? Because you care about me?"

"Caleb, stop. You know what's going to happen to me. I'm going to—"

"Do you care about me, Wraith?" he demanded, his eyes blazing, refusing to let her look away.

"Yes," she gritted out.

"Do you love me?"

She licked her lips and closed her eyes, tried to say no, but ended up choking out, "Yes."

"That's why I wanted—will always want—to spare you the pain, too. But we can't shield each other from everything, not even that. Because without pain, we have no life."

Hesitantly, she opened her eyes again. He was staring at her solemnly. "You can't love me, Caleb."

Shaking his head, he smiled. "Too late," he whispered, just as he wove his fingers through her hair, tilted her head back, and kissed her.

Whatever had numbed her pain the previous times they'd had sex was gone. She felt pain every time his lips touched hers or his bare skin brushed against hers. But she didn't flinch away from him, and she didn't cry out. Instead, she cherished it as much as she did the pleasure he gave her because in her mind they were both connected. Intertwined so that it was impossible to tell one from the other. The perfect combination of both. A balance. Symmetry in its greatest form. Caleb.

At one point, she reared back, relief bearing down on her. He cradled her face in his hand. "What is it?"

She shook her head, causing tears to fall from her eyes. The death mark. It was gone, and somehow she knew whatever had caused that particular mark to form was no longer a threat to him. She'd tell him. Explain later. But right now . . . "I'm happy," she said, pulling his mouth down to hers again. "So happy."

Later, when they lay in bed together, he said, "It was Natia. All this time."

"It appears so," Wraith said, smoothing a hand over his chest. What she didn't say was that Natia had probably been the threat that had generated the death mark. It made the most sense. It had appeared after Caleb had spurned her in favor of Wraith. Had disappeared when Caleb had held her and promised to help her. Reappeared again after Caleb had come after her. And it had stayed until he'd discovered Natia's treachery.

Wraith would make sure the feline never posed a threat to Caleb again, whatever that took. It didn't matter to her that Natia had acted out of some twisted kind of love or out of desperation. By threatening Caleb, she'd forever made an enemy out of Wraith and disintegrated any kind of pity Wraith might otherwise have felt for her.

Unaware of her protective thoughts, Caleb continued speaking. "The only thing I can't understand is Elijah. What possible reason could Natia have for wanting her brother dead? They were close. Closer than any of the other royal siblings."

"Maybe too close. Maybe Natia didn't want the closeness anymore."

When Caleb stiffened, Wraith rested her cheek against his heart and peered up at him. "After I escaped the mage, I did a lot of intel on the felines. I wanted revenge, but ultimately, I knew I couldn't blame the whole race for one feline's actions. But during my surveillance, I saw things . . ."

Caleb sat up. "What things?"

She lifted her head, but hesitated.

"Tell me, Wraith. No secrets."

No. No secrets. Not between the two of them. "Do you know felines are often bisexual?"

"Yes. And I know Natia is. She had a female lover before we were together."

"She had another male lover, too. One she might not have chosen but who might have chosen her."

Caleb looked confused, then horrified. "Elijah?" he whispered.

Wraith nodded. "I saw them together once. Acting intimately

toward each other. I thought maybe I imagined it, but given everything else we've learned today, it makes sense."

"So she had him killed? Made his death look like a by-product of War?"

Wraith shrugged. "It's a theory. My theory. Maybe she wanted to be free of him. Or from her own shame, at the very least. Maybe she blamed the heat, and that's why she's been funding the sterilization procedures."

Caleb pulled her into his arms again. "And then she targeted you. Because she knows you're special to me."

His recognition of the fact, plainly spoken, made joy sweep through her. "It must have eaten her alive. Knowing you turned her down to be with me at Knox's wedding."

"Maybe that's why Colt accepted her money. Maybe he was jealous, too."

She brushed away his attempted explanation with a slight shake of her head, clearly not wanting to talk about the man who'd betrayed her. More than willing to distract her, Caleb murmured, "Too bad Mahone had to arrive at the wedding when he did and mess things up."

She snuggled in closer to him and rested her cheek against his chest again. Closing her eyes, she relished his warmth and the beating of his heart. "Yeah. Too bad. Remind me to have a talk with Mahone about that, would you? In addition to a few other things."

He murmured his agreement and they rested in the silence for a while before he said, "What now, Wraith?"

She didn't move. She thought about pretending she hadn't heard him, but she couldn't. "Now we wait and see what fate has in store for me, Caleb. But for the first time in my life, I'm hoping she lets me stick around for a whole lot longer."

She felt him kiss the top of her head before he whispered, "Me, too."

THIRTY-NINE

Caleb got Mahone on the phone later that day.

"Alton Maddox was the man who executed Elijah, but he was just the hit man. He had governmental authorization for Elijah's torture, and the government sanctioned his actions. I want the name of the governmental authority you promised me."

Mahone sighed, and his failure to give up the name immediately had Caleb seeing red. "Damn it, Mahone, if you even try to screw me in this, I'll—"

"Hold on," Mahone snapped. "I need to make sure this line is secure. Then we'll talk."

Gritting his teeth, Caleb waited. And waited. He was beginning to think this was just another one of Mahone's tricks when he came back on the line. "Are you there?"

"Yes," Caleb said.

"We're clear. The name you want is Vanessa Morrison."

"Wh-what?" Caleb asked, certain he'd misunderstood.

This time, Mahone spoke slowly, drawing out each syllable as if Caleb were an idiot. "Va-nes-sa Mor-ri-son."

"The First Lady of the United States? She authorized Elijah's so-called torture and execution? Where are you getting your information?"

Mahone snorted. "I have my sources, O'Flare, of which you are not privy to. But I'm telling you the truth."

"I don't understand . . . Natia paid Maddox a huge sum of money just before Elijah's death. We assumed she hired Maddox to kill Elijah for her. But what connection would she have to the First Lady . . ." Remembering his recent conversation with Wraith, Caleb swallowed hard; he couldn't believe he'd been so naïve. "They were lovers?"

"Yes," Mahone said quietly. "I already knew that, but I didn't know about Natia funding Maddox or her connection to feline sterilizations. Whether she knows about Morrison's ultimate objective remains to be seen."

"What ultimate objective?"

"We have reason to believe she's part of a group called the Quorum, an organization dedicated to annihilating the peace between humans and Otherborn. I'm betting she convinced Natia that sterilization is a feline female's right and the way to give her independence and freedom."

"And the false rapes were more than just a cover?"

"Sure. They had two purposes. They were a cover, an excuse to explain the victim's infertility if and when it was discovered—after all, maybe the attacker wanted to both rape and sterilize his victims—and a way to cast suspicion on humans and dissention between humans and felines. Not difficult with someone like Harry Jenkins around, already giving us a bad name and stirring up hate."

"And Natia herself? Do you think she's been sterilized?"

"I have no idea. But we'll get our chance to find out."

"You'll have her examined when she's taken into custody," Caleb agreed.

"Something like that."

Mahone's mild response immediately put Caleb on edge. "You've already got her? Damn it, Mahone, you might have moved too soon. Bringing her into custody is going to tip off Morrison. Make her go underground."

"She hasn't been brought into custody, O'Flare. Not the way you're thinking. She's dead."

"Dead?"

"Last night she was found in an alley in Los Angeles. You wanna guess which one?"

"The alley behind Maddox's clinic? But who . . . ?" Caleb felt no remorse. No grief or regret for the female he'd kissed countless times, the last time being just before Wraith's heart had stopped beating.

"Whoever did it made it look like she overdosed on Ecstasy. When we collected her body, it wasn't a pretty sight, but it was enough to make it look like an accident. Let's just hope Morrison believes it and chalks up her lover's death as another victory for the Quorum."

"It was the vampire, Colt. He'd have the drug connections and the resources to do it."

"And the motive. After Natia's body was found, he walked into Bureau headquarters. Confessed to hiring Doug and Emmett to kidnap Wraith in order to get her away from you. He claimed his own feelings for Wraith motivated him. And he fervently denied authorizing anyone to hurt her. In fact, he said, and I quote, 'I'd kill to make sure no one hurts Wraith. I have.' Of course, he clammed up after that and brought in his attorney."

"Where is he now?"

"Out on bail. He'll probably serve his time for conspiracy to kidnap and be out on the streets in months. You gonna be paying him a visit?"

Maybe. Eventually, Caleb thought. But first, he'd tell Wraith what Colt had done. Because she deserved to know that Colt had cared enough about her to kill the female who'd endangered her. Right now, however, he had far more important things to think about. "What about Morrison?" he asked Mahone.

"We leave her alone. We want her to think she's safe. In the meantime, we have a man working his way inside. He hasn't gotten in yet, but hopefully soon. You okay with that?"

"I wouldn't say I'm okay with it, but if we bring the Quorum down in the end, that's all that matters."

"Good."

"Mahone, I want to cash in my IOU. And I need delivery to be ASAP."

"I'm pretty sure I know what you're going to ask for, and all I can say is, I'll do my best. But I'm not holding out hope at this point."

"I'm not going to rely on hope. I'm more of a take-charge kind of guy."

"Meaning?"

"Meaning, I'll do my part and you do yours, and maybe together, it'll make a difference to someone we both care about."

Wraith opened her hotel room door, frowning when she saw Lucy was alone. "Where's Dex?" The three of them had agreed to share a cab to the airport before splitting. Dex and Lucy were returning to Quantico, where Mahone would brief them on Felicia's "attack" and get their thoughts regarding the felines. Wraith and Caleb, on the other hand, would fly to Maine, where Caleb intended to access all the information the wraiths had managed to collect on the turning phenomenon. Wraith had already called Joanna, who was, despite the way Wraith had treated her in Oregon, anticipating their arrival with every intention of giving Caleb access to anything he wanted.

Caleb had told Wraith about Colt. How he suspected Colt had been the one to kill Natia after he'd found out Natia had ordered Wraith's death rather than her relocation. She tried telling herself it didn't matter, that Colt had betrayed her nonetheless, but she couldn't deny that the news brought her some comfort. For all his weaknesses and mistakes, Colt had truly cared about her. Just as Ramsey had, which had been evidenced by his newfound inability to truly hurt her, even as she asked him to. Humans were flawed and loved by flawed individuals.

Still, that love mattered.

Apparently, she was far more human as a wraith than she would've thought.

"Dex isn't ready to return to Quantico," Lucy said. "He's decided to spend a few more days in L.A. I'm pretty sure he's hoping to run into a certain vamp again."

Wraith couldn't say she was surprised. Dex had been beyond furious when he'd discovered the vamp had left before they'd reached Maddox's clinic. Jesmina had played him—with Lucy's full cooperation, of course—but there was more to Dex's interest in her than wounded pride. She studied Lucy carefully for any signs of jealousy or hurt feelings, but the mage's expression was surprisingly bland. "Are you okay with that?"

Lucy nodded. "Who would have guessed the were had such a good heart? But he's way too alpha for me. I need someone mellower. Someone like Caleb," she teased, her face lightening with her attempt at humor.

Wraith snorted. "Just goes to show how much Caleb had you fooled."

Sobering, Lucy asked, "Are we okay?"

Wraith nodded, hesitated, then awkwardly pulled Lucy into a hug. She felt the mage stiffen in surprise before she hugged her back.

"I decided to catch an earlier flight," Lucy said as she pulled away.

Surprised, Wraith struggled for the right words. "Okay, well . . . Tell Mahone, if I don't see him myself, I said thanks."

"Oh, Wraith . . ." Lucy's eyes welled with tears, and her face twisted with profound sadness.

When she felt moisture gather in her own eyes, Wraith shook her head. "None of that, now. You've got to be strong, Lucy. How else are you going to keep the guys in line?"

Lucy sniffed. "You're right. But that's more your job, Wraith. I'll sub for you while you're in Maine, but as soon as you return, I'm handing over the reins. Got it?"

"Got it," Wraith said, her affection for the mage growing despite her desperate attempt to remain unaffected.

After Lucy left, Wraith turned on the TV, hoping it would distract her until Caleb returned. He was doing some "research" on wraiths, even though she'd told him everything she knew and still none of it shed light on what their purpose was or if there was a way to avoid expiring. When he returned empty-handed, maybe he would begin to see the hopelessness of the task he'd set for them, but then again, hopeless or not, she was grateful for the excuse to spend more time with him. Maybe it showed how weak she really was, but now that she knew he loved her, she wasn't turning him away any longer. Being without him when she died scared her more than the thought of death itself.

She flipped through the channels, stopping when she came to local coverage of a college event, something called the Giving Bowl, a takeoff of the Rose Bowl, only on a much smaller scale. According to the newscaster, the game was happening as they spoke, not too far from where Wraith was staying. Admiring the simplicity and sheer whimsy of some of the floats, she jerked when the camera panned on the image of a smiling woman. She looked like a typical California girl, blond and athletic and tan. Recognition prodded at Wraith until it became a sharp pain in her temple and she winced. When the newscasters proceeded to interview the girl, Wraith turned up the volume.

". . . my sister, Annie," the blonde said, gesturing to a younger, sweeter-looking version of herself.

"So, Christina, you and your sister are here hoping to bring positive exposure to your former sorority, which your sister has recently joined. Can you tell us a little about it?"

"Sure. Delta Gamma is a sorority whose mission this year is to aid the homeless. The theme of our float is 'Shelter for All.' "

"And even though you're pretty busy with your day job, working with Red Cross, you still devote a lot of time to the sorority and the various charities it supports."

"It's a joy, even more so now that my little sister is there." Christina put an arm around her sister's shoulders and hugged her, her affection for the girl radiating in her expression. As she did, the camera closed in on Annie, and Wraith stared at the delicate necklace with a ballerina shoe pendant around Annie's neck.

It was the necklace she'd seen in her dream.

And behind her—Wraith narrowed her eyes as the camera panned out, giving her a clearer view of the mini-market behind the two girls.

She'd seen that store before. As soon as she realized that, an unexplained and unexpected knowledge flooded her brain. In a few minutes, Christina and her sister would walk the parade next to their float, then join a post-celebration party. Afterward, they'd walk home, but not before stopping at a convenience store to pick up a pack of gum.

Cinnamon gum. That same type of gum Wraith preferred.

She knew these things despite the sheer ridiculousness of the notion.

And that meant she probably knew Christina and Annie, or at least had known them in her human life. If they were going to be stopping at that store, that would be her chance to talk to them. To ask them questions. To possibly figure out.

Who. She. Was.

FORTY

It had been over fifteen years since Caleb had walked the Otherworld. The first time had been on his soul journey, just before he'd been recognized as a full shaman by his people; for two days, he'd conferred with the spirits of his grandfather and great-grandfather, learning the history of those chosen to keep balance between the earth and its inhabitants. Three years later, when Lilah Featherstone's body had been found on the reservation and there had been no trace of her little boy, Marco, Caleb had journeyed to see her spirit and discovered they'd been attacked by a stranger; before she'd died, Lilah had yelled at Marco to hide in his "special place." Three hours later, when he'd come out of his trance, Caleb had led the search parties to a set of caverns edging the river at the southernmost part of the reservation. There, they'd found Marco, huddled into a ball, his face stained with tears.

Walking the Otherworld wasn't something a shaman routinely did, and Caleb hadn't had a reason to do it again. Now, he had every reason to do it. The only problem was, he'd be going in blind, with no idea how to contact the Goddess Essenia, or whether she'd even see him.

It didn't matter. It was the only hope Wraith had. Despite their plans to go to Maine, he knew Wraith's time was running out. Thinking about that, however, made it next to impossible for him to trance himself deeply enough to enter the Otherworld. Still, he kept trying, focusing on the beauty of the surroundings he'd chosen, a conservatory surrounded by nature, just a couple of miles down the road from their hotel.

Eventually, his thoughts aligned with his slow, steady breaths and the warm pump of blood through his veins. With his eyes closed, the darkness cradled him, and he sank into pure sensation, feeling the kiss of air on his body and smelling the pungent aroma of greenery inside and out, as if the walls that enclosed him had faded away. Bright light shone through his lids, its purity warming his body and clearing his head of all conscious thought and troubles. It was only when he felt a gentle presence encircling him that he opened his eyes.

It was the spirits of his ancestors gathering around him, almost like his very own bubble, blocking the vibrant life within his body so it could walk among those who no longer possessed it.

"I ask to speak with the Goddess Essenia," he called, immediately aware of how the air around him shuddered, as if his request had disturbed his ancestors.

He looked into the vastness around him, nothing but a swirl of soft lights and shadows, and made his request again. And then again. Until he lost track of the passage of time.

And even so, his call went unanswered. Hopelessness washed over him, causing his ancestors to moan, the sorrowful sound mixing with his words like background music.

"Your desperation is a thing unwanted here, Shaman."

He didn't see her, but he knew instantly it was her: Essenia. Her voice was so sweetly melodic that Caleb instinctively closed his eyes to savor it. His body shuddered as her scent tickled each pore and hair on his body. Beautiful, he thought. Exquisite.

Her laugh made him think of rain falling into the ocean, the essence of life itself.

"Have you forgotten why you sought me out, Shaman?"

Immediately, Caleb opened his eyes. Backed by light, he could only see her silhouette, but it was enough to know that her beauty was terrifying—unlike anything any mortal was meant to see in his lifetime. And yet, instead of losing himself in her image, he formed the image of Wraith in his mind, complete with white hair, bluish skin, and hazy eyes. It gave him the focus he needed to speak.

"Goddess, I ask you to spare the Para-Ops team's wraith from the change that is awaiting her. Whatever purpose her change serves, I ask for the opportunity to meet it without requiring her death."

"You need not speak, Caleb O'Flare. I can hear your thoughts quite well. Yet I am deaf to your request. The wraith's purpose was known before her birth but now is uncertain. It is only with the change the wraith may redeem herself."

"Redeem . . ." Caleb stopped talking and let his thoughts speak for him. Redeem herself from what?

"My reason does not require your knowledge of it."

Then deprive me of the knowledge, but please, save her. I . . . I love her.

"You love her? A wraith? A being with no past and no future? How can you love her when she does not even love herself?"

The presence of Caleb's ancestors fluttered at her words, alerting him to their significance. He spoke without realizing it. "Is that what you require from her?"

He felt her ascent in the way she drew closer to him. His skin began to swelter and his hair to smolder. He stood his ground.

"It is the only way one can truly value the life given to her. Without it, my vision and love is lost, as well."

"But she's lived alone for ten years, suffering pain at anyone's touch."

"Yet she has lived. Her pain is from acting against herself. Her isolation is her own choosing."

"It would be what most choose. You ask too much of her."

That angered her. He felt it in the blast of heat that pushed him back several steps. The circle of security surrounding him wavered, then strengthened again. He, at least, wasn't alone in this, and he would lend all that he was to Wraith. "I'm sorry, but please, give her another chance. I'll teach her to love herself. I'll love her enough for both of us."

Her answer was silence, and hope welled within him. Was she considering—

"I have given her not one chance to do the right thing, but two. Most people aren't so lucky. Her test has already begun.

There's nothing I can do to change that. What's been set in motion cannot be undone. The choice is hers. It has been all along."

"I don't understand—"

"I know you don't, Shaman. But know you were destined to come together for a reason. If she loves herself as she loves you, she'll make the right choice. She'll choose her present and her future rather than her past."

He didn't miss her certainty that Wraith loved him. It struck him silent for one second, then gave him the strength to continue speaking. "Her past is what she's been looking for . . ."

"She doesn't have to look any longer."

Understanding made his body jerk. "She's learning something right now? Where is she?"

"Don't interfere, Caleb O'Flare. I warn you, if you do, it won't change matters. In fact, it might just make me angry enough to punish her again. You wouldn't want that. I wouldn't, either. Another, however, might demand it."

"Another . . . ?" He shook his head as light flashed, then dimmed. A warning, perhaps? "I won't interfere, I promise. But I need to see her again before she—before she dies."

"You're that certain she'll make the wrong choice?"

"I think she'll make the only choice you've presented her with. The deaths of every wraith prior to her prove that."

"Yet Mahone has indicated my children are all capable of growing. Perhaps he was wrong?"

"Mahone?" Caleb wondered if he'd misheard. Mahone had a direct line to the Earth Goddess? And apparently, he'd been sticking up for humans and Otherborn . . . "Mahone is a very smart man. You apparently agree. Please, if she's to meet her fate, I need to be there. I need to see her." I need to tell her I love her. I need to be able to say good-bye.

Essenia sighed, apparently hearing his thoughts and being swayed by them. "Very well, Shaman. I will allow you to see her during her final minutes. But as a spectator only. From here—"

"No!" Caleb yelled. Almost immediately, he waited for the Goddess to incinerate him for his disrespect. Instead, she merely smiled sadly.

"Take what I offer, Caleb O'Flare, for it is all you shall receive. Or go back to wait for her and hope you do not wait an eternity."

It was a mistake coming here, Caleb thought. He'd left Wraith alone to face her final test, and now he was unable to aid her. He had sidelined himself yet again, just like he had during the War, when he'd refused to help a prisoner of war and learned only later the man was the feline prince. As if identity should have made a difference. Unfortunately, it did. That was a harsh reality. And it was certainly the case now.

"Stop torturing yourself, Shaman. It displeases me. All will be as it should be. You've given the wraith all she needs to make the right decision. The rest is up to her."

Wraith waited for Caleb as long as she could. Until the urgency pressing down on her told her that if she waited any longer, her chance would be gone. Cursing, she wrote him a note and left it in the center of his bed. In it, she thanked him for seeing more in her than a bitter, hopeless ghost. She told him she'd miss him, his touch and his goodness, if she didn't make it back. And then she thanked him for loving her and teaching her how to love again, as well. Grabbing his pillow, she pressed it against her face, inhaled his essence so it gave her strength, then left.

Instinct led her, and in less than twenty minutes she'd reached the grocery store. She got there just in time.

Looking through her windshield, she could see that Christina and Annie were just walking into the grocery store. Her anticipation swelled until a beat-up old van pulled in front of the store and three bulky men armed with guns got out. They took a quick look around, then went inside.

Shit. Pounding the steering wheel, Wraith parked across the street, strapped on the weapons she'd brought with her, and ran toward the back of the store. She'd sneak in that way, gaining the element of surprise.

When she tried to open the building's service door, however, it was locked. She jimmied the lock open in under a minute, but every second pressed down on her like a dragon breathing down her neck. Silently, she opened the door and peered inside. She could hear the men taunting the girls at the front of the store.

One of the three men had stationed himself in the back storage room. He was huge, with dark, coarse hair coating his bare arms and peeking above the collar of his dingy tank top. He stood with his arms braced in the doorway, watching what his friends were doing while he called out his encouragement. From his words and the increasing hysteria in the girls' voices out front, it was apparent the men had forgotten their quest for money and were now inclined to take their booty from the girls instead.

Bastards.

". . . our lucky day, Randy! I've always wanted to fuck a college girl. Looks like this is our chance . . ."

When Wraith heard the words, spoken not by the gorilla in front of her but by one of the men up front, she flinched. Instinctively knowing what was about to happen, she threw herself forward, only her body didn't move. A sudden paralysis overtook her, locking her in place. She couldn't speak. Could hardly even breathe. The words of the man up front repeated over and over in her head, each time causing her temples to throb. The pain was so intense, she became nauseated and would have doubled over if her body had allowed it. It didn't.

Those words . . . They flooded her brain with memories. The memories of a girl named Christina. Memories of a happy childhood, parents who loved her, first kisses and first dates and dreams about other firsts . . .

In that moment, she finally understood.

She hadn't met Christina at some point in her human life. She'd *been* Christina.

She wasn't a gang member. She'd been in a sorority and the three dots on her hand had been her one act of bravado, remnants of a tattoo of the Delta Gamma Greek letters, including a triangle with three points.

Annie was *her* sister. A sister who was going to die if Wraith—

You can't save her, Wraith. That's not why you're here.

The female voice drifted through her head at the exact same moment Wraith felt her muscles unlock. With a desperate lunge, she stepped forward. The knowledge of everything she'd lost and could lose again pushed out of her in a whimper.

The man inside the room turned instantly, his gun at the ready.

"What the . . . ?" He froze when he saw Wraith, her own gun leveled on his chest. Her arms were steady but his were shaking, either from drugs or nerves. Laughter and screams were coming from the front of the store now. The man grinned and stepped toward her. "Who—or rather *what*—the fuck are you? They get a couple of sorority hotties and what? I get a dead dyke who wants to play Dirty Harry?"

Wraith pushed back her pain and grinned, knowing how scary she looked when she did so. "That's right. I'm here to make your day."

The man laughed. "Too late. They've been fucked ten ways to Sunday by now."

No, she thought. They couldn't have acted that fast. But she knew deep inside the man was telling the truth. That time had ticked by while she'd been frozen. While fate had ensured what was meant to happen would happen.

"Fuck fate," she muttered defiantly. She fired her gun twice into the man's knees in quick succession. He screamed and toppled to the ground. Racing past him, she charged into the store and nearly gagged at what she saw.

The heaviest man was on Annie, choking her. No, no, no, no. But even as Wraith fired her gun and sent him flying backward, she knew it was too late. Annie's eyes were open but lifeless, her head hanging at an odd angle. The other man, skinny with greasy blond hair, sat on top of Christina and raised his weapon. Wraith shot him dead center in between his eyes. He hung poised on the girl for two seconds before toppling off her.

Wraith rushed to Christina, praying she was still alive.

That *she* was still alive.

She was. Barely. The skirt of her dress had been pushed up, leaving her thighs obscenely splayed open. Her face was cut and bruised from where they'd hit her. She made no sound, but her gaze was focused on her sister, even when Wraith knelt beside her. Her gaze wasn't dazed as Wraith would have expected, or even hopeful, but filled with the nightmarish knowledge of what had just happened to them and that her sister was dead. As she glanced at Annie, *her sister*, Wraith felt the same despair but knew the other girl couldn't see it.

"I'm sorry. I'm so sorry," Wraith said. "I should have gotten here faster . . ."

Christina's face finally turned toward her. A furrow marred her brow. "Do I . . . do I"—she coughed, and Wraith heard the gurgle of blood in her throat—"know you?" she finished.

Wraith took her hand. "No. I mean, yes. We met a long time

ago, and I'm going to take care of you. I'm going to get you out of here and take you home, Christina."

"No."

Wraith froze. Had she imagined the girl's refusal? But the girl repeated it again, this time louder. "No. I want to die. Just let me die."

Wraith stared at her. Let her die? It was her pain talking, a pain she'd live with for a long time, her whole life in fact, but someday she'd see . . . Wraith shook her head. She felt like she'd gone crazy, talking about Christina as a wholly independent person when they were one person in two bodies . . . "I'm going to call for help." Digging into her pocket for her cell phone, Wraith took it out and flipped it open. "They can be here—"

She saw movement, and before she could react, she felt the stab of a gun's revolver against her side.

Christina had picked up her attacker's gun and now had it pointed at Wraith.

"What the . . . ?" Instinctively, she raised her own gun so it was aimed at the girl. Given her return to wraith form, it was likely the girl wouldn't be able to kill her. But for the first time in ten years, Wraith felt the uncertainty, the fear, that came with believing you could die. Maybe it was that belief that would actually kill her in the end?

"I want to die. Don't call . . . Please."

Wraith eased her finger off the trigger. "It's okay, Christina," Wraith told her. "I know you don't believe me right now, but you will be okay. Someday, you'll be able to move on."

"No . . ."

"Yes," Wraith insisted, sensing it was imperative that Christina understand the gift she'd be throwing away if she allowed death to take her. "I know. I've felt your pain, too. For ten years, I've lived with it. But eventually I knew I'd get past it. I made friends. I did good things. I . . . I even fell in love and was loved, too." Her voice broke at the end as she thought of Caleb. Knew at that moment that she'd spoken the truth. Despite all the pain she'd suffered, it had all eventually brought her to him. He hadn't been able to take her pain away, but he'd made it bearable. He'd given her a reason to keep going that truly mattered.

"Kill me or I'll kill you."

Stunned, Wraith stared at the girl. Her words hadn't gotten through. She saw the resolve in her eyes. She meant it.

Christina wanted to die, and if Wraith didn't let her go, she'd take her right along with her. But wouldn't Wraith die anyway? As soon as Christina shot herself?

This is it, she realized. This was her choice. Save her human form or her life as a wraith. But if Christina killed her, there was nothing to stop her from then taking her own life anyway.

If it wouldn't prove she'd truly lost her mind, Wraith would have laughed.

Wraith had tried to kill herself so many times in the past. Now fate wanted her to do it one last time. And she was fucked no matter which life she chose to end.

Still enclosed within the Otherworld, Caleb cursed the Goddess Essenia to hell and back.

"You're sick," he raged. "Twisted. This is the second chance you're talking about? To have her kill herself or kill her human self?"

"She gave up her human life so easily before. Maligned the great gift I'd given her. Her destiny was a special one, so it demanded I give her another chance. She has it. If she chooses to honor her new life as a wraith, I'll know my lesson has been learned. If not . . ."

"You bitch," Caleb breathed.

Fire flashed around him, enveloping him until it was eating him alive, but he refused to make a sound. Better to die now than to watch Wraith have to make such a difficult choice.

"Don't push me, Shaman," the Goddess said just before the flames ebbed. "I have watched the mistakes you've made right along with the others. You lack trust in yourself and your purpose, as well. But trust me, I love you as I love Wraith. I'll grieve her final mistake far more than you will."

His throat had been parched raw by the fire, and he could no longer speak. But there was moisture still left in him, moisture that leaked from his eyes as he turned back to the image of Wraith and Christina, kneeling on the dingy floor of a 7-Eleven with dead bodies surrounding them.

He and Essenia waited for Wraith to make her choice.

* * *

Wraith's two selves were sharing the same space. Didn't that violate the laws of physics or something? Shouldn't one of her selves, the *wrong* self, have imploded several minutes ago, before she'd ever spoken a word to the girl she'd once been?

But they were both still there, and Wraith didn't know what it meant. Even more importantly, she realized, she didn't care. All that mattered was she wasn't going to kill the girl. But she wasn't going to let the girl kill her wraith form, either.

Swiftly, she snatched the gun from Christina with her free hand.

Immediately, Christina closed her eyes, waiting for Wraith to kill her. When that didn't happen, her eyes flickered open, flashing with anger. "Do it. Please."

Wraith shook her head and holstered her gun. "That's not what Annie would have wanted for you, Christina."

Christina looked over at the lifeless, unseeing eyes of her sister and whimpered. Then she began to cry, sobs tearing from her chest. Hesitantly, Wraith enveloped the girl in her arms and, rocking both of them, began to cry, as well.

Whatever the Goddess Essenia chose for them, they were ready, and they would face it together.

When the air around her began to vibrate, and she sensed the end was near, Wraith smiled. "Hang on to me, Christina." Then she spoke for the last time. The world exploded in a blinding flash of light and took their bodies with it, but she knew those final words would somehow survive, floating in the universe until Caleb heard them. Heard her. "Caleb, I love you."

FORTY-ONE

Wraith regained consciousness slowly. Her body ached and her head throbbed, but otherwise she felt a tremendous sense of peace, as if mentally she'd been emptied of all stress, worry, and pain. Her memories were there, memories of two lives lived, first as Christina, then as Wraith, but the memories held no sway over her.

Had she died? Was she in heaven, reunited with her sister, Annie, and pondering her former lives in a lovely abstract void, knowing it was all behind her?

It was with that thought that the pain came. Because if it was all behind her, then so was Caleb. Her friends. The Para-Ops team. Even the idea of never seeing that arrogant prick Mahone gave her a twinge of regret.

She sighed, surprised when she heard sounds indicating she wasn't alone.

Her eyes popped open, but all she saw was the light that had filtered through her eyelids.

Heaven, she thought again.

"No, Wraith. You are not in the Otherworld, but in a space between your world and mine."

Sweeping the space around her, Wraith strained to attach form to voice, but there was nothing in the light but more light and yet more light. She knew who had spoken, however. "Essenia," Wraith croaked.

The Goddess laughed, the beautiful sound tinkling all around her as if she was back in her mother's belly, waiting to be born. Perhaps she was.

"That's right. I am your soul's mother. Will you curse me, Wraith? For what I've done to you?"

Wraith hesitated, then shook her head. "No," she said.

"Why not? I've given you pain. Pain upon pain. Pain to your dying breath."

"But you've also given me love," Wraith whispered. "A sister. Parents that loved me. Even as a wraith, you gave me friends. And a man . . . a man . . ."

Wraith couldn't continue. The pain was closer now. Sharper. Sneaking into her body every time she thought of Caleb, yet she couldn't stop thinking of him. Wouldn't. If thinking of him brought her pain, and pain upon pain, she'd welcome it. She'd cling to it until the Goddess destroyed her completely.

"You cling to him—to life—even now. Despite the peace that surrounds you. Why?"

"I don't know," Wraith said, even though she did. But what did it matter now? Part of her knew he was lost to her, and speaking about her feelings for him made her feel panicky, as if the words that left her would take the feelings and memories right along with them.

"You care not for your human self? You don't wonder where she is?"

"I assumed she became me, and I her once again. I remember everything. I know why you punished me. Why you punish wraiths. She gave up. I gave up. I could have fought off my attacker. I was. I was winning. But when I saw Annie die . . ."

Grief washed over her, a powerful surge of sensation accompanied by confusion. Why? Why had Annie died?

She bit her lip to keep the words inside her. She could rail at the Goddess. Condemn her for letting a young innocent like Annie die a violent death even as she saved others, but she knew exactly how that would end—with evasion or vague explanations about higher purposes and free will and fate. Annie had died right along with Christina. Wraith couldn't be blamed for Annie's death, but clearly the Goddess blamed her for her own. "I stopped," she continued. "I let him rape me. Kill me."

She felt a small pinprick of anger for her foolishness, but the irony was, if she hadn't given up, she might never have met Caleb. Could she really regret that?

"Then you've learned your lesson."

"Is it the lesson that all wraiths must learn? Is it the way to save my"—she hesitated, then lifted her chin before continuing—"to save my family?"

Essenia laughed even as her expression shifted into one of regret. "It doesn't work that way, Wraith. Each wraith has her own lesson to learn. It is not something you can reveal to her, nor I to you. But since you've learned yours, tell me—and I won't give you another chance, Wraith—why do you reject the peace I give you in order to keep your memories of Caleb O'Flare?"

"Because I love him," Wraith whispered, knowing she had no choice now. Essenia knew her fears and could take her memories of Caleb at any time. Better to obey her than risk that. "And he loved me."

"And do you think you were worthy of his love? As a wraith?"

"Yes," Wraith answered, meaning every word. "I was worth it. Mahone taught me that. My team. And Caleb. They did, too. I will always be grateful to you for bringing them to me. Now, please, either do what you're going to do or stop talking. Because I just want to rest now. Rest and think of him."

Essenia remained silent for several moments, making Wraith wonder if she was contemplating a new punishment for Wraith's insubordination. Instead, the Goddess said, "Do you want to say good-bye?"

A surge of energy passed through her, giving her awareness of her bodily form. She struggled to move her heavy limbs until she stood. "He's here?" Frantically, she looked around her.

"He's always been here, Wraith."

The light around her began to shimmer, and then she saw a form drifting toward her.

"Caleb," she whispered.

He took her hand and she *felt* him. Their bodies were solid. Alive. Warm.

She looked down at their joined hands with a frown.

"What is it?" Caleb asked.

"Your touch. I feel it, but it doesn't hurt. I . . ." She gulped in a breath. Stared. She knew it was their hands that touched, but the hand he cradled in his was tan, just shades lighter than his.

She shook her head. "Christina . . ."

He tipped her chin up with his other hand until her eyes met his. His face was vibrant with colors she now knew the names for. And she'd been right before. His eyes were the most beautiful shade of green . . .

"You *are* Christina, Wraith."

Now the fear slammed into her. The human fear that came with hope and the knowledge that it could be snatched away without warning.

"Am I dead? Are you?"

Caleb brought her hand to his lips and kissed it, then shook his head. "You're alive, Wraith. We both are. Look around you," he whispered.

She had, but she did so again.

The light faded, giving way to shapes and sounds. She was in a hospital room, she realized. No longer standing in a vastness of light, but lying in a bed with Caleb sitting next to her. Surrounded by familiar faces. Mahone. Dex and Lucy. Felicia and Knox. And . . .

She narrowed her eyes at the older couple standing closest to her. "Who . . . ?"

But she knew. Linda and Ronald Mercer. Her parents.

Annie's parents. How they must hate her for not saving her little sister. Renewed grief threatened to overwhelm her, and when she choked out, "Annie," the same grief flashed on their faces.

Caleb let go of her hand, and Wraith panicked, reaching out for him. Only to have her mother take her hand instead. "Annie's gone, Christina. But you're here. And we're so, so grateful for that."

Her mother bent and hugged her, and then her father joined them. Hesitantly at first, and then with greater and greater strength, Wraith hugged them back. They hugged and they cried and they grieved for what they'd lost, but at the same time, Wraith kept her eyes open. She kept them locked on Caleb's, and she knew, despite the pain she felt, it would get better.

FORTY-TWO

Caleb held her hand as they walked. Wraith looked around her and remembered the last time she'd been here. How the peace had enthralled and called to her. It boggled her mind that Caleb could walk this place whenever he chose to but rarely did, and even more so, that he always returned. "Are you ever tempted to stay?" she asked him.

Shaking his head, he stopped walking, cupped her face, and stared intently into her eyes. "Never. Certainly not now."

She smiled, knowing what he saw. Outwardly, she bore no resemblance to the wraith he'd once known. She was young, vibrant, and healthy again. But inside, she was still the same female. She didn't answer to the name Christina anymore—it just hadn't felt right when she'd tried. She was Wraith—once human and risen from the dead to be human again. Once painfully alone, but now bursting to the seams with family—her human parents, her wraith family in Maine, her team, and of course, Caleb. Only one thing—and admittedly it was a *huge* thing—kept her from moving on completely.

"We're almost there," Caleb said quietly.

She took in a deep breath and nodded. Tightened her fingers around his and began walking again. A short time later, he stopped. "Remember, this is a one-time thing. And Essenia said your time will be short."

"I remember. I'm thankful for whatever time she gives me. I just need to see her one last time. To make sure she's okay . . ."

"She wants the same thing."

He didn't specify who he meant, Annie or Essenia, but it didn't matter. When he bent to kiss her, she tilted her face up to his, cherishing his touch. It was something she never took for granted. She never would. Pulling away, he rested his forehead on hers.

"When we return," she murmured, "we need to talk to Mahone. He'll want to start looking for a new recruit."

"Make that two new recruits."

Surprised, she pulled back. "But I thought we decided—"

Smiling, he shook his head. "*You* decided I should stay on the team. And I will. I'll return eventually. But I have much more important things to do first. Like be with you. And watch you be a mother to our baby. I figure after a year or two, Mahone will still be able to use a healer on the team. And if he can't," Caleb shrugged, "I have trust in fate."

She swallowed hard and cupped his cheek. "So do I," she whispered.

They kissed again, and this time she took control, pouring all she was and had been and would ever be into the kiss. When she pulled back, he was still smiling, but the heat in his eyes told her he was looking forward to being alone. And horizontal. But right now . . .

He nudged her forward. "Now go. She's waiting."

Wraith turned her head and caught her breath. She squeezed Caleb's hand again before letting go. Slowly, she walked toward the glowing light and the silhouette of a young girl encased safely within it. The girl's face was split by a huge grin as she ran toward Wraith.

The sisters embraced, and Wraith felt the peace and happiness that radiated from her.

The girl's grin matched Wraith's own, and even though her sister no longer had a beating heart, Wraith's heart beat for her.

"Annie," Wraith breathed. "I love you."

* * *

This time, when Mahone sensed Essenia's presence, he barely managed to acknowledge her. It wasn't disrespect or anger or even indifference he felt; he was simply tired. Worn out. Wondering what was going to come next and if he could possibly muster up the energy to face it. Wraith's return to humanity and her happily-ever-after with O'Flare should have had him pumping his fists in the air in victory and gloating that the prophecy was well on its way to being fulfilled. Instead, he was calculating the chances that another HEA could possibly be on the horizon.

After all, in his experience, life tended to lull people into a false sense of security just before it cut their legs out from underneath them.

"Feeling sorry for yourself, Human? Regretting that you haven't gotten your own happy ending?"

Mahone smiled but kept his eyes closed, his head resting on the back of his office chair. "Not so much," he murmured. "I think I've finally accepted that's not in the cards."

He sensed her move closer to him. Felt the dual heat and chill she emanated. Felt both horror and pleasure, but somehow it was distant; he was aware of it in some plane of his mind, but once again he couldn't find the energy to respond.

She sighed and he felt the brush of something soft against his face. A gentle caress, as if from a mother to her son. Or from one lover to another?

The thought had his lids slowly lifting and her visage took up his entire line of sight, blocking out everything but who she was and what she wanted from him. What she could give him.

"I'm tired," he murmured.

"I know. And I know you crave rest. But I can't give it to you. Not yet. There's still much to be done. Many we must expose in order to defeat."

"You're powerful. You can crush us without a thought. Why can't you simply defeat those who displease you?"

Again, that soft caress despite the fact he didn't see her move. "It doesn't work that way."

"A miscalculation by whoever created us, I have to say."

She laughed and this time the sound penetrated his malaise enough to curl his toes and make his dick lengthen. What the hell?

He straightened, narrowing his eyes as she backed away. *She* backed away. *From him.*

Interesting.

"Don't be arrogant, Human. It is merely time for me to leave."

He stood, knowing that something had shifted between them. Sensing the way, for just a fraction of a second, her gaze could no longer quite meet his. Was she giving up on them? Did she realize the futility of what she'd asked of him?

"Even with Knox and Felicia's return," he said, "my team is fracturing. Their hearts are weighed down with other concerns despite the happiness they've found. Knox is obsessed with keeping Felicia safe. Wraith is no longer the weapon she once was. Our enemies are growing bolder with every defeat they suffer. Just how do you expect me to stand for your children when you won't give me full disclosure? Won't be more specific about what it is we need to do?"

"I am limited in what I can give. We both know I'm your creator but also that I am not, Mahone. I know what you speculate."

Her blatant admission shocked him. Worried him. What was behind it? "So you admit I'm right? There's someone—*something*—more powerful we're up against?"

"All I can say is creation is quite complicated. It's not as black-and-white as one would wish. Someone on your team will learn that quite well very soon."

Mahone felt his eyes round and imagined the comical picture he made. "Oh no. No. One of my team is pregnant? Who? Felicia? Wraith?" When Essenia remained silent, Mahone whispered, "Lucy?"

"We've talked quite enough, Mahone. Rest now. You'll need your energy for what's to come."

"What are you—"

His phone rang. He looked at it, then at Essenia. Watched her form fade in a flash of light.

The phone kept ringing. Ringing. Ringing.

Finally, with a soft curse, Mahone answered it. "Mahone."

"This is Dex. We've got a situation."

Keep reading for a preview of the first book
in a sexy new paranormal romance series
by Kimberly Frost

ALL THAT BLEEDS

Coming January 2012 from Berkley Sensation!

I can't believe this is happening, Alissa thought. She whirled to face her bodyguard, Mr. Clark. His lean form was rigidly straight, his expression grim as she stepped forward.

"We can't just stand by," she said in a low voice with another quick glance around the house's panic room. Oatmeal-colored walls, a stocked refrigerator, plush couches, and a bathroom with a cavernous slate-tiled shower. A person could live in the panic room for quite a while and certainly nothing, not even a demon, could get through the magically reinforced steel walls that were as thick as any bank vault's. Yes, it was safe and comfortable—if they were willing to ignore the slaughter happening in the rest of the house. The Arts & Innovation benefit had turned into a nightmare. Mr. Clark had pulled her down the hall to safety before she'd realized what was happening.

Alissa took a deep breath. The sterile air had an almost metallic tang. She straightened to her full height and beckoned for Mr. Clark's gun. He ignored her outstretched hand. She inched forward, her pink-champagne Balenciaga gown swishing over the carpet.

Beyond the bodyguard's shoulder, the giant screen showed the ballroom where an enormous demon nearly eight feet tall was holding a roomful of humans hostage. Dead security officers littered the dance floor like discarded party favors. The greasy, gray-skinned demon yawned, its toothless mouth as wide as a cavern. Would he swallow his victim whole? Like a snake? He had no weapon, but with razor-sharp claws and inhuman strength, he didn't need one.

How did the demon even cross into our world?

There had never been an incident like it in Alissa's lifetime. Or even in her mother's time. For the fifty-four years since the muses had inspired mankind to defeat the vampires during The Rising, the world had not tolerated supernatural threats. In the twenty-first century, no vampires existed and no demons rose. Humankind wrote the laws that ruled the world. And everyone had been safe. Until now.

"Mr. Clark, either go out and help those people or give me your gun so I can." Her voice was as sharp as she could make it. She might have been only twenty-one, but, as a daughter of the House of North, in a time of crisis she was prepared to lead. She kept her arms tight to her sides in hopes that he wouldn't see them tremble.

"Unless Mr. Xenakis gives the order, that door doesn't open until the creature is gone or dead," Mr. Clark said.

Alissa narrowed her eyes. Dimitri Xenakis, the Etherlin Council's president, would never give an order that would put her in danger, but he also wouldn't have locked the panic room when so many other people were still outside.

"Mr. Xenakis isn't here, but I know he would want us to help. Open the door. I'll go out and distract the demon long enough for people to escape. You can get anyone into the panic room who's too afraid or too slow to run."

Mr. Clark folded his arms across his chest, his black tuxedo jacket revealing the slight bulge on his left side where his holstered gun lay. "You expect me to use you as bait?" he scoffed.

"Yes, because I expect us to do something," she said, the irritation rising in her voice.

A flicker of movement drew her eyes to the screen. The creature attacked again. The red-violet eyes were wild. And merciless. The victim's bloodied body fell to the creature's feet. Her stomach churned, and she had to swallow against its rising contents.

Be strong! Don't let Clark see weakness. She turned from the screen, clinging to her composure.

She pushed back a strand of hair that had come loose when she'd raced down the hall. "We have to do something," she whispered.

"The silver and iron bullets bounced off it. The creature is invulnerable." Mr. Clark shook his head. "I would still face him if you weren't here, but you are. If I open the door and he catches the scent of your blood, he'll be on you in seconds once I'm dead. You know a muse's blood is irresistible to The Damned." He paused. "Nothing but Mr. Xenakis's direct order will make me open that door."

"But the demon could stay until everyone is dead," Alissa argued, holding out a hand to implore him. "We can't wait. Please. You have to let me try."

"No," he said firmly.

A tremor rocked the house, and they looked up at the screen. A figure in black strode into the ballroom. He shrugged off a black duster coat, letting it drop in his wake without slowing his stride.

"Merrick," Mr. Clark mumbled.

"Who's Merrick?" Alissa asked, staring at the dark-haired man on the screen who wore sunglasses despite the late hour. He stopped about twenty feet from the creature, then slid a knife from the sheath on his hip. He was tall and broad, but the monster was enormous.

Mr. Clark leaned forward. "He can't be serious. That blade looks like it's made of ivory. It'll crack long before it gets through a demon's hide."

Merrick's lips moved, and Alissa bent over the controls and pressed a button to un-mute the surveillance system.

To the people, Merrick said, "Get out." He nodded to the door, but when they inched toward it, the demon roared and they froze. "Go ahead," Merrick said, even as the creature crouched, ready to attack them.

Merrick clucked his tongue, drawing the demon's attention. "Come, Corthus, I'm your dance partner."

"What'd he just say?" Mr. Clark asked.

Alissa blinked, realizing that Merrick had spoken to the creature in Latin. She'd translated his words in her head without thinking. "He's goading the demon."

"Not for long," Mr. Clark said grimly.

Without warning the demon sprang forward. Alissa gasped,

her hand flying to her mouth. Merrick slid away, and the demon's claws smashed a chair but didn't get a piece of the man who continued to taunt him. As he fought, Merrick's unflinching confidence and strength amazed her.

Nothing about his body had changed, but he moved like smoke, curling close and then away. The demon cocked its head and looked down. She saw it then: blackish fluid, spraying from the demon's side. Merrick's blade had connected.

Merrick smiled at the demon's startled expression. "Come on. That can't be all you've got. I got up before noon to get here."

The demon roared and charged again. Merrick slashed and arced away, his motions fluid, almost acrobatic. The demon crumpled, moaning. Its guttural voice protested in Latin. "Impossible," it said.

"Apparently not," Merrick replied. His weapon rested casually near his thigh for a moment before he struck again, sinking the makeshift blade into the demon's skull.

Alissa recoiled, her hands in tight fists. The demon stilled.

He made that look easy when all the others couldn't even wound it. Where did he come from?

Merrick shook his head at the demon as its simmering flesh rotted rapidly into a lumpy puddle on the floor. "Not much of a peach after all," Merrick mumbled. He turned then and looked around at the bodies before he glanced up into the surveillance camera. He seemed to be staring directly at them, though with his sunglasses on it was impossible to tell for sure. The corner of his mouth curved up.

"You can come out now," he mouthed.

She blushed, embarrassed that he'd guessed that someone was hiding.

"Bastard," Mr. Clark grumbled.

"How could he know we're in here?" she asked.

"He doesn't. He's just guessing," Clark said, walking to the refrigerator at the back of the room. "It's all over. Sit and have some water."

"No," she murmured.

Onscreen, Merrick turned and strolled to retrieve his coat.

Alissa strode to the door and unlocked it, then darted out and down the corridor before Mr. Clark could stop her. The air from the ballroom smelled like asphalt and sulfur. She grimaced at the stench, but it faded as she reached the foyer.

Merrick seemed taller up close. At least six and a half feet. *Beautiful bone structure.* Even obscured by whisker stubble, she could tell.

"Mr. Merrick," she said breathlessly. He smelled spicy and masculine. Unaccountably delicious. She was almost overcome by the urge to touch him. Was it the adrenaline rush that made him seem so attractive? She extended her hand. "Please accept my thanks—"

Merrick's warm hand closed around hers just as Mr. Clark's voice boomed down the corridor. "No! Let her go, Merrick."

With his free hand, Merrick slid his sunglasses down, revealing eyes so dark they seemed to have no color at all, as black and gorgeous as midnight.

"This is an unusual party. First a demon, now an angel."

"I'm not an angel."

"Me either, as it turns out," he said with a slow smile, then opened his mouth slightly to touch the point of his tongue to the tip of a fang. Fear sluiced through her veins. *Ventala.* The by-product of the vampires' desperate attempt to save themselves by breeding with humans.

In an instant, everything she'd learned in her World Studies class came rushing back. In the early 1950s, after their unexplained mutation, shape-shifting vampires in bat form had envenomated and drained millions. Initially, bats were thought to be the vector for a new strain of plague that was universally fatal.

Eventually, the truth was suspected as un-mutated vampires hunted in the wake of their shifting counterparts. When the muses inspired the development of the V3 ammunition, humans began to fight back effectively. The tide of human fury had been boundless, and savvy vampires lacking the "Bat Plague" mutation had stopped hunting and tried aligning themselves with mankind by taking human lovers and having children with them. Ventala. It hadn't saved the vampires; it had only created a new race of bloodthirsty creatures for the world to contend with. Beautiful, deadly creatures, like the one in front of her.

Alissa studied him. Apparently amused by her surprised reaction to his fangs, Merrick cocked a mocking eyebrow. Alissa tried to withdraw her hand, but he held it. She blinked as the muzzle of Mr. Clark's gun appeared, pressing against Merrick's temple.

"I accept your thanks, Miss—?" Merrick's deep voice hummed over her skin. His breath smelled like mint leaves, making her breathe deeper.

It's a trap. Everything about him lures in his prey.

"Miss North," she said, trying to keep her voice steady as her heart beat a riot in her chest.

His gaze flicked to her neck. She wondered if he could see her pulse throbbing there. Would he sink those teeth into her throat? Bleed her dry? He might, but he seemed so in control of himself. How was that possible if the ventala were just animals in the face of a muse's blood? She knew she should draw back from him, but she didn't want to.

Innocence and mystery don't last long in each other's company. It was a quote she'd read long ago. She could taste its warning. *Don't forget what he is.*

"V3 bullets, Merrick. Unless you'd like parts of your brain leaking out of the holes I put in your skull, you'll let her go," Mr. Clark said.

Alissa grimaced. She was grateful to have the bodyguard with her, but she didn't want there to be more violence. "This isn't how the night should end, Mr. Clark. We're in Mr. Merrick's debt," she said.

Merrick's smile widened. "Beautiful manners to match the beautiful face." His low voice sent a wave of heat through her. She was attracted to him. Still. Which was foolish and made her angry with herself. "I bet your boarding school education was expensive," he said.

Yes, very expensive. And where did someone like you get educated? Charm school for killers? Her lips were dry, but she didn't dare lick them. She wouldn't tempt him. Her blood alone should have been a temptation that he couldn't resist. And yet he did resist, standing there so calmly. How? With a gun pressed to his head no less.

She swallowed slowly. "If you returned my hand, I think it would ease Mr. Clark's mind."

Merrick stared into her eyes. "Mr. Clark's. Not yours, huh?" The corners of his mouth turned up in a mocking smile.

Be still. He's toying with you.

"Too bad I was so late to the party, Miss North. If I'd gotten here earlier, I could've asked you to dance." His dark gaze seemed to light her blood on fire.

"It wouldn't have made a difference. No matter when you'd arrived, I would have had to say no." She cleared her throat. "Let go of my hand, please," she said more firmly.

"Not a peach to be had," he murmured, letting her hand fall from his. He moved past her in an instant, leaving Mr. Clark's gun pointing at empty air. When Clark noticed, he lowered it.

Relieved, and yet inadvisably disappointed, Alissa turned to watch Merrick walk through the gaping hole that he'd blown in the front of the mansion to gain entry.

"Why did he come to save us if he's one of them?" she asked.

"He didn't come to save anyone here," Mr. Clark said. "The demon was in the Varden last night, slaughtering them. Merrick came for vengeance. He's an enforcer. A common killer."

Alissa stared at the velvety darkness into which Merrick had disappeared. *Certainly a killer, but not common.*